MARTIN AMIS

THE ZONE OF INTEREST

JONATHAN CAPE
LONDON

Published by Jonathan Cape 2014

2 4 6 8 10 9 7 5 3 1

First published in Great Britain in 2014 by
Jonathan Cape
Random House, 20 Vauxhall Bridge Road,
London SW1V 2SA

www.vintage-books.co.uk

Addresses for companies within The Random House Group Limited can be found at:
www.randomhouse.co.uk/offices.htm

The Random House Group Limited Reg. No. 954009

A CIP catalogue record for this book is available from the British Library

ISBN 9780224099745 (Hardback edition)
ISBN 9780224099752 (Trade paperback edition)

The Random House Group Limited supports the Forest Stewardship Council® (FSC®),
the leading international forest-certification organisation. Our books carrying the
FSC label are printed on FSC®-certified paper. FSC is the only forest-certification
scheme supported by the leading environmental organisations, including Greenpeace.
Our paper procurement policy can be found at www.randomhouse.co.uk/environment

Typeset in Fournier MT by Palimpsest Book Production Limited,
Falkirk, Stirlingshire

Printed and bound in Great Britain by
Clays Ltd, St Ives plc

THE ZONE OF INTEREST

Round about the cauldron go;
In the poisoned entrails throw:
Toad, that under cold stone
Days and nights hast thirty-one
Sweltered venom sleeping got,
Boil thou first i' the charmed pot . . .

Fillet of a fenny snake
In the cauldron boil and bake;
Eye of newt, and toe of frog,
Wool of bat, and tongue of dog,
Adder's fork, and blind-worm's sting,
Lizard's leg, and howlet's wing . . .

Scale of dragon, tooth of wolf,
Witches' mummy, maw and gulf
Of the ravined salt sea shark,
Root of hemlock digged i' the dark,
Liver of blaspheming Jew,
Gall of goat, and slips of yew
Silvered in the moon's eclipse,
Nose of Turk, and Tartar's lips,
Finger of birth-strangled babe,
Ditch-delivered by a drab,
Make the gruel thick and slab . . .

Cool it with a baboon's blood;
Then the charm is firm and good.

                                    I am in blood
Stepped in so far, that, should I wade no more,
Returning were as tedious as go o'er.

                                    Macbeth

CONTENTS

CHAPTER I. THE ZONE OF INTEREST

1. THOMSEN: FIRST SIGHT

I was no stranger to the flash of lightning; I was no stranger to the thunderbolt. Enviably experienced in these matters, I was no stranger to the cloudburst – the cloudburst, and then the sunshine and the rainbow.

She was coming back from the Old Town with her two daughters, and they were already well within the Zone of Interest. Up ahead, waiting to receive them stretched an avenue – almost a colonnade – of maples, their branches and lobed leaves interlocking overhead. A late afternoon in midsummer, with minutely glinting midges . . . My notebook lay open on a tree stump, and the breeze was flicking inquisitively through its pages.

Tall, broad, and full, and yet light of foot, in a crenellated white ankle-length dress and a cream-coloured straw hat with a black band, and swinging a straw bag (the girls, also in white, had the straw hats and the straw bags), she moved in and out of pockets of fuzzy, fawny, leonine warmth. She laughed – head back, with tautened throat. Moving in parallel, I kept pace, in my tailored tweed jacket and twills, with my clipboard, my fountain pen.

Now the three of them crossed the drive of the Equestrian Academy. Teasingly circled by her children she moved past the ornamental windmill, the maypole, the three-wheeled gallows, the carthorse slackly tethered to the iron water pump, and then moved beyond.

Into the Kat Zet – into Kat Zet I.

*

1

Something happened at first sight. Lightning, thunder, cloudburst, sunshine, rainbow – the meteorology of first sight.

––––––

Her name was Hannah – Mrs Hannah Doll.

In the Officers' Club, seated on a horsehair sofa, surrounded by horse brass and horse prints, and drinking cups of ersatz coffee (coffee for horses), I said to my lifelong friend Boris Eltz,

'For a moment I was young again. It was like love.'

'Love?'

'I said *like* love. Don't look so stricken. *Like* love. A feeling of inevitability. You know. Like the birth of a long and wonderful romance. Romantic love.'

'Déjà vu and all the usual stuff? Go on. Jog my memory.'

'Well. Painful admiration. Painful. And feelings of humility and unworthiness. Like with you and Esther.'

'That's completely different,' he said, raising a horizontal digit. 'That's just fatherly. You'll understand when you see her.'

'Anyway. Then it passed and I . . . And I just started wondering what she'd look like with all her clothes off.'

'There you are, you see? I never wonder what Esther'd look like with all her clothes off. If it happened I'd be aghast. I'd shield my eyes.'

'And would you shield your eyes, Boris, from Hannah Doll?'

'Mm. Who'd have thought the Old Boozer would've got someone as good as that.'

'I know. Incredible.'

'The Old *Boozer*. Think, though. I'm sure he was always a boozer. But he wasn't always old.'

I said, 'The girls are what? Twelve, thirteen? So she's our age. Or a bit younger.'

'And the Old Boozer knocked her up when she was – eighteen?'

'When *he* was our age.'

2

'All right. Marrying him was forgivable, I suppose,' said Boris. He shrugged. 'Eighteen. But she hasn't left him, has she. How do you laugh that one off?'

'I know. It's difficult to . . .'

'Mm. She's too tall for me. And come to think of it, she's too tall for the Old Boozer.'

And we asked each other yet again: Why would anyone bring his wife and children here? Here?

I said, 'This is an environment more suited to the male.'

'Oh, I don't know. Some of the women don't mind it. Some of the women are the same as the men. Take your Auntie Gerda. She'd love it here.'

'Aunt Gerda might approve in principle,' I said. 'But she wouldn't love it here.'

'Will Hannah love it here, do you think?'

'She doesn't look as though she'll love it here.'

'No, she doesn't. But don't forget she's the unestranged wife of Paul Doll.'

'Mm. Then perhaps she'll settle in nicely,' I said. 'I hope so. My physical appearance works better on women who love it here.'

'. . . *We* don't love it here.'

'No. But we've got each other, thank God. That's not nothing.'

'True, dearest. You've got me and I've got you.'

Boris, my permanent familiar – emphatic, intrepid, handsome, like a little Caesar. Kindergarten, childhood, adolescence, and then, later on, our cycling holidays in France and England and Scotland and Ireland, our three-month trek from Munich to Reggio and then on to Sicily. Only in adulthood did our friendship run into difficulties, when politics – when history – came down on our lives. He said,

'You, you'll be off by Christmas. I'm here till June. Why aren't I out east?' He sipped and scowled and lit a cigarette. 'By the way, your chances, brother, are non-existent. *Where*, for instance? She's far too conspicuous. And you be careful. The

Old Boozer may be the Old Boozer but he's also the Commandant.'

'Mm. Still. Stranger things have happened.'

'*Much* stranger things have happened.'

Yes. Because it was a time when everybody felt the fraudulence, the sarcastic shamelessness, and the breathtaking hypocrisy of all prohibitions. I said,

'I've got a kind of plan.'

Boris sighed and looked vacant.

'First I'll need to hear from Uncle Martin. Then I'll make my opening move. Pawn to queen four.'

After a while Boris said, 'I think that pawn's for it.'

'Probably. But there's no harm in having a good look.'

Boris Eltz took his leave: he was expected on the ramp. A month of staggered ramp duty was his punishment within a punishment for yet another fistfight. The ramp – the detrainment, the selection, then the drive through the birch wood to the Little Brown Bower, in Kat Zet II.

'The most eerie bit's the selection,' said Boris. 'You ought to come along one day. For the experience.'

I ate lunch alone in the Officers' Mess (half a chicken, peaches and custard. No wine) and went on to my office at the Buna-Werke. There was a two-hour meeting with Burckl and Seedig, mostly concerning itself with the slow progress of the carbide production halls; but it also became clear that I was losing my battle about the relocation of our labour force.

At dusk I betook myself to the cubicle of Ilse Grese, back in Kat Zet I.

Ilse Grese loved it here.

———

I knocked on the gently swinging tin door and entered.

Like the teenager she still was (twenty next month), Ilse sat hunched and cross-ankled halfway down the cot, reading an illustrated magazine; she did not choose to look up from its pages. Her uniform was hooked on the nail in the metal beam, under which I now ducked; she was wearing a fibrous dark-blue housecoat and baggy grey socks. Without turning round she said,

'Aha. I smell Icelander. I smell arsehole.'

Ilse's habitual manner with me, and perhaps with all her menfriends, was one of sneering languor. My habitual manner with her, and with every woman, at least at first, was floridly donnish (I had evolved this style as a counterweight to my physical appearance, which some, for a while, found forbidding). On the floor lay Ilse's gunbelt and also her oxhide whip, coiled like a slender serpent in sleep.

I took off my shoes. As I sat and made myself comfortable against the curve of her back I dangled over her shoulder an amulet of imported scent on a gilt chain.

'It's the Icelandic arsehole. What's he want?'

'Mm, Ilse, the state of your room. You always look impeccable when you're going about your work – I'll grant you that. But in the private sphere . . . And you're quite a stickler for order and cleanliness in others.'

'What's the arsehole want?'

I said, 'What is wanted?' And I continued, with thoughtful lulls between the sentences. 'What is wanted is that you, Ilse, should come to my place around ten. There I will ply you with brandy and chocolate and costly gifts. I will listen as you tell me about your most recent ups and downs. My generous sympathy will soon restore your sense of proportion. Because a sense of proportion, Ilse, is what you've been known, very occasionally, to lack. Or so Boris tells me.'

'. . . Boris doesn't love me any more.'

'He was singing your praises just the other day. I'll have a word with him if you like. You will come, I hope, at ten. After our talk and your treats, there will be a sentimental interlude. That is what is wanted.'

5

Ilse went on reading – an article strongly, indeed angrily arguing that women should on no account shave or otherwise depilate their legs or their armpits.

I got to my feet. She looked up. The wide and unusually crinkly and undulating mouth, the eye sockets of a woman three times her age, the abundance and energy of the dirty-blonde hair.

'You're an arsehole.'

'Come at ten. Will you?'

'Maybe,' she said, turning the page. 'And maybe not.'

In the Old Town the housing stock was so primitive that the Buna people had been obliged to build a kind of dormitory settlement in the rural eastern suburbs (it contained a lower and upper school, a clinic, several shops, a cafeteria, and a taproom, as well as scores of restive housewives). Nevertheless, I soon found a quite service-able set of chintzily furnished rooms up a steep lane off the market square. 9, Dzilka Street.

There was one serious drawback: I had mice. After the forcible displacement of its owners, the property was used as a builders' squat for nearly a year, and the infestation had become chronic. Although the little creatures managed to stay out of sight, I could almost constantly hear them as they busied themselves in the crannies and runnels, scurrying, squeaking, feeding, breeding . . .

On her second visit my charlady, young Agnes, deposited a large male feline, black with white trimmings, named Max, or Maksik (pronounced Makseech). Max was a legendary mouser. All I would be needing, said Agnes, was a fortnightly visit from Max; he would appreciate the odd saucer of milk, but there would be no need to give him anything solid.

It wasn't long before I learned respect for this skilful and unobtrusive predator. Maksik had a tuxedoed appearance – char-coal suit, perfectly triangular white dickey, white spats. When he dipped low and stretched his front legs, his paws fanned out prettily, like daisies. And every time Agnes scooped him up and took him away with her, Max — having weekended with me — left behind him an established silence.

In such a silence I drew, or rather amassed, a hot bath (kettle, pots, buckets), and rendered myself particularly trim and handsome for Ilse Grese. I laid out her cognac and candies, plus four sealed pairs of hardy pantihose (for she disdained stockings), and I waited, looking out at the old ducal castle, as black as Max against the evening sky.

Ilse was punctual. All she said, and she said it faintly sneeringly, and deeply languidly, as soon as the door closed behind her: all she said was — 'Quick.'

———

So far as I could determine, the wife of the Commandant, Hannah Doll, took her daughters to school, and brought them back again, but otherwise she hardly left the house.

She did not attend either of the two experimental *thés dansants*; she did not attend the cocktail party in the Political Department thrown by Fritz Mobius; and she did not attend the gala screening of the romantic comedy *Two Happy People*.

On each of these occasions Paul Doll could not but put in an appearance. He did so always with the same expression on his face: that of a man heroically mastering his hurt pride . . . He had a way of tubing his lips, as if planning to whistle — until (or so it seemed) some bourgeois scruple assailed him, and the mouth recomposed itself into a beak.

Mobius said, 'No Hannah, Paul?'

I moved closer.

'Indisposed,' said Doll. 'You know how it is. The proverbial time of the month?'

7

'Dear oh dear.'

On the other hand, I *did* get a pretty good view of her, and for several minutes, through the threadbare hedge at the far end of the sports ground (as I was walking by I paused, and pretended to consult my notebook). Hannah was on the lawn, supervising a picnic for her two daughters and one of their friends – the daughter of the Seedigs, I was fairly sure. The wickerwork basket was still being unpacked. She didn't settle down with them on the red rug but occasionally dropped into a crouch and then re-erected herself with a vigorous swivel of her haunches.

If not in dress then certainly in silhouette (with her face occluded), Hannah Doll conformed to the national ideal of young femininity, stolid, countrified, and built for procreation and heavy work. Thanks to my physical appearance, I was the beneficiary of extensive carnal knowledge of this type. I had hoiked up and unfurled many a three-ply dirndl, I had eased off many a pair of furry bloomers, I had tossed over my shoulder many a hobnailed clog.

I? I was six foot three. The colour of my hair was a frosty white. The Flemish chute of the nose, the disdainful pleat of the mouth, the shapely pugnacity of the chin; the right-angled hinges of the jaw seemed to be riveted into place beneath the minimal curlicues of the ears. My shoulders were flat and broad, my chest slablike, my waist slender; the extensile penis, classically compact in repose (with pronounced prepuce), the thighs as solid as hewn masts, the kneecaps square, the calves Michelangelan, the feet hardly less pliant and shapely than the great tentacled blades of the hands. To round out the panoply of these timely and opportune attractions, my arctic eyes were a cobalt blue.

All I needed was word from Uncle Martin, a specific order from Uncle Martin in the capital – and I would act.

————

'Good evening.'

'Yes?'

On the steps of the orange villa I found myself confronted by an unsettling little character in thickly knitted woollens (jerkin and skirt) and with bright silver buckles on her shoes.

'Is the master of the house at home?' I asked. I knew perfectly well that Doll was elsewhere. He was out on the ramp with the doctors, and with Boris and many others, to receive Special Train 105 (and Special Train 105 was expected to be troublesome). 'You see, I have a high-priority—'

'Humilia?' said a voice. 'What is it, Humilia?'

A displacement of air further back and there she was, Hannah Doll, again in white, shimmering in the shadows. Humilia coughed politely and withdrew.

'Madam, I'm so sorry to impose,' I said. 'My name is Golo Thomsen. It is a pleasure to meet you.'

Finger by finger I briskly plucked off the chamois glove and held out my hand, which she took. She said,

'"Golo"?'

'Yes. Well, it was my first attempt to say Angelus. I made a mess of it, as you see. But it stuck. Our blunders haunt us all our lives, don't you think?'

'. . . How can I help you, Mr Thomsen?'

'Mrs Doll, I have some rather urgent news for the Commandant.'

'Oh?'

'I don't want to be melodramatic, but a decision has been reached in the Chancellery on a matter that I know is his paramount concern.'

She continued to look at me in frank appraisal.

'I saw you once,' she said. 'I remember because you weren't in uniform. Are you ever in uniform? What is it you do exactly?'

'I liaise,' I said and gave a shallow bow.

'If it's important then I suppose you'd better wait. I've no idea where he is.' She shrugged. 'Would you care for some lemonade?'

'No – I wouldn't put you to the bother.'

'It's no bother for me. Humilia?'

We now stood in the rosy glow of the main room, Mrs Doll standing with her back to the chimney piece, Mr Thomsen poised before the central window and gazing out over the perimeter watchtowers and the bits and pieces of the Old Town in the middle distance.

'Charming. This is charming. Tell me,' I said with a regretful smile. 'Can you keep a secret?'

Her gaze steadied. Seen up close, she was more southern, more Latin in colouring; and her eyes were an unpatriotic dark brown, like moist caramel, with a viscid glisten. She said,

'Well I *can* keep a secret. When I want to.'

'Oh good. The thing is,' I said, quite untruthfully, 'the thing is I'm very interested in interiors, in furnishings and design. You can see why I wouldn't want that to get about. Not very manly.'

'No, I suppose not.'

'So was it your idea – the marble surfaces?'

My hope was to distract her and also to set her in motion. Now Hannah Doll talked, gestured, moved from window to window; and I had the chance to assimilate. Yes, she was certainly built on a stupendous scale: a vast enterprise of aesthetic coordination. And the head, the span of the mouth, the might of the teeth and jaws, the supple finish of her cheeks – square-headed but shapely, with the bones curving upward and outward. I said,

'And the covered veranda?'

'It was either that or the—'

Humilia came through the open doors with the tray and the stone pitcher, and two platefuls of pastries and biscuits.

'Thank you, Humilia dear.'

When we were again alone I said mildly, 'Your maid, Mrs Doll. Is she by any chance a Witness?'

Hannah held back till some domestic vibration, undetectable by me, freed her to go on, not quite in a whisper, 'Yes, she is. I don't understand them. She has a religious face, don't you think?'

'Very much so.' Humilia's face was markedly indeterminate, indeterminate as to sex and indeterminate as to age (an unharmonious blend of female and male, of young and old); yet, under the solid quiff of her cress-like hair, she beamed with a terrible self-sufficiency. 'It's the rimless glasses.'

'How old would you say she is?'

'Uh – thirty-five?'

'She's fifty. I think she looks like that because she thinks she's never going to die.'

'Mm. Well, that would be very cheering.'

'And it's all so simple.' She bent and poured, and we took our seats, Hannah on the quilted sofa, I on a rustic wooden chair. 'All she's got to do is sign a document, and that's the end of it. She's free.'

'Mm. Just *abjure*, as they say.'

'Yes, but you know . . . Humilia couldn't be more devoted to my two girls. And she's got a child of her own. A boy of twelve. Who's in state care. And all she's got to do is sign a form and she can go and get him. And she doesn't. She won't.'

'It's curious, isn't it. I'm told they're meant to *like* suffering.' And I remembered Boris's description of a Witness on the flogging post; but I would not be regaling Hannah with it – the way the Witness pleaded for more. 'It gratifies their faith.'

'Imagine.'

'They love it.'

Seven o'clock was now nearing, and the room's blushful light suddenly dropped and settled . . . I had had many remarkable successes at this phase of the day, many startling successes, when the dusk, as yet unopposed by lamp or lantern, seems to confer an impalpable licence – rumours of dream-strange possibilities. Would it be so unwelcome, really, if I quietly joined her on the sofa and, after some murmured compliments, took her hand, and (depending on how that went) gently smoothed my lips against the base of her neck? Would it?

'My husband,' she said – and stopped as if to listen.

The words hung in the air and for a moment I was jarred by this reminder: the ever more bewildering fact that her husband was the Commandant. But I endeavoured to go on looking serious and respectful. She said,

'My husband thinks we have much to learn from them.'

'From the Witnesses? What?'

'Oh, you know,' she said neutrally, almost sleepily. 'Strength of belief. Unshakeable belief.'

'The virtues of zeal.'

'That's what we're all meant to have, isn't it?'

I sat back and said, 'One can see why your husband admires their zealotry. But what about their pacifism?'

'No. Obviously.' In her numbed voice she went on, 'Humilia won't clean his uniform. Or polish his boots. He doesn't like that.'

'No. I bet he doesn't.'

At this point I was registering how thoroughly the invocation of the Commandant had lowered the tone of this very promising and indeed mildly enchanting encounter. So I softly clapped my hands and said,

'Your garden, Mrs Doll. Could we? I'm afraid I have another rather shameful confession to make. I adore flowers.'

———

It was a space divided in two: on the right, a willow tree, partly screening the low outbuildings and the little network of paths and avenues where, no doubt, the daughters loved to play and hide; to the left, the rich beds, the striped lawn, the white fence – and, beyond, the Monopoly Building on its sandy rise, and beyond that the first pink smears of sunset.

12

'A paradise. Such gorgeous tulips.'

'They're poppies,' she said.

'Poppies, of course. What are those ones over there?'

After a few more minutes of this, Mrs Doll, having not yet smiled in my company, gave a laugh of euphonious surprise and said,

'You know *nothing* about flowers, do you? You don't even . . . You know nothing about flowers.'

'I *do* know something about flowers,' I said, perhaps dangerously emboldened. 'And it's something not known to many men. Why do women love flowers so?'

'Go on then.'

'All right. Flowers make women feel beautiful. When I present a woman with a plush bouquet, I know it will make her feel beautiful.'

'. . . Who told you that?'

'My mother. God rest her.'

'Well she was right. You feel like a film star. For days on end.'

Dizzily I said, 'And this is to the credit of both of you. To the credit of flowers and to the credit of womankind.'

And Hannah asked me, 'Can *you* keep a secret?'

'Most assuredly.'

'Come.'

There was, I believed, a hidden world that ran alongside the world we knew; it existed *in potentia*; to gain admission to it, you had to pass through the veil or film of the customary, and *act*. With a hurrying gait Hannah Doll led me down the cindery path to the greenhouse, and the light was holding, and would it be so strange, really, to urge her on inside and to lean into her and gather in my dropped hands the white folds of her dress? Would it? Here? Where everything was allowed?

She opened the half-glass door and, not quite entering, leaned over and rummaged in a flowerpot on a low shelf . . . To tell the truth, in my amatory transactions I hadn't had a decent thought in my head for seven or eight years (earlier, I was something of a romantic. But I let that go). And as I watched Hannah curve her body forward, with her tensed rump and one mighty leg thrown up and out behind her for balance, I said to myself: This would be a *big* fuck. A *big* fuck: that was what I said to myself.

Now righting her body, she faced me and opened her palm. Revealing what? A crumpled packet of Davidoffs: a packet of five. There were three left.

'Do you want one?'

'I don't smoke cigarettes,' I said, and produced from my pockets an expensive lighter and a tin of Swiss cheroots. Moving nearer, I scraped the flint and raised the flame, protecting it from the breeze with my hand . . .

This little ritual was of high socio-sexual signifignance – for we dwelt in a land, she and I, where it amounted to an act of illicit collusion. In bars and restaurants, in hotels, railway stations, et cetera, you saw printed signs saying Women Asked Not To Use Tobacco; and in the streets it was incumbent on men of a certain type – many of them smokers – to upbraid wayward women and dash the cigarette from their fingers or even from their lips. She said,

'I know I shouldn't.'

'Don't listen to them, Mrs Doll. Heed our poet. *You shall abstain, shall abstain. That is the eternal song.*'

'I find it helps a bit', she said, 'with the smell.'

That last word was still on her tongue when we heard some-thing, something borne on the wind . . . It was a helpless, quavering chord, a fugal harmony of human horror and dismay. We stood quite still with our eyes swelling in our heads. I could feel my body clench itself for more and greater alarums. But then came a shrill silence, like a mosquito whirring in your ear, followed, half a minute later, by the hesitantly swerving upswell of violins.

14

There seemed to be no such thing as speech. We smoked on, with soundless inhalations.

Hannah placed the two butts in an empty bag of seeds which she then buried in the lidless rubbish barrel.

'What's your favourite pudding?'

'Um. Semolina,' I said.

'Semolina? Semolina's *ghastly*. What about trifle?'

'Trifle has its points.'

'Which would you rather be, be blind or deaf?'

'Blind, Paulette,' I said.

'Blind? Blind's *much* worse. Deaf!'

'Blind, Sybil.' I said. 'Everyone feels sorry for blind people. But everyone *hates* deaf people.'

I reckoned I had done pretty well with the girls, on two counts – by producing several little sachets of French sweets and, more saliently, by dissimulating my surprise when told that they were twins. Being non-identical, Sybil and Paulette were just a pair of sisters born at the same time; but they looked not even distantly related, Sybil taking after her mother while Paulette, several inches shorter, helplessly fulfilled the grim promise of her forename.

'Mummy,' said Paulette, 'what was that dreadful noise?'

'Oh, just some people fooling about. Pretending it's Walpurgis Night and trying to scare each other.'

'Mummy,' said Sybil, 'why does Daddy always know whether I've cleaned my teeth?'

'What?'

'He's always right. I ask him how and he says, *Daddy knows everything*. But how does he know?'

'He's just teasing you. Humilia, it's a Friday but let's get their bath going.'

'Oh, Mummy. Can we have ten minutes with Bohdan and Torquil and Dov?'

15

'Five minutes. Say goodnight to Mr Thomsen.'

Bohdan was the Polish gardener (old, tall, and of course very lean), Torquil was the pet tortoise, and Dov, it seemed, was Bohdan's teenage helper. Under the swathes of the willow tree – the crouching twins, Bohdan, another helper (a local girl called Bronislawa), Dov, and tiny Humilia, the Witness . . .

As we looked on Hannah said, 'He was a professor of zoology, Bohdan. In Cracow. Just think. He used to be there. And now he's here.'

'Mm. Mrs Doll, how often do you come to the Old Town?'

'Oh. Most weekdays. Humilia sometimes does it, but I usually take them to school and back.'

'My rooms there, I'm trying to improve them, and I've run out of ideas. It's probably just a question of drapery. I was wondering if you might be able to look in one day and see what you thought.'

Profile to profile. Now face to face.

She folded her arms and said, 'And how do you imagine that might be arranged?'

'There's not much to arrange, is there? Your husband would never know.' I went this far because my hour with Hannah had wholly convinced me that somebody like her could have no fondness, none, for somebody like him. 'Would you consider it?'

She stared at me long enough to see my smile begin to curdle.

'No. Mr Thomsen, that's a very reckless suggestion . . . And you don't understand. Even if you think you do.' She stepped back. 'Let yourself in through the door there if you still want to wait. Go on. You can read Wednesday's *Observer*.'

'Thank you. Thank you for your hospitality, Hannah.'

'It's nothing, Mr Thomsen.'

'I'll be seeing you, won't I, Mrs Doll, on Sunday week? The Commandant was kind enough to ask me to attend.'

She folded her arms and said, 'Then I suppose I will be seeing you. So long.'

'So long.'

———

With impatiently quaking fingers Paul Doll upended the decanter over his brandy balloon. He drank, as if for thirst, and poured again. He said over his shoulder,

'D'you want some of this?'

'If you wouldn't mind, Major,' I said. 'Ah. Many thanks.'

'So they've decided. Yea or nay? Let me guess. Yea.'

'Why're you so sure?'

He went and threw himself down on the leather chair, and roughly unbuttoned his tunic.

'Because it'll cause me more difficulties. That seems to be the guiding principle. Let's cause Paul Doll more difficulties.'

'You're right, as usual, sir. I opposed it but it is to come about. Kat Zet III,' I began.

———

On the chimney piece in Doll's office there stood a framed photograph of perhaps half a metre square with a professional burnish to it (the cameraman was not the Commandant: this was pre-Doll). The background was sharply bisected, a hazy radiance on one side, and a felt-thick darkness on the other. A very young Hannah stood in the light, centre stage (and it *was* a stage – a ball? a masquerade? amateur theatricals?), in a sashed evening gown, cradling a bunch of flowers in arms gloved to the elbow; she was beaming with embarrassment at the extent of her own delight. The sheer gown was cinched at the waist, and there it all lay before you . . .

This was thirteen or fourteen years ago – and she was *far* better now.

They say that it is one of the most terrifying manifestations in nature: a bull elephant in a state of *must*. Twin streams of vile-smelling liquid flow from the ducts of the temples and into the corners of the jaws. At these times the great beast will gore giraffes and hippos, will break the backs of cringeing rhinoceri. This was male-elephantine *heat*.

Must: it derived via Urdu from the Persian *mast* or *maest* – 'intoxicated'. But I had settled for the modal verb. I must, I must, I just *must*.

––––––

The next morning (it was a Saturday) I slipped out of the Buna-Werke with a heavy valise and went back to Dzilka Street, where I began to go through the weekly construction report. This of course would include a mass of estimates for the new amenity at Monowitz.

At two I had a caller; and for forty-five minutes I entertained a young woman called Loremarie Ballach. This meeting was also a parting. She was the wife of Peter Ballach, a colleague of mine (a friendly and capable metallurgist). Loremarie didn't love it here, and neither did her husband. The cartel had finally authorised his transfer back to HQ.

'Don't write,' she said as she dressed. 'Not until it's all over.'

I worked on. This much cement, this much timber, this much barbed wire. At odd moments I registered my relief, as well as my regret, that Loremarie was no more (and would have to be replaced). Adulterous philanderers had a motto: *Seduce the wife, traduce the husband*; and when I was in bed with Loremarie, I always felt a sedimentary unease about Peter – his plump lips, his spluttering laugh, his misbuttoned waistcoat.

That wouldn't apply in the case of Hannah Doll. The fact that Hannah had married the Commandant: this was not a good reason to be in love with her – but it was a good reason to be in bed with her. I worked on, adding, subtracting, multiplying, dividing, and yearning for the sound of Boris's motorbike (with its inviting sidecar).

Around half past eight I got up from my desk, intending to fetch a bottle of Sancerre from the roped fridge.

Max — Maksik — sat erect and still on the bare white slats. In his custody, restrained by a negligent paw, was a small and dusty grey mouse. Still trembling with life, it was looking up at him, and seemed to be smiling — seemed to be smiling an apologetic smile; then the life fluttered out of it while Max gazed elsewhere. Was it the pressure of the claws? Was it mortal fright? Whichever it was Max at once settled down to his meal.

————

I went outside and descended the slope to the Stare Miasto. Empty, as if under curfew.

What was the mouse saying? It was saying, All I can offer, in mitigation, in appeasement, is the totality, the perfection, of my defencelessness.

What was the cat saying? It wasn't saying anything, naturally. Glassy, starry, imperial, of another order, of another world.

When I got back to my rooms Max was stretched out on the carpet in the study. The mouse was gone, devoured without trace, tail and all.

That night, over the black endlessness of the Eurasian plain, the sky held on to its indigo and violet till very late — the colour of a bruise beneath a fingernail.

It was the August of 1942.

*

19

2. DOLL: THE SELEKTION

'If Berlin has a change of heart,' said my caller, 'I'll let you know. Sleep well, Major.' And he was gone.

As you might expect, that ghastly incident on the ramp has left me with a splitting headache. I have just taken 2 aspirin (650 mg; 20.43) and shall doubtlessly rely on a Phanodorm at bedtime. Not a word of solicitude from Hannah, of course. Whilst she could clearly see that I was shaken to the core, she simply turned away with a little lift of the chin – as if, for all the world, *her* hardships were greater than my own . . .

Ah, what's the matter, dearest sweetling? Have those naughty little girls been 'playing you up'? Has Bronislawa again fallen short? Are your precious poppies refusing to flower? Dear oh dear – why, that's almost too tragic to bear. I've some suggestions, my petkins. Try doing something for your country, Madam! Try dealing with vicious spoilers like Eikel and Prufer! Try extending Protective Custody to 30, 40, 50,000 people!

Try your hand, fine lady, at receiving Sonderzug 105 . . .

Well, I can't claim I wasn't warned. Or can I? I was alerted, true, but to quite another eventuality. Acute tension, then extreme relief – then, once again, drastic pressure. I ought now to be enjoying a moment of respite. But what confronts me, on my return home? *More* difficulties.

Konzentrationslager 3, indeed. No wonder my head is splitting!

There were 2 telegrams. The official communication, from Berlin, read as follows:

BOURGET–DRANCY DEP 01.00 ARR COMPIEGNE
03.40 DEP 04.40 ARR LAON 06.45 DEP 07.05 ARR REIMS
08.07 DEP 08.38 ARR FRONTIER 14.11 DEP 15.05
JUNE 26
ARRIVE KZA(I) 19.03 END

Perusing this, one had every reason to expect a 'soft' transport, as the evacuees would be spending a mere 2 days in transit. Yes, but the 1st missive was followed by a 2nd, from Paris:

DEAR COMRADE DOLL STOP AS OLD FRIEND ADVISE EXTREME CAUTION VIZ SPECIAL TRAIN 105 STOP YOUR ABILITIES TESTED TO LIMITS STOP COURAGE STOP WALTHER PABST SALUTES YOU FROM SACRE COEUR END

Now over the years I have developed a dictum: *Fail to prepare? Prepare to fail!* So I made my arrangements accordingly.

It was now 18.57; and we were primed.

Nobody can say that I don't cut a pretty imposing figure on the ramp: chest out, with sturdy fists planted on jodhpured hips, and the soles of my jackboots at least a metre apart. And look of what I wielded: I had with me my number 2, Wolfram Prufer, 3 labour managers, 6 physicians and as many disinfectors, my trusty Sonderkommandofuhrer, Szmul, with his 12-man team (3 of whom spoke French), 8 Kapos plus the hosing crew, and a full Storm of 96 troops under Captain Boris Eltz, reinforced by the 8-strong unit deploying the belt-fed, tripod-based heavy machine gun and the 2 flamethrowers. I had also called upon a) Senior Supervisor Grese and her platoon (Grese is admirably firm with recalcitrant females), and b) the current 'orchestra' – not the usual dog's breakfast of banjoes and accordions and didgeridoos, but a 'septet' of 1st-rate violinists from Innsbruck.

(I *like* numbers. They speak of logic, exactitude, and thrift. I'm a little uncertain, sometimes, about 'one' – about whether it denotes quantity, or is being used as a . . . 'pronoun'? But consistency's the thing. And I *like* numbers. Numbers, numerals, integers. Digits!)

19.01 very slowly became 19.02. We felt the hums and tremors in the rails, and I too felt a rush of energy and strength. There we stood, quite still for a moment, the waiting figures on the spur, at the far end of a rising plain, steppelike in its vastness. The track stretched halfway to the horizon, where, at last, ST 105 silently materialised.

On it came. Coolly I raised my powerful binoculars: the high-shouldered torso of the locomotive, with its single eye, its squat spout. Now the train leaned sideways as it climbed.

'Passenger cars,' I said. This was not so unusual with transports from the west. 'Wait,' I said. '3 *classes*' . . . The carriages streamed sideways, carriages of yellow and terracotta, *Première, Deuxième, Troisième – JEP, NORD, La Flèche d'Or*. Professor Zulz, our head doctor, said drily,

'Three classes? Well, you know the French. They do everything in style.'

'Too true, Professor,' I rejoined. 'Even the way they hoist the white flag has a certain – a certain *je ne sais quoi*. Not so?'

The good doctor chuckled heartily and said, 'Damn you, Paul. Touché, my Kommandant.'

Oh yes, we bantered and smiled in the collegial fashion, but make no mistake: we were ready. I motioned with my right hand to Captain Eltz, as the troops – under orders to stand back – took up their positions along the length of the siding. The *Golden Arrow* pulled in, slowed, and halted with a fierce pneumatic sigh.

Now they're quite right when they say that 1,000 per train is the soundest 'rule of thumb' (and that up to 90% of them will be selected Left). I was already surmising, however, that the customary guidelines would be of scant help to me here.

First to disembark were not the usual trotting shapes of uniformed servicemen or gendarmes but a scattered contingent of baffled-looking middle-aged 'stewards' (they wore white bands on the sleeves of their civilian suits). There came another exhausted gasp from the engine, and the scene settled into silence.

Another carriage door swung open. And who alighted? A little boy of about 8 or 9, in a sailor suit, with extravagant bell-bottomed trousers; then an elderly gentleman in an astrakhan overcoat; and then a cronelike figure bent over the pearl handle of an ebony cane – so bent, indeed, that the stick was too high for her, and she had to reach upwards to keep her palm on its glossy knob. Now the other carriage doors opened, and the other passengers detrained.

Well, by this time I was grinning widely and shaking my head, and quietly cursing that old lunatic Walli Pabst – as his telegram of 'warning' was clearly nothing more than a practical joke!

A shipment of 1,000? Why, it comprised barely 100. As for the Selektion: all but a few were under 10 or over 60; and even the young adults among them were, so to speak, selected already.

Look. That 30-year-old male has a broad chest, true, but he also has a club foot. That brawny maiden is in the pink of health, assuredly, and yet she is with child. Elsewhere – spinal braces, white sticks.

'Well, Professor, go about your work,' I quipped. 'A stern call on your prognostical skills.'

Zulz of course was looking at me with dancing eyes.

'Fear not,' he said. 'Asclepius and Panacea wing their way to my aid. *I will keep pure and holy both my life and my art.* Paracelsus be my guide.'

'Tell you what. Go back to the Ka Be,' I suggested, 'and do some selecting there. Or have an early supper. It's poached duck.'

'Oh, well,' he said, producing his flask. 'Now we're about it. Care for a drop? It's a lovely evening. I'll keep you company, if I may.'

He dismissed the junior physicians. I too gave orders to Captain Eltz, and pared my forces, retaining only a 12-strong platoon, 6 Sonders, 3 Kapos, 2 disinfectors (a wise precaution, as it transpired!), the 7 violinists, and Senior Supervisor Grese.

Just then the little bent old lady detached herself from the hesitantly milling arrivals and limped towards us at disconcerting speed, like a scuttling crab. All atremble with ill-mastered anger she said (in quite decent German),

'Are you in charge here?'

'Madam, I am.'

'Do you realise,' she said, with her jaw juddering, 'do you *realise* that there was no restaurant wagon on this train?'

I dared not meet Zulz's eye. 'No restaurant wagon? Barbaric.'

'No service at all. Even in 1st class!'

'Even in 1st class? An outrage.'

'All we had were the cold cuts we'd brought with us. And we almost ran out of mineral water!'

'Monstrous.'

'. . . Why are you laughing? You laugh. Why are you laughing?'

'Step back, Madam, if you would,' I spluttered. 'Senior Supervisor Grese!'

And so, whilst the luggage was stacked near the handcarts, and whilst the travellers were formed into an orderly column (my Sonders moving among them murmuring '*Bienvenu, les enfants*', '*Etes-vous fatigué, Monsieur, après votre voyage?*'), I wryly reminisced about old Walther Pabst. He and I campaigned together in the Rossbach Freikorps. What sweating, snorting chastisements we visited on the Red queers in Munich and Mecklenburg, in the Ruhr and Upper Silesia, and in the Baltic lands of Latvia and Lithuania! And how often, during the long years in prison (after we settled accounts with the traitor Kadow in the Schlageter affair in '23), would we sit up late in our cell and, between endless games of 2-card brag, discuss, by flickering candlelight, the finer points of philosophy!

I reached for the loudhailer and said,

'*Greetings, 1 and all. Now I'm not going to lead you up the garden path. You're here to recuperate and then it's off to the farms with you, where there'll be honest work for honest board. We won't be asking too much of that little young 'un, you there in the sailor suit, or of you, sir, in your fine astrakhan coat. Each to his or her talents and abilities. Fair enough? Very well! 1st, we shall escort you to the sauna for a warm shower before you settle in your rooms. It's just a short drive through the birch wood. Leave your suitcases here, please. You can pick them up at the guest house. Tea and cheese sandwiches will be served immediately, and later there'll be a piping hot stew. Onwards!*'

As an added courtesy I handed the horn to Captain Eltz, who repeated the gist of my words in French. Then, quite naturally, it seemed, we fell into step, the fractious old lady, of course, remaining on the ramp, to be dealt with by Senior Supervisor Grese in the appropriate manner.

And I was thinking, Why isn't it always like this? And it would be, if I had my way. A comfortable journey followed by a friendly and dignified reception. What needed we, really, of the crashing doors of those boxcars, the blazing arc lights, the terrible yelling ('*Out! Get out! Quick! Faster! FASTER!*'), the dogs, the truncheons, and the whips? And how civilised the KL looked in the thickening glow of dusk, and how richly the birches glistened. There was, it has to be said, the characteristic odour (and some of our newcomers were sniffing it with little upward jerks of their heads), but after a day of breezy high-pressure weather, even that was nothing out of the . . .

Here it came, that wretched, that accursed *lorry*, the size of a furniture van yet decidedly uncouth – positively thuggish – in aspect, its springs creaking and its exhaust pipe rowdily backfiring, barnacled in rust, the green tarpaulin palpitating, the profiled driver with the stub of a cigarette in his mouth and his tattooed arm dangling from the window of his cab. Violently it braked and skidded, jolting to a halt as it crossed the rails, its wheels whining for purchase. Now it slumped sickeningly to the left, the near sideflap billowed skyward, and there – for 2 or 3 stark seconds – its cargo stood revealed.

It was a sight no less familiar to me than spring rain or autumn leaves: nothing more than the day's natural wastage from KL1, on its way to KL2. But of course our Parisians let out a great whimpering howl – Zulz reflexively raised his forearms as though to fend it off, and even Captain Eltz jerked his head round at me. The utter breakdown of the transport was but a breath away . . .

Now you don't go far in the Protective Custody business if you can't think on your feet and show a bit of presence of mind. Many another Kommandant, I dare say, would have let the situation at once degenerate into something decidedly unpleasant. Paul Doll, however, happens to be of a rather different stamp. With 1 wordless motion I gave the order. Not to my men-at-arms, no: to my musicians!

The brief transitional interlude was very hard indeed, I admit, as the first strains of the violins could do no more than duplicate and reinforce that helpless, quavering cry. But then the melody took hold; the filthy truck with its flapping tarps lurched free of the crossing and bowled off down the crescent road (and was soon lost to sight); and on we strolled.

It was just as I had instinctively sensed: our guests *were utterly incapable of absorbing what they had seen.* I later learned that they were the inmates of 2 luxurious institutions, a retirement home and an orphanage (both of which were underwritten by the most outrageous swindlers of them all, the Rothschilds). Our Parisians – what knew they of ghetto, of pogrom, of razzia? What knew they of the noble fury of the folk?

We all of us walked as if on tiptoe – yes, we tiptoed through the birch wood, past trunks of hoary grey . . .

The peeling birchbark, the Little Brown Bower with its picket fence and potted geraniums and marigolds, the undressing room, the chamber. I turned on my heel with a flourish the instant Prufer gave his signal and I knew the doors were all screwed shut.

Now *that's* better. The 2nd aspirin (650 mg; 22.43), is going about its work, its labour of solace, of ablution. It really is the proverbial 'wonder drug' – and I'm told that no patented preparation has ever been cheaper. God bless IG Farben! (Reminder: order in some rather *good* champagne for Sunday the 6th, to tickle Frauen Burckl and Seedig – and Frauen Uhl and Zulz, not to mention poor little Alisz Seisser. And I suppose we'll have to ask Angelus Thomsen, considering who he is.) I also find that Martell brandy, when taken in liberal but not injudicious quantities, has a salutary effect. Moreover, the stringent liquor helps soothe my insanely itching gums.

Whilst I can take a joke as well as the next man, it's clear that I'll have to have a few very serious words with Walther Pabst. In financial terms, ST 105 was something of a disaster. How do I justify the mobilisation of a full Storm (with flamethrowers)? How do I vindicate my costly use of the Little Brown Bower – when normally, in handling so light a load, you would look to the method employed by Senior Supervisor Grese on the little lady with the ebony cane? Old Walli, doubtlessly, will claim 'an eye for an eye': he's still brooding about that prank at the barracks in Erfurt with the meat pie and the chamber pot.

Of course it's an almighty pain, having to watch the pennies as closely as we do. Take the trains. If money were no object, all the transportees, so far as I'm concerned, could come here in *couchettes*. It would facilitate our subterfuge, or our *ruse de guerre*, if you prefer (as it *is* a war, and no error). Fascinating that our friends from France saw something that they were quite unable to assimilate: this is a reminder of – and a tribute to – the blinding *radicalism* of the KL. Alas, however, one can't 'go mad' and throw money around as if the stuff 'grew on trees'.

(NB. No gasoline was used, and this must count as an economy, albeit minor. Usually those selected Right go by foot to KL1, do you see, whilst those selected Left proceed to KL2 by means of the Red Cross trucks and the ambulances. But how could I induce those Pariserinnen to board a vehicle, after seeing that damned lorry? A very slight saving, agreed, but every little helps. No?)

'Enter!' I called out.

It was the Bible Bee. On the tasselled tray: a glass of burgundy, and a ham sandwich, if you please.

I said, 'But I wanted something hot.'

'Sorry, sir, it's all there is for now.'

'I do work quite hard, you know . . .'

Fussily Humilia began to clear a space on the low table in front of the chimney piece. I must confess it's a mystery to me how a woman so tragically ugly can love her Maker. It goes without saying that what you really want with a ham sandwich is a foaming tankard of beer. We're all awash in this French muck when what you desire is a decent flagon of Kronenbourg or Grolsch.

'Did you prepare that or did Frau Doll?'

'Sir, Frau Doll went to bed an hour ago.'

'Did she now. Another bottle of Martell. And that'll be all.'

On top of everything else I foresee no end of complication and expense in the proposed construction of KL3. Where are the materials? Will Dobler release matching funds? No one is interested in difficulties, no one is interested in 'the objective conditions'. The schedules of the transports I'm being asked to accept next month are outlandish. And, as if I didn't have 'enough on my plate', who should telephone, at midnight, but Horst Blobel in Berlin. The instruction he adumbrated made my flesh go hot and cold. Did I hear him aright? I cannot possibly carry out such an order whilst Hannah remains in the KL. The dear God! This is going to be an absolute nightmare.

*

28

'You're a good girl,' I said to Sybil. 'You cleaned your teeth today.'

'How do you know? Is it my breath?'

I love it when she looks so sweetly affronted and confused!

'Vati knows everything, Sybil. You've also been trying to style your hair. I'm not cross! I'm glad *someone's* taking a bit of care with their appearance. And not lounging around all day in a grubby housecoat.'

'Can I go now, Vati?'

'So you're wearing pink panties this morning.'

'No I'm not. They're blue!'

A shrewd tactic – to get something wrong every now and then.

'Prove it,' I said. 'Ahah! Homer nods.'

Now here's a common fallacy I want to knock on the head without further ado: the notion that the Schutzstaffel, the Praetorian Guard of the Reich, is predominantly made up of men from the Proletariat and the Kleinburgertum. Granted, that might have been true of the SA, in the early years, but it has never been true of the SS – whose membership rolls read like an extract from the *Almanach de Gotha*. Oh, *jawohl*: the Archduke of Mecklenburg; the Princes Waldeck, von Hassen, and von Hohenzollern-Emden; the Counts Bassewitz-Behr, Stachwitz, and von Rodden. Why, here in the Zone of Interest, for a short time, we even had our own Baron!

The bluebloods and also the *intelligent*, professors, lawyers, entrepreneurs.

I just wanted to knock that 1 on the head without additional fuss.

'Reveille is at 3,' said Suitbert Seedig, 'and Buna's a 90-minute march. They're exhausted before they begin. They knock off at 6 and get back at 8. Carrying their casualties. And tell me, Major. How can we get any work out of them?'

'Yes, yes,' I said. Also present, in my large and well-appointed office in the Main Administrative Building (the MAB), were

Frithuric Burckl and Angelus Thomsen. 'But who's going to pay for it may I ask?'

'Farben,' said Burckl. 'The Vorstand has agreed.'

At this I perked up somewhat.

Seedig said, 'You, my Kommandant, are asked only to provide inmates and guards. And overall security will of course remain in your hands. Farben will defray construction and running costs.'

'Well now,' I said. 'A world-renowned concern with its own Konzentrationslager. Unerhort!'

Burckl said, 'We'll also provide the food – independently. There'll be no back-and-forth with KL1. And therefore no typhus. So we hope.'

'Ah. Typhus. That's the crux, nicht? Though the situation was eased, I rather fancy, by the substantial selection of August 29th.'

'They're still dying', said Seedig, 'at a rate of 1,000 a week.'

'Mm. Look here. Are you planning to increase the rations?'

Seedig and Burckl glanced sharply at one another. It was clear to me that they were in disagreement on this question. Burckl twisted in his chair and said,

'Yes I *would* argue for a modest increase. Of, say, 20 per cent.'

'20 per cent!'

'Yes, sir, 20 per cent. They'll have that much more strength and they'll last a bit longer. Obviously.'

Now Thomsen spoke. 'With respect, Mr Burckl – your sphere is that of commerce, and Dr Seedig is an industrial chemist. The Kommandant and I can't afford to be so purely practical. We dare not lose sight of our complementary objective. Our political objective.'

'My thought exactly,' I said. 'And by the way. On this matter the Reichsfuhrer-SS and myself are of 1 accord.' I smacked my palm down on the desktop. 'We'll *not* stand for any pampering!'

'Amen, my Kommandant,' said Thomsen. 'This is not a sanatorium.'

'No mollycoddling! What do they think this is? Some sort of rest home?'

In the washroom of the Officers' Club what do I find but a copy of *Der Sturmer*. Now this publication has for some time been banned in the KL, and on my orders. With its disgusting and hysterical emphasis on the carnal predations of the Jewish male, *Der Sturmer*, I believe, has done serious anti-Semitism a great deal of harm. The people need to see charts, diagrams, statistics, the scientific *evidence* – and not a full-page cartoon of Shylock (as it might be) slavering over Rapunzel. I am far from alone in this view. It is the policy championed by the Reichssicherheitshauptamt itself.

In Dachau, where I launched my meteoric rise through the custodial hierarchy, a display case of *Der Sturmer*s was erected in the prisoners' canteen. It had a galvanising effect on the criminal element, and violence frequently ensued. Our Jewish brethren wormed their way out of it in typical fashion, with bribes – as they all had plenty of money. Besides, they were mainly persecuted by their co-religionists, notably Eschen, their Block Senior.

The Jews were of course aware that over the long term this foul rag actually helped their cause rather than hindered it. I offer the following as a footnote: it is well known that the editor of *Der Sturmer* is himself a Jew; and he also writes the worst of the incendiary articles it features. I rest my case.

Hannah smokes, you know. Oh, ja. Ah, yech. I found an empty packet of Davidoffs in the drawer where she keeps her underwear. If the servants talk it will soon get about that I can't discipline my wife. Angelus Thomsen is an odd bird. He's sound enough, I dare say, but there's something impudent and embarrassing about his manner. I wonder if he is perhaps a homosexualist (albeit deeply repressed). Does he have even an honorary rank, or is everything reliant on his 'connection'? Curious, because no one is more widely

31

and thoroughly loathed than the Brown Eminence. (Reminder: the lorry, from now on, to follow the more roundabout route north of the Summer Huts.) It calms you down and it numbs the gums, but brandy also boasts a third property: that of an aphrodisiac.

Ach, there's nothing wrong with Hannah that the good old 15 centimetres won't cure. When, after a final glass or 2 of Martell, I wend my way to the bedroom, she should be suitably prompt in the performance of her spousal duty. If I do encounter any nonsense, I will simply invoke that magic name: *Dieter Kruger*!

For I am a normal man with normal needs.

. . . I was halfway to the door when I was struck by an unpleasant thought. It so happens that I've not yet seen the balance sheet for Special Train 105. And I left the Little Brown Bower, that evening, without specifically telling Wolfram Prufer to bury the pieces in the Spring Meadow. Was he stupid enough to fire up a Topf & Sons 3-retorter to deal with a smattering of brats and dodderers? Surely not. No. No. Wiser heads would have prevailed. Prufer would have listened to 1 of the old hands. For example, Szmul.

Oh, Christ, what am I going on about? If Horst Blobel meant what he said, then the whole bloody lot of them'll all have to come up anyway.

I see I'd better have a brood about this. I'll sleep in the dressing room, *as usual*, and tackle Hannah in the morning. 1 of those 1s where you slip in beside them whilst they're all warm and somnolent, and ease up against them and into them. I won't stand for any hogwash. And then we'll both be in excellent spirits for our little gathering here at the villa!

For I am a normal man with normal needs. I am *completely normal*. This is what nobody seems to understand.

Paul Doll is completely normal.

3. SZMUL: SONDER

Ihr seit achzen johr, we whisper, *und ihr hott a fach.*

Once upon a time there was a king, and the king commissioned his favourite wizard to create a magic mirror. This mirror didn't show you your reflection. It showed you your soul – it showed you who you really were.

The wizard couldn't look at it without turning away. The king couldn't look at it. The courtiers couldn't look at it. A chestful of treasure was offered to any citizen in this peaceful land who could look at it for sixty seconds without turning away. And no one could.

I find that the KZ is that mirror. The KZ is that mirror, but with one difference. You can't turn away.

We are of the Sonderkommando, the SK, the Special Squad, and we are the saddest men in the Lager. We are in fact the saddest men in the history of the world. And of all these very sad men I am the saddest. Which is demonstrably, even measurably true. I am by some distance the earliest number, the lowest number – the *oldest* number.

As well as being the saddest men who ever lived, we are also the most disgusting. And yet our situation is paradoxical.

It is difficult to see how we can be as disgusting as we unquestionably are when we do no harm.

The case could be made that on balance we do a little good. Still, we are infinitely disgusting, and also infinitely sad.

Nearly all our work is done among the dead, with the heavy scissors, the pliers and mallets, the buckets of petrol refuse, the ladles, the grinders.

Yet we also move among the living. So we say, '*Viens donc, petit marin. Accroches ton costume. Rappelles-toi le numéro. Tu as quatre-vingt-trois!*' And we say, '*Faites un nœud avec les lacets, Monsieur. Je vais essayer de trouver un cintre pour votre manteau. Astrakhan! C'est toison d'agneau, n'est-ce pas?*'

After a major Aktion we typically receive a fifth of vodka or schnapps, five cigarettes, and a hundred grams of sausage made from bacon, veal, and pork suet. While we are not always sober, we are never hungry and we are never cold, at least not at night. We sleep in the room above the disused crematory (hard by the Monopoly Building), where the sacks of hair are cured.

When he was still with us, my philosophical friend Adam used to say, *We don't even have the comfort of innocence.* I didn't and I don't agree. I would still plead not guilty.

A *hero*, of course, would *escape* and *tell the world*. But it is my feeling that the world has known for quite some time. How could it not, given the scale?

There persist three reasons, or excuses, for going on living: first, to bear witness, and, second, to exact mortal vengeance. I am bearing witness; but the magic looking glass does not show me a killer. Or not yet.

Third, and most crucially, we save a life (or prolong a life) at the rate of one per transport. Sometimes none, sometimes two – an average of one. And 0.01 per cent is not 0.00. They are invariably male youths.

It has to be effected while they're leaving the train; by the time the lines form for the selection – it's already too late.

*

Ihr seit achzen johr alt, we whisper, *und ihr hott a fach.*
Sie sind achtzehn Jahre alt, und Sie haben einen Handel.
Vous avez dix-huit ans, et vous avez un commerce.

You are eighteen years old, and you have a trade.

CHAPTER II. TO BUSINESS

I. THOMSEN: PROTECTORS

Boris Eltz was going to tell me the story of Special Train 105, and I wanted to hear it, but first I asked him,

'Who've you got on at the moment? Remind me.'

'Uh, that cook in Bunatown and that barmaid in Katowitz. And I'm hoping to get somewhere with Alisz Seisser. The sergeant's widow. He's only been dead a week but she seems quite keen.' Boris gave some background. 'The trouble is she's off home to Hamburg in a day or two. Golo, I've asked you this before. I like all kinds of women, so why do I only *fancy* the lower classes?'

'I don't know, brother. It's not an unendearing trait. Now please. Sonderzug 105.'

He folded his hands behind his nape and his lips slowly parted. 'It's funny, isn't it, with the French. Don't you find, Golo? You can't quite rid yourself of the idea that they lead the world. In refinement, in urbanity. A nation of proven funkers and toadies – but they're still supposed to be better than anyone else. Better than us gross Germans. Better even than the English. And a part of you consents to it. The French – even now, when they're completely crushed and squirming, you still can't help yourself.'

Boris shook his head, as if in ingenuous wonderment at humanity – at humanity and its crooked timber.

'These things run deep,' I said. 'Continue, Boris, if you would.'

'Well I found I was relieved, no, happy and proud that the ramp was looking its best. All swept and hosed. Nobody very drunk

– it was too early. And such a pretty sunset. Even the smell had dropped. The passenger train pulls in, all festive. It could've come from Cannes or Biarritz. The people disembark unassisted. No whips, no truncheons. No cattle cars awash with God knows what. The Old Boozer gives his speech, I translate, and off we go. All so very civilised. Then along comes that fucking lorry. And the jig was up.'

'Why? What was in it?'

'Corpses. The daily berm of corpses. On its way from the Stammlager to the Spring Meadow.'

He said that about a dozen of them half flopped out over the tailboard; he said that it made him imagine a crew of ghosts being sick over a ship's side.

'With their arms swinging. Not just any old corpses either. Starveling corpses. Covered in shit, and filth, and rags, and gore, and wounds, and boils. Smashed-up, forty-kilo corpses.'

'Mm. Untoward.'

'Hardly the height of sophistication,' said Boris.

'Is that when they wailed? We heard the wail.'

'It was a sight to see.'

'Mm. And a lot to uh, construe.' I meant that it was not just a spectacle but also a narrative: it told a long story. 'A fair bit to take in.'

'Drogo Uhl thinks they never did. Take it in. But I think they just *blushed* for us – mortally blushed for us. For our . . . *cochonneries*. I mean, a lorry full of starved corpses. All a bit gauche and provincial, don't you think?'

'Possibly. Arguably.'

'So *insortable*. You can't take us anywhere.'

Misleadingly undersized and misleadingly slight, Boris was a senior colonel in the Waffen-SS: the armed, the fighting, the *battle* SS. The Waffen-SS was supposed to be less straitened by hierarchy – more quixotic and spontaneous – than the Wehrmacht, with lively disagreements running up and down the chain of command. One of Boris's disagreements with his superior, over tactics (this was in Voronezh), turned into a fistfight, from which the young major general emerged without a tooth in his head. That was why Boris was here – *among the Austrians*, as he often put it (and demoted to captain). He had nine more months to go.

'What about the selection?' I asked.

'There was no selection. They were all certainties for the gas.'

'. . . I'm thinking, What *don't* we do to them? I suppose we don't rape them.'

'Much. Instead we do something much nastier than that. You ought to learn some respect for your new colleagues, Golo. Much, *much* nastier. We get the pretty ones and we do medical experiments on them. On their reproductive organs. We turn them into little old ladies. Then hunger turns them into little old men.'

I said, 'Would you agree that we couldn't treat them any worse?'

'Oh, come on. We don't eat them.'

For a moment I thought about this. 'Yes, but they wouldn't mind being eaten. Unless we ate them alive.'

'No, what we do is make them eat each other. They mind that . . . Golo, who in Germany *didn't* think the Jews needed taking down a peg? But this is fucking ridiculous, this is. And you know the worst thing about it? You know what really rots in my craw?'

'I suspect I do, Boris.'

'Yeah. How many divisions are we tying up? There are thousands of camps. Thousands. Man hours, train hours, police hours, fuel hours. And we're killing our labour! What about the war?'

'Exactly. What about the war.'

'How does all this connect to that? . . . Oh, look at her, Golo. Her with the dark crewcut in the corner. That's Esther. Have you ever seen anything a *tenth* as sweet in all your life?'

*

38

We were in Boris's little ground-floor office, which commanded a wide and level view of Kalifornia. This Esther belonged to the Aufraumungskommando, the Clearance Detail, one of a rotating pool of two or three hundred girls who busied themselves in a shed-cluttered yard – a yard the size of a soccer field.

Boris rose to his feet and stretched. 'I came to her rescue. She was clawing up rubble in Monowitz. Then a cousin of hers sneaked her in here. She got found out, of course – because she didn't have any hair. They marked her down for the Scheissekommando. But I stepped in. It's not that difficult. Here, you just rob Peter to bribe Paul.'

'And for this she hates you.'

'She hates me.' Bitterly he shook his head. 'Well I'll give her something to hate me for.'

He tapped with his fountain pen on the glass, and went on tapping till Esther looked up. She gave a great roll of the eyes and returned to her task (she was curiously engaged – squeezing out tubes of toothpaste into a cracked pitcher). Boris got up and opened the door and beckoned.

'Miss Kubis. Take a postcard, if you would.'

Fifteen years old, and Sephardic, I thought (the Levantine colouring), and finely and tautly made, and athletic, she somehow managed to trudge, to clump into the room; it was almost satirical, her leadenness of gait. Boris said,

'Please be seated. I need your Czech and your girlish hand.' He smiled and said, 'Esther, *why* do you loathe me so?'

She plucked at the sleeve of her shirt.

'My uniform?' He handed her the fine-pointed pencil. 'Ready? *Dear Mama colon. My friend Esther's writing this for me . . . because I hurt my hand.* So, Golo, a report if you please. *While out gathering roses full stop.* How's the Valkyrie?'

'I'll be seeing her tonight. Or I certainly hope and trust I will.

The Old Boozer is having a dinner for the Farben people.'

'You know, she tends to cry off, I've heard. And it'll be deadly if she isn't there. *How to describe life in the agricultural station question mark.* You're pleased, though, so far.'

'Oh, yes. Thrilled. I even made a kind of verbal pass, and I gave her my address. I wish I hadn't in a way, because I'm always thinking she's about to knock on my door. You couldn't say she leapt at it, no, but she heard me out.'

'*The work is pretty strenuous comma.* You can't have her to your place – not with that nosey bitch downstairs. *But I love the country-side and the open air full stop.*'

'Anyway. She's magnificent.'

'Yes, she is, but there's too much of her. *The conditions are really very decent colon.* I like them smaller. They try harder. *Our bedrooms are plain but comfy open brackets.* And you can fling them about the place. *And in October they'll be giving out . . .* You're mad, you know.'

'Why?'

'Him. *And in October they'll be giving out these gorgeous eider-downs. For the colder nights close brackets semicolon.* Him. The Old Boozer.'

'He's nothing.' And I used a Yiddish expression – pronouncing it accurately enough to give Miss Kubis's pencil a momentary pause. 'He's a *grubbe tuchus*. A fat-arse. He's weak.'

'*The food is simple comma true comma but wholesome and plentiful semicolon.* Old fat-arse is vicious, Golo. *And everything is immacu-lately clean full stop.* And he has cunning. The cunning of the weak. *Huge*, underline that, please, *huge farmstead bathrooms . . . with great big free-standing tubs full stop. Cleanliness comma cleanli-ness dash. You know those Germans exclamation mark.*' Boris sighed and said with adolescent or even childish petulance, '*Miss* Kubis. *Please* look up now and then so at least I can see your face!'

*

40

Smoking cigarillos, and drinking kir from conical glasses, we looked out at Kalifornia, which resembled, simultaneously and on a massive compass, an emptied block-long department store, a wide-spectrum jumble sale, an auction room, customs house, trade fair, agora, mart, soukh, chowk – a planetary, a terminal Lost and Found.

Beetling heaps of rucksacks, kitbags, holdalls, cases and trunks (these last adorned with enticing labels of travel – redolent of frontier posts, misty cities), like a vast bonfire awaiting the torch. A stack of blankets as high as a three-storey building: no princess, be she never so delicate, would feel a pea beneath twenty, thirty thousand thicknesses. And all around fat hillocks of pots and pans, of hairbrushes, shirts, coats, dresses, handkerchiefs – also watches, spectacles, and all kinds of prostheses, wigs, dentures, deaf-aids, surgical boots, spinal supports. The eye came last to the mound of children's shoes, and the sprawling mountain of prams, some of them just wooden troughs on wheels, some of them all curve and contour, carriages for little dukes, little duchesses. I said,

'What's she doing over there, your Esther? It's a bit unGerman, isn't it? What use is a bucket of toothpaste?'

'She's looking for precious stones . . . You know how she won my heart, Golo? They made her dance for me. She was like liquid. I almost burst into tears. It was my birthday and she danced for me.'

'Oh yes. Happy birthday, Boris.'

'Thanks. Better late than never.'

'How does it feel to be thirty-two?'

'All right, I suppose. So far. You'll find out yourself in a minute.' He ran his tongue over his lips. 'You know they pay for their own tickets? They pay their own way here, Golo. I don't know how it went with those Parisians, but the norm is . . .' He bent to wipe a wisp of smoke from his eye. 'The norm is a flat third-class fare. One-way. Half price for children under twelve. One-way.' He straightened up. 'It's good, isn't it.'

41

'You could say that.'

'. . . The Jews had to come down from their high horse. Which was accomplished by 1934. But this – this is fucking ridiculous.'

———

Yes, and Suitbert and Romhilde Seedig were there, and Frithuric and Amalasand Burckl were there, and the Uhls, Drogo and Norberte, were there, and Baldemar and Trudel Zulz were there . . . I – I of course was partnerless; but they balanced me out with the young widow, Alisz Seisser (Regimental Sergeant Major Orbart Seisser having very recently passed away, in stupendous violence and ignominy, here at the Kat Zet).

Yes, and Paul and Hannah Doll were there.

It was the major who opened the front door. He reared back and said,

'Ahah, he's in full fig! And he has a commission, no less.'

'It's nominal, sir.' I was wiping my feet on the mat. 'And it could hardly be more basic, could it?'

'Rank is not a sure gauge of importance, Obersturmfuhrer. Scope of jurisdiction's the thing. Look at Fritz Mobius. He's even lower down the scale than yourself – and he's a fizzer. Scope of jurisdiction's the key. Come on through, young man. And don't worry about this. Gardening accident. I took a nasty clout to the bridge of my nose.'

And, as a result, Paul Doll had two fulminant black eyes.

'It's nothing. I know what a real wound is, I think. You should've seen the state of me on the Iraqi front in 1918. I was in bits. And don't worry about *them*, either.'

He meant his daughters. Paulette and Sybil were sitting at the top of the stairs in their nightdresses, holding hands and patiently weeping. Doll said,

'Dear oh dear. They've got their knickers in a twist about something or other. Now where's my lady wife?'

42

I had resolved not to stare. So Hannah — huge and goddessy and freshly sunburnt in an evening dress of amber silk — was almost at once consigned to the wastes of my peripheral vision . . . I knew that a long and tortuous evening was stretching out before me; and yet I still hoped to make some modest headway. My plan was to introduce and emphasise a certain theme, and thus exploit a certain rule of attraction. It was a regrettable rule of attraction, perhaps; but it nearly always worked.

Tall, slender Seedig and portly little Burckl were in business suits; all the other men loomed in dress uniform. Doll, bemedalled (Iron Cross, Silver Wand Badge, SS Honour Ring), stood with his rear to the log fire and with his legs absurdly far apart, rocking on his heels and, yes, occasionally raising a hand and letting it tremble over the gruesome whelks beneath his brows. Alisz Seisser was in mourning clothes, but Norberte Uhl, Romhilde Seedig, Amalasand Burckl, and Trudel Zulz were ablaze in velvet and taffeta, like playing cards — queens of diamonds, queens of clubs. Doll said,

'Thomsen, help yourself. Go on, get stuck in.'

On the sideboard there were many platters of canapés (smoked salmon, salami, pickled herring), plus a full bar and four or five half-empty bottles of champagne. I shuffled along with the Uhls — Drogo, a middle-aged captain, who was built like a docker, and had a split chin grey-blue with stubble, and Norberte, a frizzy, fussy presence wearing skittle-sized earrings and a gilt diadem. Not many words were exchanged, yet I made two mildly surprising discoveries: Norberte and Drogo strongly disliked each other, and they were both already drunk.

I got hold of Frithuric Burckl and talked shop for twenty minutes; then Humilia came through the double doors, gave a shy curtsey, and announced that dinner would presently be served.

Hannah said, 'How are the girls? Any better?'

'Still very bad, ma'am. I can't do a thing with them. They won't be consoled.'

Humilia stepped aside as Hannah walked quickly past, and with a grin of vexation the Commandant watched her go.

'Now you're *here*. Now you're *there*.'

Boris had solemnly warned me that the women would be seated en bloc, or else they would eat separately in the kitchen (perhaps with the children at an earlier sitting). But no – we dined in the standard coeducational style. There were twelve of us at the circular table; and if I was at six o'clock, then Doll was at eleven, and Hannah was at two (the intertwining of our calves was technically possible – but if I attempted it only the back of my head would remain on my chair). I had Norberte Uhl on one side and Alisz Seisser on the other. With white handkerchiefs noosed round their heads, the maid Bronislawa and another auxiliary, Albinka, lit the candelabrum using the long yuletide matches. I said,

'Good evening, ladies. Good evening, Mrs Uhl. Good evening, Mrs Seisser.'

'Thank you, sir, I'm sure, sir,' said Alisz.

The convention hereabouts was that you talked to the women during the soup course; after that, once general conversation started up, their voices were not really expected to be heard (and they became like padding; they became shock absorbers). Norberte Uhl had her ruddy, disappointed face slumped low over the tablecloth, and was chuckling hoarsely to herself. So without glancing at two o'clock I turned from seven o'clock to five o'clock and settled down to apply myself to the widow.

'I was very saddened, Mrs Seisser,' I began, 'to hear of your bereavement.'

'Yes, sir, thank you, sir.'

She was in her late twenties, interestingly sallow with many beauty spots (giving you a sense of continuity when, as she sat, she raised her knotty black veil). Boris was a vocal admirer of her rounded low-slung figure (and tonight it looked fluid and buoyant, despite her sepulchral tread). He also told me, in scornful detail, about the last hours of the sergeant major.

'Such a waste,' said Alisz.

'But it's a time of great sacrifices and . . .'

'That's true, sir. Thank you, sir.'

Alisz Seisser wasn't here as a friend or a colleague but as the honoured relict of a humble NCO; and she was obviously and painfully ill at ease. I wished in general to give her comfort. And for a while I searched for a redeeming feature, a saving grace – yes, a silver lining in the black thunderhead of Orbart's ruin. It occurred to me to begin by saying that the Sturmscharfuhrer, at the time of his misadventure, was at least under the influence of a potent analgesic – a large, if entirely recreational, dose of morphine.

'He wasn't feeling well on the day,' she said, revealing her feline teeth (paper-white, paper-thin). 'Not feeling well at all.'

'Mm. It is very demanding work.'

'He told me, you know, I'm not at my best, old girl. I'm not the thing.'

Before going to the Krankenbau to get his medication, Sergeant Seisser went to Kalifornia to steal enough money to pay for it. With all this accomplished, he returned to his post on the southern edge of the Women's Camp. As he neared the Potato Store (perhaps hoping for some refreshment from its still), two prisoners broke ranks and made a run for the perimeter (a form of suicide, and astonishingly rare); Seisser raised his machine gun and boldly opened fire.

'A melancholy combination of circumstances,' I said.

Because Orbart, surprised by the repercussive force of the weapon (and no doubt also surprised by the force of the drug), staggered backwards six or seven feet and, still spraying bullets, collapsed against the electrified fence.

'A tragedy,' said Alisz.

45

'One can only hope, Mrs Seisser, that the work of time . . .'

'Well. Time heals all wounds, sir. Or so it's said.'

At last the soup bowls were cleared away and we took delivery of the main course – a thick and vinous beef stew.

Hannah had just come back to the table, and Doll was in mid anecdote, telling of the visit, seven weeks earlier (in mid July), of the Reichsfuhrer-SS, Heinrich Himmler.

'I took our distinguished guest to the Rabbit Breeding Station in Dwory. I urge you to look in there, Frau Seedig. Gorgeous angora rabbits, as white and fluffy as they come. We farm them, you know, by the hundred. For their fur, nicht? To keep our aircrews warm on their missions! And there was one particular customer called *Snowball*,' said Doll, his face gradually breaking into a leer. 'An absolute beauty. And the prisoner doctor, what am I saying, the prisoner *vet*, he'd taught it all kinds of "tricks".' Doll frowned (and winced, and smiled with pain). 'Well, there was just this one trick. The main trick. Snowball would sit up on his hind legs, with his forepaws, you know, like this – and beg, they'd taught Snowball to beg!'

'And was our distinguished guest duly charmed?' asked Professor Zulz (Zulz, an honorary SS colonel, had the sinister agelessness peculiar to certain medical men). 'Was he tickled?'

'Oh, the Reichsfuhrer was tickled pink. Why, he fairly beamed – he clapped his hands! And his entire entourage, you know, they, they clapped their hands. All for this Snowball. Who looked rather alarmed but just sat there begging!'

Of course with the ladies present the gentlemen were trying not to talk about the war effort (and also trying not to talk about its local component – the progress of the Buna-Werke). During this time I never met Hannah's eye exactly, but our roundabout glances occasionally swished past one another in the candle-light . . . Elaborating on the arts of natural husbandry, the talk

46

moved on – herbal remedies, the crossbreeding of vegetables, Mendelism, the controversial teachings of the Soviet agronomist Trofim Lysenko.

'It should be more widely known', said Professor Zulz, 'that the Reichsfuhrer is highly distinguished in the field of ethnology. I'm referring to his work at the Ahnenerbe.'

'Certainly,' said Doll. 'He's assembled whole teams of anthropologists and archaeologists.'

'Runologists, heraldists, and what have you.'

'Expeditions to Mesopotamia, the Andes, Tibet.'

'Expertise,' said Zulz. 'Brainpower. Which is why we're the masters of Europe. Applied logic – that's all it is. There's no great mystery to it. Do you know, I wonder if there's ever been a leadership, a chain of command, as intellectually evolved as our own.'

'IQ,' said Doll. 'Mental capacity. There's no great mystery to it.'

'Yesterday morning I was clearing my desk,' Zulz went on, 'and I came across two memoranda clipped together. Hear this. Of the twenty-five leaders of the Einsatzgruppen in Poland and the USSR, who did some warm work I can tell you – fifteen doctorates. Now look at the Conference of State Secretaries in January. Of the fifteen attendees? *Eight* doctorates.'

'What was this conference?' asked Suitbert Seedig.

'In Berlin,' said Captain Uhl. 'At Wannsee. To finalise—'

'To finalise the proposed evacuations', said Doll, raising his chin and tubing his lips, 'to the liberated territories in the east.'

'Mm. "Over the Bug",' said Drogo Uhl with a snort.

'Eight doctorates,' said Professor Zulz. 'All right, Heydrich, rest in peace, convened and chaired. But him apart these were secondary or even tertiary functionaries. And yet. Eight doctorates. Strength in depth. *That's* how you get the optimal decisions.'

'Who was there?' said Doll with a glance at his fingernails. 'Heydrich. But who else? Lange. Gestapo Muller. Eichmann – the distinguished stationmaster. With his clipboard and his whistle.'

'That's exactly my point, Paul. Intellectual strength in depth. First-rate decisions all the way down.'

'My dear Baldemar, nothing was "decided" at Wannsee. They merely rubber-stamped a decision taken months earlier. And taken at the most exalted level.'

It was time to introduce and emphasise my theme. Under the political system that here obtained, everyone had soon got used to the idea that where secrecy began, power began. Now, *power corrupts*: this was not a metaphor. But *power attracts*, luckily (for me), was not a metaphor either; and I had derived much sexual advantage from my proximity to power. In wartime, women especially felt the gravitational pull of it; they would be needing all their friends and admirers, all their protectors. I said, slightly teasingly,

'Major. May I tell you one or two things that are not widely known?'

Doll gave a little upward bob on his buttocks and said, 'Oh yes please.'

'Thank you. The conference was a kind of experiment or pilot run. And the chairman foresaw very serious difficulties. But it was a great and unexpected success. When it was over, Heydrich, Reichsprotektor Reinhard Heydrich, had a cigar and a glass of brandy. In the middle of the day. Heydrich, who only ever drank alone. A brandy in front of the fire. With the little ticket-puncher Eichmann curled up at his feet.'

'. . . Were you there?'

I shrugged limply. I also leaned forward and, in an experimental spirit, placed my hand between Alisz Seisser's knees; and her knees clenched and her hand found mine, and I made a further discovery.

In addition to her other troubles, Alisz was mortally terrified. Her whole body quaked with it. Doll said,

'Were you there? Or was it too low-level for you?' He chewed and swallowed. 'Doubtlessly you get all this from your Uncle Martin.' The two black eyes toured the table. 'Bormann,' he said in a deeper voice. 'The Reichsleiter . . . I knew your Uncle Martin, Thomsen. We were muckers in the time of struggle.'

This was a surprise to me, but I said, 'Yes, sir. He often mentions you and the friendship you both enjoyed.'

'Give him my best. And uh, do please go on.'

'Where were we? Heydrich wanted to test the waters. To see—'

'If you mean the Lake it's bloody freezing.'

'Suitbert, please,' said Doll. 'Herr Thomsen.'

'To test the waters for administrative resistance. Resistance to what might seem to be a rather ambitious endeavour. To apply our conclusive racial strategy through the whole of Europe.'

'And?'

'As I said, unexpectedly smooth. There was no resistance. None.'

Zulz said, 'What's unexpected about that?'

'Well, think of the scope, Professor. Spain, England, Portugal, Ireland. And the numbers involved. Ten million. Perhaps twelve.'

Now the lolling shape on my left, Norberte Uhl, dropped her fork on her plate and said with a splutter, 'They're only *Jews*.'

You could hear the gustation and ingestion of the civilians (Burckl methodically slurping gravy from his spoon, Seedig rinsing his mouth with Nuits-St-Georges). Everyone else had stopped chewing; and I felt I was not alone in becoming intensely conscious of Drogo Uhl, whose head now slowly described a figure eight as his mouth widened. He turned with bared upper teeth to Zulz and said,

'No, let's not fly off the handle, eh? Let's be indulgent. The woman understands nothing. *Only* Jews?'

'"Only" Jews,' Doll sadly concurred (he was folding his napkin with a sagacious air). 'A somewhat puzzling remark, don't you think, Professor, given that their encirclement of the Reich is now complete?'

'Very puzzling indeed.'

'We didn't undertake this lightly, madam. We know what we're about, I believe.'

Zulz said, 'Yes. You see, they're especially dangerous, Mrs Uhl, because they've long understood a core biological principle. Racial purity equals racial might.'

'You won't catch them interbreeding,' said Doll. 'Oh no. They understood this long before we did.'

'That's what makes them so dire a foe,' said Uhl. 'And the cruelty. My God. Pardon me, ladies, you shouldn't have to hear it, but . . .'

'They flay our wounded.'

'They strafe our field hospitals.'

'They torpedo our lifeboats.'

'They . . .'

I looked at Hannah. Her lips were compressed, and she was frowning down at her hands – her long-fingered hands, which slowly combined and twined and intertwined, as if being sluiced under a tap.

'It's an age-old planetary racket,' said Doll. 'And we've got the proof. We've got the minutes!'

'*The Protocols of the Wise Men of Zion*,' said Uhl grimly.

I said, 'Ah now, Commandant. One gathers that some people have their doubts about the *Protocols*.'

'Oh do they,' said Doll. 'Well I hereby refer them to *Mein Kampf*, which makes the point quite brilliantly. I can't remember it word for word, but this is the gist. Uh . . . *The Times* of London says again and again that the document is a fabrication. That alone is proof of its authenticity . . . Devastating, nicht? Absolutely unanswerable.'

'Yes – put that in your pipe and smoke it!' said Zulz.

'They're bloodsuckers,' said Zulz's wife, Trudel, crinkling her nose. 'They're like bedbugs.'

Hannah said, 'May I speak?'

Doll turned on her his highwayman's stare.

'Well, it's a basic point,' she said. 'There's no avoiding it. I mean the talent for deception. And the avarice. A child could see it.' She breathed in and went on, 'They promise you the earth, all smiles, they lead you down the garden path. And then they strip you of everything you have.'

Did I imagine it? This would have been quite standard talk from an SS Hausfrau; but the words seemed to equivocate in the candlelight.

'. . . That's all undeniable, Hannah,' said Zulz, looking puzzled. Then his face cleared. 'Now, however, we're giving the Jew a taste of his own medicine.'

'Now the boot is on the other foot,' said Uhl.

'Now we're paying him back in his own coin,' said Doll. 'And he's laughing on the other side of his face. No, Mrs Uhl. We didn't undertake this lightly. We know what we're about, I believe.'

While the salads and the cheese and the fruit and the cakes and the coffee and the port and the schnapps were being steered round the table, Hannah paid her third visit to the upper floor.

'They're going down like ninepins now,' Doll was saying. 'It's almost a shame to take the money.' He held up a bulbous hand and ticked them off – 'Sevastopol. Voronezh. Kharkov. Rostov.'

'Yes,' said Uhl, 'and wait till we've punched our way across the Volga. We've bombed the stuffing out of Stalingrad. And now it's there for the taking.'

51

'You chaps', said Doll (referring to Seedig, Burckl, and me), 'might as well pack up and go home. All right, we'll still need your rubber. But we won't need your fuel. Not with the oilfields of the Caucasus at our mercy. Well? Did you spank their bottoms blue?'

Doll's question was directed at his wife, who was ducking in under the lintel and moving out of the shadows into the wriggling light. She sat and said,

'They're asleep.'

'God and all his angels be praised! What a load of bloody *nonsense*.' Doll's head slewed back round and he said, 'Judaeo-Bolshevism will be smashed by the end of the year. Then it'll be the turn of the Americans.'

'Their armed forces are *pathetic*,' said Uhl. 'Sixteen divisions. About the same as Bulgaria. How many B-17 bombers? Nineteen. It's a joke.'

'They've got trucks running around on manoeuvres,' said Zulz, 'with *Tank* painted on their sides.'

'America will make no difference,' said Uhl. 'Nil. We won't even feel its thumb on the scale.'

Frithuric Burckl, who had barely spoken, now said quietly, 'That was very far from being our experience in the Great War. Once that economy gets going . . .'

I said, 'Oh, incidentally. Did you know this, Major? There was another conference in Berlin on that same day in January. Chaired by Fritz Todt. Armaments. About restructuring the economy. About preparing for the long haul.'

'Defatismus!' laughed Doll. 'Wehrkraftzersetzung!'

'Not a bit of it, sir,' I laughed back. 'The German army. The German army is like a force of nature – irresistible. But it's got to be equipped and supplied. The difficulty is manpower.'

'As they empty the factories,' said Burckl, 'and put the lot of them in uniform.' He tubbily folded his arms and crossed his legs. 'In all the campaigns of '40 we lost a hundred thousand. In the Ostland, now, we're losing thirty thousand a month.'

I said, 'Sixty. Thirty's the official figure. It's sixty. One must be a realist. National Socialism is applied logic. There's no great mystery to it, as you say. So, my Commandant, may I make a controversial suggestion?'

'All right. Let's hear it.'

'We have an untapped source of labour of twenty million. Here in the Reich.'

'Where?'

'Sitting on either side of you, sir. Women. Womanpower.'

'Impossible,' said Doll contentedly. 'Women and war? It flies in the face of our most cherished convictions.'

Zulz, Uhl, and Seedig murmured their agreement.

I said, 'I know. But everybody else does it. The Anglo-Saxons do it. The Russians do it.'

'All the more reason why we shouldn't,' said Doll. 'You aren't going to turn my wife into some sweaty Olga digging ditches.'

'They do more than dig ditches, Major. The battery, the anti-aircraft battery that held up Hube's panzers to the north of Stalingrad, and fought to the death, they were all women. Students, girls . . .' I gave Alisz's thigh a final clasp, then raised my arms and laughed, saying, 'I'm being very reckless. And terribly indiscreet. I'm sorry, everyone. My dear old Uncle Martin likes chatting on the telephone, and by the end of the day it's coming out of my ears. Or out of my mouth. Well, what about it, ladies?'

'What about what?' said Doll.

'Joining up.'

Doll stood. 'Don't answer. Time to spirit him away. Can't have this "intellectual" corrupting the womenfolk! Now. In my house it's the gents who withdraw after dinner. Not to the Salon but to my lowly Arbeitzimmer. Where there will be cognac and cigars and *serious* talk of war. Sirs – if you would.'

————

Outside, the night was lined with something, something I had heard about but had yet to experience: the Silesian talent for winter. And it was September the third. I stood buttoning up my greatcoat, on the steps, under the coach-house lantern.

In Doll's cluttered office all the men except Burckl and me talked shoutily about the wonders being worked by the Japanese in the Pacific (victories in Malaya, Burma, British Borneo, Hong Kong, Singapore, Manila, the Bataan Peninsula, the Solomon Islands, Sumatra, Korea, and West China) and lauded the generalship of Iida Shojiro, of Homma Masaharu, of Imamura Hitoshi, of Itagaki Seishiro. There was a quieter interlude, during which it was calmly agreed that the sclerotic empires and dithering democracies of the West were no match for the ascendant racial autocracies of the Axis. Things got noisier again while they discussed the forthcoming invasions of Turkey, Persia, India, Australia, and (of all places) Brazil . . .

At one point I felt Doll's eyes on me. There was an unexpected silence and he said,

'Looks a bit like Heydrich, nicht? There's a resemblance.'

'You're not the first to see it, sir.' Apart from Goring, who might have been a burgher out of *Buddenbrooks*, and apart from the ex-champagne salesman and aristocrat-impersonator, Ribbentrop (whom London society, during his absenteeist ambassadorship there, nicknamed the Wandering Aryan), Reinhard Heydrich was the only prominent Nazi who could pass for a pure Teuton, all the others being the usual Baltic/Alpine/Danubian mishmash. 'Heydrich was in and out of the courts defending his ancestry,' I said. 'But all those rumours, Hauptsturmfuhrer, are quite baseless.'

Doll smiled. 'Well let's hope Thomsen here avoids the early

54

death of the Protektor.' He raised his voice, saying, 'Winston Churchill is about to resign. He's no choice. In favour of Eden, who's less Jew-ridden. You know, when the Wehrmacht marches back victoriously from the Volga, and from what used to be Moscow and Leningrad, they'll be disarmed by the SS at the border. From now on we'll—'

The telephone rang. The telephone rang at eleven o'clock: a prearranged call from one of the Sekretar's secretaries in Berlin (an obliging old girlfriend of mine). The room remained obediently still as I talked and listened.

'Thank you, Miss Delmotte. Tell the Reichsleiter I understand.' I rang off. 'I'm sorry, gentlemen. You'll have to excuse me. A courier is about to alight on my apartment in the Old Town. I must go and receive him.'

'No rest for the wicked,' said Doll.

'None,' I said with a bow.

In the sitting room Norberte Uhl lay like a toppled scarecrow on the sofa, attended to by Amalasand Burckl. Alisz Seisser sat rigid and staring on a low wooden bench, attended to by Trudel Zulz and Romhilde Seedig. Hannah Doll had just gone upstairs, and wasn't expected to return. To no one in particular I said that I would see myself out, which I did, pausing for a minute or two in the passage at the foot of the stairs. The distant thunder of bathwater being run; the very slightly adhesive sound of bare feet; the scandalised creaking of the floorboards.

Out in the front garden I turned and looked up. I was hoping to see a naked or near-naked Hannah through the upstairs window, gazing down at me with parted lips (and inhaling huskily on a Davidoff). In this hope I was disappointed. Only the drawn curtains of fur or hide, and the trusting rectangular light from within. So I started out.

The arc lamps moved past in hundred-yard intervals. Huge black flies furred their grillwork. Yes, and a bat skittered past the creamy lens of the moon. From the Officers' Club, I supposed, borne by the devious acoustics of the Kat Zet, came the sound of a popular ballad, 'Say So Long Softly When We Part'. But I also detected footsteps behind me, and I turned again.

Almost hourly, here, you felt you were living in the grounds of a vast yet bursting madhouse. This was such a moment. A child of indeterminate sex in a floor-length nightgown was walking fast towards me – yes, fast, much too fast, they all moved much too fast.

The small shape strutted into the light. It was Humilia.

'There,' she said and handed me a blue envelope. 'From Madam.'

Then she too turned, and walked quickly away.

Much have I struggled . . . I can no longer . . . Now I must . . . Sometimes a woman . . . My breasts ache when I . . . Meet me in the . . . I'll come to you in your . . .

I walked for twenty minutes with such imaginings in my mind – past the outer boundary of the Zone of Interest, then through the empty lanes of the Old Town until I reached the square with its grey statue and the iron bench under the curving lamp post. There I sat and read.

———

'Guess what she went and did,' said Captain Eltz. 'Esther.'

Boris had let himself in (with his own key) and was pacing the modest length of my sitting room, with a cigarette in one hand but no alcoholic glassful in the other. He was sober and restless and intent.

'You know the postcard? Is she out of her mind?'

'Wait. What?'

'All that stuff about the nice food and the cleanliness and the bathtubs. She didn't write down any of that.' With indignation (at the size and directness of Esther's transgression) Boris went on, 'She said we were a load of lying murderers! She elaborated on it too. A load of thieving rats and witches and he-goats. Of vampires and graverobbers.'

'And this went through the Postzensurstelle.'

'Of course it did. In an envelope with both our names on it. What does she think? That I'd just drop it in a mailbox?'

'So she's back shovelling Scheisse with a mortar board.'

'*No*, Golo. This is a political *crime*. Sabotage.' Boris leaned forward. 'When she came to the Kat Zet she said something to herself. She told me this. She said to herself, *I don't like it here, and I'm not going to die here* . . . And *this* is how she behaves.'

'Where is she now?'

'They've slung her in Bunker 11. My first thought was – I've got to get her some food and water. Tonight. But now I think it'll do her good. A couple of days in there. She's got to learn.'

'Have a drink, Boris.'

'I will.'

'Schnapps? What do they do to them in Bunker 11?'

'Thanks. Nothing. That's the point. Mobius puts it this way: we just let nature take its course. And you wouldn't want to get in the way of nature, would you. Two weeks is the average if they're young.' He looked up. 'You seem despondent, Golo. Did Hannah chuck?'

'No no. Go on. Esther. How do we get her out?'

And I made the necessary effort, and tried to interest myself in mere matters of life and death.

2. DOLL: THE PROJEKT

Speaking quite honestly, I'm a trifle peeved about my black eyes.

Not that I mind the actual injury, needless to say. My record speaks for itself, I venture to assert, with regard to matters of physical resilience. On the Iraqi front in the last war (where, as a 17-year-old, and the youngest NCO in the entire Imperial Army, I was quite naturally barking out orders to men twice my age), I fought all day, all night, and, ja, again all day, with my left kneecap blown clean off and my face and scalp raked by shrapnel – and I still had the strength, come that 2nd dawn, to screw my bayonet into the guts of the English and Indian stragglers in the pillbox we finally overran.

It was at the hospital in Wilhelma (a German settlement off the road between Jerusalem and Jaffa), whilst recovering from 3 bullet wounds sustained in the 2nd Battle of the Jordan, that I fell under the 'magic spell' of amatory dalliance, with a fellow patient, the willowy Waltraut. Waltraut was being treated for various psychological complaints, chiefly depression; and I like to think that our glazed meldings helped seal the rifts in her mind, as surely as they closed the great gouges in the small of my back. Today, my memories of that time are predominantly recollections of *sounds*. And what a contrast they make – on the one hand, the grunting and retching of hand-to-hand combat, and on the other the billing and cooing (often accompanied by actual birdsong, in some grove or orchard) of young love! I'm a romantic. For myself there has to be romance.

No, the trouble with the black eyes is that they seriously detract from my aura of infallible authority. And I don't just mean in the command centre or on the ramp or down at the pits. The day of the accident I hosted a brilliant dinner party for the Buna people

58

here at my attractive villa, and for long periods I could scarcely keep countenance – I felt like a pirate or a clown in a pantomime, or a koala bear, or a raccoon. Early on I became completely mesmerised by my reflection in the soup tureen: a diagonal smear of pink with two ripe plums wobbling beneath the brow. Zulz and Uhl, I felt sure, were smirking at one another, and even Romhilde Seedig seemed to be suppressing a titter. With the commencement of general conversation, however, I revived, leading the talk with all my customary assurance (and putting Mr Angelus Thomsen squarely in his place).

Now – if I'm like that in my own home, amongst colleagues and acquaintances and their lady wives, how would I comport myself with people who really matter? What if Gruppenfuhrer Blobel were to return? What if Oberfuhrer Benzler of the Reich Central Security Office should make a sudden tour of inspection? What if, heaven forbid, we received another visit from the Reichsfuhrer-SS? Why, I don't think I could even hold my head up in the company of the little Fahrkartenkontrolleur, Obersturmbannfuhrer Eichmann . . .

It was solely the fault of that bloody old fool of a gardener. Picture, if you will, a Sunday morning of flawless weather. I am at table in our pretty breakfast room, and in excellent fettle, after a strenuous albeit inconclusive 'session' with my better half. I ate the breakfast fondly prepared by Humilia (who was out at some blighted tabernacle in the Old Town). And after polishing off my 5 sausages (and draining as many mugs of capital coffee), I got up and headed for the French windows, fancying a thoughtful smoke in the garden.

Bohdan, with his back to me and a shovel over his shoulder, was on the path, stupidly staring at the tortoise as it gnawed on a cob of lettuce. And when I stepped from grass to gravel, he turned with a kind of spastic suddenness; the shovel's thick blade described a swift half-circle in the air and struck me full on the bridge of my nose.

Hannah, when she eventually came downstairs, herself bathed the site of the contusion in cold water, and gently held the slab of raw meat to my brow with her warm Fingerspitzen . . .

And now, a whole week having passed, my eyes are the colour of a sick frog – a lurid yellowy green.

'Impossible,' said Prufer (very typically).

I sighed and said, 'The order comes from Gruppenfuhrer Blobel, which means it comes from the Reichsfuhrer-SS. Understand, Haupsturmfuhrer?'

'It's impossible, Sturmbannfuhrer. It can't be done.'

Prufer, preposterously, is my Lagerfuhrer, and thus my number 2. Wolfram Prufer, young (barely 30), vapidly handsome (with a round, toneless face), quite bereft of initiative, and, in general, a desperate sluggard. Some people claim that the Zone of Interest is a dumping ground for 2nd-rate blunderers. And I would agree (if it didn't tend to reflect badly on myself). I said,

'Excuse me, but I fail to recognise the word *impossible*, Prufer. It's not in the SS lexicon. We rise above the objective conditions.'

'But what's the point, mein Kommandant?'

'What's the point? It's politics, Prufer. We're covering our tracks. We've even got to grind the ashes. In bone mills, nicht?'

'Sorry, sir, but I ask again. What's the point? It'll only matter if we lose, which we won't. When we win, which we will, it won't matter at all.'

I must admit that the same thought had occurred to myself. 'It'll still matter a *bit* when we win,' I reasoned. 'You have to take the long view, Prufer. Awkward customers asking questions and poking about.'

'The point still escapes me, Kommandant. I mean, when we

win, we're supposed to be doing a lot more of this kind of thing, aren't we? The Gypsies and the Slavs and so on.'

'Mm. That's what I thought.'

'Then why're we getting all namby-pamby about it now?' Prufer scratched his head. 'How many pieces are there, Kommandant? Do we even have a vague idea?'

'No. But there's lots.' I stood up and started pacing the floor. 'You know, Blobel's responsible for cleaning up the whole territory. Ach, he keeps nagging me for Sonders. And the rate he gets through them. I said, *Why d'you have to dispose of all your Sonders after every Aktion? Spin them out a bit, can't you? They're not going anywhere.* And does he listen?' I regained my chair. 'All right, Hauptsturmfuhrer. Taste this.'

'What is it?'

'What's it look like? Water. Do you drink the water here?'

'No fear, Sturmbannfuhrer. I drink the bottled stuff.'

'So do I. Taste it. *I* had to. Go on, taste it . . . That's a direct order, Hauptsturmfuhrer. Go on. No need to swallow.'

Prufer took a sip and let it dribble out through his lower teeth. I said,

'Like carrion, ne? Take a deep breath.' I offered him my flask. 'Have a jolt of that. There . . . Yesterday, Prufer, I was cordially invited to the civic centre in the Old Town. To face a delegation of local worthies. They said it's undrinkable no matter how many times you boil it. The pieces have started to ferment, Hauptsturmfuhrer. The water table's breached. There's no alternative. The smell is going to be unbelievable.'

'The smell is *going* to be unbelievable, my Kommandant? You don't think it's unbelievable already?'

'Stop *complaining*, Prufer. Complaining won't get us anywhere. All you ever do is complain. You just keep complaining. Complain, complain, complain, complain.'

My words, I realised, duplicated those of Blobel – when I too initially balked. And Blobel's cavils were no doubt similarly scolded by Himmler. And Prufer will unquestionably give the equivalent reprimand when he hears the demurrals of Erkel and Stroop. And so on. What we have in the Schutzstaffel is a chain of complaint. An echo chamber of complaint . . . Prufer and myself were in my office in the MAB. The room was low-ceilinged, and somewhat gloomy (and slightly cluttered), but I sat behind a desk of redoubtable size.

'So it's urgent,' I went on. 'It's objectively urgent, Prufer. You do see that, I hope.'

My secretary, little Minna, knocked and entered. In a sincerely puzzled voice she said,

'A person calling himself "Szmul" is outside, Kommandant. He's here to see you or so he claims.'

'Tell him to stay where he is, Minna, and wait.'

'Yes, Kommandant.'

'Is there any coffee? Real coffee?'

'No, Kommandant.'

'Szmul?' Prufer gulped, heaved, and gulped again. 'Szmul? The Sonderkommandofuhrer? What's he doing here, Sturmbannfuhrer?'

'That'll be all, Hauptsturmfuhrer,' I said. 'Recce the pits, accumulate the petrol refuse and the methanol if there is any, and talk to Sapper Jensen about the physics of the pyres.'

'I obey, my Kommandant.'

Whilst I sat thinking Minna bustled in with a double armful of teletypes and telegrams, of memos and communiqués. She is a personable and knowing young female, albeit far too flachbrustig (though her Arsch is perfectly all right, and if you hoiked up that tight skirt you'd . . . Don't quite see why I write like this. It isn't my style at all). And in any case my thoughts were with my wife. Hannah (I conjectured), here, during the current Aktion? No. The girls too, for that matter. I rather think that a little trip to Rosenheim is indicated. Sybil and Paulette can hobnob with those 2 reasonably harmless eccentrics, their maternal grandparents, at Abbey Timbers – the ebony beams, the hens, Karl's funny 'pull-out' drawings, Gudrun's anarchical cooking. Yes, the environs of Rosenheim. Some rural air will do them all good. And besides, with Hannah in her current 'frame of mind' . . .

Ach, would that my wife were as tractable as the languid Waltraut! Waltraut – where are you now?

'So this is a human being,' I said in the yard. 'You're an atrocious sight, Sonderkommandofuhrer.'

My eyes? My eyes are like the eyes of Goldilocks compared to the eyes of the Sonderkommandofuhrer, Szmul. His eyes are gone, dead, defunct, extinct. He has Sonder eyes.

'Look at your eyes, man.'

Szmul shrugged and glanced sideways at the hunk of bread he had thrown to the ground on my approach.

'After myself,' I said, and for a moment my mind wandered. 'You know, in the coming days, Sonder, your Gruppe will be expanded by a factor of 10. You're going to be the most important man in the entire KL. After myself, naturally. Come.'

In the truck, whilst we proceeded north-east, I thought with distaste of Obersturmfuhrer Thomsen. Despite his epicene deportment, he is, by all accounts, a tremendous scragger of the womenfolk. Famous for it, apparently. And he's no respecter of persons either, not by any manner of means. Apparently he knocked up 1 of von Fritsch's daughters (this was *after* the scandal with the catamite); and I heard from 2 separate sources that he even porked Oda Muller! Cristina Lange represents another notch on his beltstrap. They say he actually pimps for his Uncle Martin – facilitating the Reichsleiter's liaison with the actress, M. It's even rumoured that he did the deed of darkness with his own Aunt

Gerda (or with what was left of her after how many kids is it, 8, 9?). Here at the KL, as is well known, Thomsen has splashed his way through a veritable platoon of Helferinnen, including Ilse Grese (whose morals are in any case distinctly questionable). His friend, the scapegrace Boris Eltz, is apparently no better. Yes, but Eltz is a prodigious warrior, and such men – this has become more or less official policy – such men must love as freely as they fight. What's Thomsen's excuse?

In Palestine the wandlike Waltraut set me an example that I have followed all my life: without true feeling, mere congress is – let's face it – a pretty squalid business all round. In this regard I am not a typical soldier, I realise; I would never speak disrespectfully of a female; and I detest vulgar language. Thus I have been spared the world of the brothel, with its unimaginable slime and filth, likewise the 'sophisticated' lewdnesses – the court shoe squeezed between the leather boots beneath the table, the hand up the skirt in the kitchen, the rumpy waddle of the city hussy, the daubed orbits, the shaved armpits, the gossamer panties, the black stockings and the black garter belt framing the creaminess of the upper thighs . . . Such things, thank you very much, are of precious little interest to your humble servant, Paul Doll.

It wouldn't surprise me if Thomsen tries to home in on Alisz Seisser. Quite a striking thought – the cream-haired beanpole feasting on that shapely currant bun. She looked most fetching at dinner the other night. Well he'd better be quick – she'll be off back to Hamburg in a week or 2. This is her grace period, whilst she recovers from the loss of the sergeant major – the loss of Orbart, who laid down his life to foil an escape from the Women's Camp. This fact lent nobility to the mien of his survivor. Besides, black is a very becoming colour. And, as we caroused at my villa, Alisz's weeds (with that tight top) seemed to be softly ensilvered by the rays of German sacrifice. There you are, you see. Romance: there must be romance.

How long does Hannah suppose she can keep this up?

Take my word for it: there won't be sufficient petrol refuse, and I'll have to go to Katowitz *all over again*.

'Pull up here, Unterscharfuhrer. Here.'

'Yes, my Kommandant.'

Now I had not been to Sector 4IIIb(i) since July, when I accompanied the Reichsfuhrer-SS on his day-long 'look-see'. As I climbed from the truck (and as Szmul jumped down from the flatbed) I uneasily realised that I could actually *hear* the Spring Meadow. Said meadow began perhaps 10 metres beyond the mound where Prufer, Stroop, and Erkel stood with their hands pressed to their faces – but you could hear it. You could smell it, of course; and you could hear it. Popping, splatting, hissing. I joined my colleagues and gazed out at the great field.

I gazed out at the great field without the slightest trace of false sentimentality. It bears repeating that I am a normal man with normal feelings. When I'm tempted by human weakness, however, I simply think of Germany, and of the trust reposed in me by her Deliverer – whose vision, whose ideals and aspirations, I unshakably share. To be kind to the Jew is to be cruel to the German. 'Right' and 'wrong', 'good' and 'bad': these concepts have had their time; they are gone. Under the new order, some deeds have positive outcomes and some deeds have negative outcomes. And that is all.

'Kommandant, in Culenhof', said Prufer, with 1 of his responsible frowns, 'Blobel tried blowing them up.'

I turned and looked at him, and said through my handkerchief (we all had handkerchiefs), 'Tried blowing them up to achieve what?'

'You know, get rid of them that way. It didn't work, Kommandant.'

'Well I could've told him that before he started. Since when does blowing things up make them disappear?'

'That's what I thought once they'd tried. It went everywhere. There were bits hanging from the trees.'

'What did you do?' asked Erkel.

'We got the bits we could reach. On the lower branches.'

'What about the upper bits?' asked Stroop.

'We just left them there,' said Prufer.

I looked out on a vast surface that undulated like a lagoon at the turn of the tide, a surface dotted with geysers that burped and squirted; every now and then divots of turf jumped and somersaulted in the air. I yelled for Szmul.

That evening Paulette surprised me in my study. I was on an easy chair, relaxing with a glass of brandy and a cigar. She said,

'Where's Bohdan?'

'Not you too. And that's a hideous dress.'

She gulped and said, 'Where's Torquil?'

Torquil was the tortoise (and I do mean 'was'). The girls loved the tortoise: unlike the weasel, the lizard, and the rabbit, the tortoise couldn't run away.

. . . A little later I tiptoed up behind Sybil as she was doing her homework on the kitchen table – and gave her a good fright! As I then laughingly hugged her and kissed her she seemed to pull back.

'You pull back, Sybil.'

'No I don't,' she said. 'It's just that I'll be 13 quite soon, Daddy. And that's a big milestone for me. And you don't . . .'

'I don't what? No. Go on.'

'You don't smell good,' she said, and made a face.

At this my blood really started to boil.

'Do you know the meaning of the word *patriotism*, Sybil?'

She twisted her head away and said, 'I like hugging and kissing you, Daddy, but I've got other things on my mind.'

I waited before I said, 'In that case you're a very cruel little girl.'

*

And what of Szmul, what of the Sonders? Ach, I can hardly bring myself to set it down. You know, I never cease to marvel at the abyss of moral destitution to which certain human beings are willing to descend . . .

The Sonders, they go about their ghastly tasks with the dumbest indifference. Using thick leather belts they drag the pieces from the shower room to the Leichenkeller; they extract the gold-stopped teeth with pliers and chisels, and remove the women's hair with the snapping shears; they tear off the earrings and the wedding bands; then they stack the pulley (6 or 7 per consignment), which is hoisted up to the gaping retorts; finally, they grind the ashes, and the powdery dust is taken by the truckload and dispersed in the River Vistula. All of this, as already stated, they perform with dumb callousness. It doesn't seem to matter at all to them that the people they process are their comrades in race, their siblings in blood.

And do the vultures of the crematory ever show the slightest animation? Ach yech: when they greet the evacuees on the ramp and guide them through the disrobing room. In other words, they come alive only in treachery and deceit. *Tell me your trade,* they'll say. *An engineer, eh? Excellent. We always need engineers.* Or something like, *Ernst Kahn – from Utrecht? Yes, he and his . . . Oh yes, Kahn and his wife and the kids were here for a month or 2 and then decided to go on to the agricultural station. The 1 at Stanislavov.* When there is a difficulty, the Sonders are quite prepared to use violence; they frogmarch any troublemaker to a nearby NCO, who deals with the situation in the suitable fashion.

You see, with Szmul and the rest of them, it's in their interests that things should go smoothly and briskly, because they're impatient to rifle through the discarded clothes and sniff out something to drink or smoke. Or something to eat. They are always eating – always eating, the Sonders, eating the scraps filched from the disrobing room (despite the relatively generous rations they moreover enjoy). They'll sit spooning up their soup on a stack of Stucke; they'll wade knee deep through the mephitic meadow whilst munching on a hunk of ham . . .

It staggers me that they decide to persist, to last, in this way. And they do so decide: some (albeit not many), categorically refuse, despite the obvious consequence – for they too, now, have become Geheimnistrager, bearers of secrets. Not that any of them can hope to prolong their cowardly existence for more than 2 or 3 months. On this point we are quite clear and forthright: the Sonders' initiatory task, after all, is the cremation of their predecessors; and so it will go on. Szmul has the dubious distinction of being the longest-serving undertaker in the KL – indeed, in the whole concentrationary system, I shouldn't wonder. He is virtually a Prominent (even the guards accord him a modicum of respect). Szmul continues. But he knows very well what happens to them – what happens to bearers of secrets.

For myself, honour is not a matter of life or death: it's far more important than that. The Sonders, very obviously, hold otherwise. Honour gone; the animal or even mineral desire to persist. *Being* is a habit, a habit they can't break. Ach, if they were real men – in their place I'd . . . But wait. You never are in anybody's place. And it's true what they say, here in the KL: No one knows themselves. Who are you? You don't know. Then you come to the Zone of Interest, and it tells you who you are.

I waited till the girls were tucked up and then strode out into the garden. Hannah in a white shawl stood with her arms folded by the picnic table. She was drinking a glass of red wine – and smoking a Davidoff. Beyond her, a salmony sunset and a tumbling rack of clouds. I said matter-of-factly,

'Hannah, I think the 3 of you should go to your mother's for a week or 2.'

'Where's Bohdan?'

'Good God. For the 10th time, they transferred him.' And it was nothing to do with me, though I wasn't displeased to see the back of him. 'Packed him off to Stutthof. Him and about 200 others.'

'Where's Torquil?'

'For the 10th time, Torquil's *dead*. Bohdan did it. With his *shovel*, Hannah, remember?'

'Bohdan killed Torquil. You say.'

'Yes! Out of spite, I suppose. And funk. At the other camp he'll have to start again. It could be hard for him.'

'Hard in what way?'

'Well he won't be a gardener in Stutthof. It's a different kind of regime.' I decided not to tell Hannah that at Stutthof you got 25 lashes the minute you arrived. 'It was me who had to clear it all up. Torquil. Not a pretty sight, I can tell you.'

'Why should we go to my mother's?'

I hummed and hawed for a bit, claiming it was a good idea anyway. Hannah said,

'Come on, what's the real reason?'

'Oh all right. Berlin has mandated an emergency Projekt. Things'll be unpleasant here for a while. Just for a couple of weeks.'

Hannah said sarcastically, 'Unpleasant? Oh really? That'll make a change. Unpleasant in what way?'

'I'm not at liberty to disclose. War work. It may have a deleterious effect on the air quality. Here, let me top that up for you.'

A minute later I returned, with Hannah's wine and a huge glass of gin.

'Have a ponder about it. I'm sure you'll see it's for the best. Mm, nice sky. It's getting colder. Which'll help.'

'Help how?'

I coughed and said, 'Now you know we've got the Playhouse tomorrow night.'

69

Her flicked cigarette end looked like a firefly in the dusk – an upward swoop.

'Yes,' I said, 'gala performance of *And the Woods Sing For Ever*.' I smiled. 'You frown, my pet. Come on, we must keep up appearances! Dear oh dear. Who's a sulky girl then? I'd invoke the name of Dieter Kruger. But you've shown, haven't you, that you're no longer much bothered about his fate.'

'Oh, I'm bothered. Didn't you tell me that Dieter passed through Stutthof? You told me they give you 25 lashes on arrival.'

'Did I? Well only with very suspicious prisoners. They won't do that to *Bohdan* . . . *And the Woods Sing For Ever*'s a tale of rural life, Hannah.' I took a big gulp of the stringent liquor and thoroughly rinsed my mouth with it. 'About the longing for the redemptive community. The organic community, Hannah. It'll make you pine for Abbey Timbers.'

It was a joint anniversary, commemorating i) our decisive electoral breakthrough on September 14, 1930, and ii) the historic passage of the Nuremberg Race Laws on September 15, 1935. So: a double cause for celebration!

After a few cocktails in the Crush Bar, Hannah and myself (the cynosure of all eyes) made our way to our seats in the front row. The house lights dimmed, and the curtain creaked ceilingward – to reveal a thickset milkmaid sorrowing over a bare pantry.

And the Woods Sing For Ever was about a family in a farmstead during the harsh winter that followed the Diktat of Versailles. *The frost's destroyed the tubers, Otto* was 1 of its lines, and *Get your toffee nose out of that book, can't you?* was another. Otherwise, *And the Woods Sing For Ever* completely passed me by. Not that my mind went blank – on the contrary. It was most peculiar. I spent the whole 2½ hours intently estimating how long it would take (given the high ceiling as against the humid conditions) to gas the audience, and wondering which of their clothes would be salvageable, and calculating how much their hair and gold fillings might fetch . . .

Afterwards, at the party proper, a couple of Phanodorm washed down with a few cognacs soon restored my equilibrium. I left Hannah with Norberte Uhl, Angelus Thomsen, and Olbricht and Suzi Erkel whilst I had some words with Alisz Seisser. The poor little thing is off to Hamburg at the end of the week. Alisz's first item of business: see about her pension. For some reason she was white with dread.

'We'll go from west to east. There'll be 800 of you.'

Szmul shrugged, and produced, if you can believe, a handful of black olives from his trouser pocket.

'Maybe 900. Tell me, Sonderkommandofuhrer. Are you a married man?'

He said with his head down, 'Yes, sir.'

'What's her name?'

'Shulamith, sir.'

'And where is this "Shulamith", Sonderkommandofuhrer?'

It's not quite true to say that the crows of the charnel house are impervious to all human emotion. Fairly frequently, in the course of their work, they encounter someone they know. The Sonder sees these neighbours, friends, relatives, as they come in, or as they go out, or both. Szmul's 2nd-in-command once found himself in the shower room calming the fears of his identical twin. Not long ago there was a certain Tadeusz, another good worker, who looked to the end of his belt in the Leichenkeller (they use their belts, do you see, to haul the Stucke), and there was his wife; he fainted; but they gave him some schnapps and a length of salami, and 10 minutes later he was back on the job, snipping merrily away.

'Come on, where is she?'

'I don't know, sir.'

'Still in Litzmannstadt?'

'I don't know, sir. Pardon, sir, but did they see about the excavator?'

'Forget about the excavator. It's a wreck.'

'Yes, sir.'

'And they're to be carefully counted. Understand? Count the skulls.'

'Skulls are no good, sir.' He leaned sideways and expelled the last olive stone. 'There's a more reliable method, sir.'

'Oh really? Here, how long'll all this take?'

'Depends on the rainfall, sir. I'm guessing, but I'd say 2 or 3 months.'

'2 or 3 *months*?'

He turned to me, and I saw what was unusual about his face. Not the eyes (his were the usual Sonder eyes), but the mouth. I knew then, up on the rise, that Szmul, immediately after the successful completion of the present measure, would have to be dealt with, by the employment of the apt procedure.

Have garnered some further information on the sugary Herr Thomsen (despite his record, I think, deep down, he *is* '1 of those'). His mother, Bormann's much older half-sister, made an advantageous match, ne? She married a merchant banker – who also collected modern art of the most degenerate stripe. Does the mould seem familiar – money, modern art? I wonder if that 'Thomsen' wasn't once something like 'Tawmzen'. Anyway, both parents, in 1929, died in an elevator plunge in New York (moral: set foot in that Hebrew Sodom and you get what you so 'richly' deserve!). So then this only child, this princeling gets himself unofficially adopted by his Uncle Martin – the man who controls the appointment book of the Deliverer.

Now I've had to slave and sweat blood, I've had to kill myself to get where I am. But some people – some people are born with a silver . . . Now that's funny. I was about to employ the usual phrase – but then an improvement popped into my head. And it's perfect for him. Yes. Angelus Thomsen was born with a silver *Schwanz* in his mouth!

Nicht wahr?

I was bent over my desk at home, deep in weary meditation, when I heard footsteps; they neared and paused. They were not Hannah's footsteps.

And I was thinking: I am someone caught between the devil and the deep blue sea. On the one hand, the Economic Administration Head Office is always after me to do everything I can to swell the labour strength (for the munitions industries); on the other, the Reich Central Security Department presses for the disposal of as many evacuees as possible, for obvious reasons of self-defence (the Jews constituting a 5th column of intolerable proportions). I swiped my fingertips across my brow in a kind of reflexive salute. And now, I see (the teletype lay before me), that that moron Gerhard Student at EAHO is floating the bright idea that all able-bodied mothers should be worked till they drop in the boot factory at Chełmek! *Fine*, I'll tell him. *And you can come to the ramp and try separating them from their children.* These people – they just don't *think*. I said loudly,

'Whoever's out there may as well come in.'

At last came the knock. Looking very penitent and stricken, Humilia crept into the room.

'Are you just going to stand there and tremble,' I muttered (I was thoroughly out of sorts), 'or do you have something to convey?'

'My conscience is upset, sir.'

'Oh really? We can't have that. That would never do. Well?'

'I was obedient to Miss Hannah when I shouldn't have been.'

I said quite calmly, 'When I shouldn't have been, *sir*.'

*

It's the fire, do you see, it's the fire.

How to make them burn, naked bodies, how to make them catch?

We started with very modest accumulations, using wooden planks, and we were hardly getting anywhere, but then Szmul . . . You know, I can see why the Sonderkommandofuhrer leads a charmed life. He it was who made a series of suggestions which, as it happened, proved key. I lay them down, for future reference.

1) There must be but a single pyre.

2) The pyre must burn continuously, on a 24-hour basis.

3) Liquefied human fat must be used to aid combustion. Szmul organised the run-off gutters and the ladling squads, which moreover resulted in considerable economies in gasoline. (Reminder: impress this saving on Blobel *and Benzler*.)

There is at this stage only one technical difficulty that periodically confronts us. The fire's so hot you can't get near it, nicht?

Now I ask you, this is really priceless, this is, this really 'takes the cake'. All of a sudden the phone's jumping off the hook: Lothar Fey of the Air Defence Authority, angrily complaining, if you please, about our nocturnal conflagrations! Is it any wonder I'm going out of my mind?

Whilst Humilia saw fit to tell me that my wife has written and dispatched a personal communication to a proven debauchee, she was unable – or unwilling – to enlighten me as to its contents. This has ruined my concentration. Of course, the entire thing could be perfectly innocent. Innocent? *How* could it be innocent? I have no illusions about the hysterical carnality of which Hannah has shown herself to be capable, and besides it is common knowledge that once a woman loosens the sacred bonds of modesty she quickly descends to the most fantastic depravities, squatting, squelching, squeezing, squirming—

Hannah briskly knocked and entered and said, 'You wanted to see me.'

'Yes.' Biding my time, for now, I said, 'Look, there's no point in you going to Abbey Timbers. The Projekt's going to take months so you'll just have to get used to it.'

'I didn't want to go anyway.'

'Oh? What's this? Have you got a Projekt of your own by any chance?'

'Maybe,' she said, and turned on her heel.

. . . I raised my hands and rubbed my eyes. This spontaneous action, the like of which any tired schoolboy might reflexively perform over his homework, was quite painless – for the first time in I don't know how long. In the downstairs toilet I consulted the mirror. Ja, those martyred orbs of mine are still very slightly bloodshot, and slack and pouchy what with all the smoke and the late nights (it's not as if the trains don't keep coming). But my black eyes are no more.

There are the flames and the fumes; even the clearer air ripples and wriggles. No?

Like a sheet of gauze pulsating in the wind.

Now the Sonders, under Szmul's direction, have rigged up a kind of ziggurat of warped railway tracks. It is the size of the cathedral in Oldenberg.

The scene is I suppose on the very crest of the modern, but when I watch from the mound I keep thinking of the slave-built pyramids of Egypt. Using the wide ladders and the hoists they load the great lattice, then they withdraw to their wheeled towers and feed the fire, do you understand, by tossing in the pieces, sometimes by the bucketful. These towers rock like dark-age siege engines.

At night the tracks glow red. I keep glimpsing a gigantic black toad with illuminated veins even when I close my eyes.

*

75

Communication from the Geheime Staatspolizei in Hamburg: the widow Seisser is on her way back, but she returns to us with her status revised. Alisz is now an evacuee.

The Sonderkommandofuhrer was right about the best way of counting. Not skulls. Almost all the pieces were dispatched by the standard Genickschuss but often clumsily or hastily, thus splintering the crania. So skulls are hopeless. The most scientific procedure, we have established, is to count the femurs and divide by 2. Nicht?

In response to the domestic emergency I have activated the criminal Kapo I maintain in the coal mine at Furstengrube.

3. SZMUL: WITNESS

It would infinitesimally console me, I think, if I could persuade myself that there is companionship – that there is human communion, or at least respectful fellow-feeling, in the bunkroom above the disused crematory.

A very great many words are spoken, certainly, and our exchanges are always earnest, articulate, and moral.

'Either you go mad in the first ten minutes,' it is often said, 'or you get used to it.' You could argue that those who get used to it do in fact go mad. And there is another possible outcome: you don't go mad and you don't get used to it.

When work ends we gather, we who have not got used to it and have not gone mad, and we talk and we talk. In the Kommando, hugely expanded for the current collaboration, about five per cent belong to this category – say forty men. And in the bunkroom we gather a little way apart, usually around dawn, with our food, our liquor, and our cigarettes, and we talk. And I like to think that there is companionship.

I feel we are dealing with propositions and alternatives that have never been discussed before, have never needed to be discussed before – I feel that if you knew every day, every hour, every minute of human history, you would find no exemplum, no model, no precedent.

Martyrer, mucednik, martelaar, meczonnik, martyr: in every language I know, the word comes from the Greek, *martur*, meaning *witness*. We, the Sonders, or some of us, will bear witness. And this question, unlike every other question, appears to be free of deep ambiguity. Or so we thought.

*

The Czech Jew from Brno, Josef, who is gone now, wrote his testimony and buried it in a child's galosh under the hedgerow that borders Doll's garden. After a lot of disputation, and a show of hands, we resolve to exhume this document (temporarily) and acquaint ourselves with its contents. I myself am instinctively and perhaps superstitiously opposed. And as things turn out it is one of the episodes in the Lager that I would least soon relive.

Written in Yiddish, in black ink, the manuscript consisted of eight pages.

'*And there*', I began, '*a girl of five stood and. . .* Wait. I think it's a bit mixed up.'

'Read!' said one of the men. Others seconded him. 'Just read.'

'*And there a girl of five stood and undressed her brother who was one year old. One from the Kommando came to take off the boy's clothes. The girl shouted loudly, "Be gone, you Jewish murderer! Don't lay your hand, dripping with Jewish blood, upon my lovely brother! I am his good mummy, he will die in my arms, together with me." A boy of seven or eight . . .*' I hesitated, and swallowed. 'Shall I go on?'

'No.'

'No. Yes. Go on.'

'Go on. No. Yes.'

'*A boy of seven or eight*', I read, '*stood beside her and spoke thus, "Why, you are a Jew and you lead such dear children to the gas – only in order to live? Is your life among the band of murderers really dearer to you than the lives of so many Jewish victims?" . . . A certain young Polish woman made a very short but fiery speech in the—*'

'Stop.'

Many of the men had tears in their eyes – but they weren't tears of grief or guilt.

'Stop. She "made a very short but fiery speech". Like hell she did. Stop.'

78

'Stop. He lies.'

'Silence would be better than this. Stop.'

'Stop. And don't put it back in the earth. Destroy it – unread. Stop.'

I stopped. And the men turned away, they moved away, and slackly sought their bedding.

Josef, the chemist from Brno, was known to me here at the Lager, and I considered him a serious man . . . I am a serious man, and I am writing my testimony. Am I writing like this? Will I be able to control my pen, or will it just come out – *like this*? Josef's intentions, I'm sure, were of the best, even the highest; but what he writes is untrue. And unclean. A girl of five, a boy of eight: was there ever a child so fiendishly experienced that it could grasp the situation of the Sonder?

For a few moments I read on in silence, or I dragged my sight down the rest of the page . . .

> A certain young Polish woman made a very short but fiery speech in the gas chamber . . . She condemned the Nazi crimes and oppression and ended with the words, 'We shall not die now, the history of our nation will immortalise us, our initiative and spirit are alive and flourishing . . .' Then the Poles knelt on the ground and solemnly said a certain prayer, in a posture that made an immense impression, then they arose and all together in chorus sang the Polish anthem, the Jews sang the 'Hatikvah'. The cruel common fate in this accursed spot merged the lyric tones of these diverse anthems into one whole. They expressed in this way their last feelings with a deeply moving warmth and their hopes for, and belief in, the future of their . . .

Will I lie? Will I need to deceive? I understand that I am disgusting. But will I *write* disgustingly?

Anyway, I nonetheless make sure that Josef's pages are duly reinterred.

It sometimes happens that when I pass the Kommandant's house I see his daughters – on their way to school or on their way back. Now and then the little housekeeper accompanies them, but usually the mother does – a tall, strong-looking woman, still young.

Seeing Doll's wife naturally makes me think of mine.

The Polish Jews are not coming to the Lager en masse, or not yet, but some of them find their way here by a twisted road, as I did, and of course I seek them out and question them. The Jews of Lublin went to a death camp called Belzec; a great number of Jews from Warsaw went to a death camp called Treblinka.

In Łódź the ghetto is still standing. Three months ago I even got news of Shulamith: she is still in the attic above the bakery. I love my wife with all my heart, and I wish her every happiness, but as things now stand I'm glad I'll never see her again.

How would I tell her about the selections and the disrobing room? How would I tell her about Chełmno and the time of the silent boys?

Shula's brother, Maček, is safe in Hungary, and he has vowed that he will come for Shula and take her to Budapest. May it be so. I love my wife, but I'm glad I'll never see her again.

At dawn we discuss the *extraterritorial* nature of the Lager, and everything is back to normal in the bunkroom, we talk, we use each other's names, we gesticulate, we raise and lower our voices; and I like to think that there is companionship. But something is missing and is always missing; something intrinsic to human interchange has absented itself.

The eyes. When you start out in the detail, you think, 'It's me, it's just me. I keep my head dropped or averted because I don't

80

want anyone to see my eyes.' Then after a time you realise that all the Sonders do it: they try to hide their eyes. And who would have guessed how foundationally necessary it is, in human dealings, to see the eyes? Yes. But the eyes are the windows to the soul, and when the soul is gone the eyes too are untenanted.

Is it companionship – or helpless volubility? Are we capable of listening to – or even hearing – what others say?

This night at the pyre two hoist-frame plinths collapse, and I am down on all fours in a dent in the dunes banging bits of it together again when Doll's open-topped jeep draws up, thirty metres away, on the gravel road. After some rummaging around he emerges (with the engine ticking over) and moves towards me.

Doll wears thick-looped leather sandals and brown shorts, and nothing else; in his left hand he has a half-full quart of labelled Russian vodka, in his right an oxhide whip which he now playfully cracks. His spongy red chest hair is dotted with beads of sweat that sparkle in the overwhelming glare of the fire. He drinks, and wipes his mouth.

'So, great warrior, how does it go? Mm. I'd like to thank you for your efforts, Sonderkommandofuhrer. Your initiative and your dedication to our shared cause. You've been invaluable.'

'Sir.'

'But you know, I think we've got the hang of it now. We could probably muddle along without you.'

My toolbag is down by his feet. I reach for it and slide it towards me.

'Your men.' He upends the bottle over his mouth. 'Your men. What do they think is going to happen to them when the Aktion ends? Do they know?'

'Yes, sir.'

He says sorrowfully, 'Why d'you do it, Sonder. Why don't you rise up? Where's your pride?'

Again the whiplash – the leap of the cord. And again. I have the thought that Doll is disciplining his own weapon: the metal-clad tip makes its distracted leap for freedom, only to be brought to heel with an imperious twitch of the wrist. I said,

'The men still hope, sir.'

'Hope for what?' He briefly panted with laughter. 'That we'll suddenly change our minds?'

'It's human to hope, sir.'

'Human. Human. And yourself, noble warrior?'

In the canvas bag my fingers close round the shaft of the hammer; when he next tips his head back to drink I will bring it down, claw-first, on the white nakedness of his instep. He says levelly,

'You lead a charmed life, Geheimnistrager. Because you've made yourself indispensable. We all know that dodge. Like the factories in Litzmannstadt, nicht?' He took a draught that lasted several swallows. 'Look at me. With your eyes. *Look* at me . . . Yes. Rightly do you find that difficult, Sonder.'

He sluices his gums and spits skilfully between his lower teeth (the liquid ejected in a steady squirt, as if from the mouth of a ceramic fish in a municipal fountain).

'Afraid to die. But not afraid to kill. I see it in the set of your lips. You've got murder in your mouth. Such people have their uses. Sonderkommandofuhrer, I'll leave you. Work well for Germany.'

I watched him go, listing slightly (curious that drunkenness, at least at first, makes Doll more fluent in thought and speech). Geheimnistrager: bearer of secrets. Secrets? What secrets? The whole county stops the nose at them.

The snake that lives in Doll's whip is a viper, perhaps, or a mamba or a puff adder. As for the snakes that live in Doll's fire, they are pythons, boa constrictors, anacondas, every last one of them, ravenously trying to get hold of something solid in the night sky.

*

Is there companionship? When squads of heavily armed men come to the crematory and this or that section of the detail knows that it is time, the chosen Sonders take their leave with a nod or a word or a wave of the hand – or not even that. They take their leave with their eyes on the floor. And later, when I say Kaddish for the departed, they are already forgotten.

If there is such a thing as mortal fear, then there is also such a thing as mortal love. And that is what incapacitates the men of the Kommando – mortal love.

CHAPTER III. GREY SNOW

I. THOMSEN: FINDING EVERYTHING OUT

Herr Thomsen:

I want to ask you to do me a service, if you would. You remember Bohdan, the gardener? I'm told he has been arbitrarilly transfered to Stutthof.

He is also said to have been involved in a very shocking incedent, resulting in the death of poor Torquil (the tortoise), and this seemed to me so utterly out of charecter, so impossible in relation to him, that I began to doubt the truth of the story I was being given. His name is Professor Bohdan Szozeck. He was a great favourite of the girls, and of course they're inconsolible about their pet tortoise, as I think you saw tonight. I told them Torquil had just gone missing. They plan to get up at dawn tomorrow to search the garden.

I'm sorry to burden you with this but to be frank there's no one else I can ask.

Every Friday I may be found by the sandpit at the Summer Huts between the hours of four and five.

Thank you. Yours sincerley, Hannah Doll

PS. I apolagise for my spelling. They say I have a 'condition'. But I think I'm just not up to it. And it's funny, because the only thing I've ever been any good at is langauges. HD.

So, no, it was hardly the glazed summons or the desperate solicitation for which I had perhaps callowly yearned. But when after a day or two I showed the letter to Boris he tried to persuade me that it was, in its way, quietly encouraging.

'She's long lost all trust in the Old Boozer. That's good.'

'Yes, but *yours sincerely*,' I said with some petulance. 'And *Herr Thomsen*. And *there's no one else I can ask*.'

'You fool, that's the best bit. Pull yourself together, Golo. She's saying you're her only friend. Her only friend in the whole world.'

Still writhing slightly I said, 'But I don't want to be her friend.'

'No, naturally. You just want to . . . Patience, Golo. Women are very impressed by patience. Wait till the war's over.'

'Oh, sure. Wars do not observe the unities, brother.' The unities of time, place, and action. 'Wait till the war's over, indeed. Who knows what'll be left? Anyway.'

Boris obliged me and promised that he would interrogate Szozeck's Block Leader. He added,

'Adorable PS. And she's got nice handwriting. Sexy. Unselfconscious. Flowing.'

And in my solitary contemplations, with Boris's inspiring words still fresh in my mind, I looked again at Hannah's holograph – the lewd orbs of her *eh*s and *oh*s, those shamelessly plunging *jay*s and *why*s, that truly unconscionable *doubleyou*.

———

But then the whole thing froze over for nearly two weeks. Boris was sent to the subcamp of Goleschau (with orders to purge and reinvigorate its demoralised guardhouse). Before he left he had to get Esther out of Block 11; this took priority, reasonably enough, because she would have starved to death in his absence.

As a political criminal, Esther was now in the custody of the Gestapo. The non-venal Fritz Mobius, luckily, was away on leave, and Jurgen Horder, his number two, was in the Dysentery Ward of the Ka Be. Boris therefore applied to Michael Off, who, he hoped, would be considerably cheaper than Jurgen Horder.

*

85

So when I saw Hannah, at the theatre on Saturday night, I could only mime my impotence and say glancingly, while Horst Eikel loudly joked with Norberte Uhl, 'Friday next . . .' At first I felt strangely numbed (*And the Woods Sing For Ever* was about a clan of mildly famished but stoutly anti-intellectual yokels in northern Pomerania); but this very quickly and sharply changed.

A variety of physical forces seemed to be at work on me. Standing in a casual group with Hannah, I was electrically aware of her mass and body scent; she loomed huge, like a Jupiter of erotic gravity. By the time Doll took her off I was so unmoored, and so roused, that I almost pressed myself on the pale, limp, terrified figure of Alisz Seisser, and later on, as I lay in bed and stared at the darkness, it took a long time before I eventually ruled out a surprise visit to Ilse Grese.

———

And now I had another letter in front of me, as I sat drinking synthetic coffee in Frithuric Burckl's office at the Buna-Werke. 'Esteemed Sir,' it began. The correspondent was the chief personnel officer at Bayer, the pharmaceutical firm (a subsidiary of IG Farben), and the addressee was Paul Doll.

> The transport of 150 women arrived in good condition. However, we were unable to obtain conclusive results as they all died during the experiments. We would kindly request that you send us another group of women to the same number and at the same price.

I looked up and said, 'How much are women?'

'One seventy RM each. Doll wanted two hundred, but Bayer gypped him down to one seventy.'

'And what were Bayer testing?'

'A new anaesthetic. Overdid it a bit. Obviously.' Burckl sat back and folded his arms (the tonsured black hair, the thick-framed spectacles). 'I showed you that because I think it's indicative. Indicative of a faulty attitude.'

'Faulty, Mr Burckl?'

'Yes, faulty, Mr Thomsen. Did the women all die at once? Were they all given the same dose? That's the least idiotic explanation. Did the women die in batches? Did they die one by one? The point is that Bayer were repeating their mistakes. And that's what we're doing.'

'What mistakes?'

'All right. Yesterday I came through the Yard, and one of the work teams was lugging a mass of cables to the substation. At the usual swift stagger. And one of them fell down. He didn't drop anything or break anything. He just fell down. So the Kapo started clubbing the life out of him, and this Britisher from the Stalag intervened. Next thing we know a noncom got involved. Net result? The POW loses an eye, the Haftling's shot in the head, and the Kapo gets a broken jaw. And it's another two hours before the cables get lugged to the substation.'

'So what do you suggest?'

'Treating the workforce as disposable, Mr Thomsen, is hugely counterproductive. My God, those Kapos! What's the *matter* with them?'

I said, 'Well. If a Kapo isn't pulling his weight, in the noncom's opinion, then he loses his status.'

'Mm. Reduced rations and whatnot.'

'It's more serious than that. He gets beaten to death later the same day.'

Burckl frowned. He said, 'Does he? Who by? The noncoms?'

'No. The prisoners.'

Burckl went still. Then he said, 'You see, that shores up my point. The chain of violence – everyone's aquiver with it. The whole atmosphere's psychotic. And it doesn't work. We're not getting there, are we, Mr Thomsen.'

Our deadline was the middle of next year.

'Oh I don't know,' I said. 'We chug along.'

'The Chancellery is bulldozing the Vorstand. The Vorstand is bulldozing us. And we're bulldozing . . . Jesus Christ, look at it out there.'

I looked at it out there. The figures that held my attention, as always (I too had an office at Buna, and spent many hours in front of its window), the figures that held my attention were not the men in stripes, as they queued or scurried in lines or entangled one another in a kind of centipedal scrum, moving at an unnatural speed, like extras in a silent film, moving faster than their strength or build could bear, as if in obedience to a frantic crank swivelled by a furious hand; the figures that held my attention were not the Kapos who screamed at the prisoners, nor the SS noncoms who screamed at the Kapos, nor the overalled company foremen who screamed at the SS noncoms. No. What held my eye were the figures in city business suits, designers, engineers, administrators from IG Farben plants in Frankfurt, Leverkusen, Ludwigshafen, with leather-bound notebooks and retractable yellow measuring tapes, daintily picking their way past the bodies of the wounded, the unconscious, and the dead.

'I have a proposition. Oh, it's pretty radical, I admit. Will you hear me out at least?'

He righted the low stack of papers in front of him and took out his fountain pen.

'Let's go through this one step at a time. Now. Mr Thomsen, how long – what's the longest our workers last?'

I said wearily, 'Three months.'

'So every three months we're having to induct their successors. Tell me.'

From outside there came a volley of inarticulate bawling, plus two pistol shots and then the familiar rhythm of the whip. Burckl said,

'How many calories does an adult need daily in conditions of complete repose?'

'I don't know.'

'Two and a half thousand. In some of the Polish ghettoes, it's three hundred. That's dry execution. In the Stammlager it's eight. And here it's eleven, if they're lucky. Eleven, for penal labour. On eleven hundred calories, I can tell you, a heavy worker loses about three kilos a week. Do your sums. Mr Thomsen, we need to give them an incentive.'

'How're you going to do that? They know they're here to die, Mr Burckl.'

He narrowed his eyes and said, 'Have you heard tell of Szmul?'

'Indeed.'

'What's *his* incentive?'

I recrossed my legs. Old Frithuric was beginning to impress me.

'Please,' he said. 'A thought experiment. We do some sifting and settle on a core of perhaps twenty-five hundred workers. We stop beating them. We stop making them do everything at the double, unverzuglich, unverzuglich – that *terrible* swaying trot. We feed and house them decently, within reason. And they work. As Szmul works. And efficiently collaborates.' He opened out his hands towards me. 'The incentive is just the full belly and the night's rest.'

'What does Dr Seedig say?'

'I can carry him.'

'And Doll?'

'Doll? Doll's nothing. It'll be a hell of a battle, but I think the two of us together, Suitbert and I, can sway the Vorstand. Then Max Faust himself will take it to the top.'

'The top. You'll never convince the Reichsfuhrer.'

'I don't mean the Reichsfuhrer.'

'Then who do you mean? Surely not the Reichsmarschall.'

89

'Of course not. I mean the Reichsleiter.'

The Reichsfuhrer was Himmler, and the Reichsmarschall was Goring. The Reichsleiter was Uncle Martin.

'Well, Mr Thomsen?'

In my considered opinion the changes Burckl was suggesting would improve the Buna performance by two or three hundred per cent, maybe more. I coughed, politely (as if alerting him to my presence), and said,

'With respect, I fear there are certain things you don't understand. Let me—'

There was a knock on the door and Burckl's (male) secretary leaned in for a moment with a flat smile of apology. 'He's outside, sir.'

'Scheisse.' Burckl got to his feet. 'Can you give me an hour on Monday morning? You won't credit this, Thomsen – I can hardly credit it myself. Wolfram Prufer's taking me hunting. *In Russia.* Deer.'

––––––––

Outside the perimeter of the Buna-Werke, separated by about a kilometre, were the two British Kriegsgefangnisse. Between them gaped a cavernous loading bay strewn with planks and ladders, heaps of bricks and timber balks. There I saw an inmate, a burly officer in a padded overcoat and, remarkably, leather boots; he was having a sly breather, slumped against an upended wheelbarrow. I had noticed him many times before.

'*Rule Britannica,*' I cried. '*Britain shall never never . . .*'

'*Rule Britannia. Britons never never never shall be slaves. And look at me now.*'

'*Where were you took prisoner?*'

'*Libya.*'

'*. . . It says Englishmen love flowers. Do you love flowers?*'

'*They're all right. I don't mind them. Funnily enough, I was just thinking about woodbine.*'

'You like "woodbine"?'

'It's a flower. Like a honeysuckle. It's also a brand of cigarettes. That's what I was thinking about.'

'Woodbine. I do not know this. Do you like Senior Services?'

'Senior Service. Very much.'

'And Players?'

'Players are good.'

'Your name?'

'Bullard. Captain Roland Bullard. And yours?'

'Thomsen. Lieutenant Angelus Thomsen. My English I hope is not too worse?'

'It'll do.'

'I shall bring you Players or Senior Service. I shall bring them yesterday.'

'. . . You already brought them tomorrow.'

I walked on for another ten minutes; then I turned and looked. The Buna-Werke – the size of a city. Like Magnetigorsk (a city called Sparkplug) in the USSR. It was due to become the largest and most advanced factory in Europe. When the whole operation came on line, said Burckl, it would need more electricity than Berlin.

So far as the Reich leadership was concerned, Buna promised not just synthetic rubber, not just synthetic fuel. It promised autarky; and autarky, it had been decided, would in turn decide the war.

———

Early evening in the anteroom (and bar) of the Officers' Mess: sofas, armchairs, and coffee tables pillaged from the ten thousand Jews and Slavs we booted out of the Old Town two years ago, a handsome kitchen dresser with bottles of wine and spirits ranked up together with the fruit and the flowers, prisoner servants with

91

white smocks over their mattress ticking, various lieutenants and captains, either in the early stages of insobriety or the late stages of recuperation, and a noisy guest contingent of Helferinnen and Special Supervisors, among them Ilse Grese and her new fifteen-year-old protégée, freckly Hedwig, with her pigtails coiled up under her cap.

You could eat here as well as in the dining room, and Boris was opposite me at our low table for two. We were finishing the second and ordering the third round of aperitifs (Russian vodka) and deciding on our appetisers (eighteen oysters each).

He laughed quietly and said, 'Are you surprised that Ilse's gone queer on us? I'm not. *Tout s'explique*. She always said *schnell*. "Schnell." Did she say it to you?'

'Yes. Always. "Schnell." Now come on, Boris. Schnell.'

'Well here's what happened. I know the old prof wouldn't think so, but it's really quite funny. What happened was, Bohdan gave the Old Boozer a clout with a gardening tool. That's how he got his black eyes. An accident, but still.'

'This is according to who?'

'According to Bohdan's Blockaltester. Who got it from Prufer's adju. Who got it from Prufer. Who got it from the Old Boozer.'

'So. This is all according to the Old Boozer. And what became of Bohdan?'

'Golo. Why bother to ask. A Haftling can't brain the Commandant and expect to walk away. Imagine if it got around. And there's also petty *revenge* of course. You should take a lesson from this. Don't mess with the Old Boozer.'

'How long before they came for him? Bohdan.'

'That same night. Slung him in with the next trainload. And guess what. Before he knocked off work in the garden Bohdan mushed the children's pet tortoise. With the flat of his shovel.'

'Why would he do that?'

'Because he knew he was for it.'

'No,' I said. 'Bohdan Szozeck was a professor of zoology. He looked like an old poet. Anyway, what do I tell Hannah? *Finally.*'

'You could have done all this yourself. I'll show you who to ask. You don't even have to bribe her. Just a few smokes for her pains.'

'What do I tell Hannah?'

'Tell her what I'm telling you. Tell her it's Doll's version, but the only thing you know for sure is that Bohdan's grave is in the sky . . . Look at Ilse. Christ, her tomboy can't be any older than Esther.'

I said, 'Is Esther behaving? How'd you get her out?'

'Thanks for offering by the way, brother, but money's no good here any more. There's too much of it swilling around. It's like the Inflation. Because of all the jewellery. With Off I bid a thousand RM. The little slag wanted ten. I'd already given five hundred to that old prick in the Postzensurstelle. So I said, *Let her out or here and now I'll break your face.*'

'Boris.'

'I couldn't think what else to do. The car was waiting.'

We both had our eyes on Ilse, who seemed to be teaching Hedwig how to waltz.

Boris said, 'Well. There goes our Friday-night fuck in Berlin.'

This was a colloquial reference to the recent edict which forbade the running of baths, in the Reich capital, except on Saturdays and Sundays.

'I'm in her bad books as it is.'

'Oh?' I said. 'Why's that?'

'Bit shaming. Let's leave it for now. Alisz Seisser was the one I fancied . . . You know, Golo, today I came in at the end of a Behandlung.'

'Ah. I thought you seemed a bit – a bit manic.'

'The end of a Behandlung. You should see the way they get stacked.'

'Quieter, Boris.'

'Stacked upright. Sardinenpackung, only vertical. Vertical sardines. They're treading on each other's insteps. In a single wedge. With toddlers and babies slotted in at shoulder height.'

'Quieter.'

'That's thrift, that is. Zyklon B's cheaper than bullets. That's all it is.'

A meaty face at the adjacent table swung round and stared.

Boris, of course, stared back. He said loudly, 'What? *What?* . . . Oh. It's the merry beggar, is it? You like pissing money away, do you?'

And the face stared on but then withdrew.

'Remember, Golo,' he said more quietly. 'With Hannah. You're her only friend. Work on that. But listen. Treat her like a wine. Lay her down.'

'She can't come to my place,' I said, 'but there's this little hotel behind the castle. It's down an alley. An enormous bribe would do it. And, all right, the rooms aren't perfect but they're reasonably clean. The Zotar.'

'Golo.'

'I know it's in her.'

The main course was baby chicken with garden peas and new potatoes, served with a sanguinary burgundy, followed by peaches and cream and a glass or two of still champagne. Then Calvados with the walnuts and tangerines. Boris and I were by now the soberest German males in the room, and we were both very drunk.

'A single mouthful,' said Boris gravely. 'How many prisoners here? Seventy thousand? Ninety-nine per cent of them would drop down dead after a single mouthful of what we've had tonight.'

'That occurred to me too.'

'I feel like beating someone up.'

'Not again, Boris. Not so soon.'

94

'I'm champing, see. I want to go east.' He looked around. 'Yes, I want a fight, and I want a fight with someone good. So it lasts longer.'

'You won't get any takers here. After what you did to Troost.'

'It doesn't work like that. There's always some fat bastard who's heard about me and is suddenly feeling brave. Him for instance. The farmerboy by the mantelpiece.'

When we were twelve years old Boris and I had a shouting match that turned physical – and I couldn't believe the passion of the violence that came at me. It was like being run over by a frenzied but also somehow self-righteous combine harvester. My first thought when I finally got back to my feet was this: Boris must have always hated me very much. But it wasn't so. Later he wept, and stroked my shoulder, and kept on saying and saying how sorry he was.

'Golo, I had a kind of uh, anti-eureka in Goleschau. I heard . . . I heard that they were killing psychiatric patients in Konigsberg. Why? To clear bedspace. Who for? For all the men who'd cracked up killing women and children in Poland and Russia. I thought, Mm, all is not quite as it should be in the state of Deutschland. Excuse me for a moment, my dear.'

'Of course.'

Boris got up from his chair. 'You know, Bohdan was sure they'd come for him. Sat by the door, marking time. He'd given away all his worldly goods.'

'His worldly goods?'

'Yeah. His bowl, his spoon. His foot rags. You're dropping off, Golo . . . Dream about Hannah,' he said. 'And the Old Boozer's black eyes.'

I dozed for a minute or two. When I stirred and looked out, Boris was over by the mantelpiece, listening to the farmerboy, with his teeth bared and his chin up.

———

95

Friday came, so I hiked over the duney scrub, with its bubbled and knotted black hair, like wind-dried seaweed. Every eminence brought a fresh stretch of land into view, and your body hoped to see a beach, a shore, or at least a lake or a river, or a stream or a pond. But what you were confronted by was always the continuation of Silesia, the continuation of the great Eurasian plain, which stretched over twelve time zones and went all the way to the Yellow River and the Yellow Sea.

The ground levelled out, levelled out into what might have been a municipal facility in the square of some indigent township in the German north-east – two swings, a slide, a seesaw, a sandpit. There were small clusters of women on benches, one trying to read a flimsy newspaper in the wind, another knitting a yellow scarf, another extracting a sandwich from the shiny white folds of its greaseproof wallet, another merely staring into space, while time passed – Hannah Doll, with her open palms on her lap, staring into space, staring into time. Beyond, like spartan chalets, lay the pennanted Summer Huts.

'Good afternoon to you, madam,' I called out. She stood and I came up close and said, 'I don't want to sound histrionic but I was followed here and we are being watched. This is the truth.' I forced a broad smile. 'Seem at ease. Now where are those girls?'

I approached the slowly revolving roundabout. Affectingly, some might have thought, I had two bags of boiled sweets in my pockets; but they would now have to stay where they were. I asked,

'When's your birthday? I want to give you something. When is it?'

'*Years* away,' said Paulette.

'I know what I'm going to call my children,' said Sybil. 'The twins'll be Mary and Magda. And the boy'll be August.'

'Those are very good names.'

I backed off and felt Hannah draw near.

'Can you feel the season changing, Frau Doll? Ah, the alerting zest of late September. I swear to you we're being watched.'

She made as if to brighten. 'Watched? And not just by the mothers? Well. What've you got to tell me, Herr Thomsen?'

'It makes me wretched to give you bad news,' I said with every appearance of gaiety. 'But Bohdan Szozeck is no more.'

I expected her to flinch: in fact it was more like a jump, a spasm of expansion both upward and outward, and her hand flew to her mouth. Then she at once recovered, with a shake of her hair, and raised her voice, saying,

'Paulette, darling, don't bounce so hard!'

'It's what the seesaw's for! It's the whole point!'

'Gently! . . . So he didn't go to Stutthof?' she asked, smiling.

'I'm afraid he went nowhere,' I answered, smiling.

And we retained our smiles, somehow, as I followed the narrative given to me by Boris Eltz: the mishap with the garden tool, the inevitable order to Prufer, the dispatch of the Punishment Commando. I said nothing of the gas, but she knew.

'And the tortoise?'

'Bohdan's parting gesture. Apparently. This is in effect your husband's version. At several removes.'

'Do you believe all that? Bohdan?'

I shrugged stiffly. 'Mortal fear does strange things.'

'Do you believe *any* of it?'

'You see their reasoning, don't you? It mustn't get about. That a prisoner can do that to the Commandant and live.'

'Do what to the Commandant?'

'Well. Hit him even by accident. Bohdan gave him his black eyes.'

'Bohdan didn't give him his black eyes.' Her mirthless smile changed – it widened and tightened. '*I* gave him his black eyes.'

'*What would you rather?*' yelled Sybil from the distant sandpit. '*Know everything or know nothing?*'

'Know nothing,' I yelled back. *'Then you have the fun of finding everything out.'*

———

That same Friday I walked in the late dusk through the muddy alleys of Kat Zet III. Financed entirely by IG Farben, Kat Zet III had been put together, with a literalist's care, on the model of Kat Zet I and Kat Zet II. The same searchlights and watchtowers, the same barbed wire and high-tension fencing, the same sirens and gallows, the same armed guards, the same punishment cells, the same orchestra bay, the same whipping post, the same brothel, the same Krankenhaus, and the same mortuary.

Bohdan had had a Pikkolo – this was Hannah's designation. The word was ambiguous: unlike a Piepl, which meant *bumboy* and no mistake, a Pikkolo was often just a young companion, a charge, someone the older prisoner looked out for. In this case he was a fifteen-year-old German Jew called Dov Cohn. Dov was sometimes to be seen in the Dolls' garden (and I had glimpsed him on the day I paid my first visit). Hannah said that Bohdan and Dov were 'very close' . . . In common with the Buna-Werke, Kat Zet III was still under construction, and for now only a colony of builders was quartered there. According to the registrar in the Labour Section, Dov Cohn was to be found in Block 4(vi).

By this time, partly through induction, I had settled on what seemed to be the likeliest sequence of events. The morning in question: first, there is a serious altercation between husband and wife, during which Hannah deals Doll a blow to the face; over the course of the day, as the bruises pool and darken, Doll realises that he'll be needing an explanation for his disfigurement; at some point Bohdan, perhaps in an act of clumsiness, attracts his notice; he invents the story of the shovel, and relays it, together with his instructions, to Lagerfuhrer Prufer, whose adjutant notifies the

Punishment Commando . . . The only remaining mystery, so far as I could see, was the fate of poor Torquil.

My approach to Kat Zet III had been from the direction of the Buna-Werke, and I felt as certain as you could ever feel that I wasn't being followed.

With my baton I rapped on the Block door and threw it open: a barn the size of two tennis courts, containing a hundred and forty-eight three-tier bunkframes with two or three to each berth. The heat of eleven or twelve hundred men gushed out at me.

'Blockaltester! Here!'

The boss, an elder, fiftyish and well fleshed, emerged from his side room and walked hurryingly forward. I stated a name and a number and gave a sideways wag of the head. Then I stepped back into the lane, and exhaled. I lit a cheroot – to fumigate my nostrils. The smell in Block 4(vi) was a different smell: it wasn't the outright putrefaction of the meadow and the pyre, nor was it the smell diffused by the smokestacks (that of cardboard with wet rot, moreover reminding you, with its trace of charr, that human beings evolved from fish). No, it was the apologetic funk of hunger – the acids and gases of thwarted digestion, with a urinous undertang.

He stepped out, the boy, and not alone. Accompanying him was one of the Block Kapos, with his triangular green Winkel (denoting felon), his bare arms tattooed to the thickness of a sleeved singlet, his spiky pate a mere continuation of the stubble that framed his mouth. I said,

'Who are you?'

The Kapo looked me up and down. And who was I, for that matter, with my height, my frosty blue eyes, my landowner's tweeds, my Obersturmfuhrer armband?

'Name.'

'Stumpfegger. Sir.'

99

'Well leave us, Stumpfegger.'

As he turned to go he made a half gesture, raising his arm for a moment and then letting it drop. It seemed to me that he wanted to pass a proprietorial hand over the fuzz of the boy's black hair.

'Dov, walk with me a while,' I said carefully. 'Master Dov Cohn, I want to talk to you about Bohdan Szozeck. You may be unable to help me, but you should not be unwilling to help me. No harm will come to you because of it. And some good will come of it whether you help me or not.' I took out a pack of Camels. 'Have five.' What was the value of five American cigarettes – five bread rations, ten? 'Salt them away somewhere.'

For several paces the boy had been rhythmically nodding his head, and I started to feel almost sure he would give me my answer. We halted, under the ensnared lamps. It was now night, and the black sky very faintly crepitated with coming rain or coming snow.

'How did you end up here? Relax. Have some of this first.'

It was a Hershey bar. Time slowed . . . Carefully Dov freed the cellophane wrapping, stared for a moment, and gave the brown nub a reverent lick. I watched. He would be an artist with this delicacy; it would probably take him a week to carve it to nothing with his tongue . . . Hannah had talked about Dov's eyes: rich dark grey, and perfectly round, with little inlets on the line of the diameter. Eyes made for innocence, and confirmed in innocence, but now protuberant with experience.

'You're German. Where from?'

In a firm voice that nonetheless occasionally leapfrogged an octave, he told me his story. It was unexceptional. Flushed out of a Jews' House in Dresden, along with the rest of his family, in the autumn of '41; a month in the holding camp of Theresienstadt; the second transport; the leftward selection, on the spur, of his mother, four younger sisters, three grandparents, two aunts, and eight younger cousins; the survival of his father and two uncles for the usual three months (digging drainage ditches); and then Dov was alone.

'So who looks out for you? Stumpfegger?'

'Yeah,' he said, with reluctance. 'Stumpfegger.'

'And Professor Szozeck for a while.'

'Him too, but he's gone.'

'D'you know where?'

After a still moment Dov again started nodding.

'Bohdan walked here from the Stammlager to say goodbye. And to warn me not to go looking for him at the villa. Then he went back. He was waiting. He was sure they'd come.'

Dov knew everything.

On his last morning, Bohdan Szozeck went to the Ka Be (to have the dressing changed on his infected knee) and got to the villa garden later than usual, about half past nine. He was in the conservatory when the Commandant, with one hand pressed to his face, came reeling out of the glass doors of the breakfast room – in pyjamas. At first (and here I felt stirrings on the back of my scalp) Bohdan thought that Doll, swaying there in his blue and white stripes, was a *prisoner*: a Zugang (his stomach still fat, his clothes still clean), drunk or mad or just wildly disorientated. Then Doll must have caught sight of the tortoise as it inched across the lawn; he picked up the shovel and brought the flat blade down full strength on its carapace.

'And he fell over, sir. On the gravel – really hard. Backwards. His pyjama bottoms, they'd come undone and tripped him up. And he fell over.'

I said, 'Did Doll see the professor?'

'He should've hid. Why didn't he hide, sir? Bohdan should've hid.'

'What did he do?'

With a pleading face Dov said, 'He went out and helped him up. And put him on a stool in the shade. And fetched him a bottle of water. Then the Commandant waved him away.'

'So . . .' I considered. 'Bohdan knew. You said he knew they'd come for him.'

'Naturlich. Selbstverstandlich.'

'Because?'

His eyes were exophthalmic with all they knew.

'Because he was there when the Commandant showed weakness. He saw the Commandant cry.'

We walked back up the slight slope of the defile. Halfway to his Block I gave him the rest of the Camels plus ten US dollars.

'You'll put that somewhere safe.'

'Of course,' he said (almost with indignation).

'Wait. Does Doll know you were Bohdan's friend?'

'Don't think so. I only went to the garden twice.'

'. . . Okay. Now, Dov, this is our secret, all right?'

'But sir. Please. What should I tell him?'

'The Blockaltester?'

'*He* doesn't care. No. What should I tell Stumpfegger? He'll want to know what we talked about.'

'Tell him . . .' I must have been thinking about this, on some level, because the answer was ready and waiting. 'All day yesterday at the Stammlager,' I said, 'there was a man standing in the corridor between the wire and the fence. A Kapo. In handcuffs. He had a sign hanging from his neck. It said *Tagesmutter. Kleinaugen*. You know what that means?'

Dov knew.

'Tell Stumpfegger that I put him there. Tell him I'm conducting an investigation ordered by Berlin. Can you tell him that?'

He smiled and thanked me and hastened off into the dusk.

And into the snow. The first grey snow of the autumn, grey snow, the colour of ash, the colour of Dov's eyes.

Tagesmutter. Kleinaugen. *Childminder. Short Eyes.*

———

It seemed to be intermittent and non-systematic, but I *was* being followed. Being followed had happened to me often enough when I worked for Military Intelligence (the Abwehr), and you quickly developed a subsense for it. When you were being followed, you felt as if an invisible string connected you and your monitor, your sharer: depending on the intervening distance, you felt it loosen or tighten. When it was tight: that was when you twisted your head round – and saw, in your wake, a certain figure jolt or stiffen.

The man who walked behind me was a Haftling, in stripes. He was a Kapo (evident from his girth alone), like Stumpfegger, but he wore two triangles, green and red; he was a criminal and a political. This could mean a lot or it could mean almost nothing; it was possible that my shadow was merely a persistent jaywalker who had once shown some interest in democracy. But I didn't think so – he had a dour, sour look to him, a penitentiary look.

Why was I being followed? Who was the instigator? It was always foolish to underestimate the paranoia of the Geheime Staatspolizei (which here meant Mobius, Horder, Off, etc.), but they would never enlist a prisoner, let alone a political. And the only subversion I had committed so far was the tendering of bad advice.

Common sense pointed to Paul Doll. That there had been illicit contact between Hannah and me was known to only four people: the principals, plus Boris Eltz and the Witness, Humilia. Only two people, then, could have alerted the Commandant – and it wasn't Boris.

This coming Sunday Hannah and I would both attend a piano recital and drinks party in the Officers' Club, to honour the signing (with Italy and Japan) of the Tripartite Pact on September 27, 1940. I hoped to be able to tell her that Humilia had been turned.

More promisingly, the day after that, at five-thirty, I was scheduled to bump into Hannah at the Equestrian Academy. I would be feigning an interest in riding lessons. Hannah would be making

inquiries about buying or leasing a pony: Paulette and Sybil had
their eye on a shaggy Shetlander called Meinrad. In my thoughts
I was mapping out a letter; it would be a heavy call on me to
write it; I was going to say that for prudential reasons our friendship, or whatever it was, would have to end.

———

'How many bucks did you bag?'

'Me? None. I fired in the air. It's an appalling pursuit. You see
a beautiful animal nibbling on a rosebush, and what do you do?
Chew it up with two barrels' worth.' He took off his spectacles,
breathed on the glass, and applied his crumpled handkerchief (he
did this every three or four minutes). 'Quite nice countryside.
Even a decent hotel on the lake. It's not all hovels and yurts. But
why did I say yes? Wolfram Prufer. I had two dinners with him
à deux. A remarkably stupid young man. Mr Thomsen, Dr Seedig
tells me there's no ethyl acetate. I don't know what that means.
Do you?'

'Yes. No colorimetric measurements. We have the acetic acid.
But there's no ethyl alcohol.'

For a while we talked about the shortage, or the non-existence,
hereabouts, of ethyl alcohol. We then moved on to the sorry state
of the hydrogenation plant.

'Well, tell that to Berlin. Mr Thomsen, have you thought about
my proposal?'

'I have. The modifications you suggest sound quite sensible.
On the face of it. But you're forgetting something, Mr Burckl.
For the most part we're dealing with Jews.'

Burckl's large brown eyes lost all their light.

'I can assure you', I went on, 'that in the office of the Reichsleiter
there's no disagreement about this. The entire upper echelon is
unanimous on the point.'

'Yes, yes.'

'Let me summarise. And here I'll actually be quoting the very words of the Reichsfuhrer . . . Genetically and constitutionally, the Jew is averse to all work. For centuries, for millennia, he has lived very happily, thank you very much, off the host nations of the diaspora. Work, hard graft, is the preserve of the guileless Gentile, while the Jew, chuckling happily to himself, grows sleek and rich. Physical work – it simply isn't in them. You've seen the way they skive and malinger. Brute force is the only language they understand.'

'. . . Get on with it, man.'

'As for the idea of increasing their rations – that's laughable, quite frankly. Put a square meal inside a Jew and you'll never get a stroke out of him. He'll lie back thinking of milk and honey.'

'I say again – Szmul.'

'Szmul is a false analogy, Mr Burckl. Szmul works towards no foreseeable goal. Here at Buna, the Jews'll be well aware that the moment we're on line their usefulness will come to an end. So they'll impede us at every turn.'

This gave Burckl pause. He said grumblingly, 'Until six or seven years ago there were plenty of Jews at Farben. High up, too. Excellent men. Notably diligent.'

'Saboteurs. Either that or stealing patents and selling them to the Americans. It's well known. It's documented.'

From the yard came a series of screams – unusually piercing and prolonged.

'"Documented". Where? At the Ahnenerbe? You're boring me, Mr Thomsen.'

'You're disconcerting me, Mr Burckl. You're flying in the face of one of the cornerstones of Party policy.'

'Produktive Vernichtung,' said Burckl with cold resignation. 'But Vernichtung *isn't* produktiv, Mr Thomsen.' He turned his head sideways. 'I'm a businessman. I understand that here we have a people that it is opportune to exploit. How to do it ergo-nomically, that's the thing. Anyway. I won't be needing your Uncle Martin. We've got another route to the Chancellery.'

'Oh?'

'Not the Reichsleiter, not the Reichsmarschall, not the Reichsfuhrer. The Reichskanzler himself wants a meeting with an IG delegation – on quite another topic.'

'And what's that?'

'Weaponised poison gas. Mr Thomsen, I'm going to go ahead with my reforms, inasmuch as I can without your support.' He held my eye. 'You know, with the Jews I've never seen what all the fuss is about. In Berlin, half the time, I couldn't even tell a Jew from an Aryan. I'm not proud of saying this, but I was personally quite relieved when they brought in the Star. Otherwise how can you tell? . . . Go on, delate me. Have me burnt at the stake for heresy. No. No, certainly not. I've never seen one good reason for all this fuss about the Jews.'

———

On Friday, as I walked from the Old Town to Kat Zet I, I found I wasn't being followed; so I turned east and made the trek to the Summer Huts, without the least expectation that I would have company there. Swift and sticky rain, thin and cold, and smoke-soiled low-hanging clouds; the playground deserted, the sodden chalets all shuttered up. Everything answered to my mood, and to my hopes of Hannah. I pressed on through the sand and the scrub.

'Well it's all off now,' Boris had said the night before. 'Golo, I'd've liked nothing better than to see you put the horns on the Old Boozer. But it was always stupidly dangerous.'

And this from a colonel of the Waffen-SS (with three Iron Crosses) and a wild philanderer, who adored all danger . . . I said,

'It's good about the pyjama bottoms, isn't it.'

'Yes. Very. Here's a husband who tries it on with his wife and gets smashed in the face. And then falls over with his cock out in the garden. But that makes it all worse, Golo. Even murkier. The brew's too thick.'

'Maybe just once in the Hotel Zotar. I went down there and it's not *that* dirty and there's only one—'

'Don't be a moron, Golo. Listen. All the things that are laughable about the Old Boozer – they make him more of a menace, not less. And he has the powers.'

One did not make such an enemy in the concentrationary universe, where the pressure of death was everywhere; all Doll would need to do was nudge it in the direction he chose.

'Think,' said Boris. 'You – you'd probably survive it. You're a scion of the New Order. But what about her?'

Hugging my coat, I walked on. Realsexuellpolitik. All's fair in love and . . . Yes, and look how Germany waged it. The Commandant's erring wife could expect no help from the provisions of the Hague and Geneva Conventions; it would be Vernichtungskrieg – to-nothing war.

. . . I reached a coppice of decrepit birches where the smell of natural decay blessedly overwhelmed the circumambient air. Natural decay, unadulterated, and not the work of man; and a smell thick with memories . . . After a while I defeatedly dragged my thoughts elsewhere: to Marlene Muthig, the wife of an IG petrologist, with whom I often bantered in the market square; to Lotte Burstinger, a recent addition to the ranks of the Helferinnen; and to Agnes's eldest sister (the only unmarried one), Kzryztina.

Up ahead, just in front of the high hedgerow that marked the Zonal boundary, someone or other had started erecting a pavilion or gazebo – and then run out of time and timber. A planked backing, two side walls of different lengths, and half a roof. It looked like the shelter of a rural bus stop. I came round the front of it.

Paneless windows, a flat wooden bench. And Hannah Doll, in the corner, with a blue oilskin spread over her lap.

And she was dead to the world.

The hour that followed was marked by great stillness, but it was far from uneventful. Every few minutes she frowned, and the frowns varied (varieties of puzzlement and pain); three or four times her nostrils flared with subliminal yawns; a single tear gathered and dropped and melted into her cheek; and once a childish hiccup briefly shook her. And then there was the rhythm of her sleep, her breath, the surge of her soft insufflations. This was life, moving in her, this was the proof, the iterated proof of her existence . . .

Hannah's eyes opened and she looked at me with so little loss of composure that I felt I was already there, fully established in her dream. Her mouth opened along all its width and she made a sound – like the sound of the tide of a distant sea.

'Was tun wir hier,' she said steadily and unrhetorically (as if really wanting to know), 'mit diesen undenkbaren Leichenfresser?'

What are we doing here, she said, *with these unimaginable ghouls* . . .

She stood, and we embraced. We didn't kiss. Even when she started crying and we were probably both thinking how delicious it would be, we didn't kiss, not on the lips. But I knew I was in it.

'Dieter Kruger,' she eventually began.

Whatever it was, I was in it. And whatever it was, it would have to go forward.

Where now? Where to?

2. DOLL: STUCKE

If little things may be compared to large, and if a cat can look at a king, then it seems that I, Paul Doll, as Kommandant (the spearhead of this great national programme of applied hygiene), have certain affinities with the secret smoker!

Take Hannah. Yes, she will do very well, I believe, she will do nicely, I fancy, as an example of the secret smoker. And what do Hannah and myself have in common?

1stly, she has to find somewhere secluded for the gratification of her 'secret' need. 2ndly, she must bring about the disappearance of the remains: there is always the fag end, doubtlessly smeared with some loud lipstick, the butt, the stub (and to be perfectly direct about it, corpses are the bane of my life). 3rdly, she is required to deal with the odour, not only of the smoke itself but also of its residue, clinging to the clothes and especially to the hair (and in her case befouling the breath, for whilst the aroma of an expensive cigar lends authority to the internal scents of the Mensch, the reek of a penny Davidoff desecrates the salubrious waft of the Madchen). 4thly and finally, she has the obligation, if honesty is a concept she even acknowledges let alone understands, to account to herself for her *compulsion* to do what she does – stinking herself up, and wearing her guilt like some dirty little slut rancidly emerging from a strenuous joust on a hot afternoon . . .

Here the 2 of us happen to part company, and the analogy breaks down. Yes, we part company here.

For she does what she does out of wrongness and weakness. And I do what I do out of rectitude and indomitable might!

'You're wearing Mama's make-up.'
Sybil's hand flew to her face.

'You thought you'd washed it all off, didn't you? But I can still see traces of rouge. Or are you blushing?'

'. . . I didn't!'

'Don't tell lies, Sybil. You know why German girls shouldn't use cosmetics? It affects their morals. They start telling lies. Like your mother.'

'What do you mean, Vati?'

'. . . Are you excited about the pony? Better than a silly old tortoise, nicht?'

Even the most stalwart National Socialist, I think, would have to concede that the task the SS set itself in Kulmhof, in the January of this year, was exceptionally sharp. Yech, that was a somewhat extreme measure, bordering, perhaps, on the excessive – the Aktion leading to the recruitment and induction of the Sonder, Szmul. To this day it is mildly famous; people think it stands as a rare behavioural curiosity, quite possibly a 1-off. We informally call it the time of the silent boys.

(Reminder: Szmul's wife lingers in Litzmannstadt. Find out where.)

And by the way, if there are still a few fantasists who somehow retain sympathy for our Hebrew brethren, well, they ought to take a thorough look – as I was obliged to do (in Warsaw, last May) – at the Jewish Quarters in the cities of Poland. Seeing this race en masse, and left to itself, will shoo away any humanitarian sentimentality, and pretty sharpish, too, I shouldn't wonder. Nightmare apparitions, miserable destitutes, sexually indistinguishable men and women throng the corpse-strewn thoroughfares. (As a loving father, I found it particularly hard to stomach their vicious neglect of the semi-naked children who howl, beg, sing, moan, and tremble, yellow-faced, like tiny lepers.) In Warsaw there are a dozen new cases of typhus every week, and of the ½ a million Jews 5–6,000 die every month, such is the apathy, the degeneracy, and, to be quite frank about it, the want of even the rudiments of self-respect.

On a lighter note, let me describe a little incident where myself and my travelling companion (Heinz Uebelhoer, a charming 'young turk' in the offices of the Reichsfuhrer-SS) managed to alleviate the gloom. We were at the Jewish cemetery, chatting to the noted film director Gottlob Hamm (he was making a documentary for the Ministry of Enlightenment), when a Kraft durch Freude motor coach pulled up and all the Jugend disembarked. Well, Gottlob, Heinz, and myself interrupted the funeral service then under way to take a few photographs. We set up some 'genre' pictures: you know, Old Jew Stands Over Cadaver of Young Girl. The Strength through Joy schoolboys were in stitches (but these 'snaps' unfortunately came to light whilst I was visiting Hannah at Abbey Timbers and there was hell to pay. Moral: not everyone is blessed with 'a sense of humour').

And yet, and yet . . . Szmul's wife gallivants round the streets of Litzmannstadt – or 'Łódź', as the Poles call it (pronouncing it *Whoodge* or some such).

Shulamith may be needed.

I think I shall send a communication to the head of the Jewish Council there, whose name – where did I put that report? – is 'Chaim Rumkowski'.

Of course, muggins here *did* have to go down to Katowitz for more petrol refuse. I motored there (with 2 guards) in my 8-cylinder diesel Steyr 600, heading a convoy of trucks.

At the conclusion of business I took afternoon tea in the office of our civilian contractor, 1 Helmut Adolzfurt, a middle-aged Volksdeutscher (with his pince-nez and his widow's peak). Then, as usual, Adolzfurt produced a bottle and we were putting away a few drams. Suddenly he said,

'Sturmbannfuhrer. Do you know that from about 6 in the evening to about 10 at night, here in town, no one can swallow a mouthful?'

'Why ever not?'

'Because the wind turns and gusts up from the south. Because of the smell, Sturmbannfuhrer. The smell comes up from the south.'

'To here? Oh, nonsense,' I said with a carefree laugh. 'That's 50 kilometres.'

'These windows are double-glazed. It's 20 to 7. Let's go outside. If you would, sir.'

We duly traipsed downstairs and into the yard (where my men had almost finished their work). I wondered out loud,

'Is it *always* this strong?'

'It was much harsher a month ago. It's slightly better now it's colder. What *causes* it, Sturmbannfuhrer?'

'Ah, well the truth is, Adolzfurt,' I said (for I'm not unaccustomed to quick thinking), 'the truth is, we have a very sizable piggery in the agricultural station, and there's been an epidemic. Of porcine sepsis. Caused by worms. So we've had no choice, do you see, but to destroy and incinerate. Nicht?'

'Everyone talks, Sturmbannfuhrer.'

'Well tell everyone that then. About the piggery.'

The last of the tanks of benzene were now aboard. I waved the drivers on. Shortly thereafter, I forked out the 1,800 zlotys, subsequently obtaining the requisite receipt.

During the drive back, whilst the guards dozed (I myself was of course at the controls of the prestigious machine), I kept pulling over and sticking my head out of the window and taking a sniff. It was as bad as I've ever known it, and it just got worse and worse and worse . . .

I felt as if I were in one of those cloacal dreams that all of us have from time to time – you know, where you seem to turn into a frothing geyser of hot filth, like a stupendous oil strike, and it just keeps on coming and coming and piling up everywhere no matter what you try and do.

*

'They spent about 2 or 3 minutes talking, Herr Kommandant. In the enclosure behind the ranch.'

He meant the riding school. My Kapo, Steinke (a Trotskyite cut-throat in civilian life), meant the riding school – the Equestrian Academy . . . So, 2 meetings: the Summer Huts and the Equestrian Academy. And now 2 letters.

'You mean the riding school. The Equestrian Academy, Steinke. Christ, it's boiling in here . . . They talked in plain sight?'

'Yes, Herr Kommandant. There were a lot of people about.'

'And they just talked, you say. Did any documents change hands?'

'Documents? No, Herr Kommandant.'

'Written material? . . . Yes, well you see, you're not looking hard enough, Steinke. There *was* a transfer of written material. You just failed to spot it.'

'I lost sight of them for a few seconds when all these horses went past, Herr Kommandant.'

'Yes. Well you get horses at riding schools,' I said. 'Steinke, have you seen the signs mad people wear here? Saying *dumm*? Saying *Ich bin ein Kretin*? I think we'll order 1 of those for you.' Yes, and 1 for Prufer while we're at it. 'Steinke, you *get* horses at riding schools . . . And listen. From now on don't bother with him. Just monitor her. Klar?'

'Yes, Herr Kommandant.'

'How did they greet each other?'

'With a handshake.'

'With a handshake, Herr Kommandant. How did they say goodbye?'

'With a handshake, Herr Kommandant.'

We stepped aside as a group of Poles (implausibly overburdened) edged by. Steinke and myself were in 1 of the storehouses affixed to the tannery. It is here that the cheapest odds and ends of the evacuees are stacked prior to their elimination, as fuel, in the tannery furnace – cardboard shoes and plastic handbags and slabby wooden prams and so on and so forth.

'What were the respective durations of the 2 handshakes?'

'The 2nd 1 was longer than the 1st, Herr Kommandant.'

'How long was the 1st 1?'

Although I am indifferent to every aspect of 'interior decoration', I've always been pretty handy with a toolbox. Working alone, in the spring of this year, whilst Hannah tarried in Rosenheim, I successfully completed my 'pet' project: the installation of a fitted safe in the wall of the 1st-floor dressing room. Of course, I have the use of the locker in my study (and there's always the massive strongbox in the MAB). But the function of the fixture upstairs is quite otherwise. Its visible face, with the dials and tumblers, is hardly more than a facade. Open it up and what do you find? A 2-way mirror commanding a partial view of the bathroom. Alas, over the years, do you see, my wife has become rather shy, physically, and I happen to like appraising her when she's clothed in nature's garb – as is surely my conjugal right. The special 'looking glass' (and that's the *mot juste*, nicht?) I picked up on Block 10, where they were employing it to improve the monitoring of certain medical experiments. A sheet was going spare, and I thought, Hello, I'll be having that!

Well, yesterday, Hannah was just back from the Equestrian Academy (the pony) and there I was, standing to attention for the evening 'show'. Now normally Hannah turns on the taps and then rather listlessly disrobes. Whilst she's waiting for the tub to fill, repeatedly bending over to test the water's temperature – that's the best bit (her emergence is worth watching too, though she has an irritating habit of drying herself by the heated towel rack, which happens to be out of sight). It wasn't like that yesterday . . . She entered, locked the door and leaned back on it, yanked up her dress, and produced from within her panties 3 slips of light-blue paper. She studied their contents; she absorbed them a 2nd

114

time; not satisfied with that, she perused them yet again. For a moment she seemed lost in reverie. Then she moved to her left, ripping the missive to pieces; the toilet flushed, and, after the necessary interval, flushed once more.

I am now faced with the duty of recording an unpleasant truth. As Hannah read, her face 1st showed horror, then puzzled concentration, until . . . Towards the end, each time, her free Hand was at her Kehle; after a while it slid downwards somewhat, and appeared to caress the Brust area (her Schultern, in addition, were tensely turned in on themselves). How I felt, as a husband, confronted with that, may be fairly easily imagined. And that wasn't the end of it. Despite the obvious fact that she was aroused – despite the clear actuality that the female essences had stirred in her (the moistenings, the quickenings, the secret glistenings) – Hannah didn't even have the common decency to take a bath.

And ever since she's had this expression on her face. Contented, serene: in a word, unendurably smug. Moreover, she is physically abloom. She looks like she looked when she was 3 months pregnant. Full of power.

Mobius of the Politische Abteilung thinks we've got to do something about the Poles.

'How many Poles?'

'Not finalised. I'd say in the 250 range.' He tapped the file on his desk. 'A big job.'

'250.' It didn't sound very big to me – but I was by now almost unhinged by the astronomical numbers relayed to me by Szmul at the Meadow. 'Yes, I suppose that's fairly extensive.'

'And it's our own fault in a way.'

'How d'you work that 1 out?'

'All that stuff at the tannery.' He sighed. 'Slightly insensitive, don't you think?'

'I'm sorry, old boy, I don't quite follow.'

'All those odds and ends should never have left Kalifornia.'

'What odds and ends?'

'Come on, Paul – wake up.' He then said heavily, 'All that rubbish from the pacification of the area round *Lublin*. Peasant clothes. Tiny slippers. Crude rosaries. Missals.'

'What're missals?'

'Not really sure. I'm just going by Erkel's report. Some kind of filthy prayer book, I expect. They're very Catholic up there. Have you seen the condition of those men? It's a scandal. How did we let that happen?'

'Prufer.'

'Prufer. This mustn't wait. It'll be touch-and-go as it is. They aren't Jews, Paul. They aren't old ladies and little boys.'

'Do they know, the Poles?'

'Not yet. They have their suspicions, of course. But they don't know.'

'What do they hope'll happen?'

'That they'll just get dispersed. Sent hither and yon. But it's too late for that.'

'Oh well. Get the list to me tonight. Ne?'

'Zu befehl, mein Kommandant.'

As the bearer of 2 Iron Crosses (2nd class and 1st) , I am perfectly secure in my virility, thank you very much, and need make no nervous boasts about the force of my libido – in the matter of the carnal urge, as in everything else, I am completely normal.

Hannah's tragic frigidity unmasked itself fairly early on in our marriage, just after I swept her off to Schweinfurt for our honeymoon (her initial unresponsiveness, earlier, as our intimacy bloomed, I had attributed to medical considerations; but these no longer obtained). Personally, I laid it at the door of Dieter Kruger. And yet I faced the challenge awaiting me with the proverbial brash optimism of youth (or of relative youth, being 29). I felt sure that, over time, she would begin to respond to my gentleness, my sensitivity, and my extraordinary patience – a stoicism fortified by the purity of my love. But then there was a further development.

We were wed at Christmastide in '28. 1 week later, after our return to the environs of Rosenheim, Hannah's intuition was officially verified: she was 6 weeks gone. And this changed everything. You see, I happen to adhere to the doctrine propounded by that great Russian writer and thinker, Count Tolstoy, who, in an oeuvre whose title escapes me (it featured a German name, which was what piqued my interest . . . Got it! 'Kreutzer'!), calls for the eschewal of all erotic activity, not only during the months of gestation *but also throughout the period of lactation.*

It's not that I'm particularly nauseated by natural processes in a female. It's simply the principle of the thing: reverence for new life, for the priceless and inviolable formation of a fresh human being . . . We discussed it all quite openly, and Hannah, with a rueful smile, soon acceded to the superiority of my arguments. Paulette and Sybil were born in the summer of '29 – to our inestimable joy! And then my wife proceeded to nurse the twins for the next 3½ years.

The atmosphere between us, it's fair to say, grew increasingly strained. So by the time spousal relations were at last set to resume, we were – how shall I put this? – virtual strangers to each other. That 1st night, with the candlelit dinner, the flowers, the subdued lighting and soft music, the timely retirement, that 1st night was very far from being a success. After some preludial difficulties, I was in the end perfectly ready to perform – but Hannah proved quite unable to make herself mistress of her tension. It was no better the next night, or the next, or the next. I begged her to go back on her medication (or at least see the doctor and procure some sort of unguent), all to no avail.

The time was early 1933. And the Glorious Revolution was about to come to my aid. Permit me if I smile – just as Clio, the

117

muse of history, must have smiled as she relished the irony. After the Reichstag Fire (February 27), and the myriad arrests that followed it, the very man who had brought such sadness to my bedroom became the source of erotic relief. I mean friend Kruger. Ach, but that's another story.

Was it any wonder that, meanwhile, as a healthy young man with normal needs, I'd been obliged to look elsewhere?

To begin with there was a series of intensely lyrical, almost Edenic dalliances with various . . .

A knock at the door.

'Come in,' I said. 'Ah. Humilia.'

With Mobius's list.

Have you noticed, at night, whilst drowsing, that when you reach down to readjust the sheet, you often find that this necessitates lifting yourself free of it? And what an enormous effort it seems to demand of you. It's a big thing, the body, a big, heavy thing, and this is a living body, mine – all right, soggy with sleep, but buoyant with life, life!

'Vile morning, I'm afraid. Are we off then, Sturmbannfuhrer?'

'Yes yes. I'm coming for pity's sake.'

'All is well, mein Kommandant?'

I joined Prufer on the skiddy porch. A grey mist, weakly pullulating with grey snow – fat wet flakes of it. I cleared my throat and said, 'Which Bunker are we? I forget.'

. . . Stanislaw Stawiszynski, Tadeusz Dziedzic, Henryk Pileski – now and then, the night before, as I ran through Mobius's 'bill of fare', I was able to put a face to a name. And I realised that at least some of these men were truly legendary workers, veritable Stakhanovites, human sawmills and steamrollers, who regularly did a whole month in the coal mine at Furstengrube, and then (after a few weeks humping railway ties) went back for more . . .

Seated at my study desk, massaging my brow under the lamp, I began to have serious doubts about the measure Mobius proposed, and as a result (what with my other troubles) I drank far, far too much Riesling, vodka, armagnac, and above all slivovitz, and didn't get to bed until 04.07.

So I was feeling very seedy indeed when, at 06.28, I took my place on the bench behind the table in the basement of Bunker 3 (redbrick, windowless). Also present, apart from Prufer, Mobius, and myself: 2 Agents from the Political Section, plus captains Drogo Uhl and Boris Eltz. There was also a translator from the Postzensurstelle whom Prufer dismissed: the Poles, he said, were all 'old numbers' and understood German well enough ... Stacking his papers, Mobius coolly told me that he foresaw no complications. Uhl started to hum under his breath. Eltz lit a cigarette and muffled a yawn. And after a while I sat back and managed a contented albeit crapulent gurgle. I shouldn't have had that Phanodorm at 05.05. Everything I looked at seemed to blur and ripple like a radiator giving off heat.

Led by 1 armed guard (all right it was Staff Sergeant Palitzsch, but *1* armed guard?), the Poles, in columns of 5, began to fill the space. And I could hardly believe my senses. These Haftlinge were built like bears or gorillas, their striped uniforms were taut with bulk and muscle, their broad faces were tanned and glowing (and they even wore real shoes!). They were galvanic with *esprit*, too – like some crack brigade of motorised Waffen (and a sector of my heart duly if briefly ached to lead them in battle). On and on they kept sternly massing, 100, 200, 250, 300 – followed, if you please, by another casual soloist, the reviled 'ex-Pole' and long-time collaborator, Lageraltester Bruno Brodniewitsch!

Mobius frowned and nodded. 'Strammstehen!' he said with a slap of his folder on the tabletop. 'First the Kommandant will say a few words.'

This was news to me. I looked out at them. We officers had

our holstered Lugers, of course, and Palitzsch and Brodniewitsch were there with light machine guns slung over their shoulders. But I knew beyond doubt that if this battalion of bruisers scented danger – a twitch was all they'd need – there was no possibility of a single German getting out alive.

'Thank you, Untersturmfuhrer,' I said, and recleared my throat. 'Now, men, you'll doubtlessly want to know . . . You'll want to know why you were detached from your various Kommandos this morning. Ja, there'll be no work for you today.' There was a lightly appreciative murmur; and I almost went ahead and mentioned the double ration (the double ration, quite honestly, is a complete giveaway). 'So you'll have your lunch and then some free time to yourselves. Well and good. Untersturmfuhrer Mobius will explain why.'

'. . . Thank you, Sturmbannfuhrer. Now listen. You *Poles*. I'm not going to pull the wool over your eyes.'

And here I couldn't quite suppress a somewhat queasy smile. For Fritz Mobius was consummate Gestapo. Watch, listen, I thought – here comes the subterfuge. He'll play them like a lute . . .

'At some point this afternoon, probably around 5,' he said, looking at his watch, 'each and every 1 of you is going to be shot.'

I tasted vomit (and I might even have let out a cry) . . . But all that answered Mobius was silence: the silence of 300 men who had ceased to breathe.

'Yes, that's right. I'm talking to you like soldiers,' he loudly continued, 'because that's what you are. You're Home Army, the lot of you. And shall I tell you why you've been holding back? Because you can't convince your Centre that the KZ's an active asset. They think you're all bags of bones. And who'd believe there are men like you in a place like this? I can hardly believe it myself.'

The Untersturmfuhrer consulted his green file, whilst Hauptsturmfuhrer Eltz topped up the 7 glasses of soda water with a mesmerisingly steady hand.

'I shudder to think what you must've been getting away with. If you heard the word from Warsaw you'd be up our fundaments before we could blink. Men, it's over. You know full well what'll happen if there's any monkeyshines this afternoon. As I took the trouble to remind you yesterday, we have the parish registers. And you don't want your mothers and fathers and your grandparents clubbed on to the cattle wagons, you don't want your wives and children and nephews and nieces frying in the crema. Come *on*. *You know what we're like.*'

The silence gained in depth. Mobius sucked his tongue and said,

'All you can do is die like warriors. So let's keep it orderly. You show us some Polish pride and courage. And we'll show you some German respect. Oh, and you'll get your last supper. You'll get your double ration of warm bilge. Now *raus*! Hauptscharfuhrer? If you please.'

At 22.07 that night I was obliged to get out of bed and receive Prufer's oral report. From Bunker 3 I'd gone straight to the Krankenbau, where Professor Zulz gave me a vitamin shot and 2 cc's of chlorpromazine, which is supposedly an anti-emetic as well as a sedative. It didn't stop me practically sicking my ring out in the recovery bay, and I was sure I'd collapse in the slush as I stumbled home (no question of meeting the midday transport).

Now I said to Wolfram Prufer, 'Excuse the dressing gown. Come on through.' All right, I'd sworn off alcohol for the nonce, but I reckoned Prufer was due a gulp, after that kind of day, and it would've seemed unmanly not to join him. 'Ihre Gesundheit. How'd it go?'

'Pretty smooth, sir.'

In the yard of Bunker 3 a small fraction of the Polish contingent chose to die fighting (a barricade, quickly overrun), but the rest of them, 291 men, were uneventfully shot between 17.10 and 17.45.

'Quite exemplary,' said Prufer, with no expression on his unreadable face. 'In its way.'

I refilled our glasses, and we talked on, dispensing, late as it was, with the usual formalities. I said,

'Weren't you surprised Mobius was so . . . unsubtle about it? I was expecting a stratagem of some kind. You know, some form of deceit.'

'The deceit came yesterday. He told them they'd have to be taught a lesson, and he threatened to round up their families if they tried anything.'

'What's deceitful about that? That's what we do, isn't it?'

'No, not any more. Apparently it isn't worth the bother, so we stopped. Costs too much tracking them down. See, they've all been evicted and shuffled about. And besides . . .'

He proceeded to say that in any case these families, in large part, had already been bombed or strafed or hanged or starved or frozen – or, for that matter, shot in the course of *earlier* mass reprisals. Prufer drawled on,

'And those children he mentioned, ½ of them, all the 1s that're any good, have been packed off to the Reich and Germanised. So it's just not worth the sweat.'

'And those men,' I said. 'They simply . . . ?'

'No trouble at all. They had their soup and spent an hour or 2 writing postcards. When the time came a lot of them were singing. Patriotic stuff. And nearly all of them yelled out something like *Long live Poland* last thing. But that was all.'

'Long live Poland. That's a funny 1.'

Prufer stretched his neck and said, 'There was almost another cock-up – ferrying the bodies away before their mates got back from work. We covered the carts but we couldn't do anything about the blood of course. Wasn't time. The men saw. It was tense. It was tense, mein Kommandant. Mobius thinks we may have to do another batch. Repeat the whole palaver.'

'. . . Na. How's your brother, Prufer?'

'Which 1?'

'The 1 in Stalingrad. Freiherr? No. Irmfried.'

Left to myself, I engaged in an hour of soul-searching, sprawled on the easy chair by the fire with the bottle on my lap. There was I (I mused), offing old ladies and little boys, whilst other men gave a luminescent display of valour. I was of course thinking with envious admiration of the Untersturmfuhrer. Facing down those massive Polacks like that, saying, with ice in his heart, *'Ihr weisst wie wir sind.'*

You know what we're like.

That's National Socialism!

And mind you, disposing of the young and the elderly requires other strengths and virtues – fanaticism, radicalism, severity, implacability, hardness, iciness, mercilessness, und so weiter. After all (as I often say to myself), somebody's got to do it – the Jews'd give us the same treatment if they had ½ a chance, as everybody knows. They had a pretty fair crack at it in November 1918, when the war profiteers, buying cheap and selling . . .

. . . I levered myself upright and wandered out into the kitchen. Hannah was standing at the table, eating a green salad from the bowl with the wooden fork and the wooden spoon.

'Na ja,' I said, with a huge intake of breath. 'Front-line service. That's the thing. I've ½ a mind to request a transfer. To the east. Where, even as we speak, Hannah, world history is being forged. And I want to be in the thick of it, nicht? We're about to give Judaeo-Bolshevism the biggest—'

'Give who?'

'Judaeo-Bolshevism. On the Volga. We're going to give Judaeo-Bolshevism the biggest bloody nose of all time. You heard the speech? The city's virtually ours. Stalingrad. On the Volga, woman. On the Volga.'

'So soon,' she said. 'Once again you're drunk.'

'Na, perhaps I am. So might . . .' I reached into the jar for a pickled onion. Chewing vigorously, I said, 'You know, my dear, I was thinking. I was thinking we ought to do what little we can for poor Alisz Seisser. She's back. As an inmate.'

'Alisz Seisser? What for?'

'Bit of an, bit of an, an enigma. Pardon. They've got her down as an Asozial.'

'Which means?'

'Could mean anything. Vagrancy. Begging. Prostitution, heaven forbid. Or a uh, relatively minor offence. Grumbling. Painting her toenails.'

'Painting her toenails? Mm, I suppose that makes perfect sense. In wartime. A savage blow to morale.' She wiped her Mund with a napkin, and her Gesicht readjusted. 'Which is already in retreat, I hear.'

'Quatsch! Who says?'

'Norberte Uhl. Who got it from Drogo. And from Suzi Erkel. Who got it from Olbricht . . . Well then. What's the little we can do for Alisz Seisser?'

To begin with there was a series of intensely lyrical, almost Edenic dalliances, in the sylvan surrounds of our Bavarian farmstead (leased from my in-laws), with various young shepherdesses, milkmaids, and stable girls (this all started during Hannah's 2nd trimester). How often would I, in my leather shorts and embroidered tunic, vault the sheep dip and scamper through the barn doors in hot pursuit of my vernal lovely who, with an amorous yelp and a playful shimmy of her flaxen rump, would disappear on all 4s into our secret nest beneath the haystack! And how many hours would we beguile, in the idyllic paddock behind the shearing shed, Hansel with a blade of grass between his laughing lips, and his head buried in the dirndled lap of his buxom and rubicund Gretel!

Then, in '32, Hannah and myself were inexorably drawn to Munich – city of my dreams and my yearning.

Gone were the flocks, the rills, the milking stools, the cowslips, the wild thyme, and the piping maids. Whilst commuting each day to the suburb of Dachau (where I would begin *quite* a career), and whilst heading a family of 4, I still found time for a committed but eminently sensible relationship with a lady of great sophistication called Xondra, who maintained a service apartment on Schillerstrasse near the Hauptbahnhof. Quite suddenly she married a prosperous pawnbroker from Ingolstadt, but I went on to make other friends in the same flatblock – notably Pucci, Booboo, and the golden-haired Marguerite. But all that was a very long time ago.

Here in the KZ, and in wartime, too, I've never entertained the thought of any kind of 'misbehaviour'. I feel it would be utterly unGerman to compromise myself with a colleague (such as Ilse Grese), or with a colleague's wife (Berlin would *not* be amused). And otherwise you're seldom tempted, because so few of the women menstruate or have any hair. If you get desperate – well. The place in Katowitz is far too squalid, but the best 1 in Cracow is a German concern and it's as clean as an operating theatre. None of that since my wife's arrival, though. Ach, I've been the model, the ideal, the dream . . .

But now the situation has changed. And 2 can play at that game. Not so?

We do in fact have a piggery at the KL (a modest appendage to the Home Farm Station). And Alisz Seisser is a Tierpfleger – a veterinary nurse. Her uniform's the same as that of the helpers in the Haftlinge Krankenbau: white linen jacket with a red stripe daubed on the back, and a similar paintstroke down the trousers. After having a good look, I tapped on the window of her surgery, and out she popped.

'Oh thank you, thank you. Thank you for coming. It's ever so good to see you, Herr Kommandant.'

'Herr Kommandant? Paul, please,' I said with a friendly chuckle. 'Paul. No – you've been constantly in my thoughts. Poor Alisz. It must have been very difficult for you up in Hamburg. Were you in dire straits? Did the pension not come through?'

'No no. Nothing of that kind. They nabbed me at the station, Paul. When I got off the train.'

'That's odd.' On her chest she wore the black triangle of the Asozial. It had a letter sewn into it (this usually denoted country of provenance). 'What's that stand for when it's at home?' I asked with a grin. 'Zambia?'

'Zigeuner.'

I took a step back.

'Well I can't say I wasn't expecting it,' she blithely continued. 'Orbart always used to say, *If anything happens to yours truly, old girl, or if you up and leave me* – you know, joking – *then you're in the soup, love*. Sinti grandmother, see. And we knew it was in the file.'

This was a most unwelcome surprise. The Zigeuner had been workhouse fodder since the mid 1920s, and the Reichsfuhrer-SS's Central Office for Fighting the Gypsy Menace, of course, had been active for quite a while (and I noticed that just the other day these people were dispossessed and stripped of all their rights). Obviously we'd need to tackle said menace at *some* point or other . . . Although there was a Gypsy family camp in KL2 (circus people, dance-hall proprietors and the like), they were classed as internees, tattooed but unshaven and not on the labour lists. So far as I was aware, Alisz was the only Zigeuner Haftling in the entire Zone.

'Yes, so. I'll still be doing all I can for you, Alisz.'

'Oh I know you will, Paul. When they moved me from the Women's Block I could feel your hand at work. The Women's Block – it's really the end. I can't find words to describe it.'

'. . . You *seem* well enough, my dear. The crewcut's most becoming. And is that your phone number? Just joking. Nicht? Come on, Alisz, let's have a look at you then. Mm. That suit's not much help in these temperatures. You've the 2 blankets, I hope? And you're getting the Tierpfleger ration? Turn around a moment. You haven't lost any weight at least.'

She's short in the Unterschenkel, Alisz, but she has a glorious Hinterteil. As for the other stuff, the Busen and such, it's hard to say – but there's certainly no argument about the Sitzflache.

'You're better off here, you know, than in the Ka Be. I wouldn't want you in the Typhus Block. Or in Dysentery for that matter, dear.'

'No, it's not too bad at all. I'm a country girl, me. And the pigs are very sweet!'

'And I hope, Alisz, I hope you're being sustained by the sacred memory of the Sturmscharfuhrer. Your Orbart. He laid down his life, Alisz, for his convictions. And what more can we ask of a man?'

She smiled bravely. And again, for a moment, she took on that sacred glow – the holy aura of German martyrdom. Whilst she hugged herself and, with chattering teeth, hymned her sainted husband, I thought how very difficult it was to gauge a woman's figure until her clothes came off. I mean, there's an awful lot to go wrong.

'Listen, Alisz. I have a message from my lady wife. She wants you to come to the villa on Sunday.'

'The villa?'

'Oh, it'll raise an eyebrow or 2, perhaps. But I'm the Kommandant and we've a ready-made excuse. The girls' pony. It's got mange! Come and spend the afternoon.'

'Well, if you say it's all right, Paul.'

'Hannah's got some women's things she wants to give you.' I adjusted my greatcoat against the wind. 'I'll pick you up by car. And it'll be steak, spuds, and greens.'

'Oh, that would be handsome!'

'A square meal. Oh yes. And a long hot bath.'

'Ooh, Paul, I can hardly wait.'

'Till noon on Sunday. Run along now, my girl. Run along.'

I don't go out to the Meadow that often any more. Neither does Szmul. Well, he sometimes looks in around midnight, to make sure everything is processing as it should, and then goes back to his duties as a greeter. To have an exchange with Szmul, nowadays, you have to catch him on the ramp.

The first train had been dealt with, and the Sonder was seated on a suitcase, in the immediate glare of an untended arc light, eating a wedge of cheese. I came up on him from behind, aslant, and said,

'Why were you on the very 1st transport out of Litzmannstadt?'

His jaw muscles stopped working. 'The 1st transport was for undesirables, sir. I was an undesirable, sir.'

'Undesirable? A little schnook of a schoolmaster like you? Or perhaps you teach a bit of PT.'

'I stole some firewood, sir. To buy turnips.'

'. . . To buy turnips, *sir*.' I stood over him now, my jodhpurs planted well apart. 'Where did you think you were being sent? Germany? To work in Germany? Why'd you believe that?'

'They changed my ghetto scrip into Reichsmarks, sir.'

'. . . Ooh. Clever them. Your wife wasn't with you, was she, Sonder.'

'No, sir. Exempted because of pregnancy, sir.'

'Not many live births in the ghetto, I hear. Any other children?'

'No, sir.'

'So she missed that rather inelegant Aktion at Kulmhof. *On your feet.*'

He stood, wiping his greasy hands on his greasy trousers.

'You were at Kulmhof. "Chełmno", as you lot call it. You were there . . . Remarkable. No Jew gets out of Kulmhof. And I suppose they kept you on board because of your German. Tell me. Were you there at the time of the silent boys?'

'No, sir,' I lied.

'Pity . . . Now, Sonder. You know who I mean by Chaim Rumkowski.'

'Yes, sir. The Director, sir.'

'The Director. The ghetto king. I gather he's quite a "character". Here.'

And I produced from my pocket the letter I'd received that morning from 'Łódź'.

'The stamp. That's his portrait. He goes around in a wheeled carriage. Drawn by a spindly dray.'

Szmul nodded.

'I wonder if you'll live long enough, Sonderkommandofuhrer, to receive him here.'

He turned away.

'Your lips. They're always tensed and notched. Always. Even when you eat . . . You intend to *kill* someone, don't you, Sonder. You intend to kill someone "e'er you go". D'you want to kill me?' I unholstered my Luger and pressed its barrel up against his resistant brow. 'Oh, don't kill me, Sonder. Please don't kill me.' The searchlight died with a crackle. 'When your time comes, I'll be telling you exactly what to do.'

Out in the night we saw the yellow eye of the 2nd train.

'You know,' I mused, 'you know, I think we ought to make a special effort for November the 9th.'

Wolfram Prufer's round face attentively blinked and pouted.

'A proper ceremony,' I mulled on, 'and a rousing speech.'

'Good idea, Sturmbannfuhrer. Where? The church?'

'No.' I folded my arms. He meant St Andrew's in the Old Town.

129

'No. In the open air,' I conjured. 'After all, *they* did what they did in the open air, the Old Fighters . . .'

'But that was in Munich, and Munich's practically in Italy. This is East Poland, Sturmbannfuhrer. St Andrew's is like a fridge as it is.'

'Come on, there's actually not much in it, in terms of latitude. Anyway, let it snow. We'll sling up some tarps. By the orchestra stand. More bracing. It'll stiffen morale.' I smiled. 'Your brother on the Volga, Hauptsturmfuhrer. Irmfried. I trust he foresees no undue difficulties?'

'None, mein Kommandant. Losing in Russia is a biological impossibility.'

I raised my eyebrows. 'You know, Prufer, that's rather well put . . . Now what'll we do for urns?'

On Sunday evening I attended a function in the Old Town at the Rathof Bierkeller (considerably refurbished, in recent months, thanks to heavy IG custom). Yech, it was another Farben 'do', basically – we were bidding farewell to Wolfgang Bolz, who was about to return to Frankfurt after his tour. The atmosphere was pretty grim, quite frankly, and I had some trouble containing my good cheer (Alisz Seisser's visit having been an unqualified success).

Anyway, I was talking, or listening, to 3 mid-stratum engineers, Richter, Rudiger, and Wolz. The conversation centred as usual on the low levels of endeavour (and the sorry underachievement) of the Buna workforce, and how quickly they became part of the curse of my entire existence – pieces, Stucke: spitefully massive, uncompromisingly ponderous and unwieldy, mephitic sacs or stinkbombs just raring to explode.

'The Haftlinge are done in as it is, sir. Why'd they have to lug the bloody things all the way back to the Stammlager?' said Wolz.

'Why can't the Leichekommando come and pick them up, sir? Either at night or 1st thing in the morning?' said Rudiger.

'They say it's for the roll call, sir. But can't they get the numbers from the Leichekommando and just do their damned sums?' said Richter.

'Regrettable,' I absent-mindedly allowed.

'They're having to give them piggybacks, for pity's sake.'

'Because they keep running out of stretchers.'

'And there are never enough bloody wheelbarrows.'

'Additional wheelbarrows,' I put in (it was time to leave). 'Good point.'

Thomsen was present, in front of the exit – he was superciliously holding forth to Mobius and Seedig. Our eyes met, and he showed me his feminine teeth in a smile or a sneer. He drew back in dismay, and I saw the glint of fear in his white eyes, as I roughly shouldered my way out into the air.

19.51. Prufer, doubtlessly, would have been happy to run me back on his motorbike; as the frost was holding off and it was still quite light, however, I elected to walk.

During the period 1936–9, in Munich, there was an annual procession, sponsored and smiled on by the State – 'Night of the Amazons' they called it (this memory came to me as I strode through the site of the synagogue we blew up 2 years ago): columns of German damsels paraded on horseback, stripped to the waist. Tastefully choreographed, these virgins re-enacted historical scenes – celebrations of the Teuton heritage. It's said, too, that the Deliverer himself once tolerantly attended a famous nude ballet in that same city. This is the German way, do you see. The German male is in complete control of his desires. He can go at a woman like a purple genius; when the occasion demands it, on the other hand, he is happy to cast a cultured glance – yet feels no impulsion to touch . . .

I paused as I entered the Zone, steadying myself with a few stiffeners from my flask. Whatever the temperature I do like a good tramp. That's my upbringing, I suppose. I'm like Alisz. A country boy at heart.

Biggish Titten, such as those belonging to my wife, can be described as 'beautiful', smallish Titten, like Waltraut's and Xondra's, can be characterised as 'pretty', and Titten of the middlish persuasion can be designated as – what? 'Prettiful' Titten? Such are Alisz's Titten. 'Prettiful'. And her Brustwarten are excitingly dark. And see what a playful mood she's put me in!

I shall look. I shall not touch. The penalties for Rassenschande, albeit erratically imposed, can be fairly severe (up to and including decapitation) – but in any case Alisz has never stirred in me anything but the tenderest and most exalted emotions. I think of her as I would a 'grown-up' daughter – to be protected, cherished, and humbly revered.

As I passed the old crema and approached the garden gate, I contemplated my imminent rendezvous with Frau Doll; and I felt that lovely glow of surety that heats and tickles you when you're playing 2-card brag (a game far more complicated than it at 1st appears): you look round the table, and count the pips, and you're satisfied for a mathematical fact that victory is yours. She doesn't know I know about the letter she passed to Thomsen. She doesn't know I know about the missive he handed to her. I'm going 'to tie her up in knots'. I just want to see the look on her face.

Meinrad, the pony, neighed feebly whilst I ascended the steps.

Hannah was on the couch before the fire, reading *Vom Winde Verweht* to the twins. No one looked up as I settled on the revolvable stool.

'Hear me, Sybil, hear me, Paulette.' I said, 'Your mother's a very wicked woman. Very wicked indeed.'

'Don't say that!'

'An evil woman.'

'Oh what d'you *mean*, Vati?'

I slowly let my frown darken. 'Go to bed, girls.'

Hannah clapped her hands. 'Off with you. I'll be up in 5 minutes.'

'*3* minutes!'

'Promise.'

As they were getting up and moving off I said, 'Ho ho. Ho ho ho. I think it'll take a bit longer than *that*.'

In the firelight Hannah's eyes seemed to have the colour and texture of the skin of crème brûlée.

'I know something you don't know,' I said with my chin going lazily from side to side. 'I know something you don't know I know. Ho ho. Ho ho ho. I know you don't know I—'

'You mean Herr Thomsen?' she said brightly.

For a moment, I admit, I could think of nothing to say. '. . . Yes. Herr *Thomsen*. Come on, Hannah, whats your game? Listen. If you don't—'

'What are you talking about? I've got no reason to see him again. And I was sorry to impose in the 1st place. He was polite enough, but I could tell he rather resents anything that gets in the way of his mission.'

Again it was a while before I said, 'Oh really? What "mission" is this?'

'He's obsessed by the Buna-Werke. He thinks it could decide the war.'

'Well he's not wrong there.' I folded my arms. 'No, hang on. Not so fast, my girl. The letter you had Humilia give him. Yes, oh yes, she told me all about it. Some people know what morality is, you see. That letter. Perhaps you'd care to satisfy me as to its contents?'

'If you like. I asked for a meeting by the Summer Huts. At the playground. Where he reluctantly agreed to trace Dieter Kruger for me. I finally had a chance to apply to someone high up. Someone really important.'

I stood suddenly, giving my crown a glancing cuff on the mantelpiece.

'You keep a civil tongue in your mouth when you talk to me young lady!'

After a moment her head gave a penitent bow. But I didn't like the way this was going 1 bit. I said,

'And the 2nd missive – the 1 he slipped you at the riding school?'

'That was his reply, of course. His full report.'

3 minutes later Hannah said,

'I'm not telling you. Do you understand? I'm not telling you. And now, if you don't mind, I'll keep my promise to the girls.'

And with that she sashayed from the room . . . No. Our little exchange didn't go at all as I'd planned. For a while I stared into the grate – at the punily lashing flamelets. Then I picked up a bottle of something or other and went off for some testing cogitations in my 'lair'.

That night I woke up and my face was completely numb – my chin, my lips, my cheeks. As if drenched in novocaine. I rolled off the divan and dipped my head beneath my knees for an hour and a ½. It didn't help. And I thought, If any girl or woman kissed my rubbery cheeks or my rubbery lips then I wouldn't feel anything at all.

Like a dead leg or a dead arm. A dead face.

3. SZMUL: BREATHE DEEPLY

In addition we are being mocked, which is not very nice either, so to say. Mocked, and profaned. There is a Star of David on the ceiling of the airtight chamber. The foot rags they issue us with are scraps of prayer shawls. Transit Route IV, the slave-built highway from Przemsyl to Tarnopol, is laid out on the crushed rubble of synagogues and Jewish gravestones. Then there is the 'Goebbels Calendar': no holy day passes without an Aktion. The sharpest 'measures' are reserved for Yom Kippur and Rosh Hashana – our Days of Awe.

The eating. I believe I can explain the eating.

Of the five senses, taste is the only one that we, the Sonders, can partly control. The other senses are ruined and dead. It is strange about touch. I carry, drag, shove, seize – I do these things all night long. But the sense of connection is no longer there. I feel like a man with prosthetic hands – a man with false hands.

And when you consider what we see, what we hear, and what we smell, you won't deny that we do badly need to control what we taste. What would it be, the taste in our mouths, in the absence of food? As soon as you swallow and the food is gone, it comes, it returns: the taste of our defeat, the taste of wormwood.

I mean the taste of our defeat in the war against the Jews. This war is in every conceivable sense *one-sided*. We did not expect it, and for far too long we gazed with real incredulity at the incredible anger of the Third Germany.

There is a transport from Theresienstadt which includes a number of Poles. During a three-hour delay caused by the non-appearance of the Disinfektoren, I fall into conversation with the family of a middle-aged industrial engineer (a one-time member of the Jewish Council in Lublin). I am reassuring his daughter and her children about the ample meals and snug lodgings, here at the KZ, and the man trustingly takes me aside and tells me a strange and terrible story about the recent events in Łódź. It turns out to be a story about the power of hunger.

September 4, and there is a thick crowd on Fireman's Square. Rumkowski, weeping, reveals the latest German demand: the surrender, for deportation, of all adults over sixty-five and all children under ten. The next day the old will go, the young will go . . .

'They're probably all right,' I manage to say. 'You'll be all right too. Look at me. Do I look half starved?'

But of course there is more. That same afternoon the people learn that a supply of potatoes is ready for distribution. And a wave of euphoria surges through the streets of the ghetto. Now the focus of talk and thought is not the disappearance of all adults over sixty-five and all children under ten, but the potatoes.

'Don't kill me, kill someone else,' it increasingly amuses Doll to say. 'I'm not a monster. I don't torture people for the hell of it. Slay a monster, Sonderkommandofuhrer. Kill Palitzsch. Kill Brodniewitsch. Slay a monster.'

Sometimes he says (and I find, even in all this, that his diction still succeeds in offending me), 'Kill someone powerful. I'm nothing. I'm not powerful. Me – powerful? No. I'm a cog in a vast machine. I'm rubbish. I'm just a cunt. I'm shit.

'Why don't you wait for the next visit of the Reichsfuhrer? If you don't get him, try Mobius. His rank's lower than mine but he's far more weighty. Or Standartenfuhrer Blobel. Or Odilo Globocnik when he's next here.

'But don't kill Paul Doll – though of course you're welcome to try. Doll's nothing. He's shit. He's just a cunt.'

*

136

The thought I find hardest to avoid is the thought of returning home to my wife. I can avoid the thought, more or less. But I can't avoid the dream.

In the dream I enter the kitchen and she swivels in her chair and says, 'You're back. What happened?' And when I begin my story she listens for a while and then turns away, shaking her head. And that is all. It's not as if I tell her about my first thirty days in the Lager (spent in full-time exploration of the orifices of the recently dead, in collaboration with the German quest for valuables). It's not as if I tell her about the time of the silent boys.

That is all, but the dream is unendurable, and the dream knows this, and humanely grants me the power to rouse myself from it. By now I am bolt upright the instant it starts. Then I climb from my bedding and pace the floor no matter how tired I am, because I'm afraid to go to sleep.

This morning, in another of our comradely debates, we return yet again to the matter of *alleviation*. Here are a few of the things that are said.

'Every time, with every transport, we should sow panic. Every time. We should all move along the ramp whispering of murder.'

'Futile? No, not futile. It would *slow them down*. And corrode their nerves. The *Szwaby*, the *Zabójcy* – they're mortal.'

This speaker – like ninety per cent of all the Jews in the Sonderkommando – became an atheist about half an hour after starting work. But certain tenets linger. Judaism, unlike the other monotheisms, does not hold that the Devil takes human form. All are mortal. But this is another doctrine I am starting to doubt. The German is not something supernatural, but neither is he something human. He is not the Devil. He is Death.

'They're mortal. They tremble too. But when there's panic. Nightmare!'

'*Good*. So it should be.'

137

'Why make it worse for our people? Why make their last minutes worse?'

'They're not their last minutes. Their last minutes are spent jammed solid and dying. And there are fifteen of them. Fifteen minutes.'

'They're going to die anyway. We want it to cost the *Szwaby*.'

Another says, 'The fact is we *don't* sow panic. Do we. We smile and lie. Because we're human beings.'

Another says, 'We lie because when there's panic we get killed quicker.'

Another says, 'We lie because we fear the bloodlust and the rage.'

Another says, 'We lie for our lousy selves.'

And I say, '*Ihr seit achzen johr alt, und ihr hott a fach*. That's all there is. There's nothing else.'

With his shirt off and gasmask on, Doll looks like a fat and hairy old housefly (a housefly that is nearing the end of its span). He sounds like a housefly too, as he repeats the number I have given him: a sizzling whine. He asks me something else.

'I can't make you out, sir.'

We are in the 'ossuary' – a broad concavity upwind of the pyre. I am counting charred hipbones before their transfer to the grinding teams.

'Still can't hear you, sir.'

He gives a jerk of his head, and I follow him up the slope.

On level ground he frees his mouth with a gasp and says, 'So we must be nearly there, nicht?'

'We're definitely past half way, sir.'

'Half *way*?'

The pyre is sixty metres from where we stand, and the heat, though still immense, is now seamed with autumn cold.

'Well fucking get on with it . . . I know what's worrying you.

Fear not, hero. When we're done here the whole squad's for it. But you and your best fifty will proudly live on.'

'Which fifty, sir?'

'Oh, you choose.'

'. . . I select, sir?'

'Yes, you select. Go on, you've seen it done a thousand times. Select . . . You know, Sonder, I never nursed any particular hatred for the Jews. Something had to be done about them, obviously. But I'd've been content with the Madagascar solution. Or having you all neutered. Like with the Rhineland Bastards, nicht? The by-blows of the French Araber und Neger. Nicht? No killing. Just snipping. But you lot – you're neutered already, ne? You've already lost what made you men.'

'Sir.'

'I didn't decide all this.'

'No, sir.'

'I just said zu Befehl, zu Befehl. I just said ja, ja, yech, ja. Sie wissen doch, nicht? I didn't decide. Berlin decided. Berlin.'

'Yes, sir.'

'. . . You know that white-haired streak of piss who's always in civvies? You must've heard talk of Thomsen, Sonder. Thomsen's the nephew of Martin Bormann – the Reichsleiter, the Sekretar. Thomsen's Berlin.' Doll laughs and says, 'So kill Berlin. Kill Berlin. Before Berlin kills you.' He laughs again. 'Kill Berlin.'

As he starts off back to the jeep Doll turns and says, 'You live on, Sonder.' Again he laughs. 'I'm best of friends with the appropriate authority in Litzmannstadt. Maybe I can arrange a reunion. You and uh, "Shulamith". She hasn't got enough vitamin P, Sonder. *Protektsye*, nicht?

'She's still there, you know. In the attic above the bakery. She's still there. But where's her vitamin P?'

*

One morning I am in the lane passing the Kommandant's garden, and I see Frau Doll setting off for school with her daughters. She looks in my direction and she says something quite extraordinary to me. And I recoil from it as if I have smoke in my eyes. Five minutes later, standing bent behind the main guardroom, I am able to shed tears for the first time since Chełmno.

'Guten Tag,' she says.

The urge to kill is like the bore of a river, a steepsided wave coming up against the flow. Against the flow of what I am or what I was. Part of me hopes the urge is there at the end.

But if it should happen that I go to the gas (in fact I am probably too conspicuous for that, and they'll just take me aside for the shot to the nape – but imagine): if it should happen that I go to the gas, I will weave among them.

I will weave among them, saying, to the old man in the astrakhan coat, 'Stand as close to the meshed shaft as you can, sir.'

Saying, to the boy in the sailor suit, 'Breathe deeply, my child.'

CHAPTER IV. BROWN SNOW

I. THOMSEN: TOUCH THE OLD WOUND

There was a big sick bird, a kite I think it was – there was a big sick bird that hovered over the oak beyond the scaffold on the well-tended lawn (mown in stripes) facing the Appellplatz of the Farben Kat Zet.

It hovered there, in all weathers, brownish, yellowish, the colour of the healing eyes of the Commandant; and it never seemed to use its wings. It dangled – it just hung.

Now I knew a bird could do this, given a lucky confluence of currents, of rising thermals; but the sick bird did it all day long. Perhaps all night, too.

Would it *like* the upper air, you wondered? Sometimes the wind got in under its pinions, and they stirred, and you sensed effort, and you felt you could hear a distant groan of aspiration. Yet it failed to rise. The bird was aloft, merely; it couldn't fly.

Sometimes it abruptly dropped three or four metres, it lurched downwards, as if tugged by a cord. It seemed inorganic, manmade – like a *kite*, in fact, directed by a boy's inexperienced hand.

Perhaps it was mad, this ponderous predator of the air. Perhaps it was dying. You sometimes felt it was not a bird but a fish, a ray, floating, drowning, in the ocean of the sky.

I understood the bird, I absorbed it, I contained it within me.

———

This is what I passed to her at the riding school.

Dear Hannah:

Events oblige me to start with yet more bad news. Professor Szozeck's Pikkolo, Dov Cohn, has also been 'transferred' (along with a Kapo called Stumpfegger, who took an interest in him and was possibly his confidant). And this six weeks after the event. It's particularly hard to take, because I thought – didn't you? – that Dov was very well equipped to survive.

After what you told me about the circumstances of your marriage, I no longer feel the need to pay your husband even the minimal respect due to the father of Paulette and Sybil. He is what he is, and he is getting worse. If he thought he had the right to eliminate three people, one of them a child, over a single instance of compromised prestige, which in truth was an act of kindness – well. I have a measure of protection, through my uncle. You have none.

It is urgently necessary, then, that we retroactively 'normalise' our past dealings, you and I. As a qualified Referendar, I have given the thing a good deal of plodding thought, and here is the version, and the sequence, I think we should stick to. It sounds complicated but it's really very simple. The key is your certainty that Doll no longer knows the status or whereabouts of Dieter Kruger.

Now memorise this.

In the letter brought to me by Humilia, you asked me to do you a service, and said you could be found on Fridays at the Summer Huts. At our meeting there, I agreed to make inquiries about DK – reluctantly, because (of course) I resent anything that distracts me from my sacred mission at the Buna-Werke.

This second communication, the one you hold in your hand, is my report. Doll knows about the first letter, and it's likely he knows about the second (again, we were observed). If he starts to question you – then be quick to open up, freely. And when he asks you what I discovered, you should simply announce that you're not going to tell him. I will now inquire about DK (and so no doubt will your husband).

From here on we cannot meet, except communally – and no more letters. I have to say that I am deeply uneasy about what you propose for your side of it: your plan, so to speak, for the home front. As things stand, Doll will have no reason to strike out at you. But if your plan works, he won't need a reason. Still, you seem resolved, and this decision is of course yours to make.

Let me now say something from the heart.

The letter continued for another two pages.

Her plan, it should be noted, was to do everything in her power to hasten the psychological collapse of the Commandant.

'Take that look off your face, Golo. It's absolutely nauseating.'

'. . . What?'

'The meek smile. Like an altruistic schoolboy . . . I see. So there's been some kind of breakthrough, has there. And that's why you've clammed up on me.'

I was in the kitchen making breakfast. Boris had spent the night (under a heap of old curtains on the sitting-room floor) and was now crouched down rebuilding the fire, using crunched-up pages of *The Racial Observer* and *The Stormer*. Outside, the fourth week of uncompromising October weather, with low, heavy clouds, constant rain and wet mist, and, underfoot, a boundless latrine of purplish brown slime.

Referring to *The Stormer* (an illiterate hate-sheet run by Julius Streicher, the child-molesting Gauleiter of Franconia), Boris said, 'Why do you take this wank mag? Old Yid Drugs Teen Blonde. Officers aren't supposed to read *The Stormer* in camp. It's the Old Boozer's personal directive. He's that refined. Well, Golo?'

'. . . Don't worry, I won't be laying a finger on her here. Ruled out.'

'The Hotel Zotar and all that?'

'Ruled out.' I asked him how many eggs he wanted and how

he wanted them (six, fried). 'Nothing clandestine. I'll only be seeing her in company.'

'You'll be seeing her on the ninth of course.'

'The ninth? Oh yeah, the ninth. Why do they go on about November the ninth?'

'I know. You'd think they'd murder anyone who dared mention it.'

'I know. But they go on about it . . . Doll and the Poles, Boris.'

'Bunker 3?' Boris laughed happily and said, 'Oh, Golo, the state of old fat-arse. Christ. With his wall-eyed hangover. And his fluttering hands.'

'Not everyone's brave, my dear.'

'True, Golo. Excellent coffee, this. Mm, the Poles. Well, even I thought it was a bit on the sporty side. Telling three hundred circus strongmen they're about to be topped.'

'Still, you assumed . . .'

'That Mobius had done the necessary. Which he had. But Doll. We mustn't be mean, Golo. Let's just say Doll was beholden to his brown trousers.'

'And everyone could tell.'

'He gave out a whimper and sort of waggled his arms in the air. Like this. Mobius went, *Commandant!* And Doll's breath smelled of sick.'

'Anyway.' I refilled our cups, adding Boris's three sugars and stirring them in. 'Anyway, you went ahead with it.'

'They were Home Army. It was the first sensible order I'd had in months . . . Mm, they certainly knew how to die. Chest out, head up.'

We ate in silence.

'Oh, stop it, Golo. That look.'

I said, 'Indulge your old friend. I won't do it often. Most of the time I'm in agony.'

'About what? The waiting? About what?'

'Being here. This is . . . This is no place for delicate feelings, Boris.' Yes, I thought. I used to be numb; now I'm raw. 'Being here.'

'Mm. Here.'

After some thought I said, 'I'm going to take a vow of silence on Hannah. But before I do I just want you to . . . I'm in love.'

Boris's shoulders went slack. 'Oh, *no*.'

I gathered the plates and the cutlery. 'All right, I don't disagree, brother. It's hard to imagine it ending well. Now. That'll do.'

We sat smoking in the other room. The illustrious mouser, Maksik (newly arrived), his undercarriage an inch from the floor, was nosing round the low kitchen shelves; abruptly he sat and, in incensed irritation, scratched his ear with a violent hindpaw.

'She's not bad, is she . . .' Boris meant Agnes. 'Oh and Esther — Esther's fine for now, by the way. I got her off the vet detail,' he said with (I thought) a touch of smugness. 'Too much outdoor work. Yes, and I saw Alisz Seisser. Had you heard?'

'Yes. Roma or Sinti?'

'Alisz is a Sintiza,' he said wistfully. 'So sweet.'

'So she's ruled out too.'

'Mm. Give Alisz so much as a peck on the cheek, and you're breaking the law. The Law, Golo, for the Protection of German Blood.'

'And German Honour, Boris. What do you get for that?'

'Depends who you are. It's usually all right so long as you're the Aryan. And so long as you're the man, of course. But me, I'm on probation.' He took his lower lip between his teeth. 'And it'd be just like them to give me another year here. Oh, and nice news from Egypt, isn't it.'

'Mm,' I said. This was the defeat of Germany's ablest soldier, Rommel, by the British at El Alamein. 'And why's everyone gone quiet about Stalingrad?'

Boris examined the coal of his cigarette. 'I haven't done it for years, but I'm thinking more about the past. Now.'

'We all are.'

———

It was a Tuesday. That afternoon at four o'clock Hannah came out of the glass doors of the breakfast room and took a five-minute turn round the garden – under an umbrella, and wrapped up in a kind of hoodless duffel coat. She didn't look in what she knew to be my direction. I was up in the Monopoly Building, where they keep all the uniforms, the boots, the belts . . .

Paul Doll was not her first lover.

1928, and Hannah had just enrolled at the University of Rosenheim in southern Bavaria (French and English); Dieter Kruger was on the faculty (Marx and Engels). With two friends she started going to a course of lectures he was giving – for the simple reason that *he was so handsome. We all had mad crushes on him.* One day he took her aside and asked her if she felt passionate about the Communist cause; she untruthfully said that she did. He then asked her to come along to the weekly meetings he chaired in the back room of a downtown Kaffeehaus. This was the Group. So it emerged that the husky Kruger was not just an academic but also an activist, not just a don but a streetfighter (there were running battles – with guns, even grenades: the Roter Frontkampferbund versus an array of Right factions, including the NSDAP). He and Hannah began an affair and moved in together, more or less (it was known as *taking adjacent rooms*). Kruger was thirty-four; Hannah was eighteen.

He left her six months later.

I thought he must've stopped wanting to go to bed with me, she said, in the gazebo on the border of the Zone, *but it didn't seem that way. He kept coming back – you know, just for the night. Or have me go to him. He said,* You know what the real trouble is? You're not nearly Left enough. *And I wasn't. I didn't believe in it.*

146

I didn't like the Utopia. And it drove him wild when I kept falling asleep at the Group.

Paul Doll, too, was of the Group. I didn't find this surprising. At that time there were thousands of men who went back and forth from fascism to Communism without even glancing at liberalism. She went on,

Then Dieter got very badly beaten up by a gang of Browns. And it made him even more steely. He said it was 'inconceivable' that someone like him could be with a woman who wasn't really of the faith. So he went for good . . . I was pathetic. *I had a complete breakdown. I even tried to kill myself. Wrists.* And she showed me the white seams, cross-hatching the blue veins. *It was Paul who found me and took me to hospital. Paul was being very kind to me around then . . .*

I asked, wonderingly, about her parents.

D'you know what I mean by 'an autumn crocus'? Well that's what I was. I've got two brothers and two sisters a generation older than me. My mum and dad are lovely, but they'd stopped being parents. What they cared about was Esperanto and theosophy. They cared about Ludwig Zamenhof and Rudolf Steiner.

Paul was nursing me and giving me my medicine. My sedatives. I mustn't make excuses for myself but it was all like a dreadful dream. The next thing I knew I was pregnant. And the next thing I knew I was married . . .

In March 1933, of course, after the Reichstag Fire (February 27), four thousand Leftist notables were arrested, tortured, and imprisoned, and Dieter Kruger was one of them.

Dieter Kruger went to Dachau; and among his jailers, early on, was Corporal Doll.

I put aside my ambivalence and after a false start or two established contact (by teletype and then by telephone) with an old friend of my father's in Berlin, Konrad Peters of the SD – the Sicherheitsdienst Reichsfuhrer-SS, or Party Intelligence. Peters was formerly a professor of modern history at Humboldt; now he helped monitor the foes of National Socialism (sardonically specialising in the Freemasons).

'And speak freely, Thomsen,' he said. 'This line's a virgin.'

'It's very good of you to take the trouble, sir.'

'Happy to help. I miss Max and Anna.'

We shared a brief silence. I said,

'Arrested in Munich on March first. To Dachau on March twenty-third.'

'Oh. In the first batch. Under Wackerle. That must've been enjoyable.'

'Wackerle, sir? Not Eicke?'

'No. At that point Eicke was still in the lunatic asylum in Wurzburg. Then Himmler sprung him and had him declared sane. It was actually worse under Wackerle.'

Konrad Peters, although far more exalted, was like me. We were obstruktive Mitlaufer. We went along. We went along, we *went along with*, doing all we could to drag our feet and scuff the carpets and scratch the parquet, but we went along. There were hundreds of thousands like us, maybe millions like us.

I said, 'Transferred to Brandenburg Penitentiary in September. That's all I have.'

'Give me a day or two. He's not family, is he?'

'No, sir.'

'That's a relief. Just a friend then.'

'No, sir.'

———

By early November the change in the ergonomics of the Buna-Werke had become palpable: a marked relaxation of tempo (particularly evident in the Yard), and a significant burst of progress.

Accordingly I made an appointment with the head of the Politische Abteilung, Fritz Mobius.

'He'll be about half an hour,' said Jurgen Horder (thirtyish, of medium build, with slicked grey hair worn almost romantically long). 'Are you going to the thing on Monday? I haven't been invited.'

'Officers,' I said, 'and their wives. Mandatory. Your boss'll represent you.'

'Lucky him. It'll be colder than a witch's tit.'

We were on the ground floor of Bunker 13, one of the Stammlager's many three-storey slabs of dull grey brick; its few windows were all boarded up, so there was a blind quality, and a sealed quality (as well as the devious acoustics you found every-where in the Kat Zet). For the first ten minutes I could hear, from the cellars, a succession of slowly building, slowly bursting screams of pain. Then there was a long silence, followed by the sound of boots on dusty or even gravelly stone steps. Michael Off entered, wiping his hands with a tea towel (in his cream singlet he looked like the young man at the travelling funfair who synchro-nised the dodgems). Nodding, he stared at me while apparently counting his teeth with his tongue, first the lower, then the upper. He took a packet of Davidoffs from the shelf and went back down again, and the slowly building, slowly bursting screams resumed.

'Good day. Please sit. How can I help you?'

'I hope you can help me, Herr Mobius. This is somewhat embarrassing.'

Mobius was originally a penpusher at the HQ of the Secret State Police, the Gestapa – not to be confused with the Gestapo (the actual Secret State Police), or the Sipo (the Security Police), or the Cripo (the Criminal Police), or the Orpo (the Order Police), or the Schupo (the Protection Police), or the Teno (the Auxiliary Police), or the Geheime Feldpolizei (the Secret Field Police), or the Gemeindepolizei (the Municipal Police), or the Abwehrpolizei (the Counter-Espionage Police), or the Bereitschaftpolizei (the Party Police), or the Kasernierte Polizei (the Barracks Police), or the Grenzpolizei (the Border Police), or the Ortspolizei (the Local Police), or the Gendarmerie (the Rural Police). Mobius had prospered in his wing of the policing business because he turned out to have a talent for cruelty, a talent that was widely discussed, even here.

'All going forward at the Buna-Werke? You're winning? We do need that buna.'

'Yes. Funny, isn't it? Rubber – it's like ball bearings. You can't make war without it.'

'So, Herr Thomsen. What seems to be the difficulty?'

Almost completely bald, with a few shreds of straight black hair daubed round his ears and extending to the nape of his neck, dark-eyed, strong-nosed, even-mouthed, he looked like a warmly intelligent academic. Meanwhile, Mobius's most controversial novelty was his use, during interrogations, of an experienced surgeon – Professor Entress of the Hygienic Institute.

'This is awkward, Untersturmfuhrer. And slightly distasteful.'

'It's not always fun to do one's duty, Obersturmfuhrer.'

The last word was stressed with some fastidiousness (because it was voguish, in the secret police, to despise rank and other outward forms of power. Secrecy, hiddenness, was power, they knew). I said,

'Please regard all this as tentative. But I don't see any way round it.'

Mobius twitched a shoulder and said, 'Proceed.'

'At Buna progress is steady, and we'll get the thing done, and not significantly behind schedule. As long as we go on using the established methods.' I exhaled through my nose. 'Frithuric Burckl.'

Mobius said, 'The moneyman.'

150

'If he'd confined himself to a stray remark I'd have let it go. But he harps on it. He appears to have some very peculiar notions about our uh, about our Red Sea pedestrians . . . Sometimes I wonder if he has the slightest grasp of the ideals of National Socialism. Of the delicate equipoise of our inseparable twin aims.'

'Kreative Vernichtung. The postulate of all revolutions. Kreative Vernichtung.'

'Quite. Now hear this. Burckl says the Jews are *good workers*, can you believe, so long as you treat them gently. And he says they'd do even better on a full stomach.'

'Lunacy.'

'I implored him to see sense. But the man's deaf to reason.'

'Tell me, what are the objective consequences?'

'Entirely predictable. Classic erosion of the chain of command. Burckl doesn't goad the foremen, the foremen don't bully the guards, the guards don't terrorise the Kapos, and the Kapos don't thrash the Haftlinge. A kind of rot's set in. We need someone who . . .'

Mobius took out his fountain pen. 'Go on. More details, please. You're doing the right thing, Herr Thomsen. Go on.'

———

Walking reasonably steadily but unbelievably slowly, his stride somewhere between a parade march and a goose step, and with neck tipped back as if monitoring a distant aeroplane, Paul Doll came down the aisle between the two halves of the standing audience and climbed the little staircase to the low stage. It was minus fourteen Celsius, and snow, tinged brown by the pyre and the smokestacks, was purposefully falling. I looked to my right at Boris, and then to my more distant left at Hannah. We were all bundled up to the thickness of mattresses, like experienced tramps in a wintry northern town.

Doll jolted to a halt in front of the banner-draped podium.

Behind him, ranged out over the boards, fourteen wreaths leaned against fourteen 'urns' (tar-blackened flowerpots), which weakly flickered and fumed. The Commandant extended his tubed lips and paused. And for a moment it really did seem as if he had gathered us there, that murky noon, to listen to him whistle . . . But now he reached into the folds of his fleeced greatcoat and wrenched out a typescript of inauspicious bulk. The grey sky went from oyster to mackerel. Doll looked out and said loudly,

'Jawohl . . . Well might the firmament darken. Jawohl. Well might the heavens sob their burden to the ground. On this, the Reich Day of Mourning! . . . November the ninth, my friends. November the ninth.'

Although everyone knew that Doll was not wholly sober, he seemed, for now, to have dosed himself with some care. Those judicious shots of liquor had rendered him calorific (and deepened his voice); and his teeth had already stopped chattering. He now produced from a nook beneath the sloped wooden surface a large glass of colourless liquid; it gave off a faint vapour as he raised it to his mouth.

'Yech, November the ninth. A holy day of threefold import for this – for this irresistible movement of ours . . . On November 9, 1918, 1918, the Jewish war profiteers, in their crowning swindle, effectively *auctioned off* our beloved fatherland to their co-religionists in Wall Street, in the Bank of England, and in the Bourse . . . On November 9, 1938, 1938, after the cowardly murder of our ambassador to Paris by a man with the interesting name of uh, "Herschel Grynszpan"? – Reichskristallnacht! Reichskristallnacht, when the German folk, after so many years of unbearable provocation, spontaneously rose up in their simple quest for justice . . . But I want to talk to you about November 9, 1923. 1923 – as we duly honour this, the Reich Day of Mourning.'

Boris nudged me with his padded elbow. November 9, 1923, saw the ridiculous debacle of the Pub Putsch in Bavaria. On that date, about nineteen hundred assorted tub-thumpers and layabouts, cranks and freebooters, embittered militiamen, power-mad ploughboys, disillusioned seminary students, and ruined storekeepers (all shapes and sizes, and of all ages, all armed and all in ill-fitting brown uniforms, and each of them paid two billion marks, which, on that particular day, equalled three dollars and four or five cents) gathered in and around the Burgerbraukeller, near the Odeonplatz in Munich. At the appointed hour, led by a triumvirate of eccentric celebrities (the de facto military dictator of 1916–18, Erich von Ludendorff, the Biggles-style Luftwaffe ace, Hermann Goring, and, in the van, the boss of the NSDAP, the fiery corporal from Austria), they dribbled out of the basement and began their advance on the Feldherrhalle. This was to be the first leg of the revolutionary March on Berlin.

'Off they stepped,' said Doll, 'grave yet gay, iron-willed but easy-hearted, laughing but full of moist emotion as they shivered to the joyous cries of the crowd. Before them shone the inspiring example of Mussolini – and his triumphant march on Rome! Still joking, still singing – ja, even whilst they jeered and spat at the raised carbines of the Republican State Police! . . . A gunshot, a volley, a fusillade! General Ludendorff shouldered his way on, trembling with righteous fury. Goring fell, grievously wounded in the leg. And the Deliverer, the future Reichskanzler himself? Ach, despite his two broken arms he braved the flying bullets to carry a helpless child to safety! . . . And when the acrid smell of cordite at last dispersed, fourteen men, fourteen brothers, fourteen warrior-poets lay sprawled in the dust! . . . Fourteen widows. Fourteen widows, and three score fatherless bairns. Jawohl, that is what we are here to honour today. German sacrifice. They laid down their lives that we should have hope – hope of rebirth and the promise of a brighter morn.'

The brown snow had long been thinning and now quite

suddenly and silently ceased. Doll looked up and smiled with gratitude at the sky. And then in the space of a few heartbeats he seemed to falter, to tire, to tire and age; he slumped forward and took the whole lectern roughly in his arms.

'. . . Now I unfurl . . . this sacred banner – our very own Blood Flag.' He held it up for all to see. 'Symbolically stained – with Rotwein . . . Trans uh, transubstantiation. Like the Eucharist, nicht?'

Again I turned to my left – coming into disastrous contact with Hannah's eyes. She resteadied her gaze forward with a mittened hand clamped to her nose. And for the next passage of time I urgently and strenuously contended with the pressure in my chest, trying not to follow Doll's voice as it slewed and skidded on, about medals, signet rings, coats of arms, brooches, torches, chants, vows, oaths, rites, clans, crypts, shrines . . .

At last I straightened my neck. Doll, whose face now looked like a huge and unwashed strawberry, was coming to the end.

'Can a man cry?' he asked. 'Oh, ja, ja! Ach, ever and anon he must! Ever and anon he cannot but keen . . . You see me wipe away my tears. Tears of grief. Tears of pride. As I kiss this flag, badged with the blood of our hallowed heroes . . . Now. You will soon be joining me . . . in renditions of "Das Horst Wessel Lied" and "Ich Hatt' Einen Kameraden". But yet firstly, however . . . there will be a three-minute silence for . . . each of our lost martyrs. For each of the *Old* Fighters, the *fallen*. Ach, at the going down of the sun, and again in the dawn, we will remember them. To the last, to the last, they endure.

'One . . . Claus Schmitz.'

And after ten or twelve seconds it began – the diagonal blizzard of strafing hail.

There was then an instantly and maximally drunken lunch in the Officers' Club, and I moved through it, after the first half-hour (by which point Doll was laid out flat on a deep settee), as if in a mellifluous dream of peace and freedom, and there was music from the gramophone and some people danced, and although she and I kept our distance we were, I felt, intensely and continuously aware of one another, and it was hard not to submit to pressures of a different kind, different pressures on the chest, hard not to laugh and also hard not to crumple at the naively ardent lovesongs (from sentimental operettas), 'Wer Wird denn Weinen, Wenn Man Auseinandergeht?' and 'Sag' zum Abschied leise Servus'.

'Who Will Weep, As We Two Sunder?'. 'Say So Long Softly When We Part'.

———

Ten days went by before Konrad Peters called again from Berlin.

'Sorry, Thomsen, it's going to take longer than I thought. The atmosphere around this case – it's unusual. There's a certain uh, opacity. And a settled silence.'

'I was thinking,' I said. 'He couldn't have been drafted, could he, sir? Have they begun emptying the prisons?'

'Yes, but they're not conscripting politicals. Only criminals. Your man would still be considered uh, unwurdig . . . I'll keep at it. My guess is he's a red triangle somewhere. Somewhere queer – you know, like Croatia.'

For reasons that might seem more transparent than they actually were, I was ill-disposed towards Dieter Kruger. I felt scorn for what he represented – and it was a scorn long shared by all Germans of non-dependent mind. He personified the national surrender of March 1933. Obedient Kremlinites like Kruger (who *always insisted*, said Hannah, *that the Social Democrats were as bad as the fascists*) saw to it that there would be no unity, and no potency, on the Left. The whole thing seemed to have been

155

calibrated by malign yet artistic fingers. For years the Communists had done enough, and blustered enough (about their 'readiness'), to lend a kind of legitimacy to their own immediate suppression; and after the Reichstag Fire and the passage, the next morning, of the Decree for the Protection of People and State, civil rights and the rule of law became things of the past. And what did the Communists do? They unclenched their raised fists, and limply waved goodbye.

But then, too, these thoughts led to other thoughts. For instance – why did I feel like the sick bird that couldn't fly, that couldn't rise?

Uncle Martin recently told me a story about Reinhard Heydrich – the blond paladin whose fate it was to be slowly killed by a car seat (the assassins' grenade had forced leatherwork and horsehair into his diaphragm and spleen). One night, after a long session of solitary drinking, the Reichsprotektor of Bohemia and Moravia – 'the Butcher of Prague' – went upstairs and confronted his own reflection in the full-length bathroom mirror. He unholstered his revolver and fired two shots into the glass, saying, *At last I've got you, scum. . .*

The truth was that I had another reason to resent Dieter Kruger. Whatever else he might or might not have been (conceited, predatory, trust-abusing, heartless, wrong), he was capable of courage.

Hannah had loved him. And he was brave.

———

It could no longer be deferred. On the last day of November I stamped around the Yard at the Buna-Werke till I saw the thick shape of Captain Roland Bullard. I hung back and then lingeringly and watchfully followed him into one of the tool cabins between the Stalags. He had the components of a dismantled welding gun laid out on a pillowslip.

'*Players*,' I said. '*Senior Services. And – Woodbines.*'

'*Woodbine! . . . They're not the dearest, but they are the best. I take that very kindly, Mr Thomsen. Thank you.*'

'*Rule Britannia. I made some research. Hark. "The nations not so blest as thee Must, in their turn, to tyrants fall, While thou shalt flourish great and free: The dread and envy of them all."*' I said, '*Do we understand?*'

He assessed me, he took me in for the second time, and his cuboid head inclined forward.

'*Captain Bullard, I have been prying on you. Tomorrow I . . . Yesterday I saw your bending the blades of the cooling fan in the Polimerisations-Buro. And I liked it.*'

'*You liked it?*'

'*Yes. There are others as you?*'

'*. . . There are. Twelve hundred others.*'

'*Now. For reasons that do not bother us, I am fed up completely of the Third Realm. They say they will last one thousand years. And we do not wish the buggers here till . . .*'

'*Till 2933. No. We don't.*'

'*You need information? I can be help?*'

'*Certainly.*'

'*Then do we understand?*'

He lit up a Woodbine and said, '*Hark. "Thee, haughty tyrants ne'er shall tame; All their attempts to bend thee down Will but arouse thy generous flame, But work their woe and thy renown." Yes, Mr Thomsen. We understand.*'

———

It turned out that I was going to see Hannah, up close, one more time before I left for Berlin – at the Dezember Konzert (scheduled for the nineteenth). I only became aware of it when Boris seized my arm as we were crossing the parade ground of the Stammlager and said proudly (and smugly),

'Quick. This way.'

He led me to a vast and unexpected expanse of land between the Women's Camp and the outer perimeter. As we started off across it he said with a groan,

'This was quite a while ago. I had a sordid row with Ilse. In bed.'

'How very unfortunate.'

'Mm. And the consequence is that Esther's being persecuted not just by Ilse but by her little bumgirl, Hedwig.'

'What was the sordid row?'

'Not entirely creditable.' Boris's head yawed. 'I'd seen her use the lash that day. And I think it affected my mood . . . I had a fiasco.'

'Mm,' I said. 'Which gets noticed.'

'Not only that. I said to her, *Yes, Ilse, that's the best way to torture a man in bed. You don't need your knout. Just give him a fiasco.*'

'. . . Do you think there's any real harm in Hedwig?'

'Not really. It's all Ilse. They make a pet of Esther too and she says that's the worst bit. It's all Ilse. Now shsh. Behold.'

We approached a free-standing structure the size of a warehouse, with fresh wood on four sides (over which a soggy pitch roof seemed to slobber). There was frozen mud underfoot but the sky was blue and filled with huge ivory clouds rippling with hard muscles.

'Oh,' gasped Boris as he peered through the head-high window. 'A sonnet. A rose.'

It took my eyes several seconds to penetrate the stipples of grit on the glass and then adjust to the streaky light . . . The considerable space was lined with bunk beds and masses of humped equipment loosely covered in tarps. Then I saw Esther.

'She's on the triple ration. They've got to take care of her – she's their big star.'

Herself overseen by Ilse Grese in full Aufseherin gear (with cape, white shirt and black tie, long skirt, boots, the crested belt cinched tight with the whip coiled in it), Esther, in the company of five, no six, no seven other girl Haftlinge, plus Hedwig, was organising what seemed to be a slow waltz.

'Ilse cares deeply about this, Golo. Our Friday-night fuck in Berlin thinks she's been catapulted into high culture.' He said, 'It'll all hinge on the principal. And if she lets Ilse down . . .'

I watched. Esther's movements were reluctant, but helplessly fluid; and during a lull she went up on her toes (barefoot) and formed a perfect circle with her arms as her hands met above her head.

'Is she trained?' I whispered.

'Her mother was corps de ballet. Prague.'

'What happened to her mother?'

'We killed her. Not here. There. In the Heydrich reprisals . . . Do you think she'll behave, on the night? It'll be tempting for her not to. In front of that mass of SS. Look.'

The slow waltz resumed, with Esther leading.

'She was born . . .' He raised a hand and pointed to the glacial caps of the High Tatras to the south-west. 'She was born there and was a child there for ten years . . . Look at her. Look at them. Golo, look at them all dancing in their stripes.'

———

Predictably, but with unexpected starkness, the matter of Dieter Kruger was asking me a certain question.

I had just said my farewells to Frithuric Burckl, and then been introduced to his replacement (an Old Fighter, and an old Old Fighter, called Rupprecht Strunck), when Peters's call came through.

'All right,' he said. 'Transferred from Brandenburg Penitentiary to Leipzig State Prison on Christmas Day, '33. Just him. In a Steyr 220. Then the trail goes cold.'

'Why the Dienstwagen, sir?'

'Oh I think this thing goes pretty high up. As I see it there are only two possibilities. He certainly wasn't freed. So either he *escaped*, later on. And in particularly embarrassing circumstances. Either that or he was spirited away for special treatment. Very special treatment.'

'Killed.'

'Oh. At least.'

So the question was clearly framed.

Did I want the rugged Kruger at large, boldly masterminding an isolated splinter of the resistance, perhaps, hiding, planning, putting himself in harm's way – his craggy good looks gaining and maturing in nobility and honour?

Or did I want his existence reduced to an exhausted echo or two in a blood-bespattered Horrorzelle, a handful of ashes, and a scratched-out or inked-over name in a barracks register?

Well, which?

———

At four o'clock she came out of the glass doors of the breakfast room and into the garden . . .

As things now stand, Doll will have no reason to strike out at you. But if your plan works, he won't need a reason.

Let me now say something from the heart. You can stop memorising. Perhaps you should start forgetting. And if you don't already look quite leniently on me you could simply skip to the last (eleven-word) paragraph.

After we elevated to the Chancellery a known political killer who, when he spoke in public, often foamed at the mouth, a man almost visibly coated in blood and mire, and as the gross mockery settled on the lives of all but the mad: emotion, sensibility, and delicacy retreated from me, and I developed the habit of saying to myself, almost daily, 'Let it go. Let it go. What, let that go? Yes, let it go. What, even *that*? Yes, that too. Let it go. Oh, let it go.' This internal process was astoundingly well caught, in eight syllables, by the English poet Auden (writing in about 1920):

Saying Alas
To less and less.

In that gazebo or half-made pavilion, as I watched you sleep: during those sixty or seventy minutes I felt something happen to the sources of my being. Everything I had waived and ceded made itself known to me. And I saw, with self-detestation, how soiled and shrunken I had let my heart become.

When you finally opened your eyes I was experiencing something like hope.

And now I feel I am starting again – and starting from nothing. I am perpetually harassed by first principles, like a child or a neurotic, or like a trite poet in an ingenuous novelette. But this *is* the state of mind of the artist, I'm sure: the diametrical opposite of what we call *taking things for granted*. Why does a hand have five digits? What is a woman's shoe? Why ants, why suns? Then I look, with definitive incredulity, at the bald stickmen and bald stickwomen, huge-headed, in lines of five, scurrying back to slavery while the band plays.

Something like hope – even something like love. And love: what is *that*?

Everything you do and say warms and thrills and touches me. I find you physically beautiful beyond assimilation. And I simply can't help it if in my dreams I kiss your mouth, your neck, your throat, your shoulders, and the rib between your breasts. The woman I kiss is not of the here and now. She lives in the future, and she lives elsewhere.

That poem is called '*The Exiles*' (and aren't we, the sane – aren't we all *inner* exiles?). It concludes as follows:

Gas-light in shops,
The fate of ships,
And the tide-wind
Touch the old wound.

Till our nerves are numb and their now is a time
Too late for love or for lying either,
Grown used at last
To having lost,
Accepting dearth,
The shadow of death.

And to this we say an emphatic *No*.

It would infinitely reassure me if, once a week, on Tuesdays, say, at four o'clock, you would go out and take a five-minute turn in your garden. I will see you from the building up on the hill, and I'll know you are well (and that you're walking there for me).

A great void lies ahead – my one or two or perhaps three months in the Reich; but what I have I have, and I will hold it to me.

When the future looks back on the National Socialists, it will find them as exotic and improbable as the prehistoric meat-eaters (could they really have existed, the velociraptor, the tyrannosaur?). Non-human, and also non-mammalian. They are not mammals. Mammals, with their warm blood and live young.

You will now of course destroy this letter beyond retrieval. GT.

––––––––

'Esther will fail tonight – on purpose. And oh yeah. The war is lost.'

'. . . *Boris!*'

'Oh, come on. And I don't just mean the Sixth Army. I mean lost anyhow.'

162

I poured him a schnapps. He waved it away. On the Volga, Friedrich Paulus's troops were encircled (and frozen, and starving). And von Manstein's relief armour, which began its march three weeks earlier, had not yet engaged Zhukov.

'The war is lost. Esther will fail. There. Put a drop of ponce behind your ears.'

'What? What's this? Eau des Dieux . . .'

'A bit of ponce can be very appealing, Golo. On a man of exceptional virility. Behind your ears. Don't be shy. That's it. There.'

We were in his cramped flatlet in the Fuhrerheim, making ourselves especially smart and fragrant for the Dezember Konzert over in Furstengrube. With five months of his one-year demotion still to run, Boris was defiantly accoutring himself in the dress uniform of a full colonel. Full colonel, senior colonel, *active* colonel in the Waffen-SS. And Boris, this night, was levitational with nerves.

'That was a very silly idea,' he said. 'Invading Russia.'

'Oh. So you've changed your tune, have you?'

'Mm. I admit I was all for it at the time. As you know. Well. I got a little ahead of myself after France. Everyone did. No one could refuse him anything after France. So the Corporal said, Now let's invade Russia, and the generals thought, Sounds insane, but so did France. Fuck it, he's our man of destiny. And come on, while we're there we may as well indulge his fever dream about the Jews.'

'Oy. The greatest military genius of all time. Those were your words.'

'France, Golo. Smashed in thirty-nine days. Four days, really. *Much* better than Moltke. *France.*'

Boris was my blood brother, and the connection went back beyond the limits of human memory (we got to know each other, apparently, when we were one). But there had been several serious lacunae along the way. I found it impossible to be near him in the months after the seizure of power: in 1933 there were only two people in Germany who viscerally wanted world war – and Boris Eltz was the other one. Then there was that *froideur* between the invasion of Poland and the sharp setback at the gates of Moscow in December '41. And our views continued to be in less than perfect accord. Boris was still a fanatical nationalist – even though that nation was Nazi Germany. And if he knew what I was up to with Roland Bullard, Boris wouldn't hesitate. He would draw his Luger and shoot me dead.

'It still looked viable till about late September. Vernichtungskrieg, Golo, isn't really my cup of tea, but it seemed to be doing the trick ... It was a very silly idea, though, invading Russia. Step aside.'

He wanted a better view of himself in the wall mirror above the sink. Leaning back at a ludicrous angle, Boris attended to his pewtery hair with a flat brush in either hand.

'Is it very wrong, do you think,' he asked, 'to *adore* looking in the mirror? ... I know it's a crime to say it, but we've lost, Golo.'

'All right, you're nicked.'

'Christ, you could've done it on the back of an envelope. A war on two fronts? On one front, the USSR. On the other, the USA. Plus the British Empire. Christ, you could've done it on the back of an envelope. December '41.'

'November '41. I've never told you this, Boris, but they did it on the back of an envelope in November. The armaments people. And told him he couldn't win.'

Boris shook his head with a kind of admiration. 'He can't win against Russia. So what's he do? He declares war on America. It isn't a criminal regime, dear. It's a regime of the criminally insane. And we're losing.'

I said uneasily, 'There's no second front *yet*. And the Allies might bust up with Moscow. And, Boris, don't forget we're making wonder weapons.'

'So are they. With our scientists. Let me give you a little lesson on war, Golo. Rule number one: never invade Russia. All right, we kill five million and take five million prisoner, and starve to death another thirty million. That still leaves a hundred and twenty-five million.'

'Quieten down, Boris. Have some alcohol. You're too sober.'

'Not till afterwards. Listen. Even if you raze Leningrad and Moscow, then what? You'll have a boiling insurgency right down the length of the Urals for ever and ever. How do you pacify Siberia? Which is the size of eight Europes.'

'Come on, we did it last time – invaded Russia.'

'Not comparable. That was an old-style cabinet war against a dying regime. This is a war of pillage and murder. See, Golo, the Red Army's now just the vanguard. Every Russian will fight, every woman, every child . . . Until October, until Kiev, I thought murder-war was winning. I thought massacre could do the impossible.' He passed a hand over his face, and gave a wondering frown. 'I thought night was winning, Golo. I thought night *would win* and then we'd see.'

I said, 'And then we'd see what? . . . Well I'll have another finger or two, if I may.'

He appraised me with a friendly sneer. 'Mm. I suppose you can't wait to be breathing the same air as Hannah . . . Take that look off your face, Golo.'

'I only do it when I'm with you.'

'Well only do it when you're by yourself. As I told you, it's absolutely nauseating.'

In our greatcoats we hurried down Cherry Street, heading for the motor pool. In the middle distance the new Topf crematories, I and II (there would soon be III and IV), were being test-fired. How did the flames force their way up those towering funnels and come sprouting out into the black sky?

'An unsympathetic observer', said Boris with his teeth clacking in brief spasms, 'might find all this rather reprehensible.'

'Yes. Could make it look quite bad.'

'Ooh, we've got to fight like very devils now. We'll need all the victors' justice we can get. And they've got me here rotting with the fucking Viennese.'

Cherry Street forked left and became Camp Street.

'Prepare yourself, Golo. Esther Kubis. This afternoon I gave her a long lecture. And she heard me out and said, *I'm going to punish you tonight.* Why, Esther, why?'

'She's got very intransigent eyes. And she does have her grievance.'

'You know what'll happen, don't you, if she's thought to have failed? Half an hour later, she'll be flogged to death by Ilse Grese. That's what.'

I contemplated the hooded sidecar, and prepared myself for a freezing and deafening half-hour . . . *The war is lost.* This had momentarily sickened me – because for the last week at Buna I had been a witness to the ferocious innovations of Rupprecht Strunck. But now I stiffened. Yes, it was necessary to go too far, to overfulfil and superabound – anything, anything and everything, to make sure that night wouldn't win.

'In you get then,' said Boris as he straddled the driver's seat. Before attaching his goggles he took one last look at the skyscraping beacon of the firestack. 'It's all France. None of this would be happening if it wasn't for France. It's all France.'

The subcamp of Furstengrube was famous, hereabouts, not only for the self-defeating lethality of its coal mines (where the average slave lasted less than a month), but also for the venerable tonnage of its theatre (in contrast to the fabricated Playhouse at Kat Zet I). It was a churchy redbrick rotunda with a squat black dome

– requisitioned from the town for our exclusive use in the summer of 1940.

We milled about in the courtyard, officers, noncoms, privates, chemists, architects, engineers (all of us with metre-long plumes of vapour billowing from our mouths), and then gradually filtered up the steps and through the oak portal. Within, the soft reddish light had the damp sheen of gauze and worn silk; and it bore me off on a kind of memory cascade – Saturday-morning pictures in Berlin (me and Boris all bright-eyed and innocent and clutching our sweets), amateur theatricals in titivated town halls, sore-lipped necking sessions that lasted the length of whole double bills (plus newsreel) in the rear seats of provincial cinemas . . .

In the foyer I checked our coats, and by the time I caught up with Boris in the murmuring auditorium he was crooked over Ilse Grese, who had installed herself near the centre of the front row. As I approached he was archly saying,

'Everyone knows the uh, the nickname or title they have for you here, Ilse. And I'm sorry but I think it's slightly malapropos. *Half* of it's all right. Half of it's dead on.' Boris turned to me and said, 'You know what they call her? The Beautiful Beast.'

I found I was gazing at Ilse with all the freshness of discovery: the strong legs mannishly wide-planted, the hefty trunk in a black serge uniform gullibly studded with signs and symbols – lightning flash, eagle, broken cross. And I had kissed those crinkly lips, and sought favour from the voids of those borehole eyes . . .

She said tightly, 'Which half, Hauptsturmfuhrer?'

'Why, the adjective, of course. The noun I angrily repudiate. You know, Ilse, I would go before a court of law and argue under oath that you're basically humane.'

A spotlight was roaming over the blue velvet curtain. 'It's filling up,' I said.

'In a minute. Ilse,' he said intently. 'An investigator here from

167

Berlin told me you set your dogs on a Greek girl in the woods, just because she wandered off and fell asleep in a hollow. And you know what I did? I laughed in his face. *Not Ilse*, I said. *Not my Ilse*. Good evening to you, Oberaufseherin.'

A cracked electric bell was distantly sounding when they entered – the Commandant and his wife. He too was in dress uniform (with a rack of medals), and she wore a . . . But Hannah was already in shadow, and now was lost in darkness.

First, the cobbled-together chamber orchestra (two violins, guitar, flute, mandolin, accordion), and a lengthy 'medley' intended to appeal to the softer side of the praetorian heart (early Strauss, Peter Kreuder, Franz von Suppé). The stage cleared, darkened, and the players regrouped. Lights. There followed an hour-long operetta based on *The Sorrows of Young Werther*, the Goethe novella so beguilingly forlorn that it provoked an avalanche of suicides, not just in Germany but throughout Europe: the anomic hero in the bucolic village, the orphaned lass, the doomed love (for she is betrothed to another), the self-inflicted pistol wound, the slow death . . .

Curtain, and judicious applause, and silence.

An SS sergeant not yet in his twenties, tall, thin, fair, pale, and chinless, mounted a little spotlit dais and for the next forty-five minutes recited memorised verse, his face and voice grimly or gaily reenacting all the emotions that the poets had in fact mastered and formalised; while he spoke I could hear much thumping and wheeling and whispering from backstage (as well as Boris's heaving and swearing). The Unterscharfuhrer's chosen writers were Schiller, Holderlin, and, bizarrely and ignorantly, Heinrich Heine. It was an ignorance his listeners shared; the handclaps, when they came, were weary and scanty, but not because Heine was Jewish.

During the brief intermission Paul Doll took an apparently

sober but curiously wobbly stroll in the theatre's chancel, head back, lips out, and with his nose twitching censoriously as if verifying a smell . . .

The lights dimmed, the audience stopped muttering (and started coughing), and the curtains drew slowly asunder.

In a parched and childish voice Boris said, 'There Esther is at last . . .'

It was the middle act of a ballet I had seen before, *Coppelia* (music by Delibes).

A magician's lush workshop: scrolls, potions, wands, broomsticks (and the two violinists, dressed as clowns, one in each far corner). Old Dr Coppelius – played with restrained agility by Hedwig in frockcoat and grey peruke – was preparing to animate his life-size marionette. Surrounded by lesser dolls and dummies (half completed or partly dismembered), Esther sat rigid on a straight-backed chair, immaculate in tutu, spangled white tights, and bright pink slippers, reading a book (the wrong way up: Coppelius corrected her). She stared downwards sightlessly.

Now the wizard began casting his spell, with flinging gestures of the hands, as if freeing them of moisture . . . Nothing happened. He tried again, and again, and again. Suddenly she twitched; very suddenly she jumped up, and threw the book aside. Blinking, compulsively shrugging, and noisily flat-footed (and often falling over backwards like a plank into Hedwig's waiting arms), Esther clumped about the stage: a miracle of the uncoordinated, now flopsy, now robotic, with every limb hating every other limb. And comically, painfully ugly. The violins kept on urging and coaxing, but she swooned and swaggered on.

Probably nobody could have said how long it lasted, in non-subjective time, so vehement was the assault on the senses. It seemed, at any rate, as if the whole of January was coming and going. We reached the point where Hedwig – after a final few

169

thrusting flutters of her fingers – simply gave up, and stopped acting; she put her hands on her hips and turned to her mentor in the front row, who was tipping forward in her seat. Coppelia clockworked madly on.

Boris gasped, 'Oh, enough . . .'

Enough. It was enough. Now the charm took hold, the glamour took hold, the magic turned from black to white, the scowl of inanition became a willed but still blissful smile, and she was off and away, she was born and living and free. On her first tour jeté, not so much a leap as an upward glide – even at its zenith all her sinews shivered, as if trying, needing to fly even higher. The audience warmed and murmured; but I was asking myself why her movements, whose liquidity now caressed the eyes, seemed no easier to bear.

A wet snort exploded to my left; Boris was on his feet and heading for the exit, bent almost double with his arm raised to his face.

———

Very early the next morning, he and I crept drunkenly to Cracow in a Steyr 220. Up ahead, thanks to the Schutzstaffel's gift for Organisation, we had a Last-Kraft-Wagen carefully leaking sand and salt into our path. We hadn't slept.

Boris said, 'I've just realised. She was apeing the slaves. And the guards.'

'Was *that* it?'

'Staggering, strutting, staggering, strutting . . . And later, when she really danced. What was the accusation? What was she expressing?'

I eventually said, 'Her right to freedom.'

'. . . Mm, even more basic than that. Her right to life. Her right to love and life.'

As we climbed from the car Boris said, 'Golo. If Uncle Martin fucks about, I'll've already gone east when you get back. But I'll fight for you, brother. I'll have to.'

'How's that?'

'In the event of defeat,' he said, 'no one'll think you're good-looking any more.'

I held him close with my hand on his hair.

At the post-performance reception, standing in a group with Mobius, Zulz, the Eikels, the Uhls, and others, Hannah and I exchanged two sentences.

I said to her, *I might have to go on to Munich and look in the files at the Brown House.*

She said to me, nodding in the direction of Paul Doll (who was in marked disarray), *Er ist jetzt völlig verruckt.*

Boris, looking utterly beaten, sat at a table with a carafe of gin; Ilse was stroking his forearm and ducking her head down to smile up at him. At the end of the room Doll suddenly wheeled and started back towards us.

He is now completely mad.

———

I got in around midnight; and from the Ostbahnhof I groped my way through the chilled and blackened city (other people were just shadows and footsteps) to the Budapesterstrasse and the Hotel Eden.

2. DOLL: KNOW YOUR ENEMY

Cracked it!

. . . Solved it, grasped it, fathomed it, unravelled it. Cracked it!

Oh, this brain-twister cost me many, many nights of concerted cunning (I could hear myself lightly panting with guile), down in my 'lair' – as, fortified by the choicest libations, your humble servant, the stubborn Sturmbannfuhrer, outfaced the witching hour and the hours beyond! And, just minutes ago, illumination and then warmth came flooding in with the first lambent beams of morning . . .

Dieter Kruger lives. And I'm glad. *Dieter Kruger lives*. My hold on Hannah is restored. *Dieter Kruger lives*.

Today I shall call in a favour, and seek official confirmation – from the man who, they say, is the 3rd most powerful in the Reich. It's just a formality, of course. I know my Hannah and I know her Sexualitat. When she read that letter in the locked bathroom – it wasn't the thought of *Thomsen* that made her Busen ache. No, she likes real men, men with a bit of sweat and stubble, a bit of fart and armpit on them. Like Kruger – and like myself. It wasn't Thomsen.

It was Kruger. Cracked it. Kruger lives. And now I can go back to my old MO: threatening to kill him.

And when at last the harsh smell of cordite dispersed, I wrote on the lined notepad, *14 warrior-poets lay sprawled in the* . . .

'Oh what d'you *want*, Paulette?' I said. 'I'm composing an extremely important speech. And by the way you're too short and fat for that smock.'

'. . . It's Meinrad, Vati. Mami says you've got to come and look. He's got all this goo coming out of his nose.'

172

'Ach. Meinrad.'

... Meinrad is a 1-trick pony and no mistake. First mange, then blister-beetle poisoning. And what's his latest stunt? Glanders.

On the credit side, this means that Alisz Seisser's Sunday visits – the nutritious lunches, the leisurely 'soaks' – are becoming a family tradition!

It's not enough that a chap should be constantly traduced and provoked in his own home. Certain people have seen fit to call into question my professional correctitude and integrity *if you don't bloody well mind* . . .

In the office at the MAB I received a delegation of medical men – Professor Zulz, of course, and also Professor Entress, plus doctors Rauke and Bodman. Their gist? According to them I've got 'worse' at deceiving the transports.

'How d'you mean, *worse?*'

'You don't deceive them any more,' said Zulz. 'Well you don't, do you Paul. There are very unpleasant scenes nearly every time.'

'And that's all my fault, is it?'

'Keep your hair on, Kommandant. Hear us out at least . . . Paul. Please.'

I sat there seething. 'Very well. What, in *your* view, do I happen to be doing wrong?'

'Your inductionary address. Paul, my friend, it's . . . It's very basic. You sound so insincere. As if you don't believe it yourself.'

'Well of course I don't believe it myself,' I said in a business-like manner. 'How could I? You think I'm off my head?'

'You know what we're getting at.'

'. . . The business of the barrel, mein Kommandant,' said Professor Entress. 'Can we at least do away with that?'

'What's wrong with the business of the barrel?' The barrel: this was a wheeze I dreamt up in October. Concluding my speech of welcome, I'd say, *Leave your valuables with your clothing and pick them up after the shower. But if there's anything you especially treasure and can't afford to be without, then pop it in the barrel at the end of the ramp.* I asked, 'What's wrong with it?'

'It stirs unease,' said Entress. 'Are their valuables safe or aren't they?'

'Only the juvenile and the senescent fall for that 1, Kommandant,' said Zulz. 'All we ever find in the barrel's a jar of blood-thinners or a teddy bear.'

'With respect, Sturmbannfuhrer, give the megaphone to 1 of us,' said Dr Bodman. 'After all, we're trained to reassure.'

'Bedside manner, Sturmbannfuhrer,' said Dr Rauke.

Rauke, Bodman, and Entress took their leave; Zulz ominously lingered.

'My dear old friend,' he said. 'You should take a rest from the ramp. Oh, I know how dedicated you are. Go easier on yourself, Paul. I speak as a physician. As a healer.'

A healer? Ja, pull the other 1. But why did I swallow, and why did my nose itch, when he said *my dear old friend*?

So much for the smaller picture. On the macro scale, I'm overjoyed to report, the canvas is blindingly bright!

It's a good time – as autumn becomes winter, and as 1943 impends – for us to 'take stock', to have a bit of a breather and look back on the past. We're not *all* of us superhuman, not by any manner of means; and there have been moments, during this great Anstrengung of ours (like the terrifying reverse before Moscow), when I succumbed to an almost dreamlike vertigo of weakness and doubt. No longer. Ach, vindication is sweet. *Wir haben also doch recht!*

The Deliverer made it clear in his major oration of October 1 that the Judaeo-Bolshevik stronghold on the Volga was approximately ¾s overrun. He prophesied that the city would fall within the month; and although this proved overly optimistic, nobody doubts that the swastika will be rippling over the ruins in good time for Christmas. As to the remaining population, Hauptsturmfuhrer Uhl tells me that the women and children will be deported, and all the menfolk shot. And this decision, whilst stern, is surely correct – due tribute to the scale of the Aryan offering.

Triumphalism tempts me not in the slightest, for National Socialists never boast or crow. We unsmilingly turn, rather, to a mature assessment of the historic responsibilities. Eurasia is ours; we will purify even as we pacify, whilst also fanning out, as acknowledged suzerains, over the resistless nations of the West. I raise my glass to General Friedrich Paulus and his valiant 6th Army. All hail our ineluctable victory in the Battle of Stalingrad!

Szmul finally came up with a body count for the Spring Meadow.

'That's a bit steep, isn't it?'

'If anything, sir, it's probably an underestimate.'

'Na. So now I divide by 2, ne?'

'I've already done that, sir.'

The figure was always going to be fairly high, true, as it included not only the transports up to the time when cremation was first employed, but also the prisoners in the Stammlager who died of natural causes during the winter of 1941–2, when the coal-fired crema near the Ka Be was out of action for a considerable period of time.

Still. 107,000 . . .

'We were all very stirred by your speech,' said Hannah at breakfast.

I calmly buttered my roll. 'It went down tolerably well, I fancy.'

'Think. 14 Brownshirts! A massacre. Have you ever known that many men die at once?'

'Ach. It happens.'

'Brown,' she said. 'Such a gorgeous colour. With beautiful associations.'

'. . . What associations, Hannah?'

'The soil, of course. The *earth*.' She reached for an apple. 'Shame about the last hour, Pilli. How many cases of hypothermia and frostbite?'

'Yech, it should've been a 1-minute silence per martyr. Not 3.'

She said, '*Kurt and Willi*'s on at 5. I heard the little extract. Sounds intriguing. Paul, let's listen to it together. Like we used to.'

The unfamiliar congeniality of her tone put me on my guard. But what was there to fear from *Kurt and Willi*? I slapped my thigh and said, '*Kurt and Willi*? Yes, let's. I love *Kurt and Willi*. Haven't heard from Kurt and Willi for months. A bit "off ", mind you – die BBC! – but where's the harm in *Kurt and Willi*?'

Just the 1 transport that day, at 13.37. Baldemar Zulz did the necessary with the megaphone. *We apologise for the lack of sanitary facilities in the boxcars. All the more reason, though, for a hot shower and a light disinfection – because there are no diseases here and we don't want any.* Frightfully good, that, I had to admit. The stethoscope, the white coat (the black boots) – awfully good. *Oh, and would diabetics and those with special dietary needs report to Dr Bodman after supper at the Visitors' Lodge. Thank you.* Fearfully good, that, really 1st rate . . .

In the Little Brown Bower, as the atmosphere suddenly worsened and there was that dry-throated mutter we all know so well, I felt a cold damp presence invade my ungloved left hand. Took a look: I had been latched on to by a little girl of 4 or 5. My reaction was strangely slow in coming (to rear back with a snarl); I stifled it, and was able – with great effort and greater unease – to do my duty and go on standing there as required.

*

176

16.55: the master bedroom.

'Has it begun yet? . . . Oh and did Willi ever buy that car?'

Sitting on a chair with her back to the window, and warmly colourful against the damp gauze of the autumn sky, Hannah was significantly attired. There were but the 2 items of apparel (I couldn't see if she were wearing slippers): the royal-blue kimono with which I presented her on the occasion of our wedding (the fringed sash, the vast sleeves); and, next to her skin, that special white Unterkleid, or 'camisole'. This 2nd garment was also a gift bestowed on Hannah by her husband; I picked it up in Kalifornia the day before she joined me here at the KL (though when I suggested, the next night, that we 'try it out', madam seemed not best pleased). Albeit controversial, it was a gorgeous article of clothing, a semi-transparent creamy white veneering of the sheerest silk, smoother than a baby's sit-upon . . .

'Some light comedy,' I said, rubbing my hands together as I relaxed on the settee at the end of the bed. '*Kurt and Willi*'s what we want – not all that propaganda. How's Kurt's mother-in-law? That's always good for a laugh.'

She said nothing and reached for the dial.

A jaunty run on the accordion gave way to the muttering and clinking of a typical Bierstube in the Potsdamer Platz. Kurt and Willi exchanged 'the German greeting' – rather apathetically, in my view – and then we heard the accents of Berlin (you know, with the 'g' sounding like a 'y' und so, ne?).

Willi: How are you, Kurt?
Kurt: None too well, quite frankly, Willi.
Willi: Are you ailing? The good God, you look *green*.
Kurt: I know I do. That's why I'm drinking brandy.
Willi: Well tell me what's the matter.
Kurt: Ach. I just experienced something absolutely dreadful.

Above us, you know, lives a young woman, a Jewess. A scientist,

177

a serious professional lady. And today she turned on the gas valve. We found her an hour ago.

Willi: Ach.

Kurt: They'd just informed her she was being sent off to the east.

Willi: Well that *would* be upsetting!

The smile I wore was starting to become a burden to my face. I recrossed my legs and said, 'Hannah, I'm not sure this is—'

'Shoosh, Paul, I'm listening.'

Willi: I can't understand why she wasn't deported earlier.

Kurt: What? Oh. Well, she was a technician in an armaments plant. You know, Willi, we tried to encourage her, to hearten her, Lotte and I. We said it might not be too bad where she's going. And anything's better than . . .

Willi: No, my friend. A quick death in your own kitchen is far, far . . . I know this from the office. Trust me.

Hannah said, 'Where does Willi work again?'

'The Ministry of Public Enlightenment,' I said moodily.

Kurt: What are you saying? Does that really happen?

Willi: Well. It does happen.

Kurt: But why? What's the point? A little lady – part of the war effort? It's totally unnecessary!

Willi: No, Kurt. It is necessary. Why? To instil the fear of defeat. The fear of punishment.

Kurt: But what's that got to do with the Jews?

Willi: Mensch, don't you understand? The fear of retribution! Every German is implicated in the largest mass murder that has ever—'

'*Feindlicher Rundfunk*,' I burst out. 'Enemy radio! Zweifel am Sieg! Doubting victory! Feindlicher Rundfunk!'

'. . . Oh, don't blame Kurt and Willi,' she said with exaggerated torpor. 'Poor Willi. Poor *Kurt*. Listen. They're ordering more brandy. They're feeling rather sick.'

Now Hannah did something that quite dismayed me. She stood; she unfurled her sash; and she shrugged off the kimono's sapphirine folds – revealing her Unterkleid! From Kehle to Oberschenkel her body seemed to be coated in icing sugar, and I could clearly see the outlines of her Bruste, the concavity of her Bauchnabel, and the triangle of her Geschlechtsorgane . . .

'Do you know', she said, plucking at the collar, 'which dead woman you stole this from?' She smoothed it with her hands, up and down. 'Do you know?'

Hannah took up a hairbrush and went at it with arrogant eyes.

'You're . . . you're mad,' I said, and backed my way out.

And whilst we're on the subject of wives, what price 'Pani Szmul'?

To locate a Jew in a Polish ghetto one casually turns to the Uberwachungsstelle zur Bekampfung des Schleichhandels und der Preiswucherei im judischen Wohnbezirk. This used to be a sub-division of the Jewish Order Police, recruited from the pre-war underworld, and responsible to the Gestapo; but natural selection has done its work, and the spies, narks, pimps, and skankers are now running the whole show. Criminalising the gendarmerie: *that's* how you 'squeeze' a subject people, and gain access to its hoarded wealth!

Casually, limply, I turn to the Control Office to Combat Black-Marketeering and Profiteering in the Jewish Residential District – ja, die Uberwachungsstelle zur Bekampfung des Schleichhandels und der Preiswucherei im judischen Wohnbezirk.

It wouldn't have looked so scandalous in Berlin, ne? In the days when that profoundly unGerman contraption, 'democracy', was falling apart. Or in Munich, nicht? A blushful beauty of 18, as dew-bright as the fresh cornflower in her buttonhole, trailing after a burly 'intellectual' virtually twice her age?

All right in Berlin or Munich, no? But there they were in mannerly Rosenheim, with its parks, its cobblestones, its onion domes. Everybody could tell that friend Kruger was making a swine of himself with his childish ward; and it pains me to say that Hannah, for her part, was no less brazen – ach, she could barely keep her tongue out of his ear (her fingers fidgety, her colour hectic, her thighs glueyly asquirm). It was also common knowledge that they'd taken adjacent rooms at an especially disreputable boarding house in Bergerstrasse . . .

My protective instincts were sorely roused. Hannah and myself were by this juncture on the most cordial terms; friend Kruger was, as they say, a busy man, and she was nearly always 'on' for a ramble in the public gardens or a glass of tea in 1 of the many elegant cafés. I think she knew she was doing wrong, and was drawn to my air of probity and calm. Na, 1 thing was clear: she was a middle-class girl with no taste at all for the radical. This was hardly a meeting of *minds* – nicht? On a number of occasions I quietly ascended the stairs to her attic, and became aware of the most alarming ululations – they were *not* the modest coos, trills, and warbles of healthy and hygienic Geschlechtlichkeit! They were sounds of excruciation and woe; indeed, they took me back to that time in the parsonage, when I was 13, and had to listen all night to Auntie Tini giving birth to the twins.

You could feel it. These dark acts. The growing void in the moral order.

It seems, these days, these nights, that whenever I go to the ramp something dreadful happens – I mean to me personally.

'Wear that,' she said.

At 1st it seemed to be 1 of the softer transports. A smooth debouchment, an inductionary address (from Dr Rauke), a brisk selection, and a short drive through the forest, the docile evacuees, with a leaderless but competent team of Sonders discreetly murmuring among them . . . I had taken up position in the hallway between the outer door and the undressing room when a prematurely white-haired Judin approached me with a smile of polite inquiry; and I even inclined my head to attend to her question. In a spasm of animal violence she reached up and smeared something on my face – on my upper lip, my nose, the orbit of my left eye.

'Wear that,' she said.

Lice.

Of course I went straight to Baldemar Zulz.

'This could've been serious. You're lucky, my Kommandant.'

I frowned up at him (they had me lying flat on a table under a strong light). 'Fleckfieber?' I asked.

'Mm. But I know a Kamchatka louse when I see 1,' he said, showing me the filthy little crab in the pinch of his tweezers, 'and this critter's a European.'

'Na. The transport was Dutch. From Westerbork, ne?'

'You know, Paul, the Haftlinge, they'll pluck the nits off a Russian corpse and slip them under the collars of our uniforms. In the Laundry Block. Exanthematic typhus. Very nasty.'

'Yech, that's what did for Untersturmfuhrer Kranefuss. Prufer's meant to be dealing with it. Some hope there I don't think.'

Zulz said, 'Off with your togs. Fold them tidily and remember where they are.'

'What for?'

He tensed as if ready to pounce. '. . . Disinfection!'

So we had a crazed cackle about that.

'Paul, come on. Just to be on the safe side.'

Well then. A considerable relief all round!

'Wear that,' she said.

*

181

Ever since I fixed things so that Alisz Seisser got shifted to the facility in the basement of the MAB, it has been possible for she and myself to spend some precious hours together.

When my hard day's toil is done (you know, I'm sometimes in my office till well past midnight?), I consistently look in on little Alisz, bearing a 'snack', more often than not – a prune or a cube of cheese – which she then appreciatively devours!

And what do we do? Why, we simply talk. About the past, about the springtime of our lives and the experiences we share – the arbours and spinneys of our beloved German countryside. She amuses me with tales of her summer frolics on the golden sands of Pomerania, whilst I divert her with stories about the Haardt Forest and my coal-black gelding, Jonti – his flowing mane, his glittering eyes!

Of course, the arrangement is not ideal.

'But you're safe here, Alisz. At least until it passes – this mania for selections. *Wild* selections, and not just in the Ka Be. I can't be everywhere, you know.'

Her respectful gratitude knows no bounds.

'Oh, I trust you, Paul.'

There is never the slightest question of any impropriety. I regard her with the veneration due to the simple widow of a fallen comrade. More than this, I see Alisz as a kind of charge, or protégée, whom I must unswervingly guide.

She sits, rather primly, on her narrow cot with her hands folded on her lap. I myself prefer to pace, or swivel, in the little tract between the footstool and the chemical toilet.

'. . . I sometimes miss the open air, Paul.'

'Ah, but there it is, Alisz. Protective custody, nicht?'

Yech, the 'Gruppe', the weekly meetings in the cellar of the seedy Selbstbedienungsrestaurant, the interminable Dialektik! *The conversion of product into value, the superstructure above the economic base, the law of increasing immiseration* . . . Originally a theocrat, then a monarchist, then a militarist, I succumbed to the spell of Marxism – till I set *Das Kapital* aside and turned, rather, to an intensive study of *Mein Kampf*. Enlightenment was not slow in coming. Page 382: 'Marxism is only the transference, by the Jew, Karl Marx, of a philosophical attitude . . . into the form of a definite political creed . . . And all this in the service of his race . . . Marxism itself systematically plans to hand the world over to the Jews.' Well, you can't argue with logic of that calibre. No: *quod erat demonstrandum*. Next question, please.

. . . You know, there was a sort of tumbling gracelessness about Hannah in those days; she had not yet acquired the poise and bearing she would gain as Frau Paul Doll, first lady of the KL. And let's be honest – there's nothing more sick-making, in the end, than adolescent adoration: the awful way they lay themselves open, and the puppy fat, and the hot breath. I simply waited for friend Kruger to tire of her, which he eventually did (he moved out and moved on). But then what happens?

Picture, if you will, the communal lounge at the boarding house – the doilies, the cuckoo clock, the fat dachshund dozing (and silently breaking wind) in the corner. All very 'gemutlich', ne? Lovelorn Hannah and myself are seated at a little round table, and steady progress is being made by my tactful commiserations, my *petits cadeaux*, my avuncular hand-patting, und so weiter. And then the bell would sound, and, jawohl, friend Kruger would stick his snout round the parlour door. He didn't even have to snap his fingers. Hannah would lead the way upstairs for another of their groaning, shuddering trysts. This happened time after time after time.

Ah, but then fate came to my aid. On a certain night, after 1 of his sweat-soaked reunions with that fundamentally innocent child, our Marxist lion was surprised on Bergerstrasse by a crew of gaunt lads from the Sturmabteilung (Cell H). And the crunchy beating he received was so severe that his people from the KP and the Workers' Trust smuggled him off to Berlin. Our paths didn't cross for another 4½ years. And when I next saw him, friend Kruger was face down on the floor of a punishment cell in Dachau. A moment to relish to the full, no? I went on in, with a couple of comrades, and I locked the door behind us.

That was in March 1933, when it all came good, after the Reichstag Fire. After the Reichstag Fire, do you see, we took the simple step of illegalising all opposition. And the autobahn to autocracy lay clear.

Who started the Reichstag Fire?

Was it started by the fuddled lone-wolf Dutch Kommunist, van der Lubbe, with his matches and faggots and his lavish ID? No. Was it started by us? No. The Reichstag Fire was started by destiny, by providence.

On the night of February 27 the Reichstag was torched by Gott!

Hannah asked me, 'Who's that wiry man I see coming down the slope every day?'

'You must mean Szmul.'

'He's got the saddest face I've ever seen. And he never meets my eye. Never.'

'Yes, well, he's the Klempnerkommandofuhrer. Drains.'

SS-Obersturmbannfuhrer Eichmann is on the whole boyishly meticulous with his choo-choos and his chuff-chuffs; it does sometimes eventuate, however, that transports (every Kommandant's nightmare) *overlap*. And so it was in the small hours of this morning.

My hands are still aflutter and I have just washed down 3 Phanodorms.

I insisted on wielding the bullhorn, and it has to be conceded that things soon . . . But I simply don't accept that I'm getting worse at deceiving the evacuees. What's happened is that *they've* got better at not being taken in. And (come to think of it) it's easy to see why. Yes, we should have anticipated this difficulty – but you can only live and learn. The people in the target communities are drawing their own conclusions from an obvious and irrefutable truth: Nobody Has Ever Come Back. Thus they've put 2 and 2 together, and we have lost the 'element of surprise' . . . All right, I'll phrase that slightly differently: in the matter of what awaits these 'settlers' in the eastern territories, we no longer have the advantage of being unbelievable. The decisive asset of being *beyond belief*.

This afternoon the first draft collapsed pretty well immediately – they were barely out of the cattle cars. Professor Zulz and his chaps hadn't even begun the selection; there were 800 men, women, and children slewing around in the slush; and it began. A questing whimper that seems to seek and grope and probe, then the first real scream, then a whiplash, then a bodyblow, then a gunshot.

90 minutes later a kind of order had re-established itself: the 600-odd survivors had been variously bashed, flogged, and goosed by bayonet into the Red Cross vans and the ambulances. I stood on the platform, my arms akimbo, wondering just how long it was going to take to clean up *this* little lot. Somebody yelled and pointed with a truncheon. And there, 4 hours early, was the appalling apparition of Sonderzug 319, tacking its way up the slope towards us.

I will not soon forget what followed – though in fact Lady Luck, that day, smiled on we Praetorians. At 1st I thought it was 1 of those cases where Protective Custody intermeshed with another campaign for the furtherance of national hygiene, namely T4, or the Euthanasia Drive. The 2nd train was carrying a light contingent of 'incurables': in this case, the organically insane. But these weren't defective Germans: they were defective Jews – a load of nutters from the mental homes of Utrecht. Assisted by their pretty young nurses, the evacuees processed quite equably along the corpse-strewn, blood-drenched siding, with its dozen pyramids of sodden bags. To the usual sound effects were added peals of horrifying laughter.

2 old men with silver curls – twins – caught and held my eye. Their smiles expressing broad satisfaction with all they saw, they resembled a pair of hardy and even quite prosperous farmers strolling to a village fete. Up ahead a lanky, ponytailed teenager in a green canvas straitjacket tripped over a bundle of clothing and fell on her chin with a sickening snap. She rolled over and the stark white noodles of her legs kicked up and out. People looked on contentedly, and then applauded when Aufseherin Grese stepped in and yanked her up by the hair.

As I went to bed that night I prayed I wouldn't dream about the naked twins, grinning in the Little Brown Bower.

. . . If you're wearing a straitjacket, you know, and you fall over, you land on your face.

If you're wearing a straitjacket, do you see, and you fall over and land on your face, you can't get up again – not by yourself you can't.

'Did you manage to take a look at them?'

'Yes. A bit. Not really my kind of thing, Paul.'

A week ago I lent Alisz 2 monographs on ethnobiology, with a view to enriching our nightly chats. But unfortunately she has little taste for the printed word. Her days in the MAB, I fear, are not much diversified by event (for I am naturally her only visitor). Ne, not markedly alleviated by anything actually happening – just the crank of metal, at 11.30, when the food tray is shoved through the slot.

Last night we reminisced about the early days of our respective marriages – she, swept away by the virile noncom Orbart in

186

Neustrelitz, myself, mentoring the scapegrace Hannah in Rosenheim and later in Hebertshausen, near Munich. She shed a tear or 2 as she talked of her sainted husband, and I found I spoke elegiacally, as if my spouse had also passed away (in childbed, perhaps).

It was an edifying hour, and as I took my leave I permitted myself to kiss her with the utmost formality on the brow – on her 'widow's peak'.

'Ah, my darling Sybil. Why the tears, my pretty?'

'Meinrad. His throat's all bulged up. Come and see.'

After his glanders, what's Meinrad's new 1? Strangles, that's what.

As for developments on the eastern front? Loyally but anxiously I attend to my Volksempfanger; and all I hear is that somewhat puzzling silence from Berlin. Initially I thought, Well, no news is good news, nicht? Then I began to wonder.

But I'll tell you who's quite good at filling you in on the military situation. Not Mobius, not Uhl (both are dauntingly taciturn). And not Boris Eltz. Eltz is naturally high-spirited, and of course reliably gung-ho, but he's a sly, sarcastic sort of customer. Too clever by half, if you ask me (like a lot of people I could name).

No, the chap to go to, surprisingly enough, is young Prufer. Wolfram Prufer has many faults, God knows, but he's an unimpeachable Nazi. Moreover, his brother Irmfried is on Paulus's staff, no? And the mail, it seems (at least for now, as Christmas nears), is the only thing that's getting in or out of Stalingrad.

'Oh, we'll carry the day, mein Kommandant,' he said over lunch in the Officers' Mess. 'The German soldier scoffs at the objective conditions.'

'Yes, but what *are* the objective conditions?'

'Well we're outnumbered. On paper. Ach, any German soldier

is worth 5 Russians. We have the fanaticism and the will. They can't match us for merciless brutality.'

'. . . Are you sure about that, Prufer?' I asked. 'Very stubborn resistance.'

'It's not like France or the Low Countries, Sturmbannfuhrer. Civilised nations. They had the gumption and the decency to bow to superior might. But the Russians are Tartars and Mongols. They just fight till they're dead.' Prufer scratched his hair. 'They rise up from the sewers at night with daggers between their teeth.'

'Asiatics. Animals. Whilst we're still lumbered with the Christian mentality. What does this mean for the 6th Army, Hauptsturmfuhrer, and for "Operation Blue"?'

'With our zeal? Victory's not in doubt. It'll just take a bit longer, that's all.'

'I hear we're undersupplied. There are shortages.'

'True. There's hardly any fuel. Or food. They're eating the horses.'

'And the cats, I heard.'

'They finished the cats. It's temporary. All they've got to do is retake the airfield at Gumrak. Besides, privation presents no obstacle to the men of the Wehrmacht.'

'There's disease, they say. And not much medicine, I shouldn't wonder.'

'It's 30 below but they've got plenty of warm clothing. It's just a shame about the lice. And you have to be vigilant. Irmfried woke up the other night and a huge mouse had gnawed through his bedsocks and was eating his toes. He couldn't feel it because of the frostbite. Oh, and ammo. They're running out of ammo.'

'The good God, how're we going to win without ammo?'

'For a German soldier these difficulties are as nothing.'

'Isn't there a danger of encirclement?'

'The German ranks are impregnable.' Prufer paused uneasily

and said, 'If I were Zhukov, though, I'd go straight for the Romanians.'

'Ach, Zhukov's a *muzhik*. He's much too stupid to think of that. He can't hold a candle to a German commander. Tell me, how is Paulus's health?'

'The dysentery? Still bedridden, Sturmbannfuhrer. But hear me, sir. Even if we should be technically surrounded, Zhukov can't stop Manstein. Generalfeldmarschall Manstein will smash his way through. And his 6 divisions will turn the tide.'

'As you said yourself, uh, Wolfram, defeat's a biological impossibility. How can we go down to a rabble of Jews and peasants? *Don't* make me laugh.'

2 simultaneous but of course completely independent visitors from Berlin, the hulking Horst Sklarz of the Wirtschafts-Verwaltungshauptamt, and the epicene Tristan Benzler of the Reichssicherheitshauptamt. And it's the same old song.

Sklarz only has thoughts for the war economy, whilst Benzler's sole concern is national security. In other words, Sklarz wants more slaves, and Benzler wants more corpses.

I had ½ a mind to lock Sklarz and Benzler in the same room and have *them* argue the toss; but no, they came and went singly, and I was obliged to sit there getting hollered at for hour after hour.

On only 1 theme did their opinions coincide. Sklarz and Benzler both talked in extraordinarily disrespectful terms about the quality of my bookkeeping and my general paperwork.

In addition, 1st Benzler and then Sklarz dropped identical hints about my possible transfer to a subsidiary of the Inspectorate of Concentration Camps in Cologne. Both of them referred to this as a 'promotion', despite the drop in rank and the loss of all real power (not to mention the brutal cut in salary). And, what's more, Cologne is the region's Militarbereichshauptkommandoquartier, and it's forever being *bombed*.

. . . Well they're gone now. It's probably true: I should take a more orderly approach to the clerical side of things. My desktop in the MAB, as Sklarz and Benzler alike remarked, is a disgrace. A haystack upon a haystack. And where *did* I put that needle?

A cut in salary, eh? How fortunate that I've managed to put something aside – a little 'nest egg', if you will – during my custodianship of the Konzentrationslager!

'Hurry up, Paul.'

The Dezember Konzert has already come upon us!

I was behindhand, that evening, and somewhat annoyed and flustered, because Hannah, if you please, was wearing her highest high heels, and she also had her hair stacked up on her head, giving me the impression, when the 2 of us met up in the hall (the Dienstwagen awaited), that I was only ½ her height. As I've so often told her, the German girl is a natural girl: she's not *supposed* to wear high heels.

'Coming!'

Thus I dashed to my study and looked for my 'stilts'. Nicht? The leather wedges I sometimes slip into my boots for the extra few centimetres? And I couldn't *find* them, so I dismembered an old copy of *Das Schwarze Korps* and folded 4 pages into 1/16ths and used them instead. German girls aren't *supposed* to wear high heels. High heels are for the mincing sluts of Paris and New York, with their silk stockings and their satin garter belts and their—

'Paul!'

'Yes *yes*.'

When we arrived at the theatre in Furstengrube and hurried, just before the lights went down, to our seats in the middle of the front row, a murmur of envious admiration swept the house; and I confess to feeling a lovely warm glow of pride, albeit 1 tinged with poignancy. Everybody there, I'm sure, chalked up the Kommandant's tardiness to an impulsive 'bout' in the master

190

bedroom. Alas. How could they know of Frau Doll's miserable deficiencies in this sphere? I looked sadly at Hannah's beautiful face – the width of the Mund, the strength of the Kiefer, the savage Zahnen – and then the darkness came.

. . . I was soon wondering if I would ever again be able to attend a mass assemblage without my mind starting to play tricks on me. It wasn't like the last occasion, when I became gradually immersed in the logistical challenge of gassing the audience. No. This time I at once imagined that the people behind me were already dead – already dead, and recently exhumed for immolation on the pyre. And how sweet the Aryans smelled! If I rendered them into smoke and flame, the burning bones (I felt confident) would not forsake that fresh aroma!

And then, do you know, in the fever of my 'trance' (this was during the final bit, the ballet und so) it seemed to me that the Deliverer urgently needed to be apprised of my discovery. *Even as they pass through nature to eternity, the children of the Teutons do not rot and reek*. We would go together, he and I, and present these findings to the bar of history, so that Clio herself might smile and hymn the courage and justice of our cause . . . Then, dismayingly, it was all over, and the darkness fled in a cataract of acclaim.

I turned, beaming, to my wife. Who was now completely hideous – with stretched and quivering Kinn, with blood-red Augen, and a bubble of mucus in her left Nasenloch, which abruptly popped.

'Ach,' I said.

. . . There were long queues for the toilets, and when I regained the foyer my wife was standing in a group that included the Seedigs and the Zulzes, plus Fritz Mobius, Angelus Thomsen, and Drogo Uhl. Pawed at by the beaming Ilse Grese, Boris Eltz, who, clearly, was disgustingly drunk, sat to the side with his face in his hands.

'Choreographed by Saint-Leon,' Mobius was saying to Seedig. 'Music by Delibes.' He turned and gazed down at me from his great height. 'Ah here's the Kommandant. I take it you've heard, Paul. Because you don't look too clever.'

This was doubtlessly true. In the lavatory I found that the two wedges of newsprint in my boots were sopping with perspiration. As a result, perhaps, I felt intolerably parched, and I took from the rusting faucet 2 cupped handfuls of warm and yellowy water. After an uneasy couple of minutes there followed several jolts of projectile vomitus, which I skilfully directed into the tin trough of the urinal. 5 or 6 SS came and went whilst I did this. Now Mobius raised his voice, saying,

'Manstein's been turned and is in retreat. Zhukov gave him a mauling 50 kilometres to the west.'

There was silence. I swivelled and paced with my hands folded behind my back. I heard a squelching sound.

'Stepped in a puddle earlier on!' I cried with a resurgence of my customary verve. 'Both feet too. Just my luck.' At this point I felt I had to say something – all eyes were on me – in my capacity as Kommandant. '. . . So!' I began. 'The 6th Army fights on alone, nicht? It so happens that I'm quite "up" on Stalingrad. Young Prufer, no? He has a . . . I am confident,' I said, 'I am more than confident that Paulus will take all the necessary measures', I went on, 'to ensure that he doesn't get encircled.'

'Herrgott noch mal, Paul, he's already encircled,' said Mobius. 'Zhukov smashed through the Romanians weeks ago. We're noosed.'

Thomsen said, 'Farewell to the oil of the Donetz basin. Forward to the oil of the Buna-Werke. Now tell me, Frau Doll, tell me, Frau Uhl – how are your lovely girls?'

. . . The next day my Volksempfanger, which quite properly confines itself to the Nationalsozialistische station, was going on about our 'heroic stand' in the Caucasus. The 6th Army was likened to the Spartans at Thermopylae. But didn't the Spartans all get killed?

Hannah's started doing something very queer in the bathroom. I can only see her lower extremities – because she's on the chair by the towel rack, nicht? Her long-toed feet flex and stretch, as if she . . . Some sort of erotic reverie, I suppose. She's thinking of her nights (her afternoons, her mornings) doing God knows what with friend Kruger. It's thoughts of Kruger (and a post-war liaison?) that whisk her Fotze to the boil.

Well, it's nothing to do with Thomsen. They never went near each other except at functions. Now he's gone, Steinke is of course off the payroll (and to forestall any chance of future embarrassment I've had him dealt with, utilising the concordant modality).

Kruger lives. Hourly I await corroboration from the Chancellery.

Then 1 more piece of the jigsaw will slot into place.

Young Prufer, unlike his hapless sibling, went home for Christmas. And I lost little time in bearding him on his return, saying,

'Did you *know* they were encircled?'

'Yes. They've been encircled for well over a month.'

'Why didn't you tell me? I looked a real . . .'

'I couldn't risk it, Sturmbannfuhrer. It's now a very serious offence – putting something like that in a letter. Irmfried said it in baby code.'

'Baby code?'

'Our private language. So only I'd understand. I'm sorry, sir, but I didn't want to put him in a spot. I reckon he's got enough to be going on with. He says they all look like icicles. 2 weeks ago he watched some men decapitate the rotten carcass of a mule. They ate the brains with their bare hands.'

'Mm. But for a German soldier . . . How's morale?'

'Could be higher, quite honestly. On Christmas Eve the men

were weeping like children. They've convinced themselves that they're being punished by God for all those things they did in Ukraine. Last year.'

'Na. Last year.' I grew pensive, and after a while Prufer said,

'But let me put your mind at rest, mein Kommandant. There'll be no thought of surrender. Those boys aren't just crack soldiers – they're National Socialists. None more so than Friedrich Paulus, who seems to be made out of tempered steel. They'll fight to the last bullet.'

'Have they got any bullets?'

Prufer's earnest young face sustained a rise in emotion, and his voice thickened.

'A German warrior knows how to die, I trust. I think a German warrior understands what is meant by Sein oder Nichtsein. Oh, I think so. A German warrior knows what *that* involves, I believe.'

'So how will it go, Wolfram?'

'Well. The Generalfeldmarschall will have to commit suicide of course. Eventually. And the 6th will go down in a storm of glory. It'll cost the enemy dear – of that we may be certain. And who'll be the victor in the end, Paul? German prestige. And German honour, mein Kommandant!'

'Indubitably,' I concurred. I sat up straight, I drew in breath. 'You're right about the prestige, Hauptsturmfuhrer. When a ¼ of a 1,000,000 men joyfully give up their lives – in the service of an idea . . .'

'Yes, Paul?'

'*That* issues a communiqué, Wolfram, that will make the world tremble. *Guerre à mort*. No surrender!'

'Bravo, mein Kommandant,' said Prufer. 'No surrender. Hear him! Hear him!'

And it was going so well, it was going so well for once, and they were are all calmly undressing, and it was quite warm in the

194

Little Brown Bower, and Szmul was there, and his Sonders were darning their way through the throng, and it was all going so beautifully, and the birds outside were singing so prettily, and I found I even 'believed' for a moist and misty interlude that we really were looking after these deeply inconvenienced folk, that we really were going to cleanse them and reclothe them and feed them and give them warm beds for the night, and I knew someone would spoil it, I knew someone would ruin it and madden my nightmares, and she did, coming at me not with violence or anathema, no, not at all, a very young woman, naked, and tensely beautiful, every inch, coming at me with a shrug, then a gesture with her slowly raised hands, then almost a smile, then another shrug, then a single word before she moved on.

'18,' she said.

It's a bit early to say, I admit, but 1943 has thus far held more than its fair share of disappointments.

I'll unburden myself of this without further ado. Alisz Seisser, as we delicately say, is 'in different circumstances'. And so am I.

She's pregnant.

Having slept on this news, I arose at 06.30, and went downstairs for a solitary breakfast. I heard the matter-of-fact rapping on the front door, then the maid's swishy shuffle.

'Courier from Berlin, sir.'

'Put it there, Humilia. Lean it on the toast rack. And more Darjeeling.'

Coolly I progressed with my yogurt, my cheese, my salami . . .

A void surrounded the incarcerationary career of Dieter Kruger. You look at the sun for an instant too long – and your point of focus, for a while, is a pulsing blur. Hannah's lover had been hiding behind that glutinous throb. Until now.

I reached for the sharp white envelope: my name in Indian ink;

the gilt crest of the Chancellery. With steady hands I lit a cheroot and reached for a knife; I cut the letter's throat and readied myself to contemplate the status and whereabouts of friend Kruger. This is what it said:

Lieber SS-Sturmbannfuhrer Doll:
  Dieter Kruger. Leipzig, 12 Januar 1934. Auf der Flucht erschossen.
  Mit freundlichen Empfehlungen,

M.B.

. . . Shot whilst trying to escape!

Shot whilst trying to escape: a form of words, covering a large variety of destinies. Shot whilst trying to escape. Alternatively, to put it another way, shot. Alternatively, to put it yet another way, kicked or lashed or clubbed or strangled or starved or frozen or tortured to death. But dead.

There are only 2 possible explanations. Either Angelus Thomsen was himself misinformed, or else, for reasons of his own, he misinformed Hannah. And yet – why ever would he do that?

The last heroic fighters in Stalingrad, intoned my faithful Volksempfanger, *raised their hands for perhaps the last time in their lives to sing the national anthems. What an example German warriors have set in this great age! The heroic sacrifice of our men in Stalingrad was not in vain. And the future will show us why* . . .

Time: 07.43. Place: my somewhat cluttered study. I was listening to a recording of the Minister of Enlightenment's seminal address, delivered at the Sportpalast on February 18. It was a long speech anyway, and considerably protracted by bursts of the stormiest applause. During one of the more extended ovations I had time to read and reread a fine editorial in a recent copy of the *Volkischer Beobachter*. Its conclusion? *They died so that Germany might live.*

196

As for the minister, he ended his peroration with a call for total war: *People, rise up! And storm, break loose!*

When the whistling and stomping eventually died down I hurried to the Officers' Clubroom, feeling the need for solidarity and comradeship in this testing hour. There I found a like-minded Mobius, who was enjoying a morning drink.

I filled my glass and searched for something to say – something that would answer to the seemly gravity of our mood.

'Ah, Untersturmfuhrer,' I said gently. 'Greater love hath no man than him who . . .'

'Than him who what?'

'Who lays down his life for—'

'Blutige *Holle*, Paul, where do you get your information? From the Volksempfanger? They didn't *lay down their lives*. They *surrendered.*'

'Kapitulation? Unmoglich!'

'That's 150,000 dead and 100,000 captive. Have you *any idea* what the enemy's going to do with this?'

'. . . Propaganda?'

'Yes. *Propaganda.* For God's sake, Paul, get a grip.' He weightily exhaled. 'In London they're already smelting the so-called Sword of Stalingrad – "by order of the king". Churchill will personally present it to "Stalin the Mighty" at their next summit. And that's just for openers.'

'Mm, might look a bit . . . Ah, but the Generalfeldmarschall, Untersturmfuhrer. Friedrich Paulus. Like the true warrior he was, like the Roman, he took the—'

'Oh verpiss dich, like hell he did. He's hobnobbing in Moscow.'

That night I returned to the villa with a heavy heart. It was becoming clearer and clearer to me that I had been deceived – betrayed, at least in thought, by she whom I believed would always remain at my side . . . It was Thomsen. It was Thomsen who made her Busen swell. It was Thomsen who made her Saften stir. But I'm not supposed to *know* about that, am I.

I gave the door a push. Hannah was lying athwart the bed, and on the enemy radio, in impeccable high German, a voice was saying, *Now the civilised nations of the world are fully arrayed against the fascist beast. Its maniacal infamies can no longer skulk behind the fog and mist, the foul breath, of a murderous war. Soon the—*

'Who is this speaking?'

'Paulus,' said Hannah gaily.

I felt fiery whispers in my armpits. I said, 'Kruger. He's dead.'

'Mm. So I was told.'

'Then why, may I ask, are you so radiant?'

'Because the war is lost.'

'. . . Hannah, you have just committed a *crime*. A crime for which', I said, examining my fingernails (and noticing they were in need of a scrub), 'a crime for which we are entitled to exact the supreme penalty.'

'Doubting victory. Tell me, Pilli. Do you doubt victory?'

I drew myself up to my full height, saying, 'Whilst clear hegemony may elude us, there's no possibility of defeat. It's called an armistice, Hannah. A truce. We shall simply apply for terms.'

'Oh no we won't. You should listen to the enemy radio, Pilli. The Alliance will only accept unconditional surrender.'

'Unerhört!'

She lay back, on her side, in the significant Unterrock. Her brown and glowing Uberschenkeln – like those of a giantess. 'What'll they do with you,' she asked, turning over and presenting me with the cleft hillock of her Hinterteil, 'when they see what you've done?'

'Hah. War crimes?'

'No. Crimes. Just crimes. I haven't noticed any war.' She turned and smiled over her shoulder. 'I suppose they'll just string you up. Nicht? Nicht? Nicht?'

I said, 'And you'll be free.'

'Yes. You'll be dead and I'll be free.'

Of course, I didn't deign to tender a riposte. My thoughts had turned to something more interesting – the kreative Vernichtung of Sonderkommandofuhrer Szmul.

3. SZMUL: THE TIME OF THE SILENT BOYS

I'll be thirty-five in September. That declarative sentence attempts very little, I know – but it contains two errors of fact. In September I'll still be thirty-four. And I'll be dead.

At every sunrise I tell myself, 'Well. Not tonight.' At every sunset I tell myself, 'Well. Not today.'

It transpires that there's something childish about the contingent life. To exist hour by hour is childish, somehow.

How amazing it is to say it: I cannot defend myself against the charge of *frivolity*. It is frivolous, it is silly, to persist in a fool's paradise, let alone a fool's inferno.

A bewildered lull settles on the Lager after the German defeat in the east. It is like an attack – and again I admit to bathos – of mortal embarrassment. They see the size of their gamble on victory: the fantastic crimes legalised by the state, they finally understand, are still illegal elsewhere. This mood lasts for five or six days, and is now no more than a relatively pleasant memory.

There are selections everywhere – on the ramp, of course, and in the Ka Be, of course, but also in the blocks, also at roll call, and also at the gate. At the gate: the work Kommandos face selections sometimes twice a day, on the way out and on the way back in. Men the shape of gnawed wishbones – the shape of wishbones gnawed and sucked – swell out their chests and move at a jog.

The Germans cannot win the war against the Anglo-Saxons and the Slavs. But there will probably be time for them to win the war against the Jews.

Doll is different, now, on the ramp. An effort has been made. He looks less slovenly, and he's not nearly so obviously drunk or hungover (or both). His diction – this is strange – has become more confident and also more flowery. He is still very mad, in my view, and necessarily so. What can they do but turn up the dial of insanity? Doll is reconvinced; he has communed with his deepest self and discovered that, yes, murdering all the Jews is the right thing to do.

The Sonders have suffered Seelenmord – death of the soul. But the Germans have suffered it too; I know this; it could not possibly be otherwise.

I am no longer afraid of death, though I am still afraid of dying. I am afraid of dying because it is going to hurt. That's all there is attaching me to life: the fact that leaving it is going to hurt. It'll hurt.

Experience tells me that dying never lasts less than about sixty seconds. Even when it's the shot to the back of the neck, and you go down like a marionette whose strings have been snipped – the actual dying never lasts less than about sixty seconds.

And I am still afraid of that minute of murder.

When Doll next comes to see me I am in the morgue, supervising the barber Kommando and the oral Kommando. The men in the barber Kommando work with shears; the men in the oral Kommando work with a chisel or a small but heavy hammer in one hand and, to control the jaws, a blunt hook in the other. On a bench in the corner the SS dentist licks his lips in his sleep.

'Sonderkommandofuhrer. Come here.'

'Sir.'

With his Luger drawn but not raised (as if the weight of it keeps his right hand at his side), Doll has me precede him into the stockroom containing the hoses and the brooms, the brushes and the bleach.

'I want you to put a date in your diary.'

*

There is a length of wurst in front of you, and you eat it, and then it's behind you. There is a fifth of schnapps in front of you, and you drink it, and then it's behind you. There is warm bedding in front of you, and you sleep in it, and then it's behind you. There is a day or a night ahead of you, and then it's behind you.

I used to have the greatest respect for nightmares – for their intelligence and artistry. Now I think nightmares are pathetic. They are quite incapable of coming up with anything even remotely as terrible as what I do all day – and they've stopped trying. Now I just dream about cleanliness and food.

'. . . April the thirtieth. Make a mental note of it, Sonder-kommandofuhrer. Walpurgisnacht.'

It is now March 10. I feel as though I have been granted eternal life.

'Where?' he goes on. 'The Little Brown Bower? The Wall of Tears? And what time? Ten hundred hours? Fourteen hundred? And by what means? . . . You look oppressed, Sonder, by all these choices.'

'Sir.'

'Why don't you simply repose your trust in me?'

These men, the Death's Head SS, were probably once very ordinary, ninety per cent of them. Ordinary, mundane, banal, commonplace – normal. They were once very ordinary. But they are ordinary no longer.

'You're not getting off that lightly, Sonder. You'll have to do me a service before you say goodbye. Don't worry. Leave everything to the Kommandant.'

That day in Chełmno it was deafeningly cold. And perhaps that's all it is, that's all it means – the time of the silent boys.

But no. The wind was rushing through the trees, and you could hear that. From five in the morning to five in the evening the German power used whips, and you could hear that. The three gassing vans kept coming down from the Schlosslager and unloading at the Waldlager, and then firing up again, and you could hear that.

On January 21, 1942, the numbers were so great that the SS and the Orpo selected another hundred Jews to help the Sonders drag the bodies to the mass grave. This supplementary Kommando consisted of teenage boys. They were given no food or water, and they worked for twelve hours under the lash, naked in the snow and the petrified mud.

When the light was thinning Major Lange led the boys to the pits and shot them one by one – and you could hear that. Towards the end he ran out of ammunition and used the butt of his pistol on their skulls. And you could hear that. But the boys, jockeying and jostling to be next in line, didn't make a sound.

And after that, this.

'She has black hair, your wife, with a white stripe down the middle. Like a skunk. Nicht?'

I shrug.

'She is gainfully employed, your Shulamith. A skilled seamstress, she adorns Wehrmacht uniforms with swastikas. In Factory 104. At night she repairs to the attic above the bakery on Tlomackie Street. Not so, Sonder?'

I shrug.

'She will be taken on May the first. A *good* date, that, Sonder – the third anniversary of the sealing', he says, with his furry upper teeth on view, 'of the Jewish slum. She will be taken on May the first and she will wend her way here. Are you impatient to see your Shulamith?'

'No, sir.'

'Well I'll spare you. Soppy old fool that I am. I'll have her

203

killed that day in Łódź. May one. It will happen unless I countermand my order that morning. Understood?'

I say, 'Sir.'

'Tell me. Were you happy with your Shulamith? Was it a love whose month was ever May?'

I shrug.

'Mm, I suppose you'd have to explain why, in her absence, you've rather gone downhill. Let yourself go a bit. Ach, there's nothing worse than the contempt of a woman. Your one, Shulamith, she's a big girl, isn't she. Did Shulamith like you fucking her, Sonder?'

August 31, 1939, was a Thursday.

I walked home from school with my sons, in flawless and not quite serious sunshine. Then the family had a supper of chicken soup and brown bread. Friends and relatives looked in briefly, and everyone was asking the question, Had we mobilised too late? There was an atmosphere of great anxiety and even dread, but also feelings of solidarity and resilience (after all, we were the nation that, nineteen years earlier, had defeated the Red Army). There was also a long game of chess and the usual small talk, the usual smiles and glances, and that night in bed I defiantly embraced my wife. Six days later the flattened city was full of rotting horses.

When I went on that first transport, to Deutschland supposedly, expecting to find paid work, I took my sons with me – Chaim, fifteen, Schol, sixteen, both of them tall and broad like their mother.

They were among the silent boys.

And after all that, all this.

'Fret not, Sonder. I'll tell you who to kill.'

CHAPTER V. DEAD AND ALIVE

I. THOMSEN: PRIORITIES IN THE REICH

'No, I love it here, Tantchen – it's like a holiday from reality.'

'Just plain old family life.'

'Quite.'

There was Adolf, twelve (named after his godfather), Rudi, nine (named after his godfather, ex-Deputy Leader Rudolf Hess), and Heinie, seven (named after his godfather, Reichsfuhrer-SS Heinrich Himmler). There were also three daughters, Ilse (eleven), Irmgard (four), and Eva (two), and another boy, Hartmut (one). And Frau Bormann, that Christmas, had special news to announce: she was pregnant.

'Which will make eight, Tante,' I said as I followed her into the kitchen – the bare pine, the dressers, the kaleidoscopic crockery. 'Are you going to have any more?'

'Well I need ten. Then they give you the best medal. Anyway it'll make nine, not eight. I've already got eight. There was Ehrengard.'

'Indeed there was.' I went on boldly (Gerda being Gerda), 'Sorry, old thing, but does Ehrengard count? Can I help with that?'

'Oh yes.' With gloved hands and quivering forearms Gerda hoisted a tureen the size of a bidet from oven to hob. 'Oh yes, the dead ones count. They don't have to be alive. When Hartmut was born and I applied for the gold Mutterkreuz – what were they going to say? *No gold Mutterkreuz for you. One of them died so you've only got seven?*'

I stretched in my chair and said, 'Now I remember. When you moved from silver to gold, Tantchen. With Hartmut. It was a proud day. Here, can I do anything?'

'Stop being ridiculous, Neffe. Stay where you are. A nice glass of – what's this? – Trockenbeerenauslese. There. Have a rollmop. What are you giving them?'

'The children? Cold cash as usual. Strictly calibrated by age.'

'You always give them too much, Neffe. It goes to their heads.'

'. . . I was thinking, dear, that there might be a slight difficulty if your tenth is a boy,' I said (such babies were automatically called Adolf, and assigned the same godfather). 'You'll have two Adolfs.'

'That's all right. We're already calling Adolf Kronzi. In case.'

'Very wise. By the way I'm sorry I called Rudi Rudi. I mean I'm sorry I called Helmut Rudi.'

Rudi's name was changed, by court order, after Rudolf Hess, the noted mesmerist and clairvoyant (and number three in the Reich), flew alone to Scotland in May 1941, hoping to negotiate a truce with somebody he'd vaguely heard of called the Duke of Hamilton.

'Don't apologise,' said Gerda. 'I call Rudi Rudi all the time. Call Helmut Rudi, I mean. Oh and remember. Don't call Ilse Ilse. Ilse's now called Eike. Named for Frau Hess, so Ilse's now *Eike*.'

While she laid a table for seven and readied two highchairs Aunt Gerda told anecdotes about various members of her domestic staff – the (scatter-brained) governess, the (shifty) gardener, the (sluttish) housemaid, and the (thieving) nanny. Then she went still and grew thoughtful.

'They don't have to be alive,' she said. 'The dead ones count.'

Meanwhile, Gerda's husband, the Director of the Party Chancellery, the mastermind of the Wilhelmstrasse, was on his way to join us here at the old family home at Pullach in southern Bavaria. And where was he coming from? From the mountain retreat at the Obersalzberg in the Bavarian alps – from the official residence known as Berchtesgaden, or the Berghof, or the Kehlsteinhaus. Bards and dreamers called it the Eagle's Nest . . .

With sudden indignation Gerda said, 'Of course they count. Especially these days. Nobody would ever *get* to ten if they didn't.' She laughed scoffingly. 'Of course the dead ones count.'

———

It was mid morning. Uncle Martin stood bent over the hall table, sorting and stacking the vast accumulations of his mail.

'You've a good memory for the skirted staff on the third floor of the Sicherheitsdienst, haven't you, Neffe? Knowing you. You dog. I need some help.'

'How may I oblige?'

'There's a girl there I . . . Here, carry some of this, Golo. Put your arms out. I'll load you up.'

With the world war now turning on its hinges, with the geo-historical future of Germany in question, and with the very exist-ence of National Socialism itself under threat, the Reichsleiter had much to attend to.

'Priorities, Neffe. First things first. See,' he said forgivingly, 'the Chief loves his vegetable soups. You could almost say he's become *dependent* on his vegetable soups. And so might you, Golo, if you'd sworn off all meat, fish, and fowl. Well then. It transpires that his dietary cook at the Berghof is tricked out with a Jewish grandmother. And you can't have someone of that sort cooking for the Chief.'

'Obviously not.'

'I fired her. And what happens? He rescinds it – and she's back!'

'It's the vegetable soups, Onkel. Does his uh, does his companion ever cook?'

'Fraulein Braun? No. All she ever does is pick the movies. And take photographs.'

'Those two, Onkel, does he, do they actually . . . ?'

'Good question.' He quickly held an envelope up to the light. 'They certainly disappear together . . . You know, Golo, the Chief won't take his clothes off even for his personal physician? Plus he's fanatical about cleanliness. And so's she. And when it comes to the bedroom, you have to . . . you can't . . . you have to roll up your . . .'

'Of course you do, Onkel.'

'Steady it. Use your chin . . . Consider the matter from this angle, Neffe. The Chief went on from a Viennese dosshouse to become the king of Europe. It's fatuous, it's *frivolous* to expect him to be as other men are. I'd love some actual details – but who can I ask? . . . Gerda.'

'Yes, Papi,' she said, moving nearer as she passed by.

'I want an explanation.'

'Yes, Papi?' she said, backing away.

In physical outline, the Bormanns resembled the Dolls. Gerda, my age, and a grand-looking woman, with many shades of painterly beauty in her face, was just over six foot in her clogs. And Uncle Martin was an even more compressed and therefore widened version of the Commandant – but darkly and sleekly attractive in his way, with a playful air and stimulating eyes. There was something juicy about his mouth; it was always ripening for a smile. Indicatively, too, Martin never seemed at all daunted by Gerda's height; he strode along as if she made him taller, and this despite his proud paunch and his desk-job backside. He said,

'The Christmas tree.'

'They ganged up on me, Papi. They went behind my back to Hans.'

'Gerda, I thought we saw eye to eye on religion at least. One drop of that gets into them and they're poisoned for life.'

'Exactly. I blame Charlemagne. For bringing it to Germany.'

'Don't blame Charlemagne. Blame Hans. Never again. Clear?'

'Yes, Papi,' we heard her whisper as we moved on.

Uncle Martin's workroom, in Pullach: the ranks of gunmetal filing cabinets, the index-card consoles, the acres of sectioned table space, the stocky strongbox. I again thought of Doll, and Doll's office and study – those two shameful poems of irresolution and neglect.

'Onkel. What are you doing about Speer? The man's a menace.' For once I spoke feelingly: the youthful Minister of Armaments and War Production, with his startling simplifications (rational-ising, standardising), was capable, as I then saw it, of postponing defeat by at least a year. 'Why haven't you acted?'

'It's too soon,' said Uncle Martin, lighting a cigarette. 'The Cripple' – Goebbels (der Kruppel) – 'is up Speer's rump for now. And he has the ear of the Transvestite' – Goring (der Transvestit). 'But Speer will soon find out how weak he is against the Party. Which is code for me.'

Also smoking, I lay sprawled on a leather sofa to his right. I said, 'Do you know why the Chief's so sweet on him, Onkel? I'll tell you. It's not because he – I don't know – streamlined the production of prismatic glass. No, he looks at Speer and he thinks, I would've been like that, I would have been *him* – an architect, a free creator – if I hadn't been summoned by providence.'

Martin's swivel chair had slowly turned towards me. 'Well?'

'Just make him seem like any other grasping satrap, Onkel. You know, creating difficulties, whining about resources. The bloom'll soon go off him.'

'Give it time . . . All right, Golo. Buna.'

As we entered the drawing room for midday drinks Uncle Martin was saying, 'I sympathise, son. It's enough to drive you wild. I get the same endless hand-wringing about the POWs and the foreign labour.'

Rudi/Helmut, Ilse/Eike, Adolf/Kronzi, Heinie, and Eva were sitting round the tree (hung with lit candles, cookies, and apples), quietly gloating over their presents. Irmgard was at the piano; she sounded the highest key, using the mute.

'Stop that, Irma! Ach, Golo, they're saying, No corporal punishment! How can you get any work out of them otherwise?'

'How? How? But it's all right, Onkel, now Burckl's gone. No more wet-nursing. We're back to the tried and trusted.'

'There are too many of them as it is. If we're not careful, you know, we'll win the war militarily and lose it racially. Dutch gin?' Uncle Martin gave a snort and said, 'The Chief made me laugh the other day. He'd just heard that someone was trying to ban contraception in the eastern territories. It must have been the Masturbator' – Rosenberg (der Masturbator). 'And the Chief said, *Anyone tries that and I'll personally shoot them dead!* He was in a right taking. So to cheer him up I told him something I'd heard about the ghetto in Litzmannstadt. There, for their own use, they're making condoms out of babies' pacifiers. And he goes, *That's the way round it's* supposed *to be!* Salut!'

'Salut. Or as the English say, *Cheers.*'

'. . . Feast your eyes, lad. Ach. A good quiverful of kids. A crackling log fire. Outside, the snow. Over the soil. Over the Erde. And the helpmeet in the kitchen, never happier than when going about her appointed tasks. And those two guards by the gate. With cigarettes up their sleeves. Listen to this, Golo,' he said. 'It's a good one.'

Uncle Martin was losing his hair along the usual male lines, but his peaked forelock had something artistic in its shape, and still glistened. He ran his knuckles over it.

'Late October,' he said, without lowering his voice. 'I'd looked in at the SD to pick up some paperwork from Schneidhuber. I needed mimeographs, and I collared one of the girls from the pool. She's standing there looking over my shoulder as I mark up the pages. And on impulse, Golo, I slipped my left hand between her calves. She didn't even blink . . . Up and up I went, past the knees. Up and up. Up and up. And when I reached my destination, Neffe, she just – she just *smiled* . . . So I got my thumb and jammed it—'

'That *is* a good one, Onkel,' I said with a laugh.

'Ah, but that very minute, Neffe, that very minute I was called to the Wolfsschanze! Gone for a month. I come back and of course she's disappeared. No trace of her in the pool. Concentrate, Neffe. Jouncy little minx with russety hair. An absolute squiggle of curves. Begins with a k. Klara?'

'. . . Oh. She's famous. And she's not in the pool, Onkel. She goes around with the tea urn. Krista. Krista Groos.'

The Reichsleiter hooked his little fingers into the corners of his mouth and whistled so shrilly that Irmgard and Eva both burst into tears. Then you could hear the quickening gait of stout shoes and Gerda came through the doorway with a naked Hartmut on her hip.

'Neffe can reunite me', said Uncle Martin, wet-eyed, 'with my smiling redhead.'

Gerda lifted Hartmut to her shoulder. 'How well timed, Papi. Because I won't be usable by March. You see, after the third month, Golo,' she confided, 'he never comes near me. Children! The goose is served! Oh, stop snivelling, Eva.'

————

Over the next three days Uncle Martin was seen only at mealtimes. He had a series of visitors – a Max Amman (Party Publications), a Bruno Schultz (Race and Resettlement), and a Kurt Mayer (Reich Ancestry Bureau). Each of these officials, in their turn, joined the grown-ups for dinner, and they all wore the same expression, that of men who steer their ships by guidance of the highest stars.

*

211

I went on long walks with Gerda. Entertaining Gerda, absorbing Gerda, unlading Gerda: this had always been part of my function, and part of my value to the Reichsleiter. *After one of your visits, Golo*, he once said, *for weeks on end she* sings *while she scrubs the floor.*

That Christmas we shuffled arm in arm along the lawns and lanes, all swaddled up, Gerda in tweed hat and tweed scarf and tweed shawl. When I embraced her, as I quite often did (a nepotic reflex going back thirteen years), I imagined she was Hannah – the same height, the same mass. I held her shoulders steadyingly and tried to take pleasure in her face, the strong nose, the essentially tender brown eyes. But then her shapely lips would open, and she would speak . . . I embraced her again.

'You have that look, Golito. You're thinking of someone, aren't you. I can tell.'

'I can't hide anything from you, Tante. Yes. And she's your height. When I hug you I can feel your chin against my neck. It's the same with her.'

'Well. Perhaps you can settle down after the war.'

'But who knows? Wars are messy, Tante. You can't tell what'll be there at the end.'

'. . . True, Golito. True. Now how's that Boris?'

We edged on. The odourless air was magnificent. The silence was magnificent – just the steady crumplings of our tread. The whiteness of the folds and bolsters of snow was magnificent. White snow.

And what was Uncle Martin up to – with Max Amman, with Bruno Schultz, with Kurt Mayer, in the last days of 1942? He told me all about it.

With Party publisher Amman, Uncle Martin was taking steps to abolish the German alphabet. Why? Because the Chancellery

212

had surmised that the old Gothic script (whose brambly curlicues were the toast of every chauvinist) might be Jewish in origin. So the idea now was to replace it (at incalculable expense) with Roman Antiqua – throughout the Reich, in school textbooks, newspapers, documents, street signs, and all the rest.

With Schultz, of Race and Resettlement, Uncle Martin was trying to find a workable definition of the Mischlinge, or the ethnic hybrids. Having defined them, they would decide what to do about them. That December he and Schultz were 'costing' sterilisation for an estimated seventy thousand men and women, all of whom, prohibitively, would need ten days in hospital.

It was different with Racial Researcher Mayer. With Amman and Schultz, the Reichsleiter was applying himself, was enthusiastically putting himself about; with Mayer, though, he could not disguise a faint impatience with his destiny.

Uncle Martin might have been occasionally piqued by his offspring; but he was chronically tormented by his forebears. An official of his rank needed to be provably Aryan to a depth of four generations; and they kept running up against the void of his great-grandfather.

The inquisition about the Bormann genealogy had begun in January 1932.

'And it won't end,' he said (presciently). 'Even if the Russians cross the Oder and the Americans cross the Rhine – it won't end.'

Uncle Martin's great-grandfather, Joachim, was illegitimate. And Uncle Martin's great-great-grandmother, as he put it, *was the town pump* – so Joachim's paternal origin was *anybody's guess*.

'Wear full fig tonight, Neffe. To intimidate Mayer. I'm wearing mine.'

He had never raised a hand in anger, except at home, and he was not an Old Fighter, originally, but just a paymaster of Old Fighters. All the same, Uncle Martin had just received another

213

promotion, and came to dinner dressed as an SS-Obergruppenfuhrer – a lieutenant general.

————

'I'm paying for my bit. Out of my own pocket, too. But I've offered Mayer's people "proportional support" from state funds. That *might* do it. As long as I keep plugging away.'

'You work too hard, Onkel.'

'That's what I'm forever telling him, Neffe. I'm forever telling him, "Papi, you work too hard!"'

'See? That's all she ever says. *You work too hard.* Now run along, Gerda. I've certain matters to discuss with Golo.'

'Of course, Papi. Can I get you gentlemen anything?'

'Just bend over and sling in another log on your way out. Enjoy the view, Neffe. Ah. Now isn't that a good little girl?'

'What am I up to? Off my own bat you mean? Oh, not a lot. Wasted a few days covering myself with dust at the Gestapa. Red tabs, blue tabs. I'm trying to trace someone. It's nothing to me personally. I'm just obliging a lady friend.'

'That's what you're good at. You brute.'

'I'm *fairly* anxious to get back to Buna. Meanwhile, though, I'm entirely at your service. As always, Onkel.'

'. . . What do you know about the Ahnenerbe?'

'Not much. Cultural research, isn't it? Sort of a brains' trust. Pretty third-tier, I gather.'

'Here. Take it. Don't read the thing now. Just note the title.'

'"The Theory of the Cosmic Ice." What's that?'

'Mm. Well, here we're dealing with the Quack' – Himmler (der Kurpfuscher). 'Between you and me and the gatepost, I've never set much store by all that anthropology of his. Can't see the point in it. And the herbalism. Laxatives and yogurts. Don't hold with it. Can't see the point in it.'

'The oat-straw baths and so on.'

'Don't believe in it. Still, this is different, Golo. Now hear this. At the Ahnenerbe there's a meteorology department. Where they're supposedly working on long-term forecasts. But that's just a blind. What they're really working on is the cosmic-ice theory.'

'You'd better explain, Onkel.'

'It's a bit hot in here, isn't it? Give us your glass. There. Get that down you.'

'*Cheers*.'

'*Cheers*. Well. The theory is that the Aryans, the theory is that the *Aryans* aren't . . . Wait. Yes, and there's this business with the lost continent. It's pretty technical, and I don't want to elaborate now. Here. It's all in here. I want you to mug up on it, Neffe. And tell me the state of play at the Ahnenerbe.'

'The state of play on the cosmic-ice theory.'

'Now look, I'm not defending the idea on its merits. Obviously. How could I?'

'Of course you couldn't. You're no scientist.'

'I'm not scientifically qualified. On the other hand, I do know my politics, Neffe. And it isn't the theory that counts. It's who believes in it. The Quack's very sympathetic, and so by the way is the Transvestite – not that we listen to *him* any more. Thanks to me. But the Chief, Golo, the Chief. The Chief insists that if the cosmic-ice theory holds up—'

'Hang on, Onkel. Excuse me, but I thought the Chief had no time for any of that.'

'Oh, he's getting keener on it all the time. Runes, and so forth. And he lets the Cripple do his horoscope . . . See, the Chief maintains that if the cosmic-ice theory's sound, if we can substantiate it and make it stick – well. According to him, our enemies will simply down arms and apologise. And the Thousand Year Reich will have its mandate – *its mandate from heaven* is what the Chief said. So you see, Golo. I can't afford to be on the wrong side of this one.

215

It would look very bad. So find out about the cosmic ice. Klar?'

'Oh, perfectly clear, Onkel.'

'Just a gulp. Go on, boy. Help you sleep.'

'. . . I was thinking. Now I'm down here I may as well look in at the Brown House.'

'What for? It's one big cobweb.'

'Mm. But they've got the SA stuff for '33 and '34. You never know.'

'Who are you after exactly?'

'Oh. Some Communist.'

'Name? . . . Wait. Don't tell me. Dieter Kruger.'

I was sharply surprised, but I went on languidly, 'Yes. Kruger. How odd. And why's it so funny, Onkel?'

'Dear oh dear. Oh, dear oh dear oh dear. I'm sorry.' He coughed, and hawked into the fire. 'Well. In the first place the whole Kruger business is an absolute hoot. It always sets me off. And now, Neffe, to add to the gaiety of nations, you my boy, unless I'm very much mistaken, you my boy are stuffing Frau Doll.'

'Not so, Onkel. In the Kat Zet? It's hardly the place.'

'Mm. A bit on the grim side, I imagine.'

'Yes. A bit on the grim side. Now hang on, sir. You're too far ahead of me. I'm lost.'

'All right. All right,' he said and wiped his eyes. 'In early November I got a teletype from the Commandant. About Kruger. Haven't answered yet, but I'll have to. See, the thing is, Neffe, he and I have a sacred bond.'

'What a one you are for surprises tonight, Onkel.'

'The most sacred bond there is. More hallowed than the marriage vow. Complicity in murder.'

'Oh. Do tell.'

'Finish this, Golo,' he said, handing me the cognac. 'There. Early '23, Neffe. Doll's paramilitary unit identified a "traitor" in its midst. In Parchim. I was innocent, your honour! All I did was pass on permission for a beating. But Doll and his boys stayed too long in the pub, and then overdid it in the woods. I served a year. Don't you remember – no camping that summer? Doll got ten. You could say he took the fall for me, a bit. Served five. Anyway, why's he bothered about Kruger? At this stage in the game? Because Kruger fucked her first?'

'When you reply, what will you tell him? Doll.'

'Oh, I don't know.' He said through his yawn, 'Probably shot while trying to escape.'

'Was he?'

'No. That's just a form of words, of course. All it means is he's dead.'

'Is he?'

'Ach. Ach, I'm bursting to tell you the whole story, Neffe. Because I know you'd see the beauty of it. One of the moral pinnacles of National Socialism. But there can't be half a dozen men in the entire Reich who know what happened to Dieter Kruger. I'll sleep on it and have a ponder. Dear oh dear.'

'Doll. He was a Communist too, wasn't he? For a while.'

'Never. Always a sound Nazi. You can say that for him. No, he was in the pay of the Browns. And he fingered Kruger to Cell H. The Knuckledusters . . . That Hannah – why'd she marry a little coon like him? Ooh, I could've done her some damage myself, back in the day. Marvellous figure. But her mouth. Her mouth's too wide, don't you think?'

'It's a very pretty mouth. Are you still seeing the tragedienne? Manja? Or is that off?'

'No, it's on. I want her to move in here. Between films at least. Gerda's all for it – so long as I knock her up. I mean knock up Manja. As well as Gerda. Who wants ten for the Mutterkreuz. Come on, the lights. You do those ones over there.'

*

At five o'clock the next morning – on the last day of 1942 – Uncle Martin took his leave. Where was he going? First, to the mountain retreat at Berchtesgaden, by car; and thence to the field HQ in Rastenberg, East Prussia, by plane. From the Kehlsteinhaus to the Wolfsschanze – from the Eagle's Nest to the Wolf's Lair . . .

––––––––

I said at breakfast, 'No, I'll be delighted to celebrate Silvester with you, my dear. But then alas I have to get back to town. Leaving early. Hans'll give me a lift in the van. I've been entrusted with an urgent mission by the Reichsleiter.'

Gerda said abstractedly, '. . . I think Field Marshal Manstein's Jewish. Don't you? You can tell by the name . . . And after Berlin, Neffe?'

'Back to Buna. The devil makes work for idle hands, Tante.'

'What did you say?' she asked, looking elsewhere, and as if expecting no answer.

Overnight it had rained, warmed, and begun to thaw. Now a sour yellow sun was playing on the eaves and the slopes of the rooftops. All the pipes were busy, sluicing, racing; it made me think of multitudes of stampeding mice. Gerda said,

'Did Papi mention the war?'

'Barely.' I sipped tea and wiped my mouth. 'Did he mention it to you?'

'Barely. I don't think the war especially interests him. Because it's not his sphere.'

'That's true, Tante. You're right. Buna doesn't especially interest him either. Because it's not his sphere. Buna – synthetic materiel, Tantchen.'

Rivulets of melting snow sparkled like bead curtains against the misty windowpanes. Somewhere a ledge of frozen slush flopped emphatically to the earth.

'Why's Buna important?'

218

'Because it'll win us autarky.'

'That doesn't sound very good.'

'It's not like anarchy, Tantchen. Autarky. We'll be self-sufficient. And when the first five thousand tons of rubber roll out of the Werke, and when we're converting coal to oil at a rate of seven hundred thousand tons a month, this war will take on a very different complexion, I can assure you of that.'

'. . . Thank you, dearest. That's given me heart. Thank you for saying that, Neffe.'

'Is – is Uncle Martin especially interested in the Jews?'

'Well he can't very well not be, can he. And of course he's very pro.'

'Pro?'

'Pro Endlosung of course. Wait,' she said. 'He *did* mention the war. He *did* mention the war.' She frowned and said, 'Apparently they now know why we underestimated the Red Army. They got to the bottom of it. Russia had a war of its own recently, didn't it?'

'You're right as always, my love. The Winter War with Finland. Thirty-nine to forty.'

'And they botched it, isn't that right? Well they did that on purpose, Papi said. To lure us in. And another thing!'

'What, Tante?'

'Stalin was supposed to have killed half his officers. No?'

'True again. The purges. Thirty-seven to thirty-eight. More than half. Probably seven-tenths.'

'Well he didn't really. That was just another Jewish lie. And we fell for it like the simple souls we are. They're not dead. They're alive.'

Just beyond the glass doors a ruptured drainpipe swung into view, drunkenly and loutishly spewing water, and then swung away again. Plump tears had gathered in Gerda's eyes. The mice were racing and squeaking, tumbling over one another, going faster and faster.

'They're not dead, Neffe. The Judaeo-Bolsheviks. Neither disease nor filth will ever eradicate this scum. Why, dearest? Tell me. I'm not asking you why the Jews hate us. I'm asking you why they hate us so much. Why?'

'I can't think, Tantchen.'

'. . . They're not dead,' she said hauntedly. 'They're all *alive*.'

———

On New Year's Day, in my first-class carriage, 'The Theory of the Cosmic Ice' (a bulky dissertation by several hands) lay unattended on my lap. I looked out. First, the much-enlarged, seemingly interminable outskirts of Munich groaned by: untouched meadowland and woodland had now been replaced by foundries and factories, by pyramids of grit and gravel. We heard the city sirens, and the train crept into a tunnel and cowered there for over an hour. Then we picked up speed, and in harsh sunshine Germany was soon going past me like a torrent of earth tones, siennas, ambers, ochres . . .

The pitch of Uncle Martin's laughter told me that Kruger was no longer breathing. And I naturally recalled that conversation with Konrad Peters.

Spirited away for special treatment. For very *special treatment.*

Killed.

Oh. At least.

I needed to know the size of that *at least*.

It was difficult to be brave in the Third Germany. You had to be ready to die – and to die after preludial torture which, moreover, you had to withstand, naming no names. And that wasn't all. In the occupied countries the lowest criminal could resist and then die like a martyr. Here, even the martyr died like the lowest criminal, in the kind of ignominy that a German would find peculiarly terrible to contemplate. And you left behind you nothing but a wake of fear.

220

In the occupied countries such a man would be an inspiration – but not in the Third Germany. Kruger's mother and father, if he still had a mother and father, would not be talking of him, except between themselves and in whispers. His wife, if he had a wife, would remove his photograph from the mantelpiece. His children, if he had children, would be told to avert their faces from his memory.

So Dieter Kruger's death served no one. No one except me.

2. DOLL: NIGHT LOGIC

It was back in November – November 9, the Reich Day of Mourning. I awoke, I came to, in the Officers' Club. Hello, I thought, you must have nodded off, old boy. Must have taken 40 winks, no? The luncheon had long since come to an end, and that repast, embarked upon with a patriotic fervour much inflamed by my commemorative address, had clearly degenerated; around me, the dregs and leavings of a gangsters' banquet – sicked-on serviettes, toppled bottles, dog-ends upright in the trifle; and, outside, the smudged dusk of Silesia. Dusk in November, dawn in February: that is the colour of the KL.

As I lay there, trying to free my tongue from the roof of my mouth, these questions came to me . . .

If what we're doing is good, why does it smell so lancingly bad? On the ramp at night, why do we feel the ungainsayable need to get so brutishly drunk? Why did we make the meadow churn and spit? The flies as fat as blackberries, the vermin, the diseases, ach, scheusslich, schmierig – why? Why do rats fetch 5 bread rations per cob? Why did the lunatics, and only the lunatics, seem to like it here? Why, here, do conception and gestation promise not new life but certain death for both woman and child? Ach, why all der Dreck, der Sumpf, der Schleim? Why do we turn the snow brown? Why do we do that? Make the snow look like the shit of angels. Why do we do that?

The Reich Day of Mourning – back in *November*, last year, before Zhukov, before Alisz, before the new Hannah.

. . . There is a placard on the office wall that says, *My loyalty is my honour and my honour is my loyalty. Strive. Obey. JUST BELIEVE!* And I find it highly suggestive that our word for ideal obedience – Kadavergehorsam – has a corpse in it (which is doubly

curious, because cadavers are the most refractory things on earth).
The duteousness of the corpse. The conformity of the corpse.
Here at the KL, in the cremas, in the pits: *they're* dead. But then
so are we, we who obey . . .

The questions I asked myself on the Reich Day of Mourning:
they must never recur.

I must shut down a certain zone in my mind.

I must accept that we have mobilised the weapons, the wonder
weapons, of darkness.

And I must take to my heart the potencies of death.

In any case, as we've always made clear, the Christian system
of right and wrong, of good and bad, is 1 we categorically reject.
Such values – relics of medieval barbarism – no longer apply.
There are only positive outcomes and negative outcomes.

'Now listen carefully. This is a matter of the gravest moment. I
hope you understand that. Fraternising with a Haftling's serious
enough. But *Rassenschande* . . . Insult to the blood! A corporal
might get away with a reprimand and a fine. But I'm the
Kommandant. You realise, don't you, that it'd be the end of my
career?'

'Oh, Paul . . .'

The cot, the footstool, the washbasin, the chemical toilet.

'God have mercy on you if you tell anyone. Besides, it'll just
be my word against yours. And you're a subhuman. Technically
I mean.'

'Then how come you did me without 1 of them Parisians on!'

'. . . Because I ran out,' I said broodingly. 'Now watch it, my
girl. Oy. Behave. Remember. Just your word against mine.'

'But who else could it be?'

This stopped me short. Alisz had been in here for just over 3
months; and the custodial staff consisted of 2 buxom Aufseherinnen
and 1 incredibly old Rottenfuhrer.

223

'The end of your career,' she snivelled. 'What about the end of my life? You get storked up here and they go and bloody well—'

'Not neccessarily, Alisz.' I gave a brief lift of the chin. 'Well. Crying won't help you. Wha wha wha. Listen to her. Wha wha wha wha wha wha. Come on now, girl. I'm the Kommandant. I'll think of *something* or other.'

'Oh, Paul . . .'

I said, 'Stop it. Stop it. You're pregnant . . . Get *off*.'

Lately I have been applying my new mental attitude to a reconsideration of our war aims.

Objective number 1. To acquire Lebensraum, or living space, or land empire.

Even if unquestioned supremacy eludes us, a compromise can doubtlessly be hammered out (and let's ignore all that guff about 'unconditional surrender'). We'll probably have to give back France, Holland, Belgium, Luxembourg, Norway, Denmark, Latvia, Estonia, Ukraine, Belarus, Yugoslavia, and Greece, but with any luck they won't mind if we hang on to Lithuania, say, the Sudetenland and the rest of the Czech entity, plus our half of Poland (I don't think the matter of Austria will even come up).

So, objective number 1: mission accomplished!

'Now Wolfram. That shemozzle in Block 33. Please explain.'

'Well, Paul, there'd been a massive selection. And they crammed them all in Block 33. 2,500 of them.'

'2,500 in 1 block? How long for?'

'5 nights.'

'Good God. Why the delay?'

'No reason. They just didn't get round to it.'

'They let them out for roll call I assume?'

'Naturally. There's got to be *Zahlappell*, Paul. No, the trouble was they gave them some food. They don't usually bother. And it was a great mistake.'

'The food was?'

'Yes. The Kapos intercepted it. All very predictable. They went off and swapped it for alcohol. Blah blah blah. But then they came back, Paul . . . And they messed with them. The Kapos messed with the prisoners.'

'Mm. You see, that's what comes of feather-bedding. *Food*, indeed. Whose bright idea was that?'

'Probably Eikel.'

'Na. How many Stucke did you say?'

'19. Regrettable. And not to be tolerated. But it doesn't really make much odds. They'd been selected anyway.'

'. . . *Menschenskind*, Hauptsturmfuhrer! The Zahlappell! The *Zahlappell*!'

There was a silence. Prufer was frowning at me with what seemed to be intense solicitude. He gave a discreet cough and said quietly,

'Paul. *Paul*. With a Haftling headcount, Paul . . . As long as the total number tallies, there isn't any difficulty. Remember? They don't have to be alive.'

After a moment or 2 I said, 'No. No. Of course they don't. You're quite right, Wolfram. How foolish of me. Yes. They can be dead if they want. They don't have to be alive.'

My rumpy girl Friday, little Minna, knocked and put her head round the door. She asked after the whereabouts of a certain file and I told her where I thought it might conceivably be.

'How're you finding the ramp work, Wolfram?'

'Well, I can see why you got cheesed off with it, Paul.'

'It's very good of you to stand in. I'll be my old self again soon.' I tapped my desktop. 'Well. What'll we do with the Kapos? Got to be firm. Phenol? Small calibre?'

Again the look of solicitude. 'Waste of materiel, surely,

225

Kommandant. You know – simpler just to revise their status. Then, Paul, the Jews can sort it out for themselves.'

'Mm. So much better for *esprit de corps*. . . That's French, Wolfram. It means team spirit. You know, morale.'

Sybil grows lovelier with each passing day. Her abiding passion – rather reprehensibly – is still cosmetics. She filches items from her mother's dressing table. Lipstick, *nicht?* And it's rather comical. There she is, alternately smiling and pouting at me with crimson smears on her teeth.

And you should see the tangles she gets into when she tries on Hannah's brassieres!

Goal number 2. To consolidate the 1,000 Year Reich.

You know, so it lasts as long as the 1 we had before – the 1 started by Charlemagne and ended by Napoleon.

As I've already conceded, there's a bumpy patch up ahead, most probably. Once we've weathered that, however . . .

Here's a fact that's not often enough stressed. In the election of July '32 the NSDAP polled 37.5%: *the highest vote for a single party in the history of Weimar.* Solid evidence, then, of the profound affinity between the simple yearnings of the Volk and the golden dream of National Socialism. It was always there, do you see. By November '33, plebiscitary acclamation reached 88%, and by April '38 it settled at just over 99! What clearer token could there be of the rude sociopolitical health of Nazi Germany?

Ach, once we're over this somewhat rocky stretch of road, and once we've made a few modifications (including, in the fullness of time, the appointment of a rather more centrist head of state), there'll be no earthly reason why we shouldn't cruise on for the duration of the next millennium.

So. Goal number 2: mission accomplished!

*

My visit took place at the usual hour. Alisz was crouched on the stool with her hands slowly writhing on her lap.

'All right, woman, you can stop your moaning. You can switch off the waterworks. I've talked to the physician. A simple procedure. Routine. She does it all the time.'

'. . . But Paul. There are no women doctors here.'

'There are *100s* of women doctors here. They're Haftlinge.'

'The prisoner doctors haven't got any instruments. They've got toolkits!'

'Not all of them.' I had Alisz sit beside me on the bed, and I strove to reassure her for a considerable period of time. 'Better now?'

'Yes, Paul. Thank you, Paul. You always find an answer.'

And to my great surprise I felt the retreat of those higher scruples which, in the presence of a fertilised female, generally inhibit me. I said,

'Go on. Go on. Here. Just hoik it up a bit.'

And yes I went ahead and gave her 1 then and there. Thinking (and it was a form of words that I often applied to the larger situation), Well. In for a fucking penny. In for a fucking pound.

They are deeply necessary, my engagements with Alisz Seisser – for how else can I maintain my dignity and self-respect? I of course allude to the appalling conditions that obtain in the Doll villa. Alisz's unfailing gratitude and esteem (not to mention her trills of amatory bliss) form a crucial counterweight to the, to the . . .

I am afraid of Hannah. There. It takes a certain kind of courage to commit such a sentence to paper – but it's the case. How to describe this fear? Whenever we happen to be alone together, I feel a vacuum in my solar plexus, like a globe of hard air.

Starting on the night of the Dezember Konzert, Hannah has reinvented her appearance, her outward form. Whilst she was never a great 1 for the clogs and the dirndls, her raiment was always commendably demure. Now she dresses like a man-pleaser – she dresses like an experienced pleaser of men.

She puts me in mind of Marguerite, of Pucci, of Xondra, of Booboo. It isn't so much the sheeny make-up and the sections of extra Fleisch on view (and the shaven Achselhohlen!). It's the look in the Augen – the look of artful calculation. The thing about such females, do you see, is that they're continuously aware of Bett, of Sex. And whilst this is an appealing trait in a sophisticated companion, it is utterly excruciating in a wife.

I can only liken the sensation, when we're alone . . . not to the *aftermath* of sexual failure but to its *prospect*. And that defies all intuition: for the last 8 months, with Hannah, there have been no failures (and no successes).

And she continues, downstairs, to look preoccupied and smug. Is she dreaming about the effeminate charms of Angelus Thomsen? I don't believe she is. She's just sneering at the thwarted virility of Paul Doll.

. . . Last night I was in my 'lair', quietly imbibing (in moderation, however, as I've reduced substantially of late). I heard the knob give its creak, and there she was, filling the doorway in her green ballgown, gloved to the elbows, her naked Schultern taking the coiled weight of her Haar. At once I felt my blood go loath and cold. Hannah stared at me, unblinking, until I turned away.

She advanced. Very heavily, and very noisily, she sat herself down on my lap. The armchair was fairly swamped by the crackling pleats of her dress. How I wanted this weight off me – how I wanted it off, off . . .

'Do you know who you are?' she whispered (and I could feel her lips against the down of my ears). 'Do you?'

'No,' I said. 'Who am I?'

'You're a young single man, and a fucking fool of a Brownshirt, a violent fucking buffoon who marches with the Brownshirts. Who sings songs with the Brownshirts, Pilli.'

228

'Go on. If you must.'

'You're a fucking chump of a Brownshirt who, tired of thinking dirty thoughts and playing with his Viper, falls asleep in his bunk and has the worst of all possible dreams. In this dream nobody does things to you. You do things to them. Terrible things. Unspeakably terrible things. Then you wake up.'

'Then I wake up.'

'Then you wake up and you find it's all true. But you don't mind. You go back to playing with your Viper. You go back to thinking dirty thoughts. Goodnight, Pilli. Kiss.'

Aspiration number 3. To shatter Judaeo-Bolshevism once and for all.

Now let's think. We haven't had much luck, so far, with Bolshevism. As for the Judaeo side of it . . .

Not long ago there was a widely discussed murder, in Linz, where a man stabbed his wife 137 times. People seemed to think this was somehow excessive. But I immediately saw the logic of it. The night logic of it.

We can't stop now. Or what were we doing, what did we think we were about, over the last 2 years?

The war against the Anglo-Saxons does not resemble the war against the Jews. In the latter conflict, we enjoy, in military terms, a distinct advantage, as the other side has no army. And no navy and no air force.

(Reminder: have that word with Szmul *soon*.)

So let's see. Living space. 1,000 Year Reich. Judaeo-Bolshevism.

Result? 2½ out of 3. Yech, I'll drink to that.

Emergency summit in the Political Department! Myself, Fritz Mobius, Suitbert Seedig, and Rupprecht Strunck. Crisis at the Buna-Werke . . .

'This cocksucker was mixing sand with the engine grease,' said Rupprecht Strunck (a very slightly gross old party, if we're perfectly honest about it). 'To screw the gears.'

'Wirtschaftssabotage!' I lithely interjected.

'And they'd weakened the rivets,' said Suitbert. 'So they'd pop. They also skewed the pressure gauges. False readings.'

'Christ knows the extent of it,' said Strunck. 'There must be dozens of the shitpigs, with a coordinator on the floor. And there must be a mole. Inside Farben.'

'How do we know that?' asked Fritz.

Suitbert explained. The evildoers only tampered with equipment that was a long way away from 'first use'. So by the time you deployed this or that piece of machinery, and the thing jammed, stalled, collapsed, or exploded, nobody had any idea who'd put it together. Strunck said,

'They've got a fucking calendar of 1st use. Someone's given them a fucking calendar.'

I smartly said, 'Burckl!'

'*No*, Paul,' said Fritz. 'Burckl was just a sap. Never a traitor.'

'And has the apprehended culprit been interrogated?' I inquired.

'Oh yes. He spent all last night with Horder. Nothing yet.'

'A Jew I suppose.'

'No. An Englishman. An NCO called Jenkins. We've got him in the crouchbox for now. Then Off will have a go. Then Entress with the scalpel. See how he likes that.' Fritz stood, stacking his papers. 'Not a whisper of this to anyone. Not a whisper to Farben, Doktor Seedig, Standartenfuhrer Strunck. Sit on your hands, mein Kommandant. Understood, Paul? And for the love of God, *don't* go blabbing to *Prufer*.'

Of course the girls are dying to trot around on that little wreck Meinrad, but he's got *curb* now and can hardly walk. Nor, for some time, have we been able to depend on the weekly ministrations of Tierpfleger Seisser! Ach. Now we just get the odd visit from Bent Suchanek, the schludrig muleskinner loosely attached to the Equestrian Academy.

She was a rare bird, a Judin Prominent in the SS-Hygienic Institute (the SS-HI), 1 of several prisoner doctors who, under close super-vision of course, did lab work on bacteriology and experimental sera. Unlike the Ka Be (an indigent hospice or holding pound) and unlike Block 10 (a free-for-all of castrations and hysterecto-mies), the SS-HI bore quite persuasive resemblances to an estab-lishment devoted to medicine. I went there for the introductory chat, but for our 2nd meeting I had her over to a quiet stockroom in the MAB.

'Please sit.'

A Polish–German, her name was Miriam Luxemburg (and her mother was said to be a niece of Rosa Luxemburg, the famous Marxist 'intellectual'), and she'd been with us for 2 years. Now women do not on the whole age gracefully in the KL – but it's chiefly complete lack of food that does that (and even hunger, chronic hunger, can wipe away all the feminine essences in 6 or 7 months). Dr Luxemburg looked about 50, and was probably about 30; but it wasn't malnutrition that had reduced her hair to a kind of mould and turned her lips outside in. She had some flesh on her and, moreover, seemed tolerably clean.

'For security reasons it'll have to be done around midnight,' I said. 'You'll bring your own gear of course. What else'll you need?'

'Clean towels and plenty of boiling water, sir.'

'You're just going to give her a preparation, aren't you? You know, 1 of those tube pills they talk about.'

'There are no tube pills, sir. The procedure will be dilation and curettage.'

'Well, whatever you have to do. Oh by the way,' I said. 'It's possible that the directive may be subject to change.' I spoke, as it were, conjecturally. 'Yes, the orders from Berlin may quite possibly undergo modification.'

My initial offer of 6 bread rations having been dismissed with some hauteur, I now passed along a paper bag containing 2 sleeves of Davidoffs, and there would be 2 more to follow: 800 cigarettes. She intended, I knew, to expend this capital on her brother, who was struggling, somewhat, in a penal Kommando in the uranium mines beyond Furstengrube.

'Modified in what way, sir?'

'The Chancellery may yet opt', I explained, 'for a slightly different outcome. Wherein the procedure does not go well. From the patient's point of view.'

'Meaning?'

'Meaning, sir.'

'Meaning, sir?'

'There would be a further 800 Davidoffs. Of course.'

'Meaning, sir?'

'Sodium evipan. Or phenol. A simple cardiac injection . . . Oh, stare not so, "Doktor". You've selected, haven't you. You've done selections. You've separated out.'

'That has sometimes been asked of me, yes, sir.'

'And you've disposed of live births,' I said. 'There's no point in denying it. We all know it happens.'

'That has sometimes been asked of me, yes, sir.'

'Quite heroic in a way. Secret deliveries. You risk death.'

She didn't reply. For she risked death every day, every hour, just by being what she was. Yes, I thought: that'll put a few bags under your eyes and a few notches on your mouth. I gave her an interrogative stare, and she gulped and said,

'As a student, as an intern, I had such very different things in mind. Sir.'

'No doubt you did. Well, you're not a student now. Come on. What's 1 jab?'

232

'But I don't know how to do that, sir. The cardiac injection. The phenol.'

I came close to suggesting that she walk down the corridor, at the SS-HI, and put in some practice – it was called 'Room 2' and they did about 60 per day.

'It's easy, isn't it? Perfectly straightforward, I'm told. 5th rib space. All you need's a long syringe. It's easy.'

'It's easy. All right, sir. You do it.'

For a moment I turned away in thought . . . My earlier dialectic, as regards Alisz Seisser, had, in the end (after much to and fro), gone as follows: why take a chance? But the alternative wasn't free of hazard either; and there'd be the usual sullen intractability of the corpse. I said,

'Now now. Most likely the Chancellery will adhere to its original adjudication. I'm pretty sure there'll be no change of plan. Boiling water, eh?'

I suppose too that I wanted to bind her to me. For insurance, obviously. But now we are beginning to think about the exploration of darkness, we may say that I wanted her to come with me, out of the light.

'When can I assess the patient, sir?'

'What, beforehand? No, I'm afraid that's impossible.' This was literally true: there were guards down there, witnesses down there. 'You'll have to do her sight unseen.'

'Age?'

'29. She says. But you know how women are. Oh yes – I almost forgot. Is it painful?'

'Without at least a topical anaesthetic? Yes, sir. Very.'

'Mm. Oh well. We'd better have a topical anaesthetic then. You see, we can't have her making much noise.'

Miriam said she'd need money for that. 20 US, if you please. I had only 1s; I started counting them out, employing mental arithmetic.

'1, 2, 3. Your uh, great-aunt,' I said with ½ a smile. '4, 5, 6.'

Back in Rosenheim, during my Leninist period (ever a dreamer!), I used to puzzle with my future wife over the chief Luxemburgian oeuvre, *The Accumulation of Capital* (and Lenin, despite her criticisms of his use of terror, did once call her 'an eagle'). In early 1919, just after the pathetic failure of the German Revolution, Luxemburg was arrested by a Freikorps unit in Berlin, not my Rossbach boys but a pack of hooligans under the nominal command of old Walli Pabst . . .

'10, 11, 12. Rosa Luxemburg. They clubbed her to the floor and shot her in the head and threw her body in the Landwehr Canal. 18, 19, 20. And how many languages did she speak?'

'5.' Miriam straightened her gaze. 'This procedure, sir. The sooner the better. That's axiomatic.'

'Well. She's not showing,' I said (my mind was made up). 'She seemed fit enough the last time I saw her.' And it's good, not using Parisians. I expressively crinkled my nose and said, 'I think we'll leave it a bit.'

Szmul was bringing his expertise to bear on 1 of the new installations, namely Crema 4: 5 3-retorters (capacity: 2,000 per 24 hours). This particular facility had proved to be a major pain right from the start. After 2 weeks the rear funnel wall collapsed; and when we got it going again it lasted a mere 8 days before Szmul pronounced it 'burnt out'. 8 days!

'The firebricks got loose again, sir. And fell into the duct between the oven and the chimney. There's nowhere for the flames to go.'

'Shoddy workmanship,' I said.

'Poor materials, sir. The clay's been qualified. See the discoloured veins?'

'Wartime economies, Sonder. I take it 2 and 3 are holding the fort?'

'At ½ volume, sir.'

'Good God. What do I tell Communications? That I'm refusing transports? Ach, back to the pits, I suppose. And more Crap from Air Defence. Tell me . . .'

The Sonderkommandofuhrer straightened up. He shut the grate with his foot and slid the lateral bolt on the oven door. Some distance apart, we stood in the grey gloom of the vault, with its low ceiling, its caged lights, its echoes.

'Tell me, Sonder. Does it feel different? Knowing your uh – time of departure?'

'Yes, sir.'

'Of course it does. April 30th. Where are we now? The 6th. No, the 7th. So. 23 days to Walpurgisnacht.'

He took an indescribably filthy rag from his pocket and set about scouring his fingernails.

'I'm not expecting you to confide in me, Sonder. But is there anything . . . positive about it? About knowing?'

'Yes, sir. In a way.'

'Calmer and all that. More resigned. Well I'm sorry to be a killjoy. You may not relish your last duty. You may not exactly warm to the final service you'll render me. And render the Reich.'

And I gave him his assignment.

'You lower your head. You look downhearted. Take comfort, Sonder! You'll be saving your Kommandant no end of trouble. And as for your poor little conscience, well, you won't have to "live with yourself" for very long. About 10 seconds, I'd say. At the most.' I rubbed my hands together. 'Now. What are you going to use? Get your bag . . . What's this? What's this fucking *spear* here? Mm. A kind of marlinspike with a handle. Good. It'll go up your sleeve. Try it . . . All right. Now put it back.'

I made a motion. We climbed up from the basement and walked down a tunnel covered in sheets of creaking, whistling tin.

'Oh, we know where your wife is, Sonder.'

Actually, and annoyingly, this had ceased to be the case; Pani Szmul was no longer to be found in the attic above the bakery at number 4 Tlomackie Street. And when the kitchen foreman was brought in for questioning he confessed that he'd had a hand in getting her out of the ghetto – her and her brother. They were heading south. No mystery there: Hungary, where the Jews, apart from the odd razzia and massacre, were just 2nd-class citizens (and weren't even badged). And this despite the personal guarantee of President Chaim Rumkowski. Most scandalously of all (I can't get over this), most scandalously of all (I *really* can't get over this), it happened right under the noses, *right under the noses* of the Uberwachungsstelle zur Bekampfung des Schleichhandels und der Preiswucherei im judischen Wohnbezirk! And *how* much money did I disperse? I said,

'Halt.'

Na, I wasn't really discouraged. Shulamith's flit was only a theoretical or platonic reverse: the threat would still hold; the charm was still firm and good. Having taken the trouble to locate the woman, though, I found it an aesthetic irritation, somehow, to think of her strolling scot-free down the boulevards of Budapest.

'Well, Sonderkommandofuhrer. Until the 30th. Walpurgisnacht, nicht?'

Mobius took a pull on his drink. He wiped his mouth on a serviette. He sighed and said quietly,

'That cabal of little hens. Norberte Uhl, Suzi Erkel, Hannah Doll. Hannah Doll, Paul.'

'Ach.'

'Defeatism. Frivolity. Enemy radio – that's clear enough from the things they say. Now, *Paul*, I had a word with Drogo Uhl, and Norberte's kept her trap shut ever since. Likewise with Olbricht and Suzi. I had a word with *you* and . . .'

'Ach.'

'Now I didn't say this before but you can't not know that your whole . . . position here is dangling by a thread. And there's Hannah beaming and glowing at every little snippet of bad news. And you're the Kommandant! If things don't change and change soon I'll have to report it to Prinz Albrecht Strasse. I ask again. I mean it's pretty basic, isn't it? Can you, or can you not, control your wife?'

'Ach.'

I'd decided to get to bed at a prudent hour, and I was lying there curled up with the pre-war bestseller, *Die judische Weltpest: Judendammerung auf dem Erdball.*

The door swung open. Hannah. Naked but for her highest high heels. And made up to the 9s. She advanced and stood over me. She reached down and took my hair in both hands. She ground my face roughly and painfully into the brambles of her Busch, with such force that she split both my lips, then released me with a flourish of contempt. I opened my eyes, and saw the vertical beads of her Ruckgrat, the twin curves of her Taille, the great oscillating hemispheres of her Arsch.

He plays with his Viper, he plays and he plays. He plays with his viper, he plays and he plays. Darkness is a master from Germany. Look around: see how it all leaps alive – where death is! Alive!

3. SZMUL: A SIGN

It won't be this week. It won't even be next week. It won't even be the week after. It will be the week after that.

And I was ready for it. But I am not ready for this; and I should have been.

Somebody will one day come to the ghetto or the Lager and account for the near-farcical *assiduity* of the German hatred.

And I would start by asking – why were we conscripted, why were we impressed, in the drive towards our own destruction?

One day in December 1940 my wife came back from the textile plant to the small unheated room we shared with three other families – and she said to me,

'I have spent the last twelve hours dyeing uniforms white. For use on the eastern front. And who do I do this for?'

Pauperised, frozen, famished, imprisoned, enslaved, and terrorised, she was working on behalf of the forces that had bombed, shelled, strafed, and looted her city, flattened her house, and killed her father, her grandmother, two uncles, three aunts, and seventeen cousins.

There it is, you see. The Jews can only prolong their lives by helping the enemy to victory – a victory that for the Jews means what?

Nor should we forget my silent sons, Schol and Chaim, and their contribution to the war effort – the war against the Jews.

I am choking, I am drowning. This pencil and these scraps of paper aren't enough. I need colours, sounds – oils and orchestras. I need something more than words.

*

238

We are in the dank black sepulchre under Crematory IV. Doll stands there with his gun in one hand and a cigar in the other; he smooths his eyebrow with a little finger.

'All right. Let's practise your thrust. Let the weapon drop down out of your sleeve and into your hand. And spear that sack there. As fast as you can . . . Very *good*, Sonder. I think you've had a bit or practice already, ne? Listen. To repeat. They will come for Shulamith Zachariasz at noon on May the first. Unless I counter-mand my order that morning by telephone. So it's very simple. And very elegant.'

He steps forward and leans into me, chin to chin, saying bright-eyed in a spray of spittle,

'Walpurgisnacht, nicht? *Walpurgisnacht. Nicht? Nicht? Yech? Nicht? Yech? Nicht. Walpurgisnacht* . . . Sonder, the only way you can keep your wife alive', he said, 'is by killing mine. Klar?'

The earth obeys the laws of physics, turning on its axis and describing its loop round the sun. So the days pass, the land thaws, the air warms . . .

It is midnight on the spur. The transport has made good time from the camp in unoccupied France. Each boxcar was equipped with a keg of water and, even more unusually, a child's potty. The selection is beginning, and the queue, winding down the entire length of the platform (traced by the white glow of the reflectors), remains orderly. Some of the floodlights are dimmed or have their faces averted; there is calm, and a soft breeze. A sudden flock of swallows dips and climbs.

They recast you (I am muttering to myself), they recast you in their own image, they recast you as if on a blacksmith's work-slab, and, having battered you into a different shape, they grease you with their fluids, they smear you with themselves . . .

I realise I am staring at a family of four: a woman of about twenty with an infant in her arms, flanked by a man of about thirty and another woman of about forty. It is really too late to intervene; and if there is the slightest commotion I will die tonight and Shulamith will die on May Day. And yet, eerily impelled, I approach, touch the man's shoulder, draw him aside, and say as meaningly as I've ever said anything,

'*Monsieur, prenez le garçon et donnez–le à sa grand-mère. S'il vous plaît, Monsieur. Croyez moi. Croyez moi. Celui n'est pas jeune?*' I shook my head. '*Les mères ayant des enfants?*' I shook my head. '*Que pouvez-vous y perdre?*'

After several minutes of troubled hesitation he does as I say. And, when their turn comes, Professor Entress selects two, and not one, to the right.

So I delay a death – the death of *la femme*. I have, for now, saved a wife. More than this, for the first time in fifteen months I have suffered a man to look into my eyes. I take this as a *sign*.

It is not today. It is not even tomorrow. It is the day after that.

I am in the empty changing room at the Little Brown Bower. There will again be a very long delay caused by the handlers of the Zyklon B, who are both incapacitated by drugs or alcohol and will have to be replaced.

We are awaiting a transport from Hamburg, the SS and I.

The undressing area looks businesslike with its hooks and benches, its signs in all the languages of Europe; and the hosed-down gas chamber has resumed its imitation of a shower room, with nozzles (but with no drains set into the floor).

Here they come. They are filing in now, and my Sonders move among them.

An Unterscharfuhrer hands me a note from Lagerfuhrer Prufer. It says:

20 Wagons (approx. 90 in each) out of Hamburg. Stop at Warsaw: additional 2 Wagons. Total: 22 Wagons. 1,980 Settlers minus 10% found fit for work = 1,782 approx.

I see a boy, who is clearly alone, walking strangely and painfully. He is club-footed – and his surgical boot will have been left in the stack on the platform, along with all the other trusses and braces and prostheses.

'Witold?' I say. 'Witold.'

He looks up at me, and after a moment of emptiness his face flares with gratitude and relief.

'Mr Zachariasz! Where's Chaim? I went looking for him.'

'Went looking for him where?'

'At the bakery. It's shut. It's boarded up. I asked next door and they said Chaim went ages ago. With you and Schol.'

'And his mother? His mother? Pani Zachariasz?'

'They said she went too.'

'On a transport?'

'No. Walking. Her brother took her. Mr Zachariasz, I got arrested! At the station. For vagrancy. Pawiak Prison! We thought they were going to shoot us but they changed their minds. Is Chaim here?'

'Yes, he's here,' I say. 'Witold, come with me. Come on. Come.'

It is spring in the birch wood. The silver bark is peeling; the brisk wind frees droplets of moisture from the papery leaves.

I give the Kapo, Krebbs, a meaning look and say *with the authority the German power has invested in me*, 'Kannst du mich mal zwei Minuten entbehren?'

With my hand on his arm I lead Witold down the path lined with flowerpots to the white wicket gate. I stand in front of him and hold his shoulders and say,

'Yes, Chaim's here. With his brother. They're working in the home farm. In the fields. With any luck you'll get the same job. They're big boys now. They've grown.'

'What about my boot? I'll be needing my boot for the fields.'

'All the luggage will be waiting at the guest house.'

A sound makes me look up: Doll's staff car, its flabby bald tyres slithering furiously in the mud. I gesture to Krebbs.

'You'll get cheese sandwiches straight away, and then there'll be a hot meal later on. I'll have Chaim come and find you.'

'Oh, that'd be good.'

And those are his last words.

'What was going on there?' asks Doll as he watches the body being dragged behind the ambulance.

'A troublemaker, sir. He kept asking for his surgical boot.'

'His surgical boot. Yes, I could tell there was something *wrong* with him. Friday at six, Sonder. In the garden. As night falls.'

I flinch as a bird flies so low that I see its huge shadow sweep across my chest. 'As night falls, sir.'

From 1934 to 1937 Witold Trzeciak and my Chaim were as close as twins. They spent every weekend together, either in his house or our house (and sleeping, at the slightest excuse – a frightening story, a black cat glimpsed under a ladder, Halloween, or indeed Walpurgis Night – in the same single bed).

In 1938 his parents divorced, and Witold became a grimly intrepid little commuter between Łódź (father) and Warsaw (mother). He went on doing this until well after the invasion. In 1939 Witold was twelve.

Now he falls as if in a swoon. Krebbs steps back. It takes Witold less than a minute to die. About twenty seconds pass, and he is gone. There are fewer things to say goodbye to, there is less life, less love (perhaps), and less memory needing to be scattered.

It is not tomorrow, it is not even the day after. It is the day after that.

CHAPTER VI. WALPURGIS NIGHT

I. THOMSEN: GROFAZ

Any interest I might have had in the cosmic-ice theory came to an end after four or five pages of 'The Theory of the Cosmic Ice'; similarly, I satisfied myself about the thrust of volkisch Cultural Research after four or five minutes in the Ahnenerbe. So even if you included the massive handwritten exercise in hypocritical impartiality and rigour, my business in the capital was well and truly over by the last week of February.

All through the rain and wind of March I grew increasingly desperate to return to the Kat Zet. This tearing impatience did not centre on Hannah Doll (that situation, I hoped, was more or less static). No, I was in another kind of quandary: it had to do with the tempo of the Buna-Werke and the tempo of the war.

And what was keeping me? The indefinite but non-optional appointment with the Reichsleiter. Uncle Martin, at that time, seemed to be spending his entire life in the troposphere, as he shuttled between Alpine Bavaria and East Prussia, between the Eagle's Nest and the Wolf's Lair . . . Seven, eight, nine meetings were arranged, and then cancelled, by the trusted spinster Wibke Mundt – secretary to the Sekretar.

'It's this new interest of his, dear,' she said on the phone. 'He's deeply engrossed.'

'What in, Wibke?'

'It's the new craze. Diplomacy. He's been going round with all these Magyars.'

She talked on. Uncle Martin's remit was Hungary – the question of Hungary and her Jews.

'I'm sorry, dear. I know you're chafing. You'll just have to sit back and enjoy Berlin.'

———

Unlike Cologne, Hamburg, Bremen, Munich, and Mainz (together with the whole of the Ruhrgebiet), Berlin was still in one piece. There had been dozens of nuisance raids in late '40 and early '41; then these tapered off, and there was nothing at all in '42. But everyone knew for a certainty that pretty soon the sky would be black with planes.

And it happened, after the Day of the Luftwaffe (parades, march pasts, grand ceremonies): on the night of March 1/2 came the first multi-squadron bombardment. Sirens woke me (three solid chords followed by a skirling howl); I lackadaisically donned my dressing gown and went and joined the drinks party in the Eden wine cellars. Ninety minutes later the decadent levity suddenly evaporated, and it seemed that a blind, stumbling, block-straddling giant was trudging its way towards us, with a prehistoric thunderclap at every footstep; just as we were wondering *how* we were going to die (atomised, scorched, crushed, smothered, drowned), Brobdingnag or Blunderbore just as suddenly lurched and veered and went crashing off to the east.

Hundreds dead, thousands injured, perhaps a hundred thousand homeless, and a million gaunt and horrified faces. Underfoot, an endless carpet of crackling glass, and overhead a fume-laden, sulphur-yellow sky. The war was finally coming home to the place where it started – coming home to the Wilhelmstrasse.

Something was already very wrong with the city, something was already very wrong with the movements and dispositions on the streets. After half an hour you realised what it was: there were no young men. You saw lightly guarded knots of bowed work crews (labourers from subjugated lands), and municipal police, and SS; but otherwise there were no young men.

No young men, except for those on crutches or in handcarts or rickshaws. And when you ventured down the steps to the pubs of the Potsdamer Platz, you noticed all the empty sleeves and empty trouserlegs (and, of course, all the smashed faces).

At night in the corridors of the hotel you saw lines of what seemed at first sight to be amputated limbs – jackboots, left out for shoeshine.

———

'May I start with an attempt at perspective? It's been much on my mind.'

'Yes, sir, please do.'

'. . . The crime without a name began, let's say, on the thirty-first of July, '41, at the zenith of Nazi power. The letter drafted by Eichmann and Heydrich and sent to Goring, who returned it with his signature. The Fuhrer's "wish" – for a *total* solution. The letter said in effect, All month we have been assembling the manpower in the east. You have the authority. Begin.'

'For full-scale . . . ?'

'Well, they were perhaps still thinking they'd just dump them somewhere cold and barren – *after* the quick win over Russia. Somewhere beyond the Urals and up in the Arctic Circle. Extermination the long way round. But there was pressure from below – a kind of extremism contest among the plenipotentiaries in Poland. You've gone and annexed an extra three million Jews, mein Fuhrer. We can't cope with the numbers. Well? By August/ September, as the territorial answer receded – another push on the levers. The moral breakthrough had been made. And what was it, Thomsen? Killing not just the men, which they'd been doing for months, but the women and the children.'

245

March 29. Konrad Peters in the Tiergarten – the garden of beasts – with its black boles and the icing of smoky dew on the grass . . . Professor Peters was even more senior, in both senses, and even more formidable than I remembered. Short, vast, and the shape of a rugby ball, with bow tie and richly colourful waistcoat, thick spectacles, and a huge frown-riven pate that was by now almost flawlessly bald. He looked like a dandified giant cut off at the legs. I said,

'They claim there's a rationale for the children, don't they, sir?'

'Yes. Those babes in arms will grow up and want revenge on the Nazis in about 1963. I suppose the rationale for the women under forty-five is that they might be pregnant. And the rationale for the older women is *while we're at it.*'

He rocked to a halt and for a moment seemed out of breath. I looked away. Then he flung his head back and marched on.

'People, people like you and me, Thomsen, we wonder at the industrial nature of it, the modernity of it. And understandably so. It's very striking. But the gas chambers and the crematories are just epiphenomena. The idea was to speed things up, and *economise* of course, and to spare the nerves of the killers. The killers . . . those slender reeds. But bullets and pyres would've done it in the end. They had the will.'

The pathways of the Tiergarten were dotted with other amblers and wanderers, in groups of two or three, bent in donnish converse; this was the capital's equivalent of Hyde Park in London, with its Speakers' Corner (though everyone here spoke not in shouts but in whispers). Peters said,

'It's known that the Einsatzgruppen have already killed well over a million with bullets. They would've got there – with bullets. Imagine. Millions of women and children. With bullets. They had the will.'

I asked him, 'What d'you think . . . happened to us? Or to them?'

He said, 'It is still happening. Something quite eerie and alien. I wouldn't call it supernatural, but only because I don't believe in the supernatural. It *feels* supernatural. They had the will? Where did they get it from? Their aggression has sulphur in it. A real whiff of hellfire. Or maybe, or *maybe* it's quite human and plain and simple.'

'I'm sorry, sir, but how could it be?'

'Maybe all this is just what follows when you keep putting it about that cruelty is a virtue. To be rewarded like any other virtue – with preferment and power. I don't know. The appetite for death . . . In every direction. Forced abortions, sterilisations. Euthanasia – tens of thousands. The appetite for death is truly Aztec. Saturnian.'

'So modernity and . . .'

'Modern, even futuristic. Like the Buna-Werke was supposed to be – the biggest and most advanced plant in Europe. That, mixed with something incredibly ancient. Going back to when we were all mandrills and baboons.'

'Decided on, you said, at the zenith of their power. And now?'

'It will be prosecuted and perhaps completed in the colic of defeat. They know they've lost.'

'Yes,' I said. 'Berlin. The mood's completely changed, it's all flipped. Defeat is so palpable.'

'Mm. Guess what everyone's calling him now. After Africa. After Tunisgrad. Grofaz.'

'Grofaz.'

'A sort of acronym. Greatest field marshal of all time. It's just childish German sarcasm – not bad expressively, though. *Grofaz* . . . It's all changed. No more straight-arm salutes. It's Guten Tag and Gruss Gott. Making scores of millions of Germans yell out your name thirty times a day, by law. The name of that oster-reichisch *guttersnipe* . . . Well, the spell is broken. Our ten-year Walpurgisnacht is coming to an end.'

The branches of the trees were growing downy with green,

and would soon be giving the place its usual deep shadows. I asked him how long it would take.

'He won't stop. Not till Berlin looks like Stalingrad. I suppose the resistance might manage to kill him.'

'You mean the Vons – the colonels.'

'Yes, the Junker colonels. But they keep arguing among themselves about the make-up of the government-in-waiting. A laughable waste of time and energy. As if the Allies'll put another crew of *Germans* in charge. Prussians at that. Meanwhile, our petty-bourgeois Antichrist is keeping a lid on things – *by means*', said Peters, in English, '*of the nation's nineteen guillotines.*'

I said, 'Then why all the sour satisfaction? I can't get over how pleased everyone looks.'

'They feel Schadenfreude even for themselves.' He halted again, and said with a sympathetic look, 'Everyone's pleased, Thomsen. Everyone except you.'

And I told him why. I didn't attempt to vivify it; I didn't say that every other time I closed my eyes I saw a flesh-coated skeleton pegged out on the whipping horse.

'So Grofaz and Rupprecht Strunck, between them, have exposed me as a Schreibtischtater.' A writing-table perpetrator – a *desk murderer*. 'And for nothing.'

Peters scowled and raised a horizontal finger at me. 'No, it's not for nothing, Thomsen. The stakes are still enormous. Buna and synthetic fuel wouldn't win the war but they'd prolong it. And with every day that goes by . . .'

'That's what I keep telling myself, sir. Still.'

'Events will put a brake on your Herr Strunck, believe me. Very soon they'll *only* be killing the women and the children. Because they'll need the men for labour. So cheer up, eh? Look on the bright side. Shall I tell you the question that's hanging in the air?'

'If you would.'

'Who are they killing the Jews *for*? *Cui bono*? Who will wallow in the fruits of a judenfrei Europe? Who will bask in its sun? Not the Reich. There won't *be* a Reich . . .'

Just for a moment I thought of Hannah – and the unities, and what war does to them. Peters smiled and said,

'You know the people Grofaz hates most – now? Because they failed him? Germans. You watch. After he's chased out of Russia, all his efforts will be in the west. He wants the Russians to get here first. So hunker down.'

I shook his hand and I said I was grateful for his time and trouble.

He shrugged. 'Kruger? Well, now we're almost there.'

'I'm pretty sure I'll learn more. My uncle, he can't resist a good story. In which case I'll certainly . . .'

'Yes, do. I keep thinking – Leipzig, January '34. That's where and when the Dutch pyromaniac parted company with his head.' He gave a snort. 'Our Viennese visionary had his heart set on the rope. More demeaning that way. He was appalled to learn that there hasn't been a judicial hanging in Germany since the eighteenth century.' Peters gestured: in the distance, the creamy dome of the gutted and abandoned Reichstag. 'Leipzig, January '34. Do you think Dieter Kruger might've had something to do with the Fire?'

———

Wibke Mundt was a compulsive smoker – in an hour she could brim a whole ashtray with butts of brown. She was also a compulsive cougher and retcher. A full month had passed, and I now sat in her office at the Chancellery (on a bomb-damaged but efficiently repaired Wilhelmstrasse) . . . I was numbly watching the movements of another, more junior secretary, a soft-faced blonde called Heidi Richter. With abstract admiration I noted the way she leaned sideways, bent forward, crouched down, straightened up . . . During these months in town I had played the part of the privileged ascetic,

249

strolling the working-class suburbs of Friedrichshain and Wedding in the afternoons, dining early and sparely at the hotel (fowl, pasta, and other unrationed items, occasionally including oysters and lobster) before going back up to my room (where, at some personal risk, I read the likes of Thomas Mann). There were three or four Berlin girls with whom I had what we called 'understandings'; yet I let them be. Boris would have ridiculed my earnestness, but I felt that I had gained some emotional or even moral capital, and that I didn't want to deplete it, I didn't want to start living off it. And I was the man who, not so long ago, had known coition with the murderess Ilse Grese . . .

'Liebling, it's no use you pacing about,' said Wibke. 'He'll be a while yet. Here, have a cup of this filthy coffee.'

A wait within a wait: I had arrived at noon, and it was now twenty to three. So I looked again at the two letters I picked up when I settled my vast bill at the Eden.

As a supplement to his despairing weekly report, Suitbert Seedig enclosed a confidential addendum about the latest doings of Rupprecht Strunck. Strunck had abolished unverzuglich – working at the double. Now the Haftlinge were working at the treble: working at a sprint. The Main Yard, as Seedig put it, was *like an antheap in the middle of a forest fire*.

The other letter, dated April 19, was from Boris Eltz (a decidedly lax correspondent, it has to be said). Much of this was in a kind of code. What the censors wanted to hear was nearly always the exact opposite of the truth, so, for example, when Boris wrote, *I've heard that the young teetotaller is soon to be promoted for his superb efficiency and the truly exemplary burnish of his ethics*, I knew that the Old Boozer was soon to be demoted for gross incompetence and hyperactive venality.

Of Hannah he said, *I saw her at the Uhls' on Jan 30 and at the Dolls' on Mar 23.*

These must have been gangrenous occasions. January 30 was the tenth anniversary of the seizure of power; and on March 23 of the same winter the Enabling Act was passed, dissolving the constitutional state – the Law, as they called it, for the Alleviation of the People's and the Reich's Misery . . .

Boris ended his letter as follows.

At both of these receptions your friend caused our political officer to rebuke her for not falling in with the prevailing mood. She was decidedly gloomy, while everyone else, of course, scenting victory, was euphoric with nationalist fire!

To be serious, brother. I've been let out six weeks early: my time among the Austrians is at an end. Tonight and with a full heart I begin my journey to the east. Don't worry. I will fight to the death to ensure that Angelus Thomsen goes on being attractive to Aryan women. And you, my love, will do *everything in your power* to protect the blue-eyed, golden-haired 'Theres', our contrarian from the High Tatras.

As always, B.

'Heidi,' said Wibke, 'would you kindly direct Obersturmfuhrer Thomsen to the small dining room?'

————

Though not to be seriously compared with the big dining room (that atrium of a banqueting hall), the small dining room was a big dining room, its thirty-foot airspace struggling to contain many tons of crystal chandelier. I took a seat at the rectangular table and was served a cup of real coffee and a glass of Benedictine. The air was full of tobacco smoke and existential unhappiness, and a tall, fat, hot man in a tight morning suit and wing collar was reading at enormous inner cost from a sheet of paper, sweating freely as he said in fluent, formal German,

251

'We give you our warmest thanks for your typically Teutonic hospitality, Herr Reichsleiter. Our memories will especially cosset the magnificent views at the famous Eagle's Nest, the splendid performance of Richard Wagner's *Tristan und Isolde* in Salzburg, the guided tour of Munich with its poignant ceremony at the Temple of Martyrs, and, last but by no means least, the lavish repast at your own demesne in Pullach, with your beautiful children and your gracious and graceful wife. For all this, together with our stay in the glorious imperium of your capital, Herr Reichsleiter, from the bottom of our hearts we tender our—'

'Gern geschehen, gern geschehen. Now to reality,' said the Sekretar.

Looking especially eager and amused, Uncle Martin cleared his throat and straightened up in his chair. Then with dutiful if slightly inconvenienced smiles at the translator he went on,

'Berlin is eager to strengthen its stout bond with Budapest . . . Now that you're behaving like an ally again and not like a neutral . . . That's settled. On to the other matter . . . You know very well that we deplored the removal of Prime Minister Bárdossy, and we are frankly consternated . . . by the policies of Prime Minister Kállay . . . As things stand, Hungary is a veritable paradise' – ein Paradies auf Erden – 'for the Jews . . . Every hooknose' – jeder Hakennase – 'in Europe positively thirsts to penetrate your borders . . . We blush, gentlemen, we *blush*' – wir *erroten* – 'when we ponder your conception of national security! . . .'

Uncle Martin looked pityingly from face to face. A darkly bearded man of perhaps ministerial rank took a green handkerchief from his top pocket and with adolescent richness blew his nose.

'As an immediate gesture of good faith, you are asked to introduce certain measures *in accord* with the jurisprudence of the Reich . . . First, confiscation of all wealth . . . Second, exclusion from any form of cultural and economic activity . . . And third, the imposition of the Star . . . They are then to be concentrated and quarantined. Dispatch' – Absendung – 'must in due course follow . . . I come, sirs, from the Wolfsschanze itself! . . . Solemnly I am charged to deliver a personal salute to Regent Horthy.' He raised an index card and said with a smile, 'To uh, His Serene Highness the Regent of the Kingdom of Hungary . . . Who, when he blessed us with a visit just a couple of weeks ago . . . seemed strangely impervious to our recommendations . . . A salute, then, and also a promise . . . Even if you compel us to utilise the Wehrmacht, we will be having your Jews . . . We will be having your Jews. Klar? Das ist klar?'

'Yes, Herr Reichsleiter.'

'Now you stay there, Neffe, while I see our dignitaries to their motorcade.'

He returned in less than a minute. Dismissing the servants, and retaining the liqueur, Uncle Martin drank a glass standing up and said,

'There's nothing like it, you know, Golo. Telling whole nations what to do.' He took the chair beside me and asked simply, 'Well?'

I told him I'd compiled a long report, and added, 'But let me just say that it's open-and-shut.'

'Summarise, please.'

The cosmic-ice theory, Onkel (I began), also known as the World Ice Principle, holds that the earth was created when a frozen comet the size of Jupiter collided with the sun. During the trillennia of winter that followed, the first Aryans were cautiously moulded and formed. Thus, Onkel, only the inferior races are descended from the great apes. The Nordic peoples were cryogenically preserved from the dawn of terrestrial time – on the lost continent of Atlantis.

'. . . Lost how?'

'Submerged, Onkel.'

'And that's it?'

'Pretty much. It's a curious place, the Ahnenerbe. The cosmic-ice theory isn't the only thing they're trying to prove. They're trying to prove that the Missing Link wasn't an early human but some kind of bear. And that the ancient Greeks were Scandinavians. And that Christ wasn't Jewish.'

'What was he then? Is it *all* like that?'

'An Amorite. No, they do some excellent work, and they're well worth their million a year.'

Yes, I thought – worth every penny. The fact that the Ahnenerbe's employees were considered 'war essential', exempting them from military service, was militarily neither here nor there: not one of them would have passed a medical; not one of them, I sometimes thought, would have *survived* a medical. These certified Aryans had misbegotten faces that seemed to have been dreamt up by misbegotten minds – pop-eyed, buck-toothed, slobber-mouthed, slope-chinned, their noses red and runny. Most were hack researchers or semi-professional hobbyists. I once got a glimpse of the 'anatomy pavilion': a severed head boiling in a glass bowl above the Bunsen burners, a jarful of pickled testicles. The Studiengesellschaft fur Geistesurgeschichte – a waxworks, a dream disarray of charts and body parts, of calipers, abacuses, dandruff, and drool . . .

'But it's mostly propaganda. That's where its value lies, Onkel. Stoking up nationalism. And justifying conquests. Poland's just part of aboriginal Germania – that kind of thing. But the other stuff? All right, tell me this. The cosmic-ice theory – what does Speer think of it?'

'Speer? He doesn't even stoop to give an opinion. He's a technician. He thinks it's all shit.'

'And he's *right*. Distance yourself, Onkel. The Reichsfuhrer and the Reichsmarschall can gain nothing but ridicule by supporting it. Forget the cosmic-ice theory. And move against Speer. What's he got?'

Uncle Martin refilled the glasses. 'Well, Neffe, in February he claimed that he'd doubled war production in just under a year. And it's true. That's what he's got.'

'Which is precisely the danger. You see what he's building, him and Saukel, Onkel? Speer wants what is obviously yours. The succession.'

'. . . The succession.'

'If, God forbid . . .'

'Mm. God forbid . . . It's all in hand, Neffe. The Gauleiter are with me. Of course they are. They're Party. So, you know – Speer orders a trainload of machine parts and my boys take half of it along the way. And I've planted Otto Saur and Ferdi Dorsch in his ministry. He'll be stymied at every turn, and all he can do is try and get close enough to the Chief to bore him about it. Speer's just another functionary now. He's not an artist. Not any more.'

'Good, Onkel. Good. I knew you wouldn't just sit there, sir, and be cheated out of what is rightfully yours.'

A little later, when I mentioned the time of my train, the Sekretar buzzed the car pool and announced that he would accompany me to the Ostbahnhof. In the courtyard I said,

'This door. Incredibly heavy.'

'Armour-plated, Golo. Chief's orders.'

'Better safe than sorry, eh Onkel?'

'Get in . . . See? A limousine that feels almost cramped. That's the price of power. So how was your New Year's Eve?'

'It was very nice. Tantchen and I sat in front of the fire till ten past twelve. Then we drank a toast to your health and sought our beds. How was yours?'

The crouched outriders sped forward to liberate the road ahead;

we sailed through the crossings against the light; and then the bikes surged past us once again. Uncle Martin shook his head, as if in disbelief, saying,

'Ten past twelve? Can you believe, Golo, I sat up till five in the morning. With the Chief. Three and three-quarter hours we had together. Have you ever seen him up close?'

'Of course, Onkel, but just the once. At your wedding.' That was in 1929 – when Gerda and I were both on the brink of our third decade. And the leader of the NSDAP looked so much like a pale, pouchy, and cruelly overworked head waiter that every civilian there, I felt, was trying very hard not to hand him a tip. 'Such charisma. I would never dare imagine any kind of uh, tête-à-tête.'

'You know, don't you, for years people were willing to give their eyesight for five *minutes* alone with the Chief? And I get nearly four hours. Just him and me. In the Wolf's Lair.'

'So romantic, Onkel.'

He laughed and said, 'It's a funny thing. When I uh, renewed my acquaintance with Krista Groos, for whom many thanks, I felt the same excitement. Not that I . . . Nothing of that kind. Just the same *level* of elation. Have you noticed, Golo, that redheads smell stronger?'

For a quarter of an hour Uncle Martin talked of his doings with Krista Groos. Whenever I looked out through the tinted windows I instinctively expected to see a stream of raised fists and rancorous faces. But no. Women, women, women, of every age, and busy, busy, busy, not with the old Berlin busyness (getting and spending), just busy living, trying to buy an envelope, a pair of shoelaces, a toothbrush, a tube of glue, a button. All their husbands, brothers, sons, and fathers were hundreds or perhaps thousands of miles away; and at least a million of them were already dead.

'I told you she was famous,' I said as the car pulled up behind the Poland Station.

'Justly celebrated, Golo. Justly celebrated. Mm, I've got you here early for a reason. Before you go I'm going to give you a little treat. The strange tale of Dieter Kruger. I shouldn't, of course. But it can't matter now.'

'Oh you are a sport, Onkel.'

'. . . On the night before his execution, we went on a little pilgrimage to Kruger's cell. Me and a few mates. And you'll never guess what we did.'

As the Sekretar was telling his story I wound down the window to taste the air. Yes, it was true. Like the Reichskanzler (much feared in this respect by all interlocutors, even Onkel), the city suffered from halitosis. Berlin had bad breath. This was because the food and the drink were being prepared, processed, and quite possibly invented by IG Farben (and Krupp, Siemens, Henkel, Flick, and the rest). Chemical bread, chemical sugar, chemical sausage, chemical beer, chemical wine. And what were the sequelae? Gases, botulism, scrofula, and boils. Where could you turn when even the soap and the toothpaste reeked? Yellow-eyed women were breaking wind openly now, but that was only half of it. They were farting through their mouths.

'On his bare chest!' concluded Uncle Martin with his juiciest smile. 'On his bare chest. Don't you think it's a scream?'

'That *is* hilarious, Onkel,' I said, feeling faint. 'As you promised – National Socialism at its most mordant.'

'Priceless. Priceless. God how we laughed.' He looked at his watch and went quiet for a moment. 'Bloody awful place, the Wolfsschanze. It's almost like a pocket KZ, except the walls are five metres thick. But the Chief – ach, the Chief's cooking up a nasty surprise for our friends in the east. Keep an eye on the Kursk salient. When the ground hardens. Operation Citadel, Neffe. You just keep your eye on the salient at Kursk.'

'I shall. Well, Onkel. It goes without saying that I'm eternally in your debt. Give my warmest love to Tantchen.'

He frowned and said, 'Your Hannah. I have no objection to the scale of her. On the contrary. Why d'you think I married Fraulein Gerda Buch? But her lips, Golo – Hannah's lips. They're too wide. They go all the way round to her ears.'

My shoulders hunched. 'It's a very pretty mouth.'

'Mm. Well I suppose it looks all right', he said, 'if you've got your cock in it. A joy as always, dear Golo. Take excellent care.'

————

Boris had gone to war with a full heart, and I too was gravid with emotion as I prepared to set out for my own front line in the east.

Express trains to and from Poland were never crowded – because Poles weren't allowed on express trains. Or on any other trains, without special warrants, or on any trams, or on any buses. They were also banned from theatres, concerts, exhibitions, cinemas, museums, and libraries, and forbidden to own or use cameras, radios, musical instruments, gramophones, bicycles, boots, leather briefcases, and school textbooks. On top of that, any ethnic German could kill a Pole whenever he liked. As National Socialism saw it, Poles were of animal status, but they weren't insects or bacteria, like the Russian POWs, the Jews, and now also the Roma and Sinti – the Alisz Seissers of this world.

So I had a compartment to myself and two berths to choose from. All such luxuries had long been seasoned with nausea (how humiliating, how curlike it was, active membership of the master race), and I took some comfort from the fact that every visible surface of the train's interior bore a thick coating of grime. A half-centimetre of grime, in Germany: the war was lost, Germany was lost. I settled down to the eight-hour haul (and then there'd be the three hours to Cracow). But I would be back at the Kat Zet for Walpurgis Night.

There was a short delay while they attached the dining car. I would be relying, of course, on the hamper prepared for me by the heroic (and uncannily costly) kitchens of the Hotel Eden. A whistle blew.

And now Berlin started off on its journey, westward – Friedrichshain with its blocked sebaceous glands and pestilential cafeterias, the Ahnenerbe with its skeletons and skulls, its scurf and snot, the Potsdamer Platz with its smashed faces and half-empty uniforms.

———

I got back to the Old Town at four o'clock in the afternoon. It was my intention to have a bath, put on some fresh clothes, and go and present myself at the villa of the Commandant. Ah, a postcard from Oberfuhrer Eltz. *I've already picked up a knock,* wrote Boris, *a stab wound in the neck, which is a bore; but it won't stop me joining in tomorrow's assau*. . . The last two lines had been tidily blotted out.

Maksik, the storied mouser, was sitting with his eyes closed on a damp mat by the roped refrigerator. I supposed Agnes had dropped by the day before, and left Max to his work. He looked very well fed; and now, all his duties discharged, he had assumed the tea-cosy position, with his tail and all four paws tucked in under him.

Halfway across the sitting room I felt my steps slow. Something was different, altered. For the next ten minutes I scanned tabletops and quickly opened drawers and cupboards. My rooms, it was clear, had come in for scrutiny. The Gestapo approach in such matters could go one of two ways: an almost undetectably ghost-like visitation, or else an earthquake followed by a hurricane. The place hadn't been searched; it had been casually and sloppily frisked.

I washed myself with extra will and vigour, because you always felt the taint – only mildly loathsome, in this case – of violation (I imagined Michael Off rolling a toothpick in his mouth as he

259

poked through my toiletries). But as I sank back in the tub for a while before the final rinse, well, my best guess was that this was just a warning, or even a matter of routine, and that many people, perhaps the entire IG staff, had been given a once-over. I took from the closet my tweeds and twills.

When I went back into the kitchen Max was straightening up; he flexed his forepaws, and idled towards me. Although he was on the whole an unsentimental creature, occasionally, as now, he drew himself up to his full height, waited a beat, and then fainted back-first to the floor. I reached down and stroked his chin and throat, waiting for the gruff and breathy purr. But the cat did not purr. I looked at his eyes and they were the eyes of a quite different kind of feline, almost dried out with severity and animus. I whipped my hand away – but not fast enough; there was a thin red stripe on the base of my thumb, which in a minute or so, I knew, would start to seep.

'You little shit,' I said.

He didn't flee, he didn't hide. He lay there on his back staring at me with his claws unsheathed.

And it was doubly weird to see the beast in him. Because on the night train I had (prophetically) dreamt that the Zoo across the Budapesterstrasse from the Hotel Eden was being bombed by the English. SS men were running around the mangled cages shooting the lions and the tigers, the hippos and the rhinos, and they were trying to kill all the crocodiles before they slithered off into the River Spree.

———

It was five forty-five when I came down the steps and out into the square. I trudged through the rubble of the synagogue, followed the curving, dipping lanes to the flat road, and entered the Zone of Interest, getting closer and closer to the smell.

2. DOLL: THE SUPREME PENALTY

I've come to believe that it was all a tragic mistake.

Lying in bed at dawn, and readying myself for yet another immersion in the fierce rhythms of the KL (reveille, washroom, Dysenterie, foot rag, roll call, Stucke, yellow star, Kapo, black triangle, Prominenten, work teams, Arbeit Macht Frei, brass band, Selektion, fan blade, firebrick, teeth, hair), and facing 1,000 challenges to my rictus of cool command, I turn things over in my mind and, yes, I've come to believe that it was all a tragic mistake – marrying such a large woman.

And such a young woman, too. Because the bitter truth is . . .

Of course, I am not unfamiliar with hand-to-hand combat, as I showed, I think, on the Iraqi front in the Great War. However, in those cases my adversaries were nearly always gravely injured or else incapacitated by hunger or disease. And later, in my Rossbach period, whilst there were firefights und so, there was no rough stuff, no *wet* stuff, unless you count that business with the schoolteacher in Parchim, and in that instance I enjoyed a distinct numerical advantage (5 to 1, no?). Anyway, all that was 20 years ago, and since then I've just been a glorified bureaucrat, sitting at a desk with my bottom gradually oozing and seeping over the hardbacked chair.

Now I don't claim you have to be a genius to understand what I'm getting at. I cannot do the necessary – that which would restore order and contentment, and job security, to the orange villa: I can't beat her up (and then give the giant witch a sound tup in the master bedroom). She's too fucking big.

And little Alisz Seisser – Alisz is no more formidable than Paulette. She knows her place and retreats to it the very instant the Sturmbannfuhrer starts to glower!

*

261

'Stop this snivelling at once. Listen, it happens all the time all over the world. No need to make a song and dance about it.'

The stool, the chemical toilet, the cauldron of water at last starting to bubble on the office hotplate . . .

'Oh brighten up, Alisz. A clean termination. It's something you should celebrate – over a bottle of gin in a scalding bath! Nicht? Come on, let's see a smile . . . Ach. Wha wha wha. All right. It's ½ past. It's time. Wha wha wha wha wha. Now can you pull yourself together, young lady, on your own steam? Or d'you need another slap in the face?'

. . . She brought a fair bit of clobber with her, did Miriam Luxemburg.

1st she unfolded a portable stand (it looked like a miniature operating table) and laid it all out on a blue cloth: syringe, speculum, clamp, and a long wooden stick with a sharp, crenellated metal loop at the end of it. The instruments seemed to be of reasonable quality – far, far better than the gardener's kitbag to which even SS sawbones periodically resort.

'Is it just me,' I said with perfect calm, 'or was there a whisper of spring in the air today?'

A trifle miffed, perhaps, by my repeated deferments of the procedure, Luxemburg gave a wan smile, and Alisz, who had a kind of leather thong in her mouth by this stage, made no reply (and of course she hadn't been outdoors for a considerable period of time). Wearing a white singlet, the patient lay on the stripped and towel-padded cot with her legs apart and her knees up.

'How long does it take again?'

'20 minutes if things go smoothly.'

'There. Hear that, Frau Seisser? No need for all that song and dance about it.'

I had intended to make myself scarce the moment the business began, as I'm very fastidious about all matters pertaining to females and their tubes. But I stayed whilst Luxemburg

262

applied the cleansing solution and injected the local. And I lingered as she went about the process of dilation – the speculum, with its reverse-tweezer effect. And I remained for the curettage.

It was most odd. I searched my senses for squeamishness – and squeamishness just wasn't there.

When I drove Luxemburg back to the Hygienic Institute (and handed over the paper bag containing the additional 400 Davidoffs), I asked how long it would take – before little Alisz was her old self again.

On April 20th, of course, we celebrated a certain someone's 54th birthday. A rather subdued occasion in the Officers' Mess, with Wolfram doing the honours as toastmaster.

'Dem Prophet der Deutschen Status, Selbstachtung, Prestige, und Integritat restauriert!'

'. . . Einverstanden.'

'Der Mann der seinen Arsch mit dem Diktat von Versailles abgewischt!'

'. . . Ganz bestimmt.'

'Der Grosster Feldherr *aller Zeiten*!'

'. . . Richtig.'

The only partygoer who responded with any verve, apart from myself and young Wolfram (the dear boy'd got slightly sozzled), was my wife.

'So,' I murmured, 'you've entered into the birthday spirit.'

'I have,' she murmured back.

Hannah was making a thorough spectacle of herself, as usual. Dressed like a common prostitute, she cheered the myriad salutations (far too loudly), and then devoted herself to satirical titters – aimed at the decorous solemnity of the prevailing mood. I closed my eyes and thanked the Lord: Fritz Mobius was on furlough.

'Yes, I'm in the birthday spirit,' she said, 'because with any luck it'll be his last. Now how will the miserable little wanker do himself in? I suppose he's got some sordid pill – you know, put by for a rainy day. Did they give you 1 too? Do they give them to all their key wankers? Or are you not key enough?'

'High treason. And richly deserving', I said with composure, 'of the supreme penalty . . . Yes, that's the way. Get your laughing done with.'

I just want to see the look on her face.

It's aspergegillosis now: fungus on the lungs.

The equestrian academy won't hear of taking Meinrad back, so I proposed selling him to the schmierig muleskinner – as scrap. The result? Good God, no end of juvenile caterwauling. In this respect Sybil's just as bad as Paulette. They practically live in Meinrad's filthy lean-to, stroking him whilst he lies there on his side, panting hard.

You know – I *miss* Dieter Kruger!

Myself and my muckers had a very good time with him, personally, in '33, in his cell at Dachau; and he went on to become the wellspring of more vicarious amusement in the period 1934– 40. Ach, in my mind I bounced friend Kruger from prison to prison and from camp to camp – I parked him wherever I bloody well liked. And once war neared, why, I had him levelling dunes in Stutthof, quarrying in Flossenburg, licking out the clay pits in Sachsenhausen. Oh, I ran him ragged – and ingeniously enriched his sufferings (solitary, penal Kommando, starvation rations, medical experiment here, 75 lashes there). Anyway, it appears I got somewhat carried away; I overdid it, evidently, and ceased to be believed.

Kruger's fate was the only thing that held any sway over Hannah. In the old days you could even worm the odd martyred fuck out of her, on the strength of friend Kruger. Ach, how far away, now, those ecstatic meldings seem!

I *miss* Dieter Kruger.

'You going to the fireworks?' asked Fritz Mobius. We were heading for his office, walking past all the file clerks bent over their desks. Bunker 11: Gestapo.

'The girls'll be going. I'll watch it from the garden.'

No talk of Hannah, no talk of spousal discipline: Fritz was darkly preoccupied with the matter at hand.

'How was your leave?' I asked (the Mobiuses' home was in what was left of an apartment block in central Bremen). 'All beer and skittles?'

'Oh get away with you,' he said wearily as he ran his eye down the 1st page of Rupprecht Strunck's report. 'So this bastard's the coordinator on the floor?'

'Exactly. The NCO, Jenkins, fingered him and then Strunck found his calendar in the tool cabin.'

'Good. Ach, Paul. No windowpanes, no electricity, no water – it takes till lunch to organise your morning shit. You have to walk 4 blocks to fill the bucket for the flush.'

'Ja?'

'Mm. And everyone goes on about *potatoes*.' He turned a page and underlined something. 'There she is, the little woman, boring my prick off about . . . potatoes. Her mother's the same. So's her sister. Potatoes.'

'Potatoes.'

'And in the shelter, Jesus Christus, you should see the way they stare at each other's sandwiches. They *ogle*, Paul. Hypnotised. It's pathetic.' Mobius yawned. 'Tried to get some rest. So likely. Come on.'

He led the way down the crunching stone steps to the 2nd-level basement.

'And how long's this gentleman been in our care?'

'Uh, 6 days.' I said. 'Almost a week.'

'Yes, Paul,' he said over his shoulder (I could tell he was smiling), '6 days is almost a week. So. Who in Farben gave him the calendar of 1st-use?'

'He won't say.'

Fritz crunched to a halt. '. . . What d'you mean he won't *say*? He's been kennelled I take it? And the electrode up his crack?'

'Ja, ja.'

'Really? And Entress?'

'Oh, Entress had a go. Twice. Horder says this bastard's a masochist. Bullard. Bullard fucking loves it.'

'Oh, God save us.'

He yanked back the bolts. Within were 2 men, Michael Off half asleep on a stool with a pencil in his mouth, and Roland Bullard lying on his side in the dirt. I noted with fascination that Bullard's head looked like a halved pomegranate.

Mobius sighed and said, 'Oh. Excellent work, Agent.' He sighed again. 'Agent Off, a man who's been in the crouch-box for 72 hours, a man who's twice felt the probe of the professorial scalpel, is *not* going to see the light because of 1 more kick in the face. Is he now. Can you *stand up* at least when you're talking to me?'

'Ortsgruppenleiter!'

I thought that Fritz was making a very good point. A man who . . .

'Some imagination? A little creativity, Off? Oh no.'

With the tip of his boot Mobius nudged Captain Bullard under the arm.

'Agent. Go to Kalifornia and bring me some pretty little Sara. Or have you fucked things up so thoroughly that he can't even *see*? Turn his head . . . There, the eyes are gone.' Mobius drew his Luger and deafeningly fired into the straw mattress. Bullard twitched. 'All right. Well. He can't see. But he can listen.'

Again I thought that Fritz's reasoning was fundamentally sound. All right, he can't see, but as long as he can . . .

'The Brits are hopelessly sentimental. Even with Jews. Paul, I guarantee this will all be over in 2 shakes of a lamb's tail. A man like Bullard – he long ago stopped caring about *him*.'

What do I find in the Officers' Club, this breezy Friday, but a copy of *Der Sturmer*? On its front page, as usual, we are given an artist's impression of (as it might be) Albert Einstein rutting against a somnolent Shirley Temple . . .

I tirelessly insist on this: Julius Streicher has done all that is most thoughtful about our movement a great deal of harm, and *Der Sturmer* may be the sole reason why, contrary to the Deliverer's initial vision, exterminatory anti-Semitism has not 'caught on' in the West.

I've pinned up on the Club noticeboard a warning to all officers (of course you can't do much about other ranks). Anyone found in possession of this foul rag will 1) lose a month's pay, and 2) forfeit a year's leave.

Only by the most stringent measures, enforced without fear or favour, can I convince certain people that I happen to be a man who means what he says.

'Come into the garden, Hannah.'

She was ½ curled up on the armchair beside the chimney piece, with a book and a drink, her Beine not so much under her as beside her, nicht?

'Watch the Roman candles. And oh yes – humour me. Klempnerkommandofuhrer *Szmul*, no less, wants to give you a present. He worships you.'

'Does he? Why?'

'Why? Didn't you tell me you once bade him good morning? That's sufficient for a person of his sort. I let slip it was your

birthday, and he wants to give you a present. Come on, it's nice
out. I won't mind if you smoke. And there's something I have to
tell you about our friend Herr Thomsen. I'll get your shawl.'

. . . The sky was a vulgar dark pink, the colour of café blanc-
mange. Down in the dip the flames of the bonfire were darting
and wriggling. In the smoky air you caught the tang of scorched
potato skins.

'Tell me what about Thomsen?' she asked. 'Is he back?'

I said, 'Hannah, I sincerely hope there hasn't been any kind of
intrigue between you 2. Because he's a proven traitor, Hannah.
A filthy saboteur. The purest scum. He's been wrecking some
very crucial machines at the Buna-Werke.'

And I felt the charge of vindication, ½ thrill, ½ stoic disburden-
ment, as Hannah said,

'Good.'

'. . . Good, Hannah?'

'Yes, good. I admire him and fancy him all the more for it.'

'Well, he's in a great deal of trouble. I shudder to think what
the next months will hold for friend Thomsen. The only person
who can alleviate his extremity', I said, 'is myself.'

I was smiling and Hannah smiled back and said, 'Oh, sure.'

'Poor Hannah. Fatally attracted to the sweepings of our prisons.
What is it, Hannah? Were you sexually interfered with at a tender
age? When you were an infant, did you play overmuch with your
pooh-pooh?'

'Nicht? Don't you usually say *nicht*? After 1 of your jokes?'

I chuckled and said, 'All I mean is you don't seem to have much
luck with your boyfriends. Now Hannah. This could lead to an
investigation. Into you. Reassure me. You weren't involved with
his efforts in any way? Can you swear, hand on heart, that you've
done nothing to impede our project here?'

'Not nearly enough. I've made a Piepl of the Kommandant.
But that wasn't hard.'

'. . . Thank you for saying that, Hannah. Yes, that's right – get your laughing done with. Are you relishing your cigarette?'

I just want to see the look on her face.

'Why d'you need your gun?'

'Standard procedure with Haftlinge. Here he comes. With your gift. Look. He'll be taking it out for you now.'

3. SZMUL: NOT ALL OF ME

It won't be this morning, it won't even be this afternoon. It will be at the end of the day, as darkness falls.

Although I live in the present, and do so with pathological fixity, I remember everything that has happened to me since I came to the Lager. Everything. To remember an hour would take an hour. To remember a month would take a month.

I cannot forget because I cannot forget. And now at the last all these memories will have to be dispersed.

There is only one possible outcome, and it is the outcome I want. With this I prove that my life is mine, and mine alone.

On my way over there I will inhume everything I've written, in the Thermos flask beneath the gooseberry bush.

And, by reason of that, not all of me will die.

AFTERMATH

I. ESTHER: LOST IN MEMORY

Roughly chronologically . . .

Szmulek Zachariasz stopped living at about six forty-five on April 30, 1943 – an hour after my arrest.

Roland Bullard received a bullet in the back of the neck on May Day.

Fritz Mobius suffered a fatal heart attack towards the end of a nightlong interrogation on June 1.

Boris Eltz – six weeks later, on July 12 – was killed on the climactic day of the German defeat at Kursk: an engagement of thirteen thousand tanks on a battlefield the size of Wales. His frenzied Panther was just a ball of fire by the time he rammed it sideways into two charging Russian T-34s; and he was posthumously awarded the *pour le mérite*.

Wolfram Prufer, along with two other SS, got beaten to death with rocks and pickaxes in the Sonderkommando revolt of October 7, 1944.

Konrad Peters was among the approximately five thousand suspects arrested in connection with the assassination attempt of July 20, 1944; he was also among the approximately twelve thousand prisoners who died of typhus, in Dachau, during the first four months of 1945.

Uncle Martin, Martin Bormann – well, it was several years before the facts were finally verified. He was wounded by a Russian artillery shell (and then took cyanide) as he tried to flee the Chancellery in Berlin in the small hours of May 1, 1945 – after the joint suicide of the newlyweds and their subsequent immolation, which (with Goebbels) he oversaw. He was condemned to death *in absentia* on October 1, 1946.

Ilse Grese was hanged in Hamelin Prison in the British Zone

273

on December 13, 1945. She was twenty-two. All through the night she loudly sang the 'Horst Wessel Lied' and 'Ich Hatt' einen Kameraden'; her last word (spoken 'languidly', according to her executioner, Pierrepoint, who also dealt with Lord Haw-Haw) was *schnell*. *Quick*.

Paul Doll was demoted sideways in June 1943 to a clerical post at the Inspectorate of Concentration Camps, in Berlin (which was being bombed nightly, and then daily as well as nightly), and subsequently reinstalled as Commandant in May 1944. He was captured in March 1946, tried at Nuremberg, and delivered to the Polish authorities. As part of his final statement Doll wrote, 'In the solitude of my cell I have come to the bitter realisation that I have sinned gravely against humanity.' He was hanged outside Bunker 11 in Kat Zet I on April 16, 1947.

Professor Zulz and Professor Entress were among the Nazi doctors put on trial in the Soviet Union in early 1948 and sentenced to 'the quarter' – twenty-five years in the slave camps of the Gulag.

Thirteen IG Farben executives and managers (not including Frithuric Burckl) were convicted at Nuremberg in July 1948. Suitbert Seedig was sentenced to eight years' imprisonment for slavery and mass murder. Rupprecht Strunck, called out of early retirement (which began in September '43), was sentenced to seven years' imprisonment for plunder and spolia-tion, slavery, and mass murder. Not a kilogram of synthetic rubber, nor a millilitre of synthetic fuel, was ever produced at the Buna-Werke.

Alisz Seisser contracted tuberculosis of the hip, and in January 1944 was transferred to the (very occasionally Potemkinised) camp of Theresienstadt, near Prague. There is a better than even chance that she survived the war.

———

The fate of Esther Kubis is unknown, at least to me. *She won't go down*, Boris used to say. *She's rash, but in the end her spirit will refuse to give them the satisfaction.* And he often cited the first thing she ever said to him. Which was *I don't like it here and I'm not going to die here . . .*

I last saw her on May 1, 1943. We were in a sealed Block together, just the two of us. I was about to be carted off to some other camp (Oranienburg, it turned out); Esther was serving the final hours of a three-day confinement (without food or water) for not making her bed, or for not making it properly – Ilse Grese was very particular when it came to the making of beds.

We talked for almost two hours. I told Esther about the promise Boris extracted from me (to do everything in my power for her), a promise I was no longer able to keep (I had nothing to give her, not even my wristwatch). She listened to my urgings with real attention, I thought – because I was now so clearly on the wrong side of the Reich. Nor did I correct her silent inference that Boris too, perhaps, was not all he seemed.

'Esther. This insane nightmare will end,' I concluded, 'and Germany will lose. Be alive to see it with your own eyes.'

Then I dozed, having had a long and repetitive but not especially brutal night underneath the Political Department. For the first six hours I was joined by Fritz Mobius who, despite a lot of incredibly vociferous shouting (and it wasn't simulated, it wasn't an act, the millennial German anger), used no force. As the shift changed at midnight, Paul Doll looked in. To me he seemed transparently haunted and furtive; but he managed to slap my face a few times, as if in spontaneous patriotic disgust, and he punched me in the stomach (quite feebly hitting the bony ridge just above the solar plexus). From then until dawn it was Michael Off, who did a bit more of exactly the same; it appeared that someone had told them I was not to be marked.

This was curious: in his appearance Doll made me think of a

275

coal miner coming off shift. His tunic and jodhpurs minutely glinted with specks of light, and on his back there was a shard the size of a coin. It was mirror glass.

Mobius, Doll, Off – they all yelled, they all hollered fit to kill. And I vaguely and confusedly wondered if the story of National Socialism could have unfolded in any other language . . .

When I woke up Esther was standing in front of the window, with her forearms flat on the sill. It was an exceptionally clear day, and I realised she was gazing at the mountains of the Sudetenland. She had been born and raised, I knew, in the High Tatras (whose peaks were perennially capped with gleaming ice). Seen in profile, her face wore a frown and a half-smile; and she was so lost in memory that she didn't hear the door as it creaked open behind her.

Hedwig Butefisch came into the Block. She paused, then bent her knees, almost to a crouch; she moved quietly forward, and delivered a pinch to the back of Esther's thigh – not viciously, not at all, but playfully, just hard enough to give her a fright.

'You were dreaming!'

'. . . But you woke me up!'

And for half a minute they wrestled, tickling each other and yelping with laughter.

'*Aufseherin!*' shouted Ilse Grese from the doorstep.

At once the two girls recollected themselves and straightened up, very sober, and Hedwig marched her prisoner out into the air.

2. GERDA: THE END OF NATIONAL SOCIALISM

'Try and drink some of this, my dearest, my darling. I'll hold it. There.'

'. . . Thank you, Neffe. Thank you. Neffe, you're thinner. Though I'm one to talk.'

'Ah but I'm like the troubadour, Tantchen. Famished for love.'

'Pass me that. What did you say? . . . Oh, Neffe – Boris! I *wept* for you, Golo, when I heard.'

'Don't, Tante. You'll start me off.'

'*Wept* for you. More than a brother, you always said.'

'Don't, Tante.'

'At least they made a nice big fuss about him. Well, he was so photogenic . . . Is Heinie all right?'

'Heinie's fine. They're all fine.'

'Mm. Except Volker.'

'Well, yes.' Volker was her ninth child (if you included Ehrengard), and a boy. 'Volker's a little out of sorts.'

'Because this is such an unhealthy place!'

The place was Bolzano, in alpine Italy (and the time was the spring of 1946). My remaining Bormanns had met an unlikely fate: they were in a German concentration camp (it was called Bozen from 1944 to '45). But there was no more slave labour, no more flaying and cudgelling, no more starvation, and no more murder. Full of DPs, POWs, and other internees awaiting scrutiny, it was Italian now, with unabundant yet appetising food, reasonable sanitation, and many cheerful nuns and priests among the helpers. Gerda lay in its field hospital; Kronzi, Helmut, Heinie, Eike, Irmgard, Eva, Hartmut, and Volker were in a kind of military marquee nearby. I said,

'Were the Americans beastly to you, Tante?'

277

'Yes. Yes, Golo, they were. Beastly. The doctor, the doctor – not me, Neffe, but the *doctor* – told them I had to have an operation in Munich. Every week there's a train. And this American said, *That train's not for Nazis. It's for their victims!*'

'That *was* cruel, dear.'

'And they think I know where he is!'

'Do they? Mm. Well if he made it out he could be anywhere. South America, I'll bet. Paraguay. Landlocked Paraguay, that'd be the one. He'll send word.'

'And Golo. Were they beastly to you?'

'The Americans? No, they gave me a job . . . Oh. You mean the Germans. No, not very. They were dying to be beastly to me, Tante. But the power of the Reichsleiter held good to the end. Like your lovely parcels.'

'Perhaps it isn't the end.'

'True, dear. But it's the end of all his power.'

'. . . The Chief, Neffe. Killed as he led his troops in the defence of Berlin. And now it's all gone. The end of National Socialism. That's what's so impossible to bear. The end of National Socialism! Don't you see? That's what my body's *reacting* to.'

The next night she said with a vexed look,

'Golo, are you still rich?'

'No, darling. That's all disappeared. All but about three per cent.' Which was actually far from nothing. 'They took it.'

'Ah well, you see – once the Jews get a whiff of something like . . . Why the smile?'

'It wasn't the Jews, my dearest. It was the Aryans.'

She said comfortably, 'But you've still got your paintings and *objets d'art*.'

'No. I've got one Klee and one tiny but very nice Kandinsky. I suspect all the rest found their way to Goring.'

'Ooh, that fat brute. With his three chauffeurs and his pet

leopard and his bison ranch. Mascara. Changing his clothes every ten minutes. Golo! Why aren't you more indignant?'

I shrugged lightly and said, 'Me, I'm not complaining.' Of course I wasn't complaining, about that or about anything else: I didn't have the right. 'Oh, I've been very lucky, very privileged, as always. And even in prison I had lots of time to think, Tantchen, and there were books.'

She worked her shoulders up the bed. 'We never doubted your innocence, Neffe! We knew you were completely innocent.'

'Thank you, Tante.'

'I'm *certain* your conscience is completely clear.'

In fact I did feel the need to talk about my conscience with a woman, but not with Gerda Bormann . . . The thing is, Tantchen, that in my zeal to retard the German power I inflicted further suffering on men who were already suffering, suffering beyond imagination. And dying, my love. In the period 1941–4, thirty-five thousand died at the Buna-Werke. I said,

'Of course I was innocent. It was the testimony of just one man.'

'One man!'

'Testimony extorted by torture.' And I reflexively added, 'That's medieval jurisprudence.'

She slumped back, and went on in a vague voice, 'But medieval things . . . are meant to be good, aren't they? Drowning . . . throttled queers . . . in peat bogs. That kind of thing. And duels, Neffe, duels.'

This wasn't wild talk, about duels (or about peat bogs). The Reichsfuhrer-SS did briefly reintroduce duelling as a way of settling matters of honour. But Germans had already got used to living without honour – and without justice, freedom, truth, and reason. Duelling was re-illegalised after the first Nazi bigwig (an outraged husband in this instance) was briskly shot dead (by his cuckolder) . . . Now Tante suddenly opened her eyes to their full extent and cried,

'The axe, Golo! The axe!' Her head sank downwards into the

pillow. A minute passed. 'All that's meant to be good. Isn't it?'

'. . . Rest, Tantchen. Rest, my sweet.'

The next night she was weaker but more voluble.

'Golo, he's dead. I can feel it. A wife and mother can just feel it.'

'I hope you're wrong, dear.'

'You know, Papi never liked Papi. I mean, Vater never liked Uncle Martin. But I stuck to my guns, Neffe. Martin had such a wonderful sense of humour! He made me laugh. And I wasn't much of a laugher, even as a child. When I was very young I always thought, Why's everyone making that silly noise? And even later on I could never see what people found so hilarious. But Papi, he made me laugh. *How* we laughed . . . Oh, talk to me Golo. While I rest. It's the sound of your voice.'

I had a flaskful of grappa with me. I took a swallow and said,

'He made you laugh. And did you always laugh at the same things, Tante?'

'. . . Always. Always.'

'Well here's a funny story Uncle Martin told me . . . There once was a man called Dieter Kruger. I don't want to patronise you, my angel, but it was a long time ago. Do you remember the Reichstag Fire?'

'. . . Of course I do. Papi was so thrilled . . . Just go on talking, Neffe.'

'The Reichstag Fire – three weeks after our assumption of power. Everyone thought *we'd* done it. Because it was made in heaven for us.' I took another swallow. 'Anyway, we didn't. Some Dutch anarchist did it. And he was guillotined in January '34. But there was another man called Dieter Kruger. Are you awake, Tante?'

'. . . Of course I'm awake!'

'And Dieter Kruger, Dieter Kruger had a hand in one of the Dutchman's earlier arsons – a welfare office in Neukolln. So he was executed too. For good measure. Kruger was a Communist and a—'

'And a Jew?'

'No. That's not important, Tante. What's important is that he was a published political philosopher and a fervent Communist . . . So the night before the execution Uncle Martin and a few of his friends went down to death row. With several bottles of champagne.'

'What for? The champagne?'

'For toasts, Tante. Kruger was already a bit bashed about, as you'd expect, but they stood him up and ripped his shirt off, and cuffed his hands behind his back. And in a mock ceremony they awarded him all these medals. The Iron Cross with Oak Leaves. The Order of the German Eagle. The Honour Chevron of the Old Guard. Et cetera. And they pinned them on his bare chest.'

'. . . Yes?'

'Uncle Martin and his pals gave speeches, Tantchen. They eulogised Kruger as the father of fascist autocracy. Which is how he went to his death. A decorated hero of National Socialism. Uncle Martin thought that was very funny. Do you think that's very funny?'

'. . . What? Giving him *medals*? No!'

'Mm. Well.'

'. . . He started the Reichstag Fire!'

On my last night she made an effort and rallied. She said,

'We have so much to be proud of, Golo. Think of what he achieved, Uncle Martin. I mean personally.'

There was a silence. And an understandable silence. What? The intensification of corporal punishment in the slave camps. The cautious dissent on the question of the cosmic ice. The deSemitisation of the alphabet. The marginalising of Albert Speer. Uncle Martin wasn't at all interested in the accoutrements of power, only in power itself, which he used, throughout, for unswervingly trivial ends . . .

'How he took on the question of the Mischlinge,' she said. 'And the Jews married to Germans.'

'Yes. And in the end we just let them be. The intermarried ones. Pretty much.'

'Ah, but he got his Hungarians.' She gave a soft gurgle of satisfaction. 'Every last one of them.'

Well, not quite. As late as April '44, with the war long lost, the cities razed, with millions of people half starved, homeless, and dressed in singed rags, the Reich still felt it made sense to divert troops to Budapest; and the deportations began. You see, Tante, it's like that man in Linz who stabbed his wife a hundred and thirty-seven times. The second thrust was delivered to justify the first. The third to justify the second. And so it goes on, until the end of strength. Of the Jews in Hungary, two hundred thousand survived, Tantchen, while close to half a million were deported and murdered in 'Aktion Doll' in Kat Zet II.

'Mm,' she said, 'he always insisted that that was his greatest accomplishment on the world stage. You know, his greatest contribution as a statesman.'

'Indeed, Tante.'

'. . . Now, Neffe. What'll you do, my love?'

'Go back to the law, in the end, I suppose. I'm not sure. Maybe keep at it as a translator. My English is getting quite decent. I've improved it *by hook or by crook*.'

'What? It's a hideous language, so they say. And you shouldn't really work for the Americans, you know, Golo.'

'I know, dear, but I am.' OMGUS, the American Office of Military Government, and the five Ds: denazify, demilitarise, deindustrialise, decartelise, and democratise. I said, 'Tante, I'm trying to find somebody. But the thing is – what's her maiden name? I never asked.'

'Golito . . . Why couldn't you find a nice single girl?'

'Because I found a nice married one.'

'You look pained, dearest.'

'I am pained. I feel I have the right to be pained about that.'

282

'. . . Ah. Poor Golito. I understand. Who is the husband?'

'They're separated, and she won't be using her married name. He's being tried by the IMT.'

'Those swine. Jewish justice. And was he a good Nazi?'

'One of the best . . . Anyway. I'm getting nowhere. There's nothing left you can look up.' By which I meant that every file, every folder, every index card, every scrap of paper connected to the Third Reich was either destroyed before the capitulation or else seized and sequestered after it. 'There's nothing left you can look up.'

'Golito, put a notice in the press. That's what people do.'

'Mm, I already tried that. More than once. Here's a discouraging thought. Why hasn't she found me? I wouldn't be hard to find.'

'Maybe she is trying, Neffe. Or I tell you what – maybe she's dead. So many people are these days. And anyway, it's always like that, isn't it? After a war. Nobody knows where anybody is.'

With my flask on my lap I sat on at the bedside, thinking.

'I wouldn't be hard to find.' Slowly I got to my feet. 'It's time, sadly, dear. I'll have to take my leave of you, Tantchen. Tantchen?'

But Gerda was comprehensively, abysmally asleep.

'Bless you, my angel,' I said. I leaned over and put my lips to her waxy brow, and then joined the others in the truck.

———

Gerda had cancer of the uterus and died ten days later, on April 26, 1946. She was thirty-seven. And poor Volker, always a sickly baby and toddler, died the same year. He was three.

With me this had been the case for some time: I couldn't see beauty where I couldn't see intelligence.

But I saw Gerda with eyes of love and even on her deathbed she was beautiful. The stupid beauty of Gerda Bormann.

*

3. HANNAH: THE ZONE OF INTEREST

In September 1948 I sent myself on a fool's errand.

The Fourth Germany, by that time, could no longer be very faithfully described as an almshouse on a slag heap. During the hyperinflation of my adolescence, money held its worth for only a few hours (on payday everyone did their week's or their month's shopping, and did it *instanter*); by contrast, in the post-war period money was worthless to begin with. Once again the answer lay in a change of banknote. The currency reform of June 20 put an end to the Zigaretten Wirtschaft – a state of affairs in which a Lucky Strike became too valuable to smoke – and introduced the Soziale Marktwirtschaft, or the free market (no rationing, no price controls). And it worked.

In the quixotic spirit of that summer, I procured a car, a filthy old Tornax (whose blackened and oft-needed crank kept making me think of a broken swastika), and boldly drove south-east. My purpose? My purpose was to get closer to the end of hope – to exhaust it, and so try to be rid of it. I was quieter, older, greyer (hair and eyes losing colour); but my somatic health was good, I quite liked translating for the Americans (and I had become genuinely passionate about a *pro bono* job I was doing on the side), I had men friends and even lady friends, I was plausibly to be seen in the office, in the PX store, in the restaurant, at the cabaret, at the cinema. Yet I could not construct a plausible inner life.

My OMGUS colleagues liked to say that 'Ich Wusste Nichts Uber Es' was the new national anthem (I Didn't Know Anything About It); and yet all Germans, around then, as they slowly regained consciousness after the Vernichtungskrieg and the Endlosung, were meant to be reformed characters. And I too was a reformed character. But I could not construct a self-sufficient

284

inner life; and this was perhaps the great national failure (which, at least, I did not seek to relieve by 'joining' anything). If I looked inside myself, all I saw was the watery milk of solitude. In the Kat Zet, like every perpetrator, I felt doubled (this is me but it is also not me; there is a further me); after the war, I felt halved. And when I entertained memories of Hannah (a frequent occurrence), I didn't have the sense of a narrative gallingly unfinished. I had the sense of a narrative almost entirely unbegun.

Earlier I said that you couldn't live through the Third Germany without discovering who you were, more or less (always a revelation, and often untoward); and without discovering who others were, too. But now it seemed that I had barely made the acquaintance of Hannah Doll. I remembered and still tasted the complex pleasure I derived from her, from the shape of her stance, the way she held a glass, the way she talked, the way she crossed a room – the warm comedy and pathos it filled me with. And where exactly were these interactions unfolding? And what was that syrupy stench (which walls and ceilings were powerless to exclude)? And was *that man* her husband? . . . The Hannah I knew existed in a sump of misery, and in a place that even its custodians called *anus mundi*. So how could I defend myself from thoughts of a Hannah reborn and reawakened? Who would she be – who would she be in peace and freedom, trusting, trusted? Who?

Under National Socialism you looked in the mirror and saw your soul. You found yourself out. This applied, *par excellence* and *a fortiori* (by many magnitudes), to the victims, or to those who lived for more than an hour and had time to confront their own reflections. And yet it also applied to everyone else, the malefactors, the collaborators, the witnesses, the conspirators, the outright martyrs (Red Orchestra, White Rose, the men and women of July 20), and even the minor obstructors, like me, and like Hannah Doll. We all discovered, or helplessly revealed, who we were.

Who somebody really was. *That* was the zone of interest.

285

And so it came about that I resumed my search for a maiden name.

————

Hannah met Paul Doll in Rosenheim, and they spent time together in Rosenheim, and it seemed reasonably likely that they were married in Rosenheim. So I went to Rosenheim. With much snorting, knocking, and pinking, and then stalling, and then bounding, the terrible Tornax completed the sixty kilometres from Munich.

Rosenheim comprised eighteen boroughs, each with its own Standesamt: births, weddings, deaths. My project, therefore, would effortlessly consume an entire week's leave. Well, 'furloughs', by now, were being audaciously referred to as 'vacations'. Besides the abruptly available goods and services, there was something unrecognisable in the air. Whatever it was, it was not the return of normality. There had been no normality to return to, not after 1914, not in Germany. You had to be at least fifty-five to have an adult recollection of normality. But there was something in the air, and it was new.

I arrived on the Sunday, and established myself at a guest house on the fringe of the Riedergarten. First thing the next morning, in solemn consciousness of futility, I cranked the Tornax and started on the concentric circles of my rounds.

At five in the afternoon of the following Saturday, sure enough, I was drinking a glass of tea at a stall in the main square, my throat inflamed and my eyes weakly watering at the far corners. After the expenditure of much drudgery, cunning, obsequiousness, and money (those valiant new Deutschmarks), I had managed to peruse a total of three ledgers; and without the slightest edification. The trip, the enterprise, in other words, had been a ridiculous failure.

*

And so I stood there, dully looking out at the peace and freedom of the town. That was undeniable: there was peace and freedom (the capital was under blockade, and there was little peace, and no freedom, in the Russian mandate to the north-east, with rumours of hectare-wide mass graves). And what else? Many years later, I would read the first dispatch from an American journalist posted in Berlin, which consisted of four words: *Nothing sane to report*. The year was 1918.

In January 1933, when the NSDAP picked up the keys to the Chancellery, a narrow majority of Germans felt, not just horror, but the dreamlike fuddlement of the unreal; when you went outside, you were reminded of the familiar, though only as a photograph or a newsreel reminded you of the familiar; the world felt abstract, ersatz, pretend. And that was what I was a witness to, maybe, that day in Rosenheim. The beginning of the German compromise with sanity. Social realism was the genre. Not fairy tales, not Gothic novelettes, not sagas of swords and sorcery, not penny dreadfuls. And not romance, either (an outcome I was beginning to accept). Realism, and nothing else.

From this certain questions would inevitably and persistently follow.

From above? said Konrad Peters in the Tiergarten – fastidious Peters, who died in Dachau covered in nightsoil and lice. *From above, Bismarckian Realpolitik degraded to the nth degree. Combined with hallucinatory anti-Semitism and a world-historical flair for hatred. Ah, but from below – that's the real mystery. It's a common slander of the Jews, but it's no slander of a huge fraction of the Germans. They went like sheep to the slaughterhouse. And then they donned the rubber aprons and set to work.*

Yes, I was thinking, how did 'a sleepy country of poets and dreamers', and the most highly educated nation the earth had ever seen, how did it yield to such wild, such fantastic disgrace? What made its people, men and women, consent to having their souls

287

raped – and raped by a eunuch (Grofaz: the virgin Priapus, the teetotal Diónysus, the vegetarian Tyrannosaurus rex)? Where did it come from, the need for such a methodical, such a pedantic, and such a literal exploration of the bestial? I of course didn't know, and neither did Konrad Peters, and neither did anyone in my sight, families, limping veterans, courting couples, groups of very young and very drunken GIs (all that strong, cheap, and delicious Lowenbrau), tin-rattlers collecting for causes, black-clad widows, a moving, threading line of boy scouts, and sellers of vegetables, sellers of fruit . . .

Then I saw them. I saw them over a great and populous distance – and they were receding from me, walking away from me to the far edge of the square. It was the configuration – that was all. A mother and her two daughters, the three of them in straw hats, swinging straw bags, and dressed in crenellated white.

I hurried after them through the holiday crowd.

———

'You're too old now', I said shakily (with a fizz of distress in my sinuses), 'and too tall for ice cream.'

'No we're not,' said Sybil. 'We'll never be too old for ice cream.'

'Or too tall,' said Paulette. 'Oh come on, Mami . . . Mami! Oh *please*. Come on.'

I bought the girls banana splits in the lounge at the Grand. Their mother eventually agreed to have an orange juice (and I ordered a large schnapps) . . . When I touched her shoulder, at the foot of the sloping alley, and as I said her name, Hannah turned. Her face took on the stasis of recognition; and then all she did was widen her eyes and raise a white-gloved hand to her mouth.

In a thick voice I was saying,

'The fancy word, young ladies, is *lustrum*. Five years. And there's no other lustrum that changes a person as much as thirteen to eighteen. You've changed particularly, Paulette, if I may say so. Your beauty has come in.'

And this was incidentally and providentially true; she had grown five or six inches, and you could look at her now without seeing the long upper lip and the cluelessly staring nostrils of the Commandant.

'What about eighteen to twenty-three?' said Sybil.

'Or nought to five?' said Paulette. 'There. What about nought to five.'

A smart shopping arcade adjoined the glassy atrium of the hotel; and I had the expectation that the twins, in the end, would be unable to resist the pressure of the neon lights, the costly materials, and the scents and blooms of the florist's.

'Can we, Mami?'

'Not now . . . Oh, okay. Five minutes. No longer.'

The girls ran off.

I leaned forward with my hands on my thighs. 'Forgive me,' I said. 'I didn't realise you'd remarried.'

She straightened up. 'Re*married*? Yes, I'm really good at that, aren't I? My status', she said slowly, 'is *widow*.'

'. . . I'm due back in Munich tomorrow evening,' I said (I had intended to leave that night, and my suitcase was already in the rusty boot of the Tornax). 'Can I see you very briefly before I leave? Morning coffee, say?'

She had that flustered look, as if the room temperature was too high for her, and her left knee was bobbing up and down. Most ominously of all, she was repeatedly closing her eyes – the upper lids staying where they were while the lower glided heavenward. And when a man sees a woman doing that, all he can do is mumble something polite and make his way to the door. She said,

'No. No, I don't think there's any point. Sorry.'

I thought for a moment and asked her, 'Can I show you

289

something?' I reached for my wallet and extracted a small strip of newsprint. It was an ad I had placed in the personal columns of the *Munich Post*. 'Would you do me the honour of reading this?'

She took it from my fingers and said, '*Lawyer and translator, thirty-five, seeks a) professional tuition in Esperanto, and b) professional guidance in theosophy. Please reply to . . .*'

'In case your parents saw it. And now I'm thirty-eight.' I managed not to try and nudge her curiosity by promising an account of the last hours of Dieter Kruger. I just said, 'You're too generous to deny me a little of your time. If you would. Please.'

At this point she made a decision and matter-of-factly told me where and when, and for how long. On my asking she even gave me her address.

'Part of the trouble', I said, 'was that I didn't know your maiden name.'

'It wouldn't have been much use to you. Schmidt. Now where are those girls?'

———

It seemed to be a dusk-to-dawn delirium, and of viral force — shallow, semi-conscious nightmares, nightmares of impotence. I strained to lift or shift an endless series of cumbrous and almost immovably heavy objects; then I tried and failed to force my way through thick portals made of gold and lead; in shameful incapacity I fled from or cowered before grinning enemies; naked, and shrivelled to nothing, I was laughed and taunted out of bedrooms, boardrooms, ballrooms. Finally my teeth began to waltz around my jaws, changing places, hiding behind one another, till I spat them all out like a mouthful of rotten nuts and thought, It is done. I cannot eat, talk, smile, or kiss.

Outside the weather was neutral, only exceptionally still.

*

Hannah had told me to meet her at the bandstand behind the Freizeitgelande – the recreation ground. *Everyone knows it.* She also said that she had an hour. This was stated, simply. I resolved of course to be punctual; and I would be punctual in my leaving, too.

I went downstairs and ordered a breakfast I couldn't eat. So I went back up and bathed and shaved, and when it was half past ten I took from the sink the bunch of flowers I had bought the evening before, in the Grand, and started off.

———

Three times I asked the way, and three times I was directed with the same grave attentiveness (as if these passers-by were prepared to accompany me – or even carry me – to my rendezvous). I circled the train station, which was evidently functioning (though you could see in the middle distance a giant's climbing frame of mangled track), and crossed two block-sized bomb sites, cleared of rubble but still redolent of doused gasoline. All this (according to one of my guides) from the raids of mid April '45, the last of them on April 21, by which time the Russians were in Berlin and already shelling the Chancellery. The bombers were British – the least hateful and the least hated (and the least anti-Semitic) of all the combatants. Well, I would later think, wars get old; they get grizzled and smelly and rotten and mad; and the bigger they are the faster they age . . .

Next, the playing field (three teenagers with a soccer ball each, playing keepy-uppy), and the circular pond – a clan of ducks, a lone swan. The great bell of St Kaspar's, with portentous three-second intervals, was gonging eleven as I settled on a bench in plain sight of the circular bandstand, where a few old bods in worn blue serge with gilt buttons were packing up a few old trumpets and trombones. Against a sky as colourless and as neutral as tracing paper, rather sedately dressed in matching jersey and

291

long skirt, all cotton, all dark blue, here she came – reduced (we were all reduced), but still tall, broad, and full, and still light-footed. I stood up.

———

'These of course are for you. To make you feel like a film star.'

'Amaryllis,' she said, in sober identification. 'With stems as thick as leeks. Give me a moment and I'll wedge them in the water.'

She had to kneel to do it. When she straightened up, and removed a blade of grass from her sleeve, I felt again that complex pleasure, with its strange elements of pity and delight. Doing this, or that, this way, and not that way. Her habits, her choices, her decisions. With sharp desire, and also with a press of dread, I knew that her hold on my senses was intact and entire; it was plangent but also humorous somehow, this hold, making me want to laugh, making me want to cry.

'Please be assured that my expectations are very low.' I had my hands face to face as if in prayer, but they moved, too, nodding in time as I said, 'A correspondence. Perhaps some kind of friendship . . .'

This was acknowledged. I said,

'Because it may well be that nothing can be salvaged. That wouldn't surprise us, I don't think.'

'No, it wouldn't.' She looked around. 'Nothing else has lasted, has it, from that time. Not even a building or a statue.'

I produced a pack of Lucky Strike; we both took one, and the flame of my lighter was solid and still (no wind, no weather). 'Mm, I suspect I know why you were unhappy when I – when I reappeared.'

'Look, I don't want to be mean. But what makes you think I've stopped being unhappy? I've gone on being unhappy. I'm unhappy now.'

292

This in turn was acknowledged. She said,

'Don't think it's just you. I've been living in dread of seeing anyone at all from back then. I don't think I could even bear seeing little Humilia. Who's all right, by the way.'

Her tone was untheatrical — flat and straight, like the level address of her eyes. The dense dark brown hair was the same, the wide mouth was the same, the manly squareness of the jawbone was the same. Two vertical furrows had established themselves on either side of the bridge of her nose — and that was all.

'I have to be in town by three anyway. At noon I'll be gone.'

'. . . If that's neurotic, or just plain weak, then I'm just plain weak. It was too much for me. I wasn't up to it.'

My eyebrows continued to undulate sympathetically, but I found that the whole of my being, and not just my heart, resisted this — rejected it; and with a firmness I couldn't yet understand. I said nothing.

'I can't stop imagining I'll see Doll. That's how nuts I am. I'd die if I saw him.' She shuddered, she writhed, and said, 'I'd certainly die if he touched me.'

'He can't touch you.'

There was a long silence. There had been several long silences. And now St Kaspar's reproachfully sounded the quarter-hour.

'Can we talk more blandly for a while? Go on about your job. And then I'll calm down.'

'Well, it's not quite a change of subject,' I said; but I too felt the need to talk more blandly, for a while. So I told her about my job. The eight million completed questionnaires, and the five grades of classification, all the way from Nonincriminated to Major Offender.

'The fifth one. That's the one my late husband qualified for.'

'Sorry. Yes.' I hesitated. 'But let me — let me be earnest and tell you about the side of it that really interests me.'

293

My extracurricular work had little to do with victors' justice (as if, after a war, there was any other kind). It concerned itself with the Bundesentschadigungsgesetz, or the guidelines on reparations: victims' justice. In this case indemnities for murdered relatives, for years lost to slavery and terror, and for persisting physical and mental debility (and for the theft of all assets and belongings). My friend David Merlin, a Jewish lawyer and a captain in the US Army (and one of our most brilliant and reviled denazifiers), had recruited me a year earlier; and at first the whole thing felt deeply pertinent and also deeply fanciful – who, at that stage, could imagine a Germany, not only sovereign and solvent, but also sorry? No longer. The new reality – emergent Israel, back in May – was like an injection or an impregnation; and Merlin was already planning an exploratory mission to Tel Aviv. She said,

'That's the best thing you could be doing. And all power to you.'

'Thanks. Thanks. So, anyway, my days are full. I'm busy at least.'

'Mm. I'm not.'

She said she was having to do more for her folks now – her mother's hips, her father's heart.

'And I teach conversational French for five hours a week. I can't do any written stuff because of my spelling. You know, the dyslexia. So all I do, really, is raise the girls.'

Who now appeared, drifting into view at the far end of the pond as the half-hour sounded. They came to a halt – and it was clear that they'd been assigned to come and check on their mother. Hannah waved, and they waved back before drifting off again.

'. . . The twins like you.'

I swallowed hard and said, 'Well I'm very glad, because I like them and always have. And isn't it nice that Paulette can now walk tall with Sybil? There you are, I'll be a friend of the family. I'll come down every now and then on the train and take you all out to lunch.'

'. . . I'm sorry, but I can't take my eyes off that swan. I hate that swan. See? Its neck's clean enough, but look at the feathers. They're grimey-grey.'

'Like the snow in Poland.' First white, then grey, then brown. 'When did you leave?'

She said, 'I probably left the same day you did. When they bundled you off. May the first.'

'Why so soon?'

'Because of the night before. Walpurgisnacht.' Just for a moment she brightened. 'Apart from the obvious, what do you know about Walpurgisnacht?'

'Go on.'

'Back there, the girls were very excited. Not only about the bonfire and the fireworks and the roast potatoes. They had this book they liked terrorising themselves with. Walpurgisnacht is meant to be the time when you can cross the boundary between the seen and the unseen worlds. Between the world of light and the world of darkness. They loved that. Can I have another cigarette?'

'Of course . . . A friend of mine, a late friend of mine said the Third Reich was one long Walpurgisnacht. And he talked about the boundary, but the boundary between life and death, and how it seemed to have disappeared. April the thirtieth. Wasn't that the night when the curious creature in the Wilhelmstrasse put himself out of his misery?'

'Was it? Well, it's also my birthday. Anyway.' In an intent tone she said, 'I do want to ask you about this because I'm not sure I saw it right. Look how vile-natured that swan is.'

The swan – the furiously affronted question mark of its neck and beak, its black-eyed stare.

With slight unease I said, 'Oh yes. There's a bit about Walpurgisnacht in – can it be *Faust*? *The witches fuck, the he-goat shits*. . .'

'That's *good*.' She flexed her brow and went on, 'He asked me into the garden. Watch the roman candles. He said Szmul, he said Szmul wanted to give me a birthday present. Now try and imagine you're there.'

The three of them in the gaining twilight. Beyond, down the slope, the Walpurgisnacht blaze and, perhaps, the upward whoosh of a rocket. The sunset, the first stars. Sonderkommandofuhrer Szmul was on the other side of the garden fence. In his stripes. The atmosphere, she said, was like nothing she'd ever experienced or read about or heard about. Looking glazed, the prisoner drew from his sleeve a long tool or weapon, a kind of spike with a narrow crosspiece. And all was uncertain, all was pretend.

Doll kicked the gate open and said, *Come on then* . . .

Szmul stood his ground. He parted his shirt and put the point to his chest. (As she said this she held out her joined hands at arm's length.) And Szmul looked her in the eye and said to her,

Eigentlich wolte er dass ich Ihnen das antun.

And Doll said, *Oh, what use* are *you then?*

And shot him in the face. He had his gun out and he shot him in the face. Then he crouched down and shot him in the back of the neck.

When Szmul stopped quivering Doll turned slowly on his haunches and stared up at her.

Eigentlich wolte er dass ich Ihnen das antun. *Really he wanted me to do this to you.*

'As he said it Szmul looked me in the eye. I used to see him almost every day and he never did that. Looked me in the eye.' For a moment she seemed surprised by the cigarette she was holding, and drew on it and dropped it to the ground. 'Doll was covered in blood. God, what a bullet does . . . And still trying to smile. I suddenly knew who he'd been all along. There he was, a nightmarish little boy. Caught doing something plainly disgusting. And still trying to smile.'

'So you . . .'

'Oh. Straight away I got the girls and took them to Romhilde Seedig's. And we left the minute we could.' She placed a flat hand just beneath her throat. 'And I knew who he was. Now, Herr Thomsen, the Referendar, what do you make of all that?'

I spread my hands. 'You've had five years to think. You must've got somewhere with it.'

'Mm. Well in the end the worst thing, really, was that he stopped Szmul from killing himself by his own hand. Instead he destroyed his face. You know, I used to say good morning to Szmul in the lane. And whatever else he was he wasn't a violent man . . . Now this is right, isn't it? Doll had, I don't know, persuaded Szmul to hurt me or even kill me.'

'The thing I always feared. Persuaded him, put pressure on him. I wonder how.'

'That's what I wonder too.'

'For the rest you saw it right, I think.'

St Kaspar's ponderously reminded us that it was eleven forty-five. A Sunday, but no other church bells were audible, in this city of a hundred spires.

'Do you want to know what happened to Dieter? What did Doll say happened to him?'

'Well he said he was dead. Which is the case, isn't it? Oh, Doll said all kinds of things. And kept misremembering and contra-dicting himself. He said they cut all the nerves in his groin. They locked him naked in a kind of fridge of dry ice. Then they—'

'No, no, none of that's true.'

'I could tell it couldn't *all* be true.'

'He was martyred,' I said firmly. 'He died for his cause, but it was quick. And early on. January '34. I learned that from the Reichsleiter.'

297

'. . . You were in prison, weren't you? Not in a camp.'

'Camps at first, then prison, thank God. Compared to camp, prison is bliss. Stadelheim, eighteen months in the political wing . . . I'll tell you about it another time. If there is another time.'

It was eleven fifty-four, and I had to speak.

'Hannah, I wasn't imagining it, was I? You did have some feeling for me, back then?'

She lifted her face and said, 'No, you weren't imagining it. And it seemed, I don't know, it felt right when you hugged me in the pavilion that time. And I went out into the garden for you and I was glad to do it. I thought about you a lot. A lot. And I wished I hadn't had to destroy your letter. And I tracked down the poem you quoted from. *"The Exiles".'*

'Gas-light in shops, The fate of ships.'

'And the tide-wind Touch the old wound . . .'

She nodded sorrowfully and went on, 'But something's happened. Back then, you were my figure for what was sane. For what was decent and normal and civilised. And now all that's been turned on its head. I'm . . . It's sad. You aren't normal any longer, not to me. When I see you, I'm there again. When I see you I smell it. And I don't want to smell it.'

I eventually said it grieved me to admit that this made a kind of sense.

'Can you believe, I was married to one of the most prolific murderers in history. Me. And he was so coarse, and so . . . prissy, and so ugly, and so cowardly, and so stupid. Dieter was hopeless too in his way. A head full of someone else's ideas. Stalin's. See? I'm no good at it. I'm just not up to it. Doll. Doll. The thought of being with a man is alien to me now. I haven't given them a glance in years. I'm finished with them. I'm so finished.'

I considered for a moment – or for a moment I stopped considering. 'You haven't got the right to say that.'

'Haven't got the *right?*'

'No, you haven't, I don't think you have. Only a victim has the right to say there's no coming back from it. And they hardly ever do. They're desperate to restart their lives. The ones that are truly broken are the ones we never hear from. They're not talking to – they're not talking to anybody. You, you were always your husband's victim, but you were never a *victim.*'

She shook her square head at me. 'It depends on the person, doesn't it? Suffering isn't relative. Don't they say that?'

'But oh yes suffering is. Did you lose your hair and half your body weight? Do you laugh at funerals because there's all this fuss and only one person died? Did your life depend on the state of your shoes? Were your parents murdered? Were your girls? Do you fear uniforms and crowds and naked flames and the smell of wet garbage? Are you terrified of sleep? Does it hurt and hurt and *hurt?* Is there a tattoo on your soul?'

She straightened again and was still for a moment, but then said steadily, 'No. Of course not. But that's exactly what I mean. The thing is we don't deserve to come back from it. After that.'

I said, 'So they've prevailed, have they? In the case of Hannah Schmidt? True? *Till your nerves are numb And your now is a time Too late for love. Saying Alas To less and less.*'

'Exactly. *Grown used at last To having lost.* And I don't mean the war.'

'No. *No.* You're a fighter. Like the time you gave Doll those black eyes. With one punch – Christ, you're like *Boris.* You're a fighter – that's who you really are.'

'No it isn't. I was never less myself than I was back then.'

'And is *this* who you really are? Cowering in Rosenheim. And finished.'

She folded her arms and looked to the side.

'Who I am doesn't matter,' she said. 'It's simpler than that. You

299

and me. Listen. Imagine how disgusting it would be if anything good came out of that place. There.'

The first gong sounded: thirty-six seconds.

'I will arise and go now.'

And I arose. Overhead, above the grey – more grey, and no ghosts of blue. Again I swallowed hard, and said quietly,

'May I write? May I visit? Allowed? Forbidden?'

The refolded arms, the second look to the side.

'Well I'm – well I'm not forbidding it, am I. That would be . . . But you're wasting your time. And my time. Sorry. I'm sorry.'

I swayed before her. 'You know, I came to Rosenheim hoping to find you. And now you're near and not lost, I can't give up.'

She looked out at me. 'I'm not asking you to stay away. But I am asking you to – to give up.'

My knees creaked as I made a shallow bow and said with a show of briskness, 'I'll let you know when I'm coming. Please prepare the girls for high tea in the Grand. With their Uncle Angelus.'

The tower tolled nine, tolled ten.

'You can of course be trusted to remember your flowers.' My legs felt even weaker, and I had the knuckles of my left hand pressed tight against my brow. 'Will you do something for me? When we part, this Sunday afternoon, say so long softly.'

'Mm, I remember. Yes, all right. Sure.' She breathed out. '. . . So long.'

Now the twins were drifting back into sight, beyond the tall white bird in the round water.

'So long,' I answered, and turned and walked away.

ACKNOWLEDGMENTS AND AFTERWORD: 'THAT WHICH HAPPENED'

I am of course greatly indebted to the *loci classici* of the field – the works of Yehuda Bauer, Raul Hilberg, Norman Cohn, Alan Bullock, H. R. Trevor-Roper, Hannah Arendt, Lucy S. Dawidowicz, Martin Gilbert, Ian Kershaw, Joachim C. Fest, Saul Friedländer, Richard J. Evans, Richard Overy, Gitta Sereny, Christopher R. Browning, Michael Burleigh, Mark Mazower, and Timothy Snyder, among many others. These writers have established the macrocosm. I now intend to discharge some obligations on the level of the *meso* and the *micro*.

For the moods and textures of daily life in the Third Reich: Victor Klemperer's magisterial *I Shall Bear Witness* and *To the Bitter End*; Friedrich Reck's spitefully intelligent *Diary of a Man in Despair*; Marie Vassiltchikov's captivating and politically incisive *Berlin Diaries, 1940–1945*; and Helmuth James von Moltke's *Letters to Freya*, a monument of moral solidity (and uxoriousness), all the more convincing for his self-confessed equivocation after the defeat of France in June 1940.

For IG Farben, the Buna-Werke, and Auschwitz III: Diarmuid Jeffreys's finely executed *Hell's Cartel*; Robert Jay Lifton's *The Nazi Doctors*; Rudolf Vrba's *I Escaped from Auschwitz*; Laurence Rees's *Auschwitz*; Witold Pilecki's *The Auschwitz Volunteer: Beyond Bravery*; and the Primo Levi of *If This Is a Man*, *Moments of Reprieve*, and *The Drowned and the Saved*. For the ethos and structure of the SS, Heinz Höhne's *The Order of the Death's Head* (with its excellent appendices) and Adrian Weale's *The SS: A New History*.

For background, and for random details and insights: Golo Mann's *The History of Germany Since 1789*; Robert Conquest's *Reflections on a Ravaged Century*; Peter Watson's *The German Genius* and *A Terrible Beauty*; Paul Johnson's *A History of the Jews* and *A History of the Modern World*; Antony

Beevor's *Stalingrad, Berlin: The Downfall,* and *The Second World War;* Niall Ferguson's *The Pity of War* and *The War of the World;* the three-volume *Nazism: A History in Documents and Eyewitness Accounts,* edited by J. Noakes and G. Pridham; *Bomber Command, Armageddon,* and *All Hell Let Loose,* by Max Hastings; Heike B. Görtemaker's *Eva Braun;* Jochen von Lang's *The Secretary* (on Bormann); Eric A. Johnson's *Nazi Terror: The Gestapo, Jews, and Ordinary Germans;* Edward Crankshaw's *Gestapo* and, more especially, his exquisite *Bismarck;* and the death-cell memoir, *Commandant of Auschwitz,* by the fuddled mass murderer Rudolf Höss (from Primo Levi's introduction: 'despite his efforts at defending himself, the author comes across as what he is: a coarse, stupid, arrogant, long-winded scoundrel').

For the tics and rhythms of German speech my principal guide was Alison Owings and her *Frauen: German Women Recall the Third Reich.* Time and again Owings probes, coaxes, humours, and inveigles her way into cosy intimacy with a wide range of housewives, heroines, diehards, dissenters, ex-prisoners, ex-guards. Her subjects are historically anonymous except for one; and the centrepiece of this amusing, frightening, and consistently illuminating book is a long interview, in Vermont, with Freya von Moltke, close to half a century after the execution of her husband. Owings writes:

> I had assumed, while nervously boarding ever smaller planes to get to her home, that I would find a woman of bravery and dignity, and I did. I was not prepared to find a woman in love.
>
> . . . 'Women who lost husbands in the horrendous war and even here, in this country, experienced far worse than I. For them it was horrible, the men going off to war and then never coming back. Many lost husbands who hated [the regime] and they nonetheless were killed. That is *bitter*. But for me, everything was worthwhile. I thought, he has fulfilled his life. And he did. Definitely.
>
> 'When you talk with me for a long while,' she said, 'you understand that one lives a whole lifetime from such an experience. When

he was killed, I had two delightful children, two dear sons. I thought, so. That is enough for a whole life.'

For the survivors and their testimonies I want to single out from the huge and forbidding archive a volume that deserves permanent currency: Anton Gill's *The Journey Back from Hell*. It is an extraordinarily inspiring treasury of voices, and one grounded and marshalled by the author with both flair and decorum. Indeed, these reminiscences, these dramatic monologues, reshape our tentative answer to the unavoidable question: What did you have to have to survive?

What you had to have is usually tabulated as follows: luck; the ability to adapt, immediately and radically; a talent for inconspicuousness; solidarity with another individual or with a group; the preservation of decency ('the people who had no tenets to live by – of whatever nature – generally succumbed' no matter how ruthlessly they struggled); the constantly nurtured conviction of innocence (an essential repeatedly emphasised by Solzhenitsyn in *The Gulag Archipelago*); immunity to despair; and, again, luck.

Having communed with the presences in Gill's book, with their stoicism, eloquence, aphoristic wisdom, humour, poetry, and uniformly high level of perception, one can suggest an additional desideratum. In a conclusive rebuke to the Nazi idea, these 'subhumans', it turns out, were the cream of humankind. And a rich, delicate, and responsive sensibility – how surprising do we find this? – was not a hindrance but a strength. Together with a nearly unanimous rejection of revenge (and a wholly unanimous rejection of forgiveness), the testimonies assembled here have something else in common. There is a shared thread of guilt, the feeling that, while they themselves were saved, someone more deserving, someone 'better' was tragically drowned. And this must amount to a magnanimous illusion; with due respect to all, there could have been no one better.

He has so far gone unnamed in this book; but now I am obliged to type out the words 'Adolf Hitler'. And he seems slightly more manageable, somehow, when escorted by quotation marks. Of mainstream historians, not one claims

305

to understand him, and many make a point of saying that they don't understand him; and some, like Alan Bullock, go further and admit to an ever-deepening perplexity ('I can't explain Hitler. I don't believe anyone can . . . The more I learn about Hitler, the harder I find it to explain'). We know a great deal about the how – about how he did what he did; but we seem to know almost nothing about the why.

Newly detrained at Auschwitz in February 1944, and newly stripped, showered, sheared, tattooed, and reclothed in random rags (and nursing a four-day thirst), Primo Levi and his fellow Italian prisoners were packed into a vacant shed and told to wait. This famous passage continues:

> . . . I eyed a fine icicle outside the window, within hand's reach. I opened the window and broke off the icicle but at once a large, heavy guard prowling outside brutally snatched it away from me. '*Warum?*' I asked him in my poor German. '*Hier ist kein warum*' (there is no why here), he replied, pushing me inside with a shove.

There was no why in Auschwitz. Was there a why in the mind of the *Reichskanzler*-President-Generalissimo? And if there was, why can't we find it?

One way out of the quandary involves an epistemological rejection: thou shalt not seek an answer. And this commandment can take different forms (leading us into a sphere known as the theology of the Holocaust). In *Explaining Hitler* – a work of almost uncanny percipience and stamina – Ron Rosenbaum is sympathetic to the spiritual queasiness of Emil Fackenheim (author of, for example, *The Human Condition After Auschwitz*); however, he quietly derides the secular but self-righteous Claude Lanzmann (maker of *Shoah*), who calls all attempts at explanation 'obscene'. Rather, Rosenbaum inclines to the position of Louis Micheels (who wrote the painfully intimate memoir, *Doctor 117641*): '*Da soll ein warum sein*: There must be a why.' As Yehuda Bauer tells Rosenbaum, in Jerusalem, 'I'd like to find it [the why], yes, but I haven't': 'Hitler is explicable in principle, but that does not mean he *has* been explained.'

Still, we shouldn't forget that the mystery, the why, is divisible: first, the Austrian *artist manqué* turned tub-thumper, second, the German – and Austrian – instruments he carried with him. Sebastian Haffner was a popular historian who studied both ends of the phenomenon, from below in *Defying Hitler* (a memoir of life in Berlin 1914–33, written in 1939, just after he got out) and from above in *The Meaning of Hitler*, an intense exegesis that appeared in 1978, when Haffner was seventy-one (in 1914 he was seven). The first book went unpublished in his lifetime, and there is no attempt at uniting the two perspectives. But we can attempt it; and the connections are unignorable.

In moods and mentalities, it seems, *Volk* and Führer partook of the same troubled Danubian brew. On the one hand, the people, with their peculiar 'despair of politics' (as Trevor-Roper has put it), their eager fatalism, their wallowing in petulance and perversity, what Haffner calls their 'resentful dimness' and their 'heated readiness to hate', their refusal of moderation and, in adversity, of all consolation, their ethos of zero-sum (of all or nothing, of *Sein oder Nichtsein*), and their embrace of the irrational and hysterical. And on the other hand the leader, who indulged these tendencies on the stage of global politics. His inner arcanum, Haffner believes, floridly manifested itself during the critical hinge of the war: namely the two-week period between November 27 and December 11, 1941.

When the *Blitzkrieg* in the east began to collapse, Hitler notoriously remarked (November 27):

> On this point, too, I am icily cold. If one day the German nation is no longer sufficiently strong or sufficiently ready for sacrifice to stake its blood for its existence, then let it perish and be annihilated by some other stronger power . . . I shall shed no tears for the German nation.

By December 6, as the War Diary of the Wehrmacht Operations Staff records, Hitler had acknowledged that 'no victory could any longer be won'. And on December 11, four days after Pearl Harbor, he boldly, gratuitously, and suicidally declared war on the USA. Where, here, is the Führer's why? According to Haffner, he was 'now coveting defeat'; and he wanted that defeat to be 'as complete and disastrous as possible'. Thereafter his aggression veered in on a new target: Germans.

This reading offers a framework for December '41–April '45, and helps make some sense of the Ardennes offensive in late '44 (which effectively opened the eastern door to the Russians) and the two disobeyed 'Führer Orders' the following March (for mass civilian evacuation from the west, and the 'Nero Order' for scorched earth). We now ask, How far back did it go – the subconscious drive towards self-destruction, and later its treasonable corollary, the conscious drive towards 'national death'? And the answer seems to be that it went back all the way.

Hitler's core notion, 'living space', announced with settled pomp in *Mein Kampf* (1925), was from the start a ridiculous anachronism (the reasoning is 'pre-industrial'); and its *sine qua non*, the quick win over Russia, was ruled out in advance by demographics and geography. When the dissident diarist Friedrich Reck, who came from an old military family, learned of the attack on Russia (June '41) he reacted with 'wild jubilation': 'Satan's own have overreached themselves, and now they are in the net, and they will never free themselves again'. Thus in Haffner's words, the 'programmatician', as Hitler liked to call himself, 'programmed his failure'.

Both Haffner's books give you the rare excitement of impending (if perhaps fugitive) clarity; and read in tandem they do seem to inch us a little closer to coherence. But we are continuing to beg an enormous question: the question of sanity. After all, Hitler's other core notion, the one about the Jewish world conspiracy, comes straight out of a primer on mental diseases – it is the schizophrenic's first and most miserable cliché. In the street, then, gutter Judaeophobia (or at best the unnatural 'indifference' adduced by Ian Kershaw), a fulminant nationalism, and herd docility punctuated by 'mass intoxications'; in the Chancellery, the slow *felo de se* of a mind now putrescing with power. And madness, if

308

we impute it (and how can we exclude it?), is bound to frustrate our investigation – because of course we will get no coherence, and no legible why, from the mad.

What is the unique difficulty in coming to terms with 'that which happened' (in Paul Celan's coldly muted phrase)? Any attempt at an answer will necessarily be personal, and for this reason: 'the Nazi genocide', as Michael André Bernstein has written, 'is somehow central to our self-understanding'. Not everyone will feel that way about the events in eastern Europe 1941–5 (and I am reminded of W. G. Sebald's dry aside to the effect that no serious person ever thinks about anything else). But I accede to Bernstein's formulation; it is surely one of the defining elements of the singularity.

My own inner narrative is one of chronic stasis, followed by a kind of reprieve. Here is an illustration. I first read Martin Gilbert's classic *The Holocaust: The Jewish Tragedy* in 1987, and I read it with incredulity; in 2011 I read it again, and my incredulity was intact and entire – it was wholly undiminished. Between those dates I had worked my way through scores of books on the subject; and while I might have gained in knowledge, I had gained nothing at all in penetration. The facts, set down in a historiography of tens of thousand of volumes, are not in the slightest doubt; but they remain in some sense unbelievable, or beyond belief, and cannot quite be assimilated. Very cautiously I submit that part of the exceptionalism of the Third Reich lies in its unyieldingness, the electric severity with which it repels our contact and our grip.

Soon after this negative eureka (I have not found it, I cannot understand it), my eye was caught by a new edition of Primo Levi's *The Truce* (his comedic and affirmatory companion volume to the darkness of *If This Is a Man*). And here I came across an addendum I hadn't seen before – 'The Author's Answers to His Readers' Questions', which covers eighteen pages of small print.

'How can the Nazis' fanatical hatred of the Jews be explained?' asks question number seven. In reply Levi lists the most commonly cited root causes, which, nevertheless, he finds 'not commensurate with, not proportional to, the facts that need explaining'. He goes on:

> Perhaps one cannot, what is more one must not, understand what happened, because to understand is almost to justify. Let me explain: 'understanding' a proposal or human behaviour means to 'contain' it, contain its author, put oneself in his place, identify with him. Now, no normal human being will ever be able to identify with Hitler, Himmler, Goebbels, Eichmann, and endless others. This dismays us, and at the same time gives us a sense of relief, because perhaps it is desirable that their words (and also, unfortunately, their deeds) cannot be comprehensible to us. They are non-human words and deeds, really counter-human . . . [T]here is no rationality in the Nazi hatred; it is a hate that is not in us; it is outside man . . .

Historians will consider this more an evasion than an argument. To non-discursive writers, though (and we remember that Levi was also a novelist and a poet), such a feint or flourish may be taken as a spur. Here, Levi is very far from hoisting up the no-entry sign demanded by the sphinxists, the anti-explainers. On the contrary, he is lifting the pressure off the why, and so pointing to a way in.

*

My special thanks go to Richard J. Evans for checking my typescript, for drawing my attention to some historical implausibilities, and for tidying up several grave errors in the novel's garnish of German; and thanks also to my friend of almost half a century, Clive James, for his suggestions and his thoughts. As I said to Professor Evans at the outset, my only conscious liberty with the factual record was in bringing forward the defection to the USSR of Friedrich Paulus (the losing commander at Stalingrad) by about seventeen months. Otherwise, I adhere to that which happened, in all its horror, its desolation, and its bloody-minded opacity.

*

310

To those who survived and to those who did not; to the memory of Primo Levi (1919–87) and to the memory of Paul Celan (1920–70); and to the countless significant Jews and quarter-Jews and half-Jews in my past and present, particularly my mother-in-law, Elizabeth, my younger daughters, Fernanda and Clio, and my wife, Isabel Fonseca.

- fatsia
- sage